The
BITTER FRUIT
BENEATH

JULIE EVANS

To Eden, born 27th January 2020.
A ray of light at a time of darkness.

"To all those who seek to bury the past. Beware the man with the shovel."

ABOUT JULIE EVANS

 After training as a lawyer, Julie returned to her native Cornwall to establish her own law firm and to raise her three children. After years building a successful legal practice it was time for a new adventure and she decided to write the stories she had formulated in her head over the years about her community and the lives of those who find themselves on the wrong side of the law.

THE BITTER FRUIT BENEATH is Book Three in Julie's new **CORNISH CRIME** series.

Book One *RAGE* and Book Two *A SISTERHOOD OF SILENCE* are available to buy now on Amazon. Book Four *A BAPTISM OF FIRE* is due to be released in late 2021.

If you would like to read more about Julie, visit her website at **www.cornishcrimeauthor.com** where you will be given the opportunity to join her readers' club and receive free downloads and inside information exclusively available to members, including a **FREE** novella in the **CORNISH CRIME** series, *THE ROSARY PEA What's Your Poison?*

ONE

Hoping to God the zip didn't burst, Eden Gray wheeled her squeaky trolly through the sun-flooded atrium of the Truro Crown Court. It bulged with papers ditched by the barrister she'd instructed on the gruelling four-day trial she had just lost in spectacular style. Mumbling his apology, the QC had made a dash for the door on the pretext of catching the four-thirty train back to Bristol. They both knew despite his eye-watering fee, he'd made a pig's ear of it. No wonder he was running for the Mendips.

Her mind whirred with things she could have done better, not least instructed counsel with an eye for detail. He'd been slack; all style and no substance. Their defence had crashed and burned and her client had been sent down for fraud.

She shouldn't be surprised; everyone knew barristers were the rock stars of the legal profession. After the gig they leapt into their limousines and headed back to the hotel, leaving the sweaty roadies like her to mop up the mess. She'd been the one expected to visit the client in the cells and apply the sticking plaster before he'd been carted off to Exeter jail to serve a six-year sentence. She ought to be able to afford a paralegal to help but money was tight. She could barely afford her secretary, Agnes. Until the final payment of her divorce settlement came through she'd be stuck with the grunt work.

Apologizing to the po-faced usher for the rubber marks left by the limping wheels, she crossed the terrazzo floor, through the enormous glass revolving door, out into the real world, to be greeted by an ironically optimistic sky that felt like a slap in the face.

She paused to take off her jacket and to light a much-needed cigarette. She'd quit smoking five years earlier but always kept an emergency supply and a Bic lighter in an old sunglasses case at the bottom of her bag for shit days like this. Inhaling deeply, she slipped her aching feet free of her shoes, settling on the wall to take in the scenery.

Built on the site of a medieval castle, the Court enjoyed spectacular views over the tiny city dominated by the three spires of its cathedral. It was a shame the so-called temple to Justice behind her had none of its soaring majesty. Despite the town planner's promises, it had turned out to be yet another low-slung homage to concrete; the gleaming god of architects.

The word *architect* caught like a barb in her heart for a split-second, reminding her of her ex, Andrew. She liked to keep him pixilated whenever possible but the word *architect* had a habit of switching him to high resolution. Taking a final puff of her cigarette, she stubbed out his image before it took hold.

Though past four o'clock, the heat hung around. Overdressed and clammy in her court suit, she watched with unabashed envy, a middle-aged couple, the woman in a flimsy summer top, climb into a blue convertible. She imagined they'd enjoyed a late lunch in the courtyard garden of the swanky fish restaurant around the corner. She, on the other hand, knew of convicted killers with a better chance of day release than her and couldn't remember what it was like not to eat lunch on the hoof. It was salt in the wound living in Cornwall, where on days like this every man and his tail wagging dog seemed to be on holiday.

After the day she'd had she would normally have rushed home, grabbed her board and let the surf reinstate some perspective, but the renovations to the beach house were far from finished and until the rewiring was complete, she was stuck renting the airless flat above the florist's in the main street. She decided she'd check how the work was going this weekend and if necessary give her cousins who were handling the project a hefty kick up the backside.

Friends had warned her not to employ family, especially family too easily distracted by the prospect of a day catching waves.

"Like putting alcoholics in charge of an off-licence."

Eden couldn't blame them for being side-tracked. She'd made a point of siting her study at the back of the beach house, fearing she'd never get any work done if it faced the ocean. The Atlantic breakers etched their mark on every Cornish child. Salt water ran through their veins, altering their DNA. It turned them into "blue-bloods," her dad always joked. She knew what he meant. Raised within spitting distance of the sea, she felt trapped and unsettled without it. Too much terra firma set her adrift. As a student in London, she'd tried to compensate by filling her room with posters of seascapes and sand dunes. She'd even carted a three-foot piece of driftwood on the train back from Cornwall to hang above her headboard. Winter was bearable but the airless, scorching afternoons spent revising in the park to escape the sticky streets, brought unbearable melancholy. Fountains and lakes filled with tamed water were a poor remedy for the type of seasickness she suffered from.

Undoing the top button of her blouse, she slipped her jacket over her arm and began the bumpy descent past the line of cafes and gift shops strung like bunting along the steep hill to her office. Her heart sank on reaching the bottom of the slope as she noticed not for the first time, the peeling paint and tarnished brass plaque in need of a polish;

Eden Gray LLB: Solicitor and Commissioner for Oaths.

She'd barely had chance to heave the rebellious trolley over the threshold before Agnes busied towards her; bingo wings flapping; face flushed with excitement.

'Don't bother to sit, you're needed at the station.'

Pretending she hadn't heard, Eden carried on walking through reception, Agnes nipping at her heels like a rabid Jack Russell.

'They called … there's a client waiting.'

'I've just left court; can't someone else on the rota do it?'

'The client's mother asked for you specifically. I expect she wants a female solicitor and you're the only one available.'

A back-handed compliment if ever there was one.

'What's the case? Shoplifting? A domestic?'

'A teenager has killed her baby; well sort of her baby.'

That got Eden's attention. '*Allegedly* killed her baby,' she corrected, 'and is it her baby or not?'

'She's one of them surrogates; you know one of them who gets paid by couples who can't have kiddies. She's taken their money then gone and killed the baby ... *allegedly*.'

'A termination?'

'No, they've found a body,' Agnes lowered her voice almost to a whisper; '*buried* and with that lot, there's bound to be more to it.'

'What lot?'

'The Luteys; that's the client, Rowan Lutey. She's one of the Tregarren Luteys. Mother wouldn't go near that place. She always said the Luteys were cunning.'

Agnes scattered her dead mother's homilies about like broken beads, each one a pearl of wisdom. The older Agnes got, the more reactionary and self-serving her late mother's opinions became. Nevertheless, her encyclopaedic knowledge from beyond the grave; of the community, who was married to who, what they did for a living, maiden names and decades of misdemeanours was sometimes useful, but despite her curiosity being kindled, Eden was not in the mood today. She was tired and hungry; running on fumes.

'Give the station a ring and say I'm on my way and not to interview the girl until I get there. I need the loo and a coffee; can you put the kettle on and grab me something to eat?'

'What do you want me to do first, call the station or play office junior?'

Eden heard the peeve and clocked the passive aggressive stance; reading body language was part of the job. Agnes was right of course but she simply didn't have the energy to make something herself or take the bait.

She'd inherited her secretary, along with the threadbare carpets and tatty furniture from her predecessor; a sole practitioner for whom Agnes had worked for twenty years. Without her it was impossible to decipher everything from the archaic filing system to how the boiler worked. A year on, like the moth-eaten armchairs in reception, despite the frayed exterior, Agnes felt a tolerable fit. A newer model would no doubt be comfier and less likely to lose its casters in a spin but would need to be broken in and would make the rest of the place look shabby.

'Whichever suits you best; you choose,' Eden smiled, adding under her breath; 'you usually do,' as she swapped her court shoes for her trainers.

When she got back from the loo, there was a sorry looking cheese sandwich and a black coffee on her desk. Ignoring the deliberately forgotten milk, she took a gulp, burnt her tongue, thrust the sandwich into her jacket pocket and left for the station.

***

Swinging into the car park she spotted Detective Inspector Luke Parish parking under the shade of the sycamores in the far corner. She hoped to God he hadn't noticed her. The last time she'd seen him at the magistrates' court they'd had words about Thea.

Luke and her younger sister had history; a curdled romance, turned sour when Thea walked out without notice, taking their daughter with her. She now lived in London with the latest of a long line of boyfriends and made it her mission to make it as difficult as possible for Luke to have access to Flora, now five.

Eden understood his frustration but objected to him taking her to task in public and his presumption she held any sway over her wayward sister. Thea liked to throw a grenade and walk away from the damage. Their eternally tolerant parents put her behaviour down to her artistic temperament, which seemed to Eden to be an excuse for anything; "she paints, darling".

So did Hitler, Eden thought but never vocalised.

Over time she'd learnt to dodge the shrapnel and resented being dragged back into the warzone by anyone, including Thea's disgruntled ex.

Things were further complicated by the fact Luke had been her friend long before he'd met Thea. They might have been more, had her effervescent sister not seven years before, crashed a beach barbeque Eden had organised for Luke's twenty-fifth birthday.

5

That day she had learnt a valuable lesson; never underestimate an eighteen-year-old in a pink stringed bikini.

She watched Luke stride to his boot and retrieve two plastic evidence bags; waiting until he was inside the building before making her way up the steps to report to the custody officer.

'Ms Gray,' greeted Jake Fairchild. 'I won't ask to what do we owe this pleasure because I got a call from the lovely Agnes to say you were on your way for the Lutey girl?'

'So, what's the story, Jake?'

'You'd better ask the DI here.'

She swivelled to face Luke. He avoided eye contact as he marshalled her behind the front desk into the corridor leading to the cells.

'In here. I'll give you a bit of background before we go down,' he said, opening a side door. His angular face and intense dark eyes, topped with black unruly eyebrows should have cast him as a comic book villain; but for his smile. His lips stretched in a smile so perfect it shot him up the tinder scale from a mediocre six to a full blown nine-and-a-half and probably explained Thea's reluctance to cut him loose; her constant use of Flora to reel him back in.

'We can talk here,' she said, stepping back. Most there knew their connection and she had no intention of adding grist to the gossip mill or getting another ear-bashing.

'Okay, your shout.'

Eden noticed the flash of annoyance and decided to keep this as brief and professional as possible.

'So, why have you arrested my girl?'

'We have a statement from a local woman, Jessica Marshall who says Rowan Lutey was pregnant.'

'Last time I looked motherhood wasn't a crime?'

Luke's jaw twitched. 'Jess and Phil Marshall say they paid Rowan ten grand to be their surrogate. She's a waitress at their restaurant in Truro. Things were going to plan with the pregnancy until last Wednesday when she didn't turn up for her evening shift. Jess tried ringing her but her phone kept diverting to voicemail. She wanted to go round to check on the girl right away but they had a large

6

party booked in and her husband persuaded her to leave it, which she did. Next morning, Jess went round to Rowan's flat and found her groggy and disorientated, so much so, Jess thought she was drunk or high on something. She questioned her and they argued. Rowan told her she could stick her job and her money because the baby was gone. She refused to elaborate and threw Jess out, along with the bag containing most of the cash she'd been paid previously. Jess called Phil and they reported the matter to us.'

'And you brought Rowan in; a bit heavy handed even for you lot?'

'We're not looking for work,' he bristled. 'The couple were told it was a contractual matter and they should consult their solicitor. We assumed Rowan was lying about the baby and had changed her mind until yesterday afternoon when the body of a near term newborn was found in a shallow grave by an archaeological team working at Tregarren, the village near the girl's family farm. One of the PCs on duty connected the two incidents and the decision was taken to visit Rowan this afternoon. She was evasive and unwilling to explain her behaviour or confirm she was still pregnant. When she refused to come in voluntarily we arrested her on suspicion of manslaughter.'

'Manslaughter?'

'I know, I know; you're thinking infanticide but that's only an option when a *biological* mother is charged. Your client won't confirm whether she has a genetic link with the child or not.'

Legal soup, cold through neglect, slopped around at the back of her mind; a distant tutorial about the distinction between the fertilisation of an egg belonging to the surrogate and the implantation of someone else's. She was pretty sure the latter was illegal in the UK. What she didn't know was how it impacted on her defence. Had she been thinking straight - not reeling from her last case - she would have looked it up before she'd set off. Infanticide was serious enough but generally carried a non-custodial sentence, manslaughter on the other hand would mean anything between two years and life imprisonment. Caught on the backfoot she wished she'd gone into the side room with him, rather than suffer the indignity of a law tutorial within earshot of his team. No doubt the smug bastard had already consulted the lawyers at the CPS and was taking great pleasure in educating her. She'd been ambushed but could still flip this if she kept her nerve.

'So, there is no DNA evidence to link my client to the child you've found?'

'She let us take a buccal smear which will tell us soon enough but I'm thinking, whether she's the biological mother or not, her DNA will be on the body if she gave birth to that baby. If there's a match, she's in the frame.'

'You're kidding, you took a cheek swab before she'd taken legal advice?'

'Look, before you get on your high horse, we offered her another brief because we were told you were tied up in court but she turned us down because her mother had already called your office. We told the girl she should wait until you arrived but she didn't want to. You can check the custody record if you like?'

She swallowed her fury. 'I'd rather see my client if you don't mind?'

'I'll take you now.'

Luke led the way down the narrow staircase to the interview room. 'She's in here.'

It was a dismal windowless space, khaki green walls bathed in artificial light; contriving to induce unease and claustrophobia in equal measure. The girl jumped to her feet as they entered.

Eden waited for Luke to leave before she spoke. 'Please sit down, Rowan. I'm Eden Gray, your solicitor. Your mum called me. I'm here to help you.'

Greasy hanks of black hair hung like wet curtains around the girl's face. Trembling, she looked scared to death.

'You're cold?' Eden said, shouldering off her jacket and wrapping it around the girl.

'Thank you,' Rowan mumbled, her fingers drumming a frantic rhythm on the chipped Formica table. Her eyes darted from the clock to the concrete floor then up to the strip-lit ceiling, as if searching for an escape route.

'Do you know why you're here?'

The girl briefly locked eyes with her lawyer, before beginning her nomadic scan again. The tap … tap … tap, continuing until Eden, unable to bear it any longer, reached across to fold the girl's delicate hands in her own.

'Rowan, you've been arrested on suspicion of killing your baby.'

'It shouldn't have come yet; it's not time … it's not time.' The voice was small; like a child's. It was no surprise she'd given a sample. She'd give her soul to get out of there.

'Can you tell me about the baby … about the birth?'

'I don't remember, I can't remember; it wasn't time.'

'Are you saying you have absolutely no recollection of having the baby?'

The girl looked at her blankly.

'But you were definitely pregnant?' Eden asked becoming more and more concerned.

Rowan nodded again.

Eden was venturing into unfamiliar territory. She had no idea what it felt like to give birth and the way things were going with her love life at the moment she probably never would, but she'd seen enough documentaries and episodes of *Call the Midwife* to know it wasn't a piece of cake.

This girl was vulnerable. Whether it was because of the circumstances she found herself in or there was something more going on she wasn't sure. What's more, without the benefit of some background history along with medical and psychiatric reports she could do more harm than good here. She needed to get her client out of there fast and buy them both some time.

'It's okay,' she said patting the girl's hand. Would you like to go home?'

Tears brimmed in terrified eyes.

Eden hammered on the door and five minutes later she was back upstairs with Luke.

'That girl wasn't fit to give consent to a sample, or to be questioned come to that. Was any attempt made to have her examined when she arrived?'

'No one was available.'

'Then I think you've jumped the gun. I have serious concerns about her mental health. I don't want her questioned again until she's had a medical examination, to assess her physical and mental state. Unless you want to spend the night on suicide watch I see no reason for you to hold her until then and suggest you release her on condition to report back once all the facts are at our fingertips.'

'Alright, alright … but this isn't going away.'

'Don't worry I know that.'

An hour later Eden bundled Rowan into a car with her mother and brother. She was relieved her tactic had bought her time. She wouldn't be found wanting again.

Back in the carpark she pulled the sagging sandwich from her pocket and took a bite, before lobbing the unappetising mess into the hedge just as Luke emerged from the station. For a split second, she wondered whether as a good law-abiding citizen she should get out, retrieve it and find a bin, then thought; what the hell; what's he going to do, arrest me?

TWO

She'd felt exhausted earlier, but now the adrenaline was pumping, she thought she might just be able to catch the boys before they downed tools for the day if she headed to the beach house now. They'd said they were working evenings to catch up after spinning a yarn about difficulty getting materials and finding woodworm in the rafters. It would be good to let them know she intended to hold them to their promise to knuckle down and get the plumbing finished by the end of October by which time she'd have her share of the London flat sale and be able to press ahead with the new bathroom and kitchen.

She'd been cutting out pictures from magazines for months and couldn't wait to make it her own in a way she never could with the houses she'd shared with Andrew. He always took over presuming she had no interest or if she did, it didn't count for much. After all, he had letters after his name to prove he was the tastemaker. She had wandered around the finished product feeling like a chocolatey-fingered toddler in an art gallery.

She pulled off left before she hit the village, taking the narrow cliff road to the beach house. Everyone called it a house but it was more of a hut. It had started out as a Heuer's shelter for fishermen on the lookout for approaching shoals of pilchards.

Perched on the cliff edge among the dunes it offered a bird's eye view of the fish driven inshore to be caught in their thousands. In the sixties a well-known artist saved it from demolition, converting it into her studio. She left it to the local bird watchers association who short of funds to repair the place, eventually put it up for sale just as she was contemplating her move back to Cornwall. When her dad rang to say it was on the market she thought he was mad for thinking she'd even consider it but out of nostalgia and sheer nosiness had rung the agents. They had shown uncharacteristic integrity; admitting it was 'in lerrups' which was Cornish for a shithole. Nevertheless, the minute she'd stepped through the battered door of the perfectly round two-storey building, with its broken windows and walls Jackson Pollocked with seagull mess, its simplicity drew her in. From that moment she thought of it as home.

She knew all about simplicity. Andrew had lectured her for four years on its merits; simplicity of line, simplicity of function and form, in fact, simplicity of everything except the marriage itself following the chaos that ensued with his confession he was leaving her for the middle-aged divorcee whose house he'd designed and built. When through her tears she asked him why he was doing this to her, he'd waxed lyrical about self-cleaning glass, iroko handrails, and a lap pool in the basement and it slowly dawned on her he wasn't leaving her for another woman but for a three-story townhouse in Primrose Hill with a view of the park.

The beach house was her revenge; her answer to his *maison de l'amour*.

The summer season would be over when she moved in. She couldn't wait. The thought of waking in the house; walking to the window, coffee in hand to look out on a stretch of pristine sand; not a stripy windbreak in sight, filled her with joy.

She parked up by the skip overflowing with twisted window frames and rotten floorboards. She'd have to make sure she ordered another one; another five hundred quid to find from somewhere. Her cousin's van wasn't there but a couple of deckchairs perched on the cliff edge and a half-filled mug of warm tea said they weren't long gone. She walked around to the front of the house. The door was padlocked, awaiting the arrival of its replacement which hopefully wouldn't warp the way this one had. She was pleased to see the hand-built windows were finally in. As the marmalade glow of the dipping sun lit up the interior she could tell some progress had been made inside too and her spirits lifted.

It was only money after all. This was hers, and the view alone was worth every penny. She slumped into one of the deckchairs, watching the last of the kittiwakes swoop above the ocean painted silver in the dying light and tried to relax away all thoughts of Rowan Lutey and the baby, leastways until she got home.

She wondered why she could never recapture the limp, heavy, tiredness she'd felt as a child; so different from the sweaty, aching variety after a workout at the gym, or the anxious lawyer's fatigue she regularly suffered after a sleepless night worrying about a pending court case. She pictured herself in the back of her mother's battered Volkswagen, She and Thea crammed in together, along with the surf boards, beach bags and towels, leaning against each other and licking each other's arms like puppies. This was a game they played to see whose skin tasted the saltiest, as if it determined who'd had the most fun. It would set them off giggling until her mother told them to pack it in. They'd be quiet until she turned on the radio, and then sing along to Joni or Aretha; sandy feet up on the back of the seats, tapping their toes until kissed by Morpheus, they fell asleep. She remembered being woken when they got home and how the bath that followed tingled her skin and left sand around the plughole. How she longed for that old, contented slackness.

Slipping off her trainers she felt the tickle of marram grass on her ankles; the cool sand between her toes and permitted herself to let her worries ebb away until the sun dipped behind Chapel Rock.

THREE

As soon as she'd got home she had trawled her legal database for case law on infanticide. An offence in its own right and a defence to a charge of murder or manslaughter, a mother had to; *kill her child in its first year, as a direct result of a disturbance of the mind caused by giving birth.* Irrespective of the present uncertainty about her biological link to the child, Rowan didn't remember the birth. How could she be traumatised by a non-event?

Grabbing her car keys, she hoped her client was in a better frame of mind this morning; ready to give her something ... anything, she could hang her defence upon. She'd crawled into bed with more questions than answers and didn't like the feeling one little bit.

Soon smart Victorian terraces gave way to corrugated roofs and stock proof fences as the lane, ribboned through the valley, following the River Kenwyn out of Truro towards the Lutey farm.

The road opened up as she entered the tiny hamlet of Tregarren, with its smattering of tidy cobb-walled cottages and characterless nineteen-seventies bungalows. A sign swinging above a wall of herringboned slates, known locally as 'Jack 'n' Jills', announced the converted water mill on the right was open for B&B and she made a mental note in case she needed to accommodate expert witnesses from further afield in the weeks ahead. The Luteys lived on the other side of the village and as she got closer her hands gripped the steering wheel a little tighter; anxiety pecking.

Hunkered down in the valley, Warnock Farm was smarter than she'd imagined; a slate-capped giant, cloaked in fiery Virginia Creeper. Harvest-stubbled fields like massive arms, stretched out across the parched landscape, it was an advert for good husbandry. The double gates fronting the road were open and the curtains twitched as she drove through. No sooner had she parked; Matthew Lutey was inviting her in; his muscular frame filling the doorway.

'Ma and our Rowan are through there, in the kitchen,' he said, face reddening as he turned to leave via the back way, taking the granite steps two at a time.

The low autumn sun sliced the room, blinding Eden for a second as she entered. Blinking away the psychedelic assault on her retinas, she could make out the two women sitting at a broad pine table; scrubbed within an inch of its life. On it a batch of yellow buns cooled on a wire rack; spicing the air with saffron. An ancient dresser clung to one wall. Eden skimmed the cluttered blue and white china but her eyes were irresistibly drawn to the far end of the kitchen where a line of children's socks hung drying beside a cast iron range. She willed away an image of giant ovens and gingerbread houses as she moved towards the women, ducking to avoid the dusty posies of dried flowers and herbs hanging from the rafters.

'Good morning, Miss Gray,' greeted Rowan's mother, pulling out a chair for her, 'thank you so much for helping our Rowan with all this.'

She hadn't had the chance to take a good look at Carmen Lutey the night before. In her late forties, her blue eyes and cinnamon hair were a stark contrast to Rowan's dusky, gothic looks. Though not a large woman by any means there was a sturdiness about her, lacking in her will-o-the-wisp daughter.

'They look lovely,' Eden flattered nodding at the buns as she pulled her dictating machine from her bag. The mother loomed large in this family; she needed to keep her on side.

'Help yourself; they're fresh baked,' offered Carmen, pouring her tea before she had time to decline.

'Did you manage to sleep last night?' she asked, diverting attention to Rowan.

The girl nodded; bleary eyes telling a different story. Clean hair scraped back; multiple piercings through her eyebrow and nose not on show the evening before; silver rings encasing every finger, she looked older. Eden wasn't sure if she'd armoured up to fight her corner or to confess.

'I'm going to record our interview but before we go on, are you happy to talk with your mum in the room. There may be things you don't feel comfortable telling me in front of her?'

'No, I want her here. I've got nothing to hide.'

'You're sure?'

'I'm sure.'

The girl had unglued at the station but here, with her mother in tow, the fidgety anxiety seemed to have waned. Last night there had been insufficient evidence to charge her. Her job was to keep it that way but if Rowan intended to own up to this, her role would be limited to a plea of mitigation; on the back of psychiatric reports. It might not be the worst thing that could happen given her misgivings about this case. Under resourced, she felt uneasy committing to a manslaughter trial and a client as needy as Rowan at the expense of all others. She had to resist her usual urge to jump in feet first until she knew exactly what she was dealing with here.

She pressed record.

'Firstly, let's recap on the evidence the police have, the most important of which is, of course, the baby's body. At the moment there is no DNA to link you to the child but it's only a matter of time before they complete their analysis of the saliva sample you gave. I will try and exclude it but we can't pretend it doesn't exist. Until then, all they have is Jessica Marshall's statement which says you were pregnant and she and her husband paid you ten thousand pounds to have a baby for them.'

Eden noticed Carmen look away.

'It was for expenses and anyway, I gave the money back, well, most of it,' Rowan protested.

Eden couldn't hide her surprise at the stroppy tone so at odds with the way the girl had been the day before.

'No one's disputing you gave it back but that's not the point. The point is you told them you could no longer comply with the arrangement. So, either you changed your mind, or you couldn't give them the baby because you no longer had it? Until the baby was found the police believed it was the former but finding the baby changed all that.'

'They don't even know it's the same baby?' Rowan said sulkily.

'They know you're booked in for a medical examination tomorrow morning which will confirm if you've recently given birth?'

'I can tell you now, she has,' Carmen gulped, eyes fixed on her daughter. 'I don't need a doctor to confirm it. Lift your pullover, Rowan.'

The girl lifted her shapeless grey jumper over her head to reveal two small wet patches darkening her vintage Metallica T-shirt. The minute she was sure Eden had seen, she struggled back into her sweater, pulling at the sleeves so only the tips of her bitten nails remained visible.

Despite her determination to keep her emotions in check, Eden welled with sympathy for the girl, little more than a child herself.

'I know this is painful, but I have to ask you; could it be your baby they've found?'

'No ... I ... I don't know? I don't remember anything.'

'But you remember Jessica coming to the flat and you admit giving back the money. Are you saying you gave it back because you knew you'd had the baby and it was ...' she chose the word carefully, 'gone?'

A flush swept Rowan's cheeks as she looked to her mother for reassurance. None was forthcoming. It was clear whilst the mother was supportive, she couldn't help with the missing detail.

'I suppose so,' she stuttered into the neck of her jumper.

'Answer the question,' Carmen urged, reaching across to lift her daughter's chin; 'Miss Gray is trying to help. Did you know the baby was dead?' she asked her face laddered with worry.

Eden waited for the emotional collapse she'd seen so many times before, the reversion to childhood by a young offender; the revelation of guilt and hysterical plea for forgiveness but surprisingly, it didn't come. Instead, the girl straightened in her seat.

'No ... no I didn't; I just knew it wasn't inside me no more. That doesn't mean I killed it, does it, Ma ...?'

A storm gathered on Carmen Lutey's face. 'No, it doesn't, my love,' she reassured before turning to Eden. 'My girl wouldn't kill a baby, I know that much, whether hers or someone else's. She's been a silly … silly girl but she'd not harm a child. She's never harmed a living creature in her life. None of my children would harm a living thing unless it was for eating.'

Eden knew she'd got as far as she could with Carmen present. It was instinctive for a mother to protect her young. Whether Rowan possessed the same impulse she didn't know. What she did know was nothing about this client's story added up. She turned off her dictating machine.

'I think that's enough for today. I'd like to see you at my office early tomorrow afternoon once you've been examined by your GP. You're obliged to report to the station the day after but I'll be with you and it's nothing to worry about. The police may call to arrange for you to see a psychologist to check you are fit to be questioned before then. Remember, the conversations we have are between us and for no one else's ears. If they try to question you on the details of this case, say nothing; volunteer nothing, just call me right away, understood?'

Rowan nodded.

Eden turned to Carmen. 'There's no need for you to come tomorrow, although I may need to speak to you separately over the next few days if that's alright; about the place where the baby was found? As a matter of fact, I'm off to the site now. I've arranged to meet with the chief archaeologist.'

Carmen looked daggers; goodwill slipping to the flagstone floor.

'I'm sorry, have I said something to offend you?' apologised Eden, annoyed she may have lost the woman's trust with one ill-judged comment.

'Don't believe everything you hear that's all; them types might think they know everything but things aren't always what they seem.'

Eden didn't press her for further explanation but for the first time since she arrived she felt a chill cut through the stifling heat.

FOUR

Carmen watched the solicitor's car drive away. She trusted Eden Gray, although she didn't take kindly to her attempts to exclude her and worried about her interest in the site. She needed time to think.

'I'm going up the lane to pick a few blackberries for a crumble; you alright on your own for a bit, love?' she asked, pulling an old ice cream tub from the back of the cupboard.

Rowan nodded and replaced her ear pods.

The lane was dust dry. There had been little rain all summer. The crops suffered, the cabbages bolted and the harvest came early, but at least they'd gathered in the hay without any downpours. There wasn't a sniff of rain and the seaweed on the draining board remained crisp. When it got back its rubbery bounce, she'd know to expect a storm.

She'd always loved blackberry picking; striding out with the children, excited at the promise of the purple fruit, plump and juicy, bursting in their mouths and staining their fingers and tongues. It was the way the fruit ripened at the close of summer when the land seemed lazy. They were the last hooray.

Wilting, she blew down the front of her shirt. The late September sun scorched the back of her neck leaving her sticky with sweat as she stretched to pluck three fat berries nestling high up in the hedgerow. Eden Gray probably didn't do blackberry picking, why would she when she could buy the giant knobbly beetles Tesco sold all year round?

It had been a mad panic to find a solicitor yesterday. She'd known something was wrong when she'd heard a car speeding up the lane and could tell by the boy-racer gear changes she'd warned would burn out the clutch, it was Matthew. It was odd for him to be there in the afternoon and not at the garage. She'd watched the bright red Subaru screech to a halt and her son jump out, run into the farmhouse, then out again.

'Ma … are you there, Ma?' he'd bellowed from the middle of the yard.

All her children had a tendency to stand where they were and holler for her; summoning her in, like she did the cows for milking.

'I'm in the barn,' she'd shouted back.

'I've been trying to call you,' he said, red-faced and dishevelled in his green work overalls.

She'd felt for her mobile, then realised she'd left it in the kitchen.

'It's our Rowan, she's been arrested.'

Fair hair, stuck to his sweaty forehead; eyes wild and wide as saucers he'd looked much younger than his twenty years and she could tell he wasn't joking.

As soon as he'd told her about the baby she'd got it into her head she wanted a woman lawyer and when they'd looked on the local Law Society website, Eden Gray had been the standout candidate and to be fair she seemed genuinely concerned about Rowan, considering this was just another case to her. Perhaps she didn't have much else in her life? She must be in her mid-thirties, and good-looking, but there was no wedding ring. Then again, that meant nothing. In fact, who was she to talk? Four children by two fathers and not a husband in sight; scandalous but then, her family was used to scandal.

Things weren't so bad these days; not like when she and her sister Morvah were growing up, when they were branded by the past; their name tainted with fear and revulsion. She remembered the small fabric pouch sewn by her gran, filled with mustard seeds and tansy hung around her neck, tucked in under her vest to ward off evil. How she'd slip it off as soon as she left the house, knowing if someone smelt its pungent odour, she'd be ridiculed for being strange. Strange to a child was so much worse than anything else.

Mother warned them to ignore the village children who followed them name-calling after school and generally they did. Although she remembered one-time Morvah shouted at them for netting Cabbage Whites, telling them they shouldn't trap butterflies

20

because they were the souls of dead children. Some boys chased them throwing stones, striking her on the shoulder. Her little sister had spun around and raised her hand in a hex. She'd been pretty sure Morvah had no idea what a hex was, let alone how you cast one. It was just a word she'd heard, but the twist of her fingers and the flash of those black eyes of hers had done the trick and for a few magical weeks, they'd been free to gather fluffy hawthorn blossom to make into cordial and burn for Beltane and to play in the stream, until the bullies returned.

It was learnt behaviour, passed down and suffered by every generation of her family; the fact they didn't believe in Christmas or going to chapel twice on Sundays was excuse enough back then in the buttoned-up Methodist community. Unlike their God-fearing neighbours, their lives were measured by the seasons and the festivals they brought with them. Beltane with fire, Samhain at the end of October when they remembered the dead, Yule and Imbolc; the Celtic new year and festival of birth, containing the rite most sacred to her family, when they poured ewes' milk on the ground in a blessing. Their celebrations were played out against a backdrop of humdrum normality. If they'd lived like the generations before, without *Doctor Who* and *Top of the Pops*, things might have been easier. Seeing the outside world through the TV screen made it worse somehow, made them aware they were different.

It was only after Gran died and the last pit was dug, things had changed. Though her mother kept the feast days, she cleared the house of all signs of Wiccan. They still didn't go to chapel but by then neither did anyone else much.

Visitors came from up country, with no idea of their history. They bought milk and veg from them and holidayed in the barns they converted. They had moved on and when mother died, Morvah left home to train as a nurse and she as the eldest, took over the farm. People had begun to forget.

Now, with this baby being found in one of the pits the past would be raked up again and the finger-pointing would start and this time it wouldn't be only the villagers. Once the news got out, they'd find themselves in the centre of something they couldn't turn their backs on and walk away from. Dropping the last jewelled berry in the tub, she began the steady stroll back down the track. To make matters worse, she was sure Rowan was lying, or rather wasn't telling the whole truth. She knew it as certainly as she knew there would be no rain today.

A memory, like a weevil, burrowed; early summer, her seventeen-year-old daughter standing at the sink in a baggy shirt and leggings washing dishes after Sunday lunch. It was a scorcher and her two youngest children Maisy, six, and Jago, eight, in their bathers were being chased around the yard by Matthew with the hose pipe. She'd told her to leave the dishes, put on her costume and join them. Usually, Rowan would have jumped at the chance, but she'd said she didn't want to play stupid games. Noticing her usually stick-thin daughter had put on a little weight, she'd wondered if the puppy fat was why she didn't want to strip off. She'd put the thicker waist down to working in the cafe; being tempted by the staff freebies. Since then, she'd rarely seen Rowan out of baggy, shapeless clothes.

Now as she placed the ice cream tub on the draining board, she knew it was something else she'd been trying to hide; new life ripening; swelling her belly; bitter fruit. Lifting the seaweed from the windowsill, she crumpled it to dust.

FIVE

Eden had learnt through experience to start with the where and how. The why came later. By visiting the crime scene, she could form her own opinion; not be misled by the police or bamboozled by expert evidence. It was also a good way to test a client's integrity, especially when they claimed they'd never been there.

She'd casually throw out a few false facts about a place and wait for them to put her right. It was surprising how often it worked; how easily they tripped themselves up. It was crucial to know the true measure of your client, not the filtered Facebook gloss they put out to the world. Being innocent of the crime didn't mean they had nothing to hide and the false alibi the, *I've never been there in my life*, was often what got them convicted. Once a jury knew they were capable of lying about that, it was an easy stretch for the prosecution to convince them they were lying about the rest. Eyes glazed as they remembered all the liars they'd known; the unfaithful husband; the boss who had promised promotion. Realising how gullible they'd been they'd vow; *not this time. I won't be fucked over again.*

She'd kept the phone call with Elspeth Fuller, the Chief Archaeologist, brief, telling her Rowan was helping with enquiries and no more. In her experience, the most fruitful interviews were those without the benefit of a script.

Following her sat-nav, she turned left out of the farm gate, passing a postcard-perfect cottage the same vivid shade of pink as the ant-acid medicine in her dad's bathroom cabinet, before veering back into dappled woodland where hawthorns bent double by the wind stooped to shake arthritic hands above her head. The hedge, no doubt gilded in spring with cowslips and yellow gorse, had escaped a summer flail and brambles ran riot; clawing at her wing mirrors. Eyes peeled for oncoming vehicles or dogwalkers requiring her to slam on the brakes, she nearly missed the hairpin turn onto the unmarked muddy track leading to the site; avoiding the verge by inches as she swerved to make the corner.

She was relieved when the track finally widened and she was able to pull onto an area of level hardcore; parking next to a battered green Jeep. Beyond, stood a caravan and a large prefab and to the left, trapped on one side by a dense coppice, a flat, muddy field dotted with wooden markers and criss-crossed aluminium planking. In the far corner, cordoned off with flapping yellow tape, a police incident tent, where she guessed the body of the baby was found. She examined the perimeter with the targeted eye of an Exocet missile. The open aspect made it difficult for anyone to bury a baby secretly in daylight, whilst in the dark, the roped-off areas and muddy ground pitted with trenches dug by the archaeologists rendered it treacherous and confusing. Whoever buried the baby needed to know the lay of the land and exactly where they were heading.

Spotting a woman working on something through the open door of the prefab, Eden retrieved her wellies from the passenger footwell. She wished she'd worn proper socks instead of the sports variety, which slipped off her heel and balled in the toe of her boot. Tucking her notepad into her bag she sucked her way through the mud towards the woman.

'Professor Fuller …?' she shouted above the noise of the squeaky conveyor belt to her side feeding soil and rubble into a rusty sieve.

Fuller, didn't look up as she spoke. 'Come through but remove your boots. I'm at a critical point.'

Irish; the tone Dublin academic and distracted. Eden hoped this wasn't going to be a complete waste of time.

The interior was cramped. Trestle tables and a site plan spread out across one, others were piled high with plastic trays, full of broken pottery, stones and other fragments, took up much of the room. Shelves stacked with jars of murky anonymous liquids lined three of the walls. Tools hung on the other.

Eden guessed Fuller was in her mid-sixties. At a distance, she'd looked younger, largely down to her dolly-mixture clothes. She wore a boxy multi-coloured striped jumper not unlike one Eden's mum knitted her when a kid from odd ends of wool. Fuller's version had shrunk in the wash; the sleeves ending abruptly halfway up her arms. Skinny; her jeans hung off her backside, secured with a man's belt; tan leather flapping against her thighs. Lilac-tinted grey frizz, piled high and secured in a spotted bandana, completed the eccentric garb.

She was preoccupied, submerging slivers of muddy green fabric into a few centimetres of liquid, before placing them carefully in a container, covering them with a lid and labelling the side. Pulling off her gloves, she finally looked up, stepped forward and shook Eden's hand.

'Elspeth Fuller.' The handshake was vigorous and firm; rough palms and grouted nails a testimony to hard work and Eden guessed the tools hanging from the walls, were not just for show.

'Eden Gray. I rang earlier; Rowan Lutey's solicitor?'

'Ah yes, you mentioned the Lutey girl was helping the police with their enquiries. It's only we have to be careful who we let on site. We've had to put up with all sorts of comings and goings over the last few days; it's difficult to keep track of who's who. I've sent the rest of my team home until we get the all-clear.'

'You're here alone?' Eden asked, surprised. It was a glorious Autumn day but the place still felt heavy with gloom.

'For the time being. The police have agreed to send a patrol around at night. We're worried once word gets out about the baby's body, the press will be all over it and we'll attract ghouls from miles around.'

'Ghouls?'

'Weirdos, who like to view scenes of crime. Then there's the witch thing. Once the press cotton on to it, we'll be inundated with the wretched Wicca brigade.'

'Witch thing, I'm sorry I don't follow?'

'The witch pits; the baby was found in one of them; I assumed you knew? Shallow pits dotted across an area of about half an acre;

forty centimetres square, dug into the earth then lined and covered. The earliest has been carbon dated and is circa sixteen-forty, the most recent the nineteen-eighties. We found a particular brand of binder twine in that one, only produced then. This is a site of Pagan ritual; to some, of witchcraft.'

Luke had said a shallow grave. He'd said nothing about 'witch pits'.

'Of course, it's the contents we're primarily interested in.'

'Contents?'

Eden's stomach roiled, speculating Elspeth might mean human remains; that the baby was one of many bodies found.

'The votive offerings buried in each one. The oldest was lined with a swan's pelt. I can show you if you like?'

Relief; the word *ritual* had thrown her. To an archaeologist, it probably covered a multitude of sins but to someone like her; working in the Criminal Justice system the word conjured images of balaclava-clad rapists and serial killers.

Elspeth led her to the far side of the prefab, through a locked door into a stuffy windowless cubical. With the flick of a switch, the room was saturated with eerie, ultraviolet light.

'The finds are organic and subject to material degradation in all but the most controlled environments. The site is full of natural springs so the anaerobic boggy ground has preserved them. Our job is to keep them that way.'

Carefully lifting a large plastic box labelled Pit 32 from a side shelf, Elspeth manoeuvred it onto the table, raising the lid to reveal the contents. Though no longer soft or snowy white, the damp quills were visible; forged together to form a stiff cape reminding Eden of something draped over the shoulders of a bright young thing from the roaring twenties.

'It was buried with several pebbles found at only one beach in the county, a remote sort of place used by locals; Swanpool.'

Eden knew it well. It had been a childhood favourite because across the road from the beach was a large freshwater pond where you could hire small rowboats and catch tadpoles in spring.

'I know the place. I went there a lot when little.'

Fuller peered closely at her as if seeing her for the first time. 'Ah, yes … I can see it now I look at you.'

Eden wasn't sure what she meant.

Fuller must have sensed her hesitation. 'I don't mean to pry but you have an interesting face. It's the anthropologist in me; always on the lookout for unique histories and those are often written on the face. The Brythonic Celts have been my specialist area of study for several years now. It's in the bone structure you see and the colouring of course; like a roadmap when you know how to read it. It's extremely rare; red hair; the real stuff like yours I mean. The gene is seventy-thousand years old and originated in West Asia but is recessive, so in theory, it could disappear completely in a few years from now.'

Eden didn't have a clue what the woman expected her to do with the knowledge she was teetering on the brink of extinction and was annoyed she'd managed to slide under the archaeologist's microscope. She needed to nip this in the bud. She was here to ask the questions not the other way around and swiftly turned the conversation back to the pits.

'Do you know why it was important the pebbles came from there?'

'We're not sure but the place name is significant. We suspect the site was used for rituals to do with fertility. The swan is a symbol of fertility both in Greek and Celtic mythology. It's been carried through the Christian tradition. Saint Bridget is often represented in the form of a swan with a gold chain around her neck. She of course is the patron saint of midwifery. It's from her the word bride derives and indeed Bride is the Celtic goddess associated with spring and re-birth.'

Eden wondered if she should be taking notes for a test at the end of the impromptu lecture.

'Other birds were used as well; one pit contained two magpies. You know the saying; one for sorrow, two for joy, etcetera. Folklore has it a lone magpie carries a drop of the Devil's blood under its tongue. It's why the locals salute a single bird, so it won't curse them.' Walking a couple of steps to the back of the room Elspeth retrieved another plastic container; smaller this time. 'And there were these of course.'

Eden wasn't sure at first what she was looking at, then focusing, realised the pitiful tableau comprised the disintegrated remains of four eggs, each containing the scrawny twisted body of a naked bug-eyed chick.

'It's peculiar, isn't it? The chemicals in the soil dissolved the shells over time, leaving only the membrane around them. It seems they were buried in the pit just before they were about to hatch.'

'Buried alive?'

The woman's face twisted in surprise as if this macabre detail was news.

'Gruesome when you say it like that.'

The cloying stench of preservatives caught the back of Eden's throat. She had to get some air. 'And the baby. Could you show me exactly where you found the body?'

'The place is still technically a crime scene but I can show you on the plan if you like?' offered Elspeth, clipping the lid back on the chicks, turning off the light and closing the door behind them.

'I didn't find it myself. It was one of the student volunteers but I got there soon after. It was sheer chance it was found at all,' she said, pointing to one of many tiny red stickers dotting the plan. 'We completed excavations in that area a couple of months ago. The boy snuck off for a cigarette and noticed a fallen marker. He went to replace it; saw the ground had been disturbed and called my assistant. They lifted the cover and found the child. Quite a shock.'

'I can imagine.'

'It was clear it was a recent burial. There was decomposition of course but the remains were obviously not ancient. We called the police and the rest is history as us archaeologists say,' she grinned; pleased with the pun.

'I'm wondering how many people know about this place. I've never heard of it myself?'

'We try to keep it under the radar, like I said before, we don't want to attract undesirables. The land is owned by the council and the dig is privately funded, so we're not dependent on public donations.'

'How many people are involved?'

'I would say about twenty-five in all, including the undergraduates who help in the summer vacation. I can provide names if you like?'

'Was Rowan Lutey a volunteer, or known to someone else who worked here?'

'Not as far as I'm aware, but she'd know all about it of course because of her family.'

'Sorry, I don't understand?'

'She's a member of the family who dug the pits in the first place. Can you imagine, generation upon generation of Lutey women digging these pits over the centuries? They've always been known in the area as *cunning folk*; witches in common parlance, although I prefer to think of them as custodians; women charged with keeping Pagan ritual alive.'

There it was; that word again.

So that's what Agnes meant when she said the Luteys were cunning. She'd thought her secretary was inferring they were undesirables; didicoys or pikeys. Agnes and her dead mother often ranted on about didicoys and pikeys; political correctness not being their strong point. She must have been desperate to point the finger and yell, 'WITCH'.

'It was good of you to show me around. It's been helpful,' thanked Eden, pulling on her boots.

'If you need any further information, I have an office at the museum. I or one of my team is there every day. No need to make an appointment, just let them know who you are at reception. My mobile's on there but the museum is the best place to reach me,' offered Elspeth, handing Eden her card; her school teacher tone leaving Eden in no doubt she was dismissed.

Walking back to her car, she glanced across the field towards the police tent trying to make sense of the archaeologist's comments about the Lutey family and their connection to the site. It at least explained Carmen's reaction earlier.

Driving away, she attempted to dissect her day, only to conclude whilst she'd had an interesting history lesson at the feet of Elspeth Fuller and another in maternal safeguarding from Carmen Lutey, she was none the wiser about the one thing that mattered, whether Rowan was telling the truth or not, or if her reaction, her unwillingness to remember, was more to do with what happened afterwards; the burial rather than the birth.

Elspeth had examined her history in her features. What heritage would she find etched on Rowan's face if she had a mind to look? One thing was for certain, short of a broomstick and a pointy hat Eden wasn't sure she'd be able to spot a witch if one poked her in the eye.

SIX

She knew she probably ought to get back to the office but couldn't muster any enthusiasm. Her diary was free of clients, so at least there would be no one languishing in the waiting room, suffering sideways glances and short shrift from Agnes. She could see from her phone she had a new voicemail from Luke.

'Hi, it's me,' long pause. 'I'm ringing to give you the heads up. SOCO have finished at the site. I rang your office but Agnes said she hadn't seen you. I couldn't say much yesterday at the station with everyone around but I wanted to apologise for having a go at you about Thea the other day. It was unprofessional and it won't happen again. It's only I worry about Flora and …'

Beeeep.

He was out of time, thank God.

He'd said the forensic results would be out on Friday. It didn't give her long to get her ducks in a row. Luke hadn't said if the autopsy had determined how the child died.

She'd bought Rowan time on the basis she was mentally unfit but things were moving fast and the next time the girl attended, the police would be prepared. Tired as she was, she had a long evening ahead of her and headed home.

The flat felt chilly despite the heat of the last few days. She longed for a bath; a leisurely soak but knew it would likely propel her into a sleep she could ill afford so settled for a shower, letting the near scalding water pound her clean. When finished, she towel-dried her hair, slipped on her robe and was about to switch off the light when she caught a glimpse of herself in the steamy bathroom mirror.

Wiping away the condensation with the heel of her hand, she revealed the face Elspeth Fuller had made so much of and supposed 'interesting' was as good an adjective for it as any other. Though not princess pretty like Thea with her forget-me-not eyes and small, neat nose, she looked okay. Her features were angular and when tired, like this evening, her skin had a tendency towards transparency; a bluish tinge looming beneath her pale grey eyes. Elspeth had gone on about her red hair and in the harsh bathroom light, it gleamed. She usually got her hairdresser to run a few caramel highlights through it but things had been hectic lately and she hadn't been for a couple of months.

Thea was blonde like her mum; petite like her too, whereas she was tall and willowy. Flat-chested and awkward in her teens, she'd adopted an ungainly stoop whenever around them until one of her mother's more perceptive friends quietly suggested she take up surfing to make her more body aware; to give her core strength and balance. It worked and these days she embraced her height. Victoria's Secret had solved the other problem.

Striking was the word often used to describe her. She'd seen other women's eyes narrow as they weighed up the threat and enough men had complimented her over the years; some she hoped because they meant it but their compliments often felt inquisitorial like Elspeth's questions that afternoon; a prelude to a conversation about her background. Sooner or later, they'd expect to exchange histories and she'd be forced to tell her whole sorry story only to be left feeling diminished.

She'd known she was adopted for as long as she could remember. Her parents sat her down for 'the talk,' when she was five, shortly after her mum and baby sister, came home from the hospital and they felt the need to explain why there were no photographs of her in her mummy's tummy or on day one like there were of Thea; why she didn't seem to exist until she was a toddler. She had accepted the news; what choice did she have?

The partners she'd had over the years handled her adoption well enough but her abandonment was just too tragic to leave alone. They seemed intent on picking the scab in the hope of being the one to make it all better. In her opinion, nothing dampened a romance like exposing scar tissue. It was one of the reasons she'd liked Andrew when they met. He didn't seem to care about the past. He was focused on the future; his rather than hers as it turned out.

Examining her features in the mirror, she wondered what it must be like to own them the way people do when they know they have their mother's dimples or their father's eyes? She wrapped a towel around her hair, switched off the light and wandered to the kitchen to retrieve a bottle of wine. A lover who didn't ask questions and would keep her company as she worked through the night.

It was past ten and she hadn't eaten. Popping a couple of slices of bread in the toaster she opened the fridge on the off chance there was something vaguely edible to stick on top and found a tub of cream cheese still in date. She finished the meagre supper watching *Newsnight* before carrying the wine and her laptop to the bedroom.

Propping her pillows behind her, she settled on the bed and logged in. The police would be able to determine whether Rowan had given birth to the baby from the DNA residue on its body. They had Jessica Marshall's testimony which confirmed Rowan looked distraught and was aware the baby had gone. She handed back the money knowing she could no longer fulfil her part of the bargain. How did she know and why hadn't she reported the missing baby to the police? It's what everyone would expect her to do. Unless of course she already knew there was no point because the child was already dead and buried in a witch pit?

Then there were the pits themselves. There was no denying the family link. Rowan was one of the few people who knew about them and their macabre contents.

She typed *surrogacy* into her search engine; hesitated, deleted and re-typed *Celtic Sacrifice*.

SEVEN

Carmen looked in on Rowan, her face buried in the pillow; hair a tangled bird's nest. It was good to have her home. Her flat belonged to the Marshalls who'd been only too pleased to let the police in to search for evidence and leave the message she wasn't wanted back.

Though they'd talked after Eden left, she'd not managed to get anything else out of her and she'd resisted pressing too hard. Her daughter needed to recharge her batteries before her medical and her interview with Eden that afternoon. There would be time to talk later. Right now, she had something to do; something she dared not put off.

Most people wouldn't be up for hours but she was used to rising at the crack of dawn to see to the animals. She could hear a solitary robin singing outside. Those like her who rose in the dark knew it was the robin, not the lark who sang first. The old folk song played in her head.

And when they were dead the robins so red, brought strawberry leaves and over them spread.

Poor babes in the wood, poor babes in the wood. Oh, don't you remember those babes in the wood.

Although not steep, the attic stairs were narrow and in need of dusting. It was easy to forget them behind the door at the end of the landing. She felt for the light pull before remembering the bulb had gone the last time she'd come up to store some of Maisy's old toys. Thankfully there was another at the top which, when switched on would give the room a nicotine glow which would have to do.

The attic extended the width of the house but was of little use for anything other than storage; the criss-cross of oak beams

34

making it difficult to manoeuvre your way through without bumping your head. She picked her way to the far corner where the battered ox-blood trunk lay under a pile of dust sheets. She pulled them aside. The leather had long ago lost its shine; the catch staining her fingertips with rust as she opened the lid.

What she was looking for rested at the bottom, under a tangle of tarnished horse brasses, their black leather dusted with the powdery kiss of mildew. She supposed she should give them a polish and sell them on eBay. They'd been her first man's pride and joy but he was long gone and she had no use for them on the Farrow & Ball painted walls of the shabby-chic cottage she let to holidaymakers. The local pub had a fair collection; reproductions, hanging alongside the inglenook and she wondered whether they might take them.

She lifted them to one side and there it was. Wrapped in buttery kid leather, tied with string, it had been a decade or more since she'd opened it and didn't have time to do so now. She had to get it out of the house and somewhere it wouldn't be found so easily. If the police got hold of it, it could make matters worse for Rowan. They wouldn't understand its secrets; secrets not hers to tell - a story from dead lips, recorded on foxed and curling pages. She lifted the book carefully, feeling its smooth leather blanket, thin and worn. It smelt of the past; of pipe tobacco and wax. Tucking it under her arm, she piled the tangle of brasses back inside the trunk, closed the lid and replaced the dust sheets before retracing her steps to the landing. Pausing there for a moment, she listened for movement but everything was quiet as she tiptoed downstairs and out of the door.

The air was heavy and it had started to drizzle. She was relieved. They needed rain to soften the earth for the winter veg. Sliding the book under her jumper to keep it dry, she looked down at her slippers. The wet cobbles, slicked purple and black were treacherous and she needed to take care as she tottered across the yard.

Autumn was finally here. She'd light a fire when she got back. It would be the first time the twist of smoke appeared from the chimneys since last winter.

Unlocking the padlock to Flossie's Barn, named after her grandfather's favourite mare, she headed for the hiding place; behind the old tin water butt steadily rusting away in one corner. She'd holed up there as a child when there were chores to be done. Now she needed to hide the past.

EIGHT

Eden overslept, waking on top of the duvet cover, hair still wrapped in the damp towel. A sour fur coated her tongue and she remembered she'd finished off the wine. Scraping her unruly curls into a topknot, she changed, brushed her teeth and headed for the office to look through the post and drop off a tape for Agnes to type up. Afterwards, she'd make straight for the museum, where she hoped to catch Elspeth.

She'd fallen asleep reading about how the Celts were known to practice human sacrifice to help prophesy during Samhain when the veil between this world and the world of spirits lifted. These rituals took place in woodland where the remains of their victims were buried in pits often with animal bones.

Carmen's reaction the day before had warned her off any talk of witch pits while she was around, but Rowan would be alone when they met later and she needed to know whether the burial of the baby's body in one was a coincidence or something else? She didn't like the turn this was taking. If her client was involved in some Celtic mystic crap she needed to know sooner rather than later because if she was thinking this way so would others once they knew the Luteys' history.

Agnes was busy on the phone as she sauntered past the reception desk to her office at the back of the building. Other than for the few minutes following her disastrous fraud trial, she'd barely been there for the best part of a week; the lopsided trolley abandoned in the corner a rickety reminder of her recent failure.

The room was airless, fumy with the smell of photocopier ink, and laced with a sickly whiff of rotten fruit from a half-eaten apple turning brown where she'd left it on the bookshelf next to *Stone's Justices' Manual.*

The stack of papers gathering dust on top of the filing cabinet raised a sigh of frustration. She'd have to make time to catch up later but for now, the Lutey case had to take priority; things were about to ratchet up a notch.

After forty minutes sifting through her in-tray, prioritising everything screamingly urgent with aide-memoires on yellow post-it notes, she tidied her desk, plopped the wrinkly apple in the bin and escaped via the back door, taking the narrow cut through to River Street.

Wedged between a Vietnamese nail bar and a tiny gentlemen's outfitters whose window display was a history lesson in itself, the grand sandstone façade of The Royal Cornwall Museum dominated the otherwise modest street. The salty lure of fried bacon beckoned from the cafe next door but despite her rumbling stomach, she resisted the urge to take advantage of the two for one panini offer and veered left, up a couple of shallow steps to the museum foyer. The woman behind the desk, busy sticking reduced-price labels on a stack of calendars nearing their year-end, looked up.

'Visitors buy them for the shots of Cornish beauty spots,' she said clearly feeling the need to explain.

Eden decided not to ask if they'd heard of postcards. 'I'm here to see Professor Fuller.'

The woman arched forward; itching to hear more. 'Are you a journalist? We've had a lot of journalists since the discovery of the baby.'

'I'm not but if you tell her it's Eden Gray, I'm sure she'll see me.'

Unimpressed, the gossipy gatekeeper lifted the receiver and dialled an internal number.

'You can go on through,' she huffed, 'it's up the stairs on the first floor; second door on the left.'

Eden hadn't been to the museum for years and was amazed at the changes to the main exhibition room since the days when it topped her school trip list. Back then it had been a marvellously quirky place, where Celtic torques sat wedged between miniature mine engines and stuffed weasels sporting velvety waistcoats. The exhibit she'd loved best; the one that sent her imagination racing was the shrivelled, black cadaver in an open coffin; the wizened mummy of an Egyptian priest, Iset Tayef Nakht. The curator had let her and her classmates touch him; actually, allowed them to stroke his shiny ebony forehead and make a wish.

Whenever she told this story to friends from out of county, their reaction was one of disbelief and she'd begun to wonder if she'd imagined the whole thing until recently she'd read the mummy was undergoing a makeover to undo the carnage done by the numerous coats of varnish applied by his original Victorian caretakers. Now, more educational experience than old curiosity shop, she couldn't deny the transformation but missed the loopy chaos.

Taking the wide marble staircase to the first floor, she was pleased on reaching the landing to discover the portrait of 'The Cornish Giant' still held pride of place. As a teenager, used to watching obese recluses being craned out of bedroom windows on TV, she hadn't thought he was much to write home about. But today, resplendent stomach testing the seams of his crimson yeomanry uniform, and lace-frilled collar snug beneath his treble chin, he looked more dignified than she remembered and she gave a respectful nod in his direction in recognition of his portly grandeur.

Along the corridor, was the door labelled, Professor E. Fuller. She was about to knock when it flew open.

'Eden … so glad you've come. I can see what Elspeth meant about the hair.'

Her hand instinctively lifted to her head. The greeting was so unnervingly familiar, for one embarrassing moment, she thought she must have met the young man before.

'I'm afraid Elspeth's not in today, she told me you might turn up. I'm her assistant, James Ferris.' In his late twenties; he wore a pale green designer jumper and skinny jeans. Handsome in a contrived way, his fair beard was carefully trimmed, his hair slicked back in a perfect hipster quiff. Eden couldn't help wondering how he got along with his dishevelled boss?

The room was sparse save for a large table in the centre piled high with papers, books and files.

'You're interested in the pits?'

She wasn't sure if he knew the connection between her interest and her client.

'Yes, in the history behind the excavation, especially the link to the Lutey family.'

'And you think it will help prove Rowan's innocence?'

It was a good question. She wasn't sure it would help at all.

'Actually, she's not been charged yet.'

'No … of course not,' he blushed. 'Elspeth told me about Rowan, well not exactly, she told me you were her solicitor but I put two and two together because the police asked if she'd been hanging around in the days before the body was found? I was one of the first on the scene. The student who found the body was working with me at the time.'

'And had you?'

'What?'

'Seen Rowan at the site?'

'Never, none of the Luteys have visited despite Elspeth trying to get them to. It's a shame they're not interested because there's a big gap in our knowledge about the ritual surrounding the pits, but I guess you'd like me to tell you what we do know?'

'That would be helpful.'

She took notes as he talked. Every now and then he'd visit one of the piles of paper and pluck out a Pagan symbol or a photograph of a standing stone. Other times he'd grab a book, letting it fall open on a particular page which he'd then read aloud.

Eden envied his enthusiasm for his chosen profession; how certain he was of its worth. Once, she'd believed in justice the way James Ferris believed in history. Nowadays she believed only in her own ability and even that confidence was beginning to waver. Justice in her experience was a well-prepared case. She only hoped she was up to the job.

When she first told her left-wing parents, she wanted to be a lawyer, they'd assumed she meant in immigration or civil rights, working out of a crowded inner-city law centre for legal aid rates. She could never have done that. She had no memory of her less-than-perfect start in life, but people would have automatically assumed she did and it gave her some intrinsic understanding of their predicament. In reality, she hadn't a clue what it meant to be abused or underprivileged, so how could she help those who were? She'd have felt a complete fraud. In the end, she'd compromised and become a criminal defence lawyer.

'The site dates back to pre-Christian times. No one knows how far back the Luteys can trace their links to it; maybe as far? We know for certain they were involved by the eighteen-hundreds because they appear on the High Sheriff's list of pellars operating in the county.'

James told her about the people who came from far and wide each spring to visit 'cunning folk' or pellars to renew their good fortune. How the captains of the Packet trading fleet and local fisherman requested charms to bring them luck on their voyages.

'Are you talking about spells, when you say charms?'

'In a way, but tangible; often little bags worn around the neck, filled and blessed by the pellar.'

'Filled with what?'

'Earth, sand, teeth, the bones of small birds, herbs, any number of things. Sometimes magic symbols or a verse on slips of paper.'

'And the Luteys were pellars?'

'I'm talking about the early to mid-nineteenth century. Back then, Cornwall was full of pellars. Every village had someone called in to bless the harvest or the ground before planting. Usually, they were women able to help with childbirth or herbal remedies when people fell ill. The Luteys were special, they were conjurors.'

'Magicians?'

'Not like David Blaine or Dynamo,' James laughed and Eden noticed his teeth were perfect. 'They were said to be able to conjure up spirits.'

A shiver licked the back of Eden's neck.

'This is a period in history when science and superstition overlapped. Some thought electricity magical, others it was the work of the Devil. On the one hand, seances were at their height, on the other there was a religious revival in play. The Methodist

Church in Cornwall was able to thrive because of its emphasis on the supernatural; the movement of the spirit in the congregation. Speaking in tongues and swooning at the word of God wasn't that removed from the incantations and possessions of the conjurors they were used to. There was plenty of work for conjurors but they called themselves something else, spiritualists or mediums.'

'Smoke and mirrors?'

'Some yes but not the Luteys. They were concerned with the spirits of the living rather than the dead. They worked charms to conjure new life.'

'Elspeth told me the pits were believed to contain offerings to Saint Bride.'

'That's what we think. You saw the eggs?'

'Yes.'

'Eggs have always been a symbol of rebirth. The Romans and the Egyptians gave eggs as gifts during the Spring Equinox just as Christians give Easter eggs in remembrance of Christ's resurrection. The egg is the symbol of life. Its shape has no beginning and no end.'

Eden shuddered, remembering the chicks buried alive.

'We think the Luteys were paid to dig the pits by women having trouble conceiving. Right up until Rowan's grandmother died people went to her for help when they couldn't get pregnant. It was always discreet you understand; not something you wanted to shout from the rafters but in the centuries before, they would have needed to be even more careful. If they weren't, they were in danger of being branded witches. James I's *Daemonologie* published in 1597 started a frenzy of persecution involving everything from ducking stools to tormenting with needles to find the spot on the body impervious to pain which defined a witch. The last witch trials in the county took place in seventeen twelve but the oldest pit we've found is seventy years older. It was dangerous for the Luteys and the women who went to them for help. Secrecy was crucial but it was not an indication of evil or guilt, but fear.'

'From what you say, it was pretty harmless; a bit of hope before IVF came on the scene?' Eden said thinking of Jessica Marshall.

'Correct.'

'So, where exactly does the buried baby come into all this?'

'Nowhere; it would be sacrilege. The ground is sanctified to bring life. To bring a dead baby there would curse it forever.'

'Thanks, you've been really helpful.' she said, closing her notebook.

'No problem and if you need anything else feel free to call in again, or you can reach me at the site.'

Grabbing a latte from the cafe on her way out, Eden wandered slowly back to the office. It was a lot to take in. If James was right and Rowan was true to her family's beliefs, she would never bury a dead baby in one of the pits, but if she didn't, who did? She didn't believe in the supernatural, or magic, black or white, but plenty did and their appetites would be fed by the reporters already sniffing around. Once they put their fire and brimstone spin on this, she didn't rate her client's chances of a fair trial. No one would be interested in something as mundane as the truth.

NINE

Rowan arrived on time and to Eden's relief, alone. Ushering her into her office before Agnes got the chance to reach for the thumbscrews, she began with the update received via Luke's voicemail the evening before.

'I've heard from the police. The forensics team has finished their investigation. It means we need to get ready for their findings.'

'What's that mean, for me?'

'It means we need to be prepared.'

'For what?'

'For when the police question you again. My guess is they'll telephone tomorrow to ask me to bring you in.'

'What if I refuse?' Rowan said; chin tilted in defiance.

Her mulish arrogance reminded Eden of Thea.

'It's simple. If you don't go voluntarily, they'll come and get you. We need to be prepared and to be prepared I need to know everything; good and bad.'

Eden wasn't convinced the girl's silent acceptance was sincere. 'I asked you to come alone so we could speak frankly. I know you said you have no secrets from your mum and that's good. I'm not trying to encourage you to keep things from her.'

'But you think I'm lying, don't you? You think I killed my own baby and buried it in one of the pits. Well, you're wrong; I didn't. *My* baby could be alive somewhere else and no one's looking for it.'

Eden wasn't going to back off. Attack was always Thea's first line of defence too.

'I want to believe you ... I do. You're right, at this moment there is still a remote possibility this is another child but why do you think you don't remember what happened? You were pregnant, that's certain isn't it, that's what you've told me and that's what I assume the doctor confirmed today?'

'Yes,' Rowan agreed; anger giving way to an expression of confusion.

'But then the Wednesday before last you say you woke up having taken a nap knowing you'd given birth?'

'Yes.'

'How exactly did you know?'

Like everyone, Eden had heard stories of naive teenagers delivering unexpected bundles of joy into the toilet basin but even those girls couldn't ignore the evidence once it arrived. Here, there was no mewing infant to testify this had ever happened; only a feeling. The doctor's examination had hopefully at least given substance to a story that at first blush looked like the product of an overactive imagination.

'Let's go back. You say you took a nap and the next thing you knew it was early evening and you were no longer pregnant?'

'Yes.'

'Were you in pain when you woke?'

'Not pain exactly. I felt sort of ... empty.'

Rowan's hand drifted down to her abdomen.

'You no longer felt the baby moving; is that it?'

'More than that; I knew there was nothing there anymore.'

'You definitely felt it moving before?'

'Yeah, all the time; that's why I was so tired. I hadn't got much sleep the night before and wasn't due in for my shift until lunchtime, so decided to go back to bed. The next thing I knew it was evening.'

'So, you're convinced everything was normal up until the point you fell asleep. There was nothing to suggest you were about to give birth: no contractions, no waters breaking?'

'No, nothing out of the ordinary, just the usual ... you know, the baby moving around inside and I felt so tired.'

'And when you woke, was there any physical evidence you'd had the baby; blood for instance, on your sheets?'

'No.'

'What about your clothes; were you wearing a nightdress or pyjamas; were you dressed?'

'Pyjamas, and there was a little blood on them. When I woke up, I went to the loo and I noticed there was something.'

'What did you think?'

'I still wasn't quite with it and thought I'd started my period. That's what it felt like, cramping, you know like before you come on. I felt groggy, like when you're hungover and don't quite know where you are. Then I thought, I can't be having my period because I'm pregnant. I felt my stomach and it felt flatter and then I knew the baby was gone.'

'But you hadn't been drinking or taking drugs?'

'No,' the girl replied flatly.

'So, what did you do then?'

'I lay there on the bathroom floor for a while. Then, I started to look for it.'

'For the baby?'

'Yeah.'

'Where … where did you look?'

Agitated, the girl began to fiddle with her eyebrows, plucking out the tiny hairs. She probably needed a break but Eden knew it would be difficult to pull the interview back if she stopped now. Rowan was talking and she needed to extract as much as possible before she retreated again.

'I pulled the covers off the bed, then looked under the bed; in case it had slipped underneath. In the drawers, in the wardrobe. I pulled all the clothes out. I searched the kitchen cupboards, everywhere.'

Eden listened with growing disbelief. 'Go on Rowan, you're doing really well,' she encouraged, her nose twitching with the overpowering stink of deceit. She'd seen this girl as a bit of a cause, someone to be protected, championed even, but the girl was talking nonsense and you didn't have to be a lawyer to spot it.

'I even emptied the bin onto the kitchen floor. That was when I was sick; vomited all over the tiles.'

'Poor you. Why didn't you call an ambulance or the police?'

'I don't know … I panicked, I suppose.'

Eden closed the file on her desk. 'Look Rowan, the police are going to ask you these questions and they won't be as sympathetic as me, I can tell you. I want you to be ready. Why didn't you call anyone?'

The girl's face crumpled.

'It's perfectly understandable you should get upset talking about this,' said Eden but we have to go through it and what you're telling me doesn't make sense.'

'I felt so strange, like it was a dream and I thought the baby would turn up.'

'Turn up?'

'I thought, maybe this was how it happens with surrogacy, maybe you fall asleep and have the baby, then someone comes and takes it, you know? I didn't want to get anyone into trouble. I kept thinking whoever had delivered the baby and taken it, would let me know once they'd checked it was okay.'

'But who? Who do you think would do that, the Marshalls; your GP?'

'My GP knew nothing about it. I was worried he'd tell Mum. I know he shouldn't, but I was worried he would. He's been the family doctor for years. You should have seen his face today when he examined me. He looked like he was about to have a fit.'

'You mean to say you had no antenatal care throughout this pregnancy?'

'Not from my usual doctor.'

'Then who examined you; who gave you check-ups to make sure you and the baby were okay?

Rowan hesitated, plucking at her eyebrows again.

This girl will be hopeless in a witness box, Eden thought, you can read her like a book.

'Morvah,' she whispered.

'Who?'

'Morvah, my auntie. Mum's younger sister. She's a midwife.'

'And she knew you were pregnant and about the Marshalls having paid you to have the baby?'

'Only about the pregnancy bit, at first.'

'Why didn't she tell your mother?'

'Because I made her promise not to and because Mum and her don't speak. They haven't spoken since Gran died and Mum got the farm.'

'But you're still close to her?'

'I was until all this. I knew how much Mum thought of her and how much she missed her. I kept in touch hoping I could help them sort things out and be friends again. Then, when I knew I was having the baby I asked if she'd take care of me during the pregnancy and she went along with it.'

'She must have known she'd lose her job if found out?'

'Yeah, that's why she said she could only look after me until I was about three months gone. After that, I'd have to go to a proper clinic. If I didn't, she'd tell Mum.'

'So, you told her you'd go to your GP?'

'Yeah.'

'But you didn't?'

'No. Jess contacted a private clinic and every three weeks I went there for a check-up. They gave me one of them blood pressure kits and some urine testing strips and Jess tested me in between visits.'

'And you cut ties with Morvah?'

'Not right away. She still took an interest; wanted to know how I was and all that. It was only when I told her about the surrogacy, we fell out.'

'What about?'

'Nothing really.'

'Tell me and I'll decide whether it's nothing.'

'She tried to get me to change my mind, not to give the baby to the Marshalls; not to take the money. She said it was a terrible thing to do, to take money for a child. She said if I was determined to give the baby up, I should put it up for adoption, then the parents would be checked out to make sure they were suitable so the baby would get the best chance in life.'

Eden listened, her own memories surfacing about her status as an adopted child and how things turned out for her. She'd been lucky with her parents but it was still the biggest event of her life and the one she'd had the least say in.

'What was your response?'

'I told her, as far as I was concerned it was the Marshalls' baby, not mine, and I'd taken the money to get away from here.'

'What did she say to that?'

'She flipped, said I was a bad person, unnatural, that no woman should be capable of giving up a baby to strangers especially a Lutey woman. She went on about how our family had at our own cost tried to give women the gift of motherhood and how I was turning my back on all that. I argued with her. I said I was doing exactly the same as the family had always done, only I wasn't doing it with stupid spells, or for free; that's a mug's game.'

'Did she see your point of view?'

'No way. She said I was a disgrace and I haven't seen or spoken to her since. When I told Jess, she said Morvah wasn't to come near me or the baby ever again.'

There was a childish petulance in the girl's tone and Eden was becoming increasingly concerned that apart from a few tears at the outset of their conversation Rowan was showing no obvious grief for this child. It may have, in her mind, belonged to Jess Marshall but she had carried it for nigh-on nine months. Either she was in complete denial or she was unnervingly cold-hearted. Eden cut to the chase.

'Rowan, what do you know about the witch pits?'

'Nothing.'

'Surely you know about your family's connection with them?'

'I suppose so.'

'Well, don't you find it interesting? I know I would if it was my family. I've spoken to the archaeologist involved with the dig, it's fascinating stuff.'

Rowan seemed interested suddenly.

'Who did you talk to?'

'Who … you mean the name of the archaeologist? I spoke to Elspeth Fuller.'

'Oh her,' she grimaced, 'well she might find it fascinating digging around in the dirt to get her name on some university paper no one reads, but I don't.'

Eden was beginning to realise this girl revealed the most about herself when she was angry.

'So, you do know about the burial offerings made by your family as a fertility rite and the discoveries made on the dig?'

'Yeah, but Mum wants nothing to do with it. Morvah's the only one who gives a damn. She's the one who believes in all that Wiccan stuff.' The girl's anxiety bubbled to the surface again and Eden knew she'd touched a nerve even though she had no idea which one.

'Even so, you must understand why it's an amazing find?'

'But it's not a find to us, is it? We've known about it all along and what good has it done us? Beltane and Imbolc and all that other crap and that woman, the archaeologist, isn't interested in paying us for telling her stuff.'

'I know she's tried to talk to Carmen. Are you saying your mother asked for money?'

'Of course not. Mum wants the past to go away. She's happy working all hours on the farm and running around after the holidaymakers.'

'I see.'

'People like us get nothing for free. All those women my family helped never had to pay a penny; they gave *donations*; food and stuff. It would have been bad luck to take money Mum said. Stupid if you ask me.'

'Is that why you took the money for your baby, Rowan?'

She paused, thinking about her answer. 'I suppose, if they wanted it so badly, why shouldn't they pay for it? They'd spent loads of money on waste of time fertility treatments. Why should I give them a baby for free?'

'But now the baby's gone and the money's gone too.'

'Exactly, so ask yourself, why would I leave myself with nothing? Why would I carry around a baby I didn't want; not be able to drink or go out with my mates; not be able to tell my mum. Why would I do all that to end up worse off?'

She was right of course. She was mercenary and selfish and the more Eden saw of her the less she liked her, but Rowan had a good commercial brain and the child's murder made no commercial sense. The problem was it wasn't a defence likely to go down well with a jury. Eden had one more question she was determined to ask.

'So, tell me, who's the baby's father?'

'What's that got to do with anything?' she glared.

'Maybe nothing, but until we know what happened to this baby, we have to keep an open mind about everyone who has a connection with it and that includes the father.'

'Well good luck with that, I haven't got a clue who he is; some holidaymaker I met in a club and slept with on the beach one night.'

'Really?'

'Yeah, what's wrong with that?' she said defiantly.

'Nothing absolutely nothing. It doesn't seem the sort of thing you'd do, that's all.'

'How would you know, the sort of thing I'd do?'

'You're right … but—'

Rowan shot up. 'I've got to go. I've got that psychiatric whatsit they've booked for me.'

'I'll pick you up tomorrow morning at ten-thirty.'

'Whatever,' she shouted over her shoulder before slamming the door behind her.

For two pins she'd tell her to find a new lawyer; one willing to put up with her paroxysms and sketchy memory; not to mention the routine lying and she was lying, she would bet Rowan knew exactly who the father of her baby was.

Eden slammed her file shut.

TEN

She had just settled down with a coffee to read Rowan's psychiatric evaluation e-mailed overnight when she got the text from Luke confirming the request her client attend at the station for further questioning. She didn't answer the text. Instead, she scanned the report hoping it would give her a let out. The author Bill Duffy was an astute and independent professional she trusted and used for her own reports. It concluded:

Whilst Rowan Lutey presents somewhat disconnected from her current situation, she can distinguish between right and wrong and make informed decisions based upon information relayed to her. She does not present with any indications of psychosis nor is there any reference in her medical records to previous lapses into fugue states or episodes of drug or alcohol-induced automatism. There is no evidence she has suffered any physical trauma to the head that may be responsible for her amnesia. It is my professional opinion therefore that whilst this young lady is suffering from anxiety and fatigue, she is nonetheless (subject to close and monitored supervision and an ongoing review by a suitably qualified health professional as to her physical wellbeing after giving birth) fit to be questioned under the provisions of PACE.

Not much help there and to add to her dilemma there was no heads up in Luke's text on the results of the forensics carried out on the baby's body on cause of death. She printed off the report, finished her coffee and set off to collect her client.

***

She could tell something was up, long before she caught sight of the farm, by the number of abandoned cars parked along the verge. Maybe local hunt followers? It was the right time of year, but the cars were not of the battered vans and Land Rover variety she'd expect. Perhaps a funeral in the church, or coffee morning in the village hall? As she got nearer, it was clear what was going on. The place was crawling with press; the farm gate blocked by a camera crew filming a perky female reporter Eden recognised from the regional news.

Putting her foot down, she drove past, following the road to the back lane, she remembered from her previous visit led to the rear of the farm. For the moment it was clear. She pulled in around the corner and rang Rowan's mobile. Carmen answered.

'It's Eden. I'm trying to get to you, but cars and reporters are barring the way. What the hell is going on?'

'The first of them arrived at about eight this morning and there's been a steady stream since. They were right up to the door until Matthew went out and told them they were trespassing.'

The woman's voice was remarkably calm considering her family was under siege. Eden admired her fortitude. Many in her situation would have crumbled.

'They're not around the back at the moment, I'll try to get through this way.'

'How are you going to get Rowan out?' Carmen asked, her voice less controlled.

'I'm going to call the police and tell them to come and move these people off.'

'It'll make matters worse if the police turn up. Can't I talk to the reporters; tell them our Rowan's done nothing wrong?'

'No, no you can't. You could be tricked into saying something you'll regret. I'll talk to the press if and when I think it's the best thing to do. You shouldn't engage with them at all. It could prejudice Rowan's case. I can't understand why they're here?'

'Haven't you heard?'

'Heard what?' asked Eden absentmindedly; checking over her shoulder no one had followed her.

'It's been on the local radio. The baby ...' Eden caught a quiver in Carmen's voice, 'they're saying the baby was suffocated and it may have happened when it was buried?'

Eden's stomach fell away as she grappled with the implications of those terrible words. Why hadn't Luke told her; he must have known when he texted? No wonder the press was there. The grim discovery of the baby's body was newsworthy enough, but even the most inventive hack couldn't have imagined this. This new horror and the girl's family history was an irresistible draw; a scoop worthy of every tabloid out there.

'Carmen, I have to ring the police. I have to alert them to the situation.'

'Alright … I suppose you know best, but Rowan's petrified. She's locked herself in her room.'

'Keep talking to her. Try and get her out. I'll take the back lane down to you. I'll call when I'm outside.'

Eden phoned the station. 'This is Eden Gray, I'm calling about my client Rowan Lutey. She's due to report for interview this morning.'

'Rowan Lutey you say and how do I spell that?'

Eden could barely contain herself. 'Really? Exactly how many manslaughter suspects have you got on the books?' she replied sarcastically. 'Try spelling it the same way you spelt it when you brought her in for questioning. You need to send a car to pick up my client and to get rid of the press camping outside. Had someone thought to tell me about this, I would have made sure she didn't come back here last night. DI Parish must have known about the forensics when he texted me this morning. The reporters have been here since eight so they certainly bloody knew. It was on the local morning news for god's sake but you lot didn't think to tell me?'

She was too furious to care whether the young woman on the other end of the line was part of the conspiracy. She needed to vent and only disconnected when she was satisfied she'd got her message across.

Grabbing her bag and an old coat from the boot of the car, she pulled the hood over her head. She couldn't do much about the smart suit creasing beneath the makeshift disguise but swapped her kitten heels for the wellies she'd worn on her visit to the site. Keeping close to the hedge, she clambered down into the lane, over the small stile, down the granite steps to the back door of the farmhouse. The door opened on the first ring to Rowan's mobile.

Matthew stood guard at the kitchen window, looking out across the farmyard towards the ever-growing body of people outside the gate. It had begun to rain and those without umbrellas took shelter under the trees; among them a smattering of activists carrying banners, scrawled with slogans; DEVIL'S SEED … BABY KILLER … WITCH.

Eden read the hateful words and shuddered.

The two younger children had been planted at the kitchen table playing 'Who's Who,' no doubt set up as a distraction.

'Maisy, it's your turn,' encouraged Carmen. 'Why don't you ask Jago if his man's got a hat on?'

'Don't keep telling er, Ma.'

'Has your man got a hat on?' mimicked Maisy.

'No, so there.'

Eden watched as the little girl flipped down the faces of two characters with a flourish.

'So … it *is* a man then?' she said with a triumphant grin.

'Ma …' Jago whined.

'Now quiet, Jago, I need to talk to Miss Gray; play with your sister nicely.'

Carmen steered Eden towards the other end of the kitchen.

'She still won't come out; she's taken the news badly,' she whispered, then nodding in the children's direction, 'I've not been able to take them to school. We couldn't get out and I couldn't leave Rowan anyway.'

'I understand. The police will see the press off. If it's them leaking this stuff I'll find out, don't you worry.'

Matthew hollered from his lookout, 'It's them, they're here; two police cars at the gate. They're coming in and there's another one blocking the way behind.'

Eden touched Carmen on the shoulder in a gesture of solidarity as she moved towards Matthew to look for herself. Luke was the first out of the car along with a young female officer Eden recognised as DS Denise Charlton.

'Let them in, Matthew,' she said, nodding at Carmen, 'you stay with these two, I'll talk to them.'

Carmen didn't argue. Something in the way she slumped back down into the chair next to the two giggling children told Eden she knew her only option was to weather this storm.

Luke faced Eden's inquisitorial gaze the minute he walked through the door.

'Now, before you say anything, none of this is down to us. We don't want the press around this investigation any more than you do. In fact, we've already had a call from the council about the security at the site. Reporters are camped out there too. It's a massive headache. Whoever leaked this … it wasn't the investigative team, believe me.'

'Believe you? Yeah right. Never mind the press; what about you leaking a bit of information my way. Why didn't you see fit to put me in the fucking picture about the baby this morning when you called?'

The expletive caused the children to look up from their game and a frown shadowed Carmen's face.

'Can we have a quiet word?' Luke chided, grabbing her arm and leading her towards the hallway, out of earshot of the others. Eden pulled away, annoyed she'd lost it whilst he, once again, was coming across as the grown-up.

'Listen, when I texted to you this morning, I didn't know all the information. I don't know why I didn't, because I should have been told, but for some reason, I wasn't. I'm as angry as you about it.'

'It's convenient though, isn't it? I bring my client in for questioning and you drop the bombshell the baby was buried alive. If that's not an ambush I don't know what is?'

'If I'd known, I'd have told you. Think about it. If I'd dropped the *bombshell* in the interview, you'd have stopped it. You're a good lawyer. You'd never have allowed me to continue to question the girl.'

He was right of course. The advantage of surprise may well have been short-lived but at least she would have got Rowan's reaction.

Her first reaction might have confirmed guilt or innocence for both her and Luke, now, neither had been privy.'

'Alright I believe you,' she conceded.

Luke let out an unmistakeable sigh of relief. 'So, where's she now?'

'Upstairs, locked in her room.'

'Well, we'd better get her out, and so you don't accuse me of withholding anything else or breaching the Code, I assume you got Bill Duffy's report this morning? I called in a favour to get it done quickly because of the seriousness of the charge.'

She wasn't sure what he wanted from her. If it was congratulations, he'd have a long wait.

'And the DNA; any news on that front?' she asked.

'Not yet. You know the score it'll be a couple of weeks at least before the results are back, but we're confident from the talks we've had with the Marshalls she's the baby's mother, but I expect you know that already?'

Eden ignored the question; not wanting to admit she was as much in the dark as anyone.

'Which room is Rowan's?' she shouted through to Carmen.

Before she had time to answer, the door at the top of the stairs opened.

'It's okay, I'm coming down.'

They watched the girl descend; eyes puffy and red-rimmed, every step an effort.

'I'm going to take you to the station,' said Luke kindly. 'I know you intended to go with Eden but we need to get you through the reporters blocking the gate. Eden will follow.'

'Can I have a quick word with my client?'

'Okay, but make it quick, there'll be plenty of time for talking at the station.'

Eden guided the girl to the other end of the hallway, out of earshot of the detectives.

'It's okay, I'll be right behind you,' she reassured. 'DI Parish and the other officer will not question you in the car, or at the station until I arrive. Once we start the interview don't answer anything unless I indicate you should. You're going to say 'no comment' to every question they put to you. You can confirm who you are but that's it. They'll reveal the evidence they have in their questions but you give nothing away,' she said, desperately trying to drill into the teenager the importance of her advice.

'I need to speak to Mum before I go; she's worried.' Rowan brushed past her through to the kitchen.

Eden grabbed the opportunity to talk to Luke alone. 'Promise me, you won't let anyone question her; no tricking her into talking about the baby, or the pregnancy, or anything else for that matter.'

'You know it would be inadmissible. There's no need for me to promise.' He was obviously offended and she said nothing more, satisfied her client was safe with him, for the time being at least. She'd seen the way he handled her. Many wouldn't be so compassionate given the circumstances. If Rowan did this, she could expect no sympathy; not from the police, the press, or the public. She'd be regarded as the most hated of creatures; a mother who killed her young.

Turning to leave, Eden overheard Maisy's gleeful shout, 'I won; I know … I know who you are.'

ELEVEN

The atmosphere changed the minute they walked through the door. Conversations stuttered to an uncomfortable halt; all eyes on Rowan, nothing but contempt in any of them.

Eden was used to police stations and the inevitable wave of resentment whenever she entered from those who believed defence lawyers operated on the dark side, but she'd only experienced this brand of searing animosity, the kind that crackled like static, once in her career, when as a newly qualified solicitor she'd been seconded onto the defence team of wealthy businessman Carl Pearson; a high-profile serial rapist. She'd loathed Pearson and every slimy excuse and self-serving platitude that trailed from his lying lips about the young women he'd abused. Nonetheless, she had defended him and although he'd been jailed, he'd been acquitted on several of the charges. It had led to a string of cases defending equally reprehensible types until eventually, she discovered that through their chat rooms and forums she'd become their go-to person. She had been forced to face an unpalatable truth; she had built her reputation defending monsters. After the initial shock she was left feeling sullied; shamed and isolated. She stopped trying to justify representing the indefensible; trying to uphold her role in a system requiring the prosecution evidence to be tested and guilt to be proven. The truth was no one wanted to hear her excuses. No matter how enlightened her friends were, she, through association had become as bad as Pearson. Worse still she had begun to worry they were right.

She'd moved back home to Cornwall because statistically, she was less likely to be called upon to represent the worst humanity could throw up. She was hiding in plain sight, championing a system she no longer believed in but was too invested in to ditch. This case would place her in the pillory again and the spectacle would pull a crowd. Her own connections; her past cases, everything, would be scrutinised.

Cop-shop banter was replaced with stiff formality as the custody officer signed them in. Out of the corner of her eye, Eden noticed a young female PC biting her bottom lip with such ferocity she worried she might draw blood. As they walked Rowan through to the interview room, Eden heard the woman mutter, 'bitch,' under her breath.

Eden hoped Rowan hadn't heard and soon as they were in the corridor, she took Luke aside.

'Did you hear that officer?'

'She and her husband are paying for IVF. Police are people like everyone else but I'll have a word.'

His holier than thou attitude was beginning to niggle.

'I'd look there for your press leak if I was you,' Eden said, following him into the room to wait while Rowan was prepared for interview. She used the time to read Bill Duffy's report again. It didn't improve on second reading. There was nothing else for it; she'd have to rely on her own experience and her client's willingness to listen to her advice to make no comment.

One look at Rowan as she entered told her things were unlikely to go to plan. The shaky waif who had descended the stairs an hour earlier looked pissed off and cocky. Neither of which in her experience went down well in a police interview room.

Luke nodded to Denise Charlton to start the recording.

'For the purposes of the tape, present are Rowan Lutey, Eden Gray, solicitor, DI Luke Parish and DS Denise Charlton.'

Luke turned his attention to Rowan. 'Although you were cautioned following your arrest, I must now caution you again as the circumstances have changed since your release under investigation. Do you understand?'

Rowan nodded.

'Can you please indicate verbally for the record?'

'Yes.'

'Rowan Lutey, you do not have to say anything but it may harm your defence if you do not mention when questioned something you later rely on in court. Anything you do say may be used in evidence against you. You understand?'

'I understand.'

'Okay good. Both your GP and Doctor Duffy have confirmed you are fit to be questioned.'

'I never said I wasn't.'

Luke shuffled his papers.

Eden bit her lip.

'The results from the forensic examination of the baby reveal asphyxiation. Whilst the DNA analysis of the saliva sample you provided hasn't come back yet from the lab, the evidence we do have indicates you are its natural mother. Your medical examination confirmed you have recently given birth. I assume you accept that much?'

'My client accepts she recently gave birth,' Eden interjected.

'Fine, let's move on,' Luke said, raising an eyebrow.

'Can you explain to me how your baby came to be buried at the site at Tregarren?'

Eden glared at Rowan, willing her not to comment.

'No, I can't.'

'You expect us to believe you gave birth, mislaid the baby and then miraculously a baby turns up dead; buried at an archaeological dig close to where you live and that it has nothing to do with you?'

'I don't care what you believe: it's the truth.'

'So, what's the explanation?'

'You tell me? I don't know … I don't remember having the baby, I told you. I don't remember any of it.'

'Rowan that's not true, is it? It can't be true.'

Eden tried to catch Rowan's eye. The girl was totally ignoring her advice. She interrupted before she alienated her interrogator further.

'My client has said repeatedly she doesn't remember. She can't be expected to give an account of something she doesn't remember.'

'Well, let's approach this another way. Rowan, do you take drugs or drink heavily on a regular basis?'

Rowan looked flustered.

'You don't need to answer that,' counselled Eden, becoming more exasperated by the minute.

'No comment.'

Hurray, she's finally listening, Eden thought.

'Okay, but if you weren't drunk and hadn't taken anything, how do you explain your amnesia?'

'I don't know,' Rowan mumbled, picking at her fingernails.

'Do you have any medical condition; say epilepsy or something else that might cause you to blackout or suffer memory loss?'

Eden noted the sarcasm in his tone and interjected.

'You have a medical report from an expert. You don't need my client to confirm this.'

Luke moved on. 'Can you see why we're having trouble believing you? You were pregnant: then you weren't. You told Jessica Marshall the baby was gone. We can take from that, you knew the baby was missing, but didn't report it or try to find the child. Why not?'

'I did try.'

Eden knew what was coming and how unconvincing it would sound. Why the hell wouldn't this girl just do as she was told and shut the hell up?

'I looked everywhere around the flat for the baby; everywhere, but it wasn't there.'

Disbelief built on the detective's face.

'Look Rowan, if you tell us you were distraught and panicked; took the baby and buried it, not knowing it was alive, we might be able to help you. Why would you know? It was a traumatic thing for you to go through alone. Maybe, the baby didn't cry? People would understand. You wanted to get rid of it; wanted to pretend none of it had ever happened. You gave the money back to the Marshalls and walked away. You buried the baby thinking it was dead, trying to do the best you could. Is that how it happened, Rowan?'

Eden hoped to God she agreed to the scenario being laid out on a plate for her. It would mean a plea of infanticide and a non-custodial sentence. Her heart sank with Rowan's response.

'No … no. I didn't bury the baby and I don't remember. I don't … I don't.' She began to sob.

'My client is distressed. Can we please take a break?'

Luke leaned back in his chair. 'Interview paused at thirteen-thirty.'

As soon as they were alone, Eden tackled Rowan.

'Why didn't you stick to no comment like I told you to? If you are not going to listen to me, frankly there's little point in me being here.'

The girl fidgeting in her seat said nothing.

Eden took a deep breath, relenting a little. 'Well, we are where we are. Now you have engaged with them you need to think carefully about what they're offering. They are at a loss to know who else would have done this, if not you? If I'm honest I'm having the same trouble. They're giving you the chance to tell them your side of the story. Like DI Parish said, if you had the baby, thought it was dead and panicked, people will understand but they'll find it impossible to believe you knew nothing. If you are trying to protect someone else or if there is someone you suspect of being involved, now is the time to say.'

The girl seemed to be gathering her thoughts and for a moment Eden believed she was getting through to her until lifting her head, Rowan's words hit like rifle bullets.

'You're as deaf as that lot,' she shouted. 'I've told … you … all … I … know.'

The door opened. Luke's usually mobile face was frozen, officious and unreadable.

'Eden, can I have a word?'

'I'll be right back.'

Luke's expression didn't soften once they were out in the corridor.

'I've just spoken to the Crown Prosecution Service and provided them with the details of the interview. In their opinion, there's sufficient evidence to charge her.'

'With what, infanticide?'

'Manslaughter. They say the DNA's a formality and the chance of this being someone else's baby is remote beyond possibility. They want this thing dealt with ASAP given the press interest and the public's response.'

'But even if she killed the baby, however she did it, her actions and her lack of memory are bound to be linked to the trauma of the birth?'

'You heard me in there. I gave her every chance to put her case. If she had, the charge may well have been different but she's given us nothing and I have to tell you my gut says there's something not right here. Not once … not fucking once did she even ask the sex of the child. We haven't revealed it, because evidentially we wanted to keep that bit of information back, but she gave birth to that baby and hasn't even bothered to ask.'

He was right.

'Maybe she knew from the scans and didn't need to ask?'

'The Marshalls didn't want to know the sex so no one knew, including Rowan, I checked. You know the constable you took objection to on the way in? It was the first thing she asked when she heard. *Was it a little boy or little girl?*'

'So, my client's not maternal.'

'These have just been sent through.' Luke opened the folder he was carrying to pull out a photograph. 'Look at that, then talk to me about maternal feelings,' he said, thrusting a photograph under her nose, 'and in case your client is remotely interested, it was a little boy.'

Eden gasped at the photo, unable to hold back her horror. The tiny body lying on the mortuary slab, lifeless and waxy; eyes tightly closed, rosebud lips slightly apart, looked like a child's doll; perfect in every way except the only one that mattered. The baby boy looked so alone splayed out like one of Elspeth's specimens; stripped of every kindness. Eden wanted to cover him; to keep him warm. Pushing the photograph away she stared at Luke, tears brimming.

'That's the reaction I'd expect from anyone; male or female; maternal or not. There's a sergeant in the office back there; on the police boxing team, hard as you like; when I showed him this two minutes ago he buckled; had to steady himself. Your client's cold, unfeeling, and they're the traits of a killer. The CPS thinks so too. The charge is manslaughter and she's lucky it's not murder. If you want to plead Infanticide as a defence it's up to you.'

Luke walked away.

'Hang on a minute, we haven't finished,' Eden said grabbing his arm.

'Yes, we have Eden; we have,' he snapped, shaking her free.

Back in the interview room, DS Charlton pushed the button on the recorder.

'Interview resumed thirteen forty-five. Those present, as before. Rowan, I want you to look at this photograph.'

Luke slid the piteous image across the table towards the girl.

Rowan glanced down briefly before pushing it back to him and Eden shared the detective's disgust as he returned the photograph to its folder.

'Miss Lutey, have you got anything to add to what you've said previously now you have had the opportunity to consult further with your solicitor?'

The girl looked first at Eden then back to Luke. 'No.'

'Then, given you cannot, or are unwilling to offer any explanation and, on the evidence, we have and you have been made aware of, we are terminating this interview.'

Five minutes later they were in front of the custody sergeant.

'Rowan Lutey you are charged that on or around the twentieth of September Two Thousand and Nineteen you unlawfully killed your infant child contrary to common law. You will be remanded in custody pending any bail application made on your behalf by your solicitor. Do you understand?'

Rowan made no reply; her eyes fixed firmly on her trainers.

'Give me strength,' Luke shouted, slamming his fist down on the desk, so the custody sergeant's pen landed on the floor. 'Do you understand?'

'Yes, I understand.' Rowan spat; insolent black eyes burning with contempt.

TWELVE

After telephoning Carmen to break the news her daughter had been charged with manslaughter and would be in custody until her bail application on Monday morning, Eden didn't feel like going home. She'd failed Carmen as much as she'd failed her daughter; perhaps more so, given Rowan had made no attempt to save herself.

She decided to drive to her parents' house. Although they only lived a few miles away she hadn't called or spoken on the phone for weeks. She'd seen them briefly on their return from their month-long tour of India, but it was a fleeting visit. She hadn't hung around for the slideshow or the vegetarian curry cooked 'the way they'd had it in Mumbai'. She didn't know why she was heading there now, other than something about this case touched a nerve.

The front door was open as usual and as she walked straight through to the kitchen, she was greeted with a terrible stench.

'What the hell is that smell?'

'Hello darling, I'm making Comfrey stew. You soak the leaves, then let it stand outside in a tub for a couple of weeks. I scoop up a little bit into the watering can and add water; it's brilliant stuff, a feed and pesticide all in one and totally organic of course.'

'It stinks. I'm not surprised the insects run away.'

'Does it? I hadn't noticed, I must be used to it,' smiled her mother, stirring the thick green devil's brew.

'Where's Dad?' Eden asked, grabbing the least brown banana from the bowl on the kitchen table and walking through to the sitting room.

Her dad taught pottery part-time at the local college whilst her mum was an art therapist at a special needs unit in Falmouth. They grew their own vegetables and kept a few chickens for the eggs, although her mother never ate them now she was a committed vegan.

'In the studio, loading the kiln. He'll be in soon. Do you want a drink?'

Eden knew she meant rhubarb cordial so tart it stripped the roof of your mouth, or water. Her parents didn't do hot drinks or alcohol.

'No, I'm fine thanks.'

'I'll finish off here. This is about done.'

The sitting room was a mess and she had to move a stack of newspapers from the settee to make room to sit. Castro, the family mongrel, lay on the rag rug by the hearth where once burned a fire before her parents decided not to contribute to the consumption of fossil fuels and instead, wore layers of jumpers to fend off the cold.

'Hello boy,' Eden said stooping to give him a pat.

The elderly dog didn't move, probably not wanting to lose his prime position in case his owners had a rethink on the grounds of animal welfare.

'Mum, can I put the news on?' Eden shouted.

'The radio's out here on the windowsill?'

'No, I was wondering if I could put the telly on. I think there might be something about the case I'm on at the moment.'

'We usually try not to put it on until after nine, but of course, if it's important?'

Eden lifted the remote they'd been forced to buy when everything went digital. It had hardly been used since, other than to watch *Gardeners' World* or *Blue Planet*. Eden wanted to see the South West news. She caught the end of the weather forecast and waited for the switch to the regional channel. As she thought Rowan's arrest was the lead story.

'A local girl has been charged with the manslaughter of the new-born baby found earlier this week in a shallow grave at an archaeological dig in Cornwall. We're going now to our reporter Sindy Raybald at the site where the body was found.'

She assumed the report would feature coverage taken that morning at the Lutey's Farm or perhaps from outside the police station, but they were live from outside Elspeth Fuller's prefab. She guessed they'd not been allowed near the pit itself. To her surprise, James Ferris, not Elspeth, was the one being interviewed by Little Miss Perky.

'I'm here with James Ferris one of the archaeologists working at the dig and the person who found the baby. What was your immediate feeling when you first saw the child, James?'

'Well, of course, I was shocked. It was a terrible thing to have to find like that.'

Eden wondered why he hadn't mentioned the boy who'd been with him at the time but guessed he'd been told beforehand about the limited slot and to keep it brief.

'As an experienced archaeologist, you must have found human remains before?'

James smiled widely at the young blonde; it was the same boyish grin he'd given Eden at the museum when telling her about his work. Then, it had been engaging; now it seemed totally inappropriate.

'Yes, I've worked around the world on a fair number of ancient burial sites in my career but nothing quite prepares you for something like this.'

'No … no of course not.' Sindy Raybald's voice dropped to a respectful tone for a nanosecond, before ratcheting up again. 'There has been a lot of speculation about what you've previously discovered at the site. There is talk locally your findings are associated with witchcraft, is that true?'

'Let's say Pagan ritual rather than witchcraft. I feel witchcraft is a rather emotive word.'

'Yes, but do you think the child murder and burial here is linked to witchcraft; a satanic killing?'

'To talk about Satan is unhelpful,' he replied sharply, impatience shrouding the affable casualness he'd displayed earlier. 'It's naive and dangerous to analyse the religious beliefs of the past in the context of modern times. Historically, the Devil and God were as real to people as say celebrities are to us today. Though you never met them, they were present on a daily basis. Back then the supernatural world was every bit as real as the natural to the population. These rituals were their way of bridging the two. The Devil is of course a modern concept nothing to do with Paganism but derived from the Celtic worship of the horned god Cernunnos, the god of nature and to the Christian mind chaos and sexual abandonment. We have found no horns here and that's surprising. Fertility rituals usually involve male and female symbolism, but not here.'

The reporter's head waggled in mock understanding.

'So, you believe the person who did this - possibly the girl charged today - believes in witchcraft?'

James was a drowning man. 'I cannot comment. I can only tell you about the finds and their importance in our understanding of Celtic ritual. We have made a ground-breaking and unique discovery here of forty pits ... that ...'

'Yes, yes fascinating but back to Rowan Lutey, the woman charged with killing the child. She is, we understand, a member of a family believed to be witches by generations of local people. They are the ones who dug the pits you've excavated, isn't that so? Do you think the child's death is linked?'

'There is no historical basis for that hypothesis.'

'But didn't some contain live offerings?'

'Yes but ...'

'So, do you think the baby was buried as an offering?'

'Look I really can't say. I don't ...'

Sindy Raybald cut him off, turning away to schmooze with the camera. 'That was James Ferris, archaeologist here in Cornwall. Neither the Lutey family nor their solicitor Eden Gray were available to comment.'

Up flashed a photograph of Eden leaving the Lutey farm earlier.

'Now back to the studio for the rest of the day's news.'

What a disaster.

Eden didn't expect Elspeth to be pleased either. She was pretty sure she wouldn't have given the interview at all but if she had, she'd have given a better account of herself. As it was, James had made sure the very people, Elspeth wanted to stay away from the site would soon be camping on her doorstep. More importantly, he'd done nothing to help Rowan's defence. He hadn't denied the Lutey's involvement or shut down the references to witchcraft. Now the black cat was out of the bag, there was no putting it back.

'Are you defending the Lutey girl then?'

It was her dad, standing in the doorway wiping the last of the white clay dust from his fingers.

'Yes, I am and that hasn't made it any easier,' she said pressing the off switch on the remote.

'So, do you think she did it?'

Eden didn't discuss the details of her cases with anyone. It was a breach of confidentiality and dangerous, but she always sought out her father when her work gave her sleepless nights. He had the knack of rallying her when she floundered.

'The evidence of manslaughter is weak, but if the DNA proves the baby is hers, she knew about the pits and not many did. Did you know about them?'

'No, I didn't but I must say it's all fascinating stuff. You can see why the press is interested in this one.'

'I know. I'm going to have to deal with them and all the nutcases who according to the chief archaeologist are bound to climb on the bandwagon.'

'Was the young chap on the telly the chief archaeologist? He looked about twelve to me.'

'Everybody looks about twelve to you, Dad. He's her assistant. She'd have done a better job. She's been determined to keep this dig low-key. I can't for the life of me understand why she let him give a live interview.' She'd give Elspeth a call later to see what the hell was going on?

Her mother emerged from the kitchen in a waft of steam.

'Are you staying for something to eat, darling?'

'No, you're alright, Mum. I need to do a shop on my way home. I'll get something then.'

'You need to look after yourself,' she said frowning, 'all this processed food, eating on the run, it's playing havoc with your long-term health not to mention the damage it's doing to the environment.'

Not wanting another lecture on meat is murder she kissed her on the cheek.

'Bye, Mum, love you.' Brushing past her father she whispered, 'You can escape to McDonald's with me if you like?'

'Don't tempt me,' he whispered back. 'Just seeing Eden to her car,' he shouted as he followed her outside.

'How's the building work going?' her father asked holding open the car door for her.

'Slowly.'

'Do you want me to go and have a word?'

'Would you mind?'

'Not at all. I did warn you about having family do work for you.'

'You and everyone else. Anyway when did you get so wise?'

'When I got so old,' he smiled.

Her dad wasn't old. Her mother's strict health regime saw to that. He was lithe and fit for his sixty-three years.

Getting back into the car, she suddenly remembered her sister. 'Dad … have you and Mum heard from Thea lately?'

'I know Mum called her when we got back from our travels but I don't think she's been in touch since; why do you ask?'

'Luke is the investigating officer on the case and it's a bit awkward that's all. I thought you might be able to give me the heads up on what's going on with those two. I get the impression he hasn't seen Flora for several weeks. He had a bit of a rant at me the other day … outside court…before all this.'

'What did he expect you to do about it?'

'God knows; you'd think he'd realise by now Thea's a law unto herself. If she does ring perhaps you could persuade her to be a little more cooperative. He genuinely misses Flora and given Thea's history, worries when he can't get hold of her. I don't want things to escalate and find myself in the middle.'

'Okay, I'll try and have a word but I make no promises it'll do any good.'

'Thanks, Dad and while you're at it, check she's taking her meds. All this seems a bit random even for her.'

Thea had finally been diagnosed when aged twenty-three with bipolar disorder. If she took her medication, she was relatively stable but if she forgot, or went on one of her many forays into alternative therapies, things were apt to spiral quickly into chaos.

'Do your best, love. I know you'll do your best for that poor kid,' said her father leaning in to kiss her cheek.

'I will, though I've got a feeling it won't be easy.'

Driving away she felt a little better. This case had begun to tip her off balance. She'd needed to touch base with those who loved her and had no agenda, although she was glad her mother hadn't seen the news. She would have added to the pressure; politicised Rowan's struggle, made her the victim of sexual prejudice. She hadn't ruled out portraying Rowan as the victim; it was the whole basis of the infanticide defence. At the moment she had nothing else. All she could do was play the sympathy card; the scenario Luke had offered Rowan and she'd so foolishly rejected.

The battle would have to be won in the media first. It was clear they were intent on demonizing the girl. She would need Elspeth's help and Luke's co-operation. She hoped at least, after her conversation with her father, the latter would prove less problematic.

THIRTEEN

The supermarket was busier than she'd imagined on a Saturday evening.

Avoiding the temptation to pick up a basket and fill it with a couple of ready meals and a bottle of Rioja, she grabbed a trolley. Perhaps her mother was right, if she got some decent food in her, everything would fall into place; perhaps broccoli was the answer to all her problems?

The middle-aged man in the Barbour ahead of her at the checkout was taking his time, loading a box with the special wine deal. She remembered she'd forgotten eggs, and leaving her trolley, ran to grab a dozen. Walking back, she spotted Luke lifting a six-pack of Peroni from the shelves. Head down, she stole a sneaky peek into his basket as she passed; lasagne for one. Clearly, he was living the dream. He looked up. She couldn't pretend she hadn't seen him.

'Eggs?' he said.

'Quite the detective,' she quipped.

'I'm sorry about today,' he said blushing slightly, 'but the CPS was adamant. They're under scrutiny now the press has got hold of this. They have to be seen to be doing something.'

'It's fine,' she conceded, feeling a little sorry for him. 'You're doing your job and I'm going to do mine. No need for either of us to apologise. I've got to go; I'm parked by the till.'

The cashier was about to call someone to move her trolly out of the way as she re-joined the queue.

'Sorry ... sorry,' she apologised, holding the egg box aloft.

The stony-eyed woman behind muttered to her husband. 'Stupid bitch.'

Eden turned. 'I'm sorry what did you say?'

'I don't know how you can live with yourself defending that evil little cow?'

'What evil little cow would that be?'

'The cow that's murdered her baby.'

Eden's heart flapped like a trapped bird in her chest but she couldn't bring herself to let this pass.

'Who made you judge and jury?' she said turning to face them.

The people in the queue began to shuffle uneasily.

'You think you're so bloody clever, don't you; what gives you the right to think you're smarter than us?' the woman's rabid husband snarled.

'Well, let me think … half a brain?'

The woman puffed out her sizable chest, 'Paedo loving bitch.'

'What did you say to me?' Eden asked, stunned.

'You heard her,' spat the husband, face puce with rage.

'That's enough,' a voice boomed from behind. It was Luke. He'd taken his warrant card from his pocket and people were staring. 'Shut it down or I'll arrest the pair of you,' he warned the irate couple.

'Oh yeah, stick up for her, never mind protecting decent people who look after their kids.'

'Oh, grow up; one more word and I swear …'

His phone rang and he walked away to take the call, leaving Eden to unload her groceries, hands trembling, any appetite for the food she'd bought dwindling with every barcode beep.

She felt a sharp tap on her shoulder and braced herself for another onslaught.

To her relief it was Luke. 'The farm's on fire.'

'What?'

'Come on, leave that, I'll give you a lift.'

FOURTEEN

The stench seeped through the car vents, burning their nostrils and smarting their eyes as they watched in disbelief the swirling kaleidoscope of purple, orange and red smoke billowing across the valley.

At the end of the lane, they were directed by a police officer towards a cordoned off layby by the farm gate where Luke parked behind a string of police cars.

Flames engulfed the timber barn to the left of the farmhouse.

As they got out, Eden felt the heat blister her cheeks, and stepped back.

'I need to look for my team,' Luke hollered above the din, 'are you okay here?'

'Yeah fine; you go on.'

It was hard to think amidst the cacophony of machinery, as faceless shadows darted about the courtyard shouting orders above the sizzle and crack of burning wood. Every now and then a beam crashed to the ground, launching embers, like furnace fireflies into the night. She looked around for Carmen and the children and saw them standing on the verge, wrapped in blankets, transfixed; eyes shining like beads. She rushed towards them.

'Carmen, thank God you're all safe. What on earth happened?'

'I don't know. I woke and smelt smoke, came downstairs and saw the barn was on fire.'

Eden, afraid the woman might topple, helped her to sit on the hedge.

'Was it a bonfire that got out of hand?'

'No, we've been stuck in the house all afternoon. There were people here into the evening until it got dark. Matthew didn't even get out to feed the animals till gone seven.'

'The reporters have been here since this morning?'

'No not them. They moved off soon after you left. I mean the others, the ones with the placards covered with those awful lies about Rowan. More and more of them arrived during the day; marching up and down, shouting foul things. I've had the TV turned up as loud as possible to drown them out so the kids couldn't hear the filthy stuff they were shouting.'

'Like what?'

'Nothing I've not heard before but not for young ears,' she said her eyes settling on the children.

'What about the police, why didn't they move them off?'

'They said as they were on the public highway and as they weren't obstructing or causing a breach of the peace there wasn't much they could do about it. I told them, they're obstructing *me* and breaching *my* bloody peace but they shrugged it off. It's been driving me mad stuck indoors but I thank God for it now. I went to bed early. I usually sleep like the dead until I get up for the animals but I've been doing nothing all day, then tossing and turning worrying about our Rowan. If I hadn't been, I might not have woken until it was too late.'

'Is the house okay?'

'There will be smoke damage but luckily the wind is in the other direction, so the flames haven't jumped the gap between the barn and the house. Thank God the holiday cottage was empty and the damage there is minimal. We're booked up for half-term.'

Eden noticed she was clutching something close to her chest under the blanket. It looked like a book. She guessed it was something precious; probably a photograph album. Isn't that what everyone always said they'd grab if their house caught fire; the stuff which couldn't be replaced?

Luke jogged across to talk to Carmen.

'I've spoken to the head of the fire crew. He says they've got the fire under control but it'll be morning before the buildings are considered safe for you to go back into the house. Do you have somewhere to go tonight?'

'I can go to my girlfriend's but she hasn't got the room for the rest,' Matthew said.

'Anywhere you can think of Carmen?'

'No, not really. I could book into a hotel but my purse is in the house and I'm not allowed back in.'

'Well, I'm sure we can arrange something for you.'

'I've only got one bedroom, but if you take the bed with the children, I'm happy to take the settee,' Eden offered.

'It's kind of you,' Carmen said, eyes glistening, 'but only if you're sure?'

'I'm sure. Come on, let's get these two to bed. Can you drive us Matthew; can we all fit in?'

'Yeah, no problem.'

'I'm not sure I should leave,' choked Carmen, looking towards the house and bursting into tears.

'Look, there's nothing you can do here. The firemen have got everything under control. You'll have plenty of cleaning up to do tomorrow. You could do with the rest tonight,' Eden comforted.

She couldn't imagine trying to get the smell out of a house or clearing away the charred remains of the barn once the fire was extinguished. It was the last thing the family needed right now.

'It was Flossie's Barn,' Carmen sobbed.

'Oh no, were their animals in there?' Eden asked, a faint queasiness rising.

'No, it's the name my grandfather gave it. It's been there forever and now in a matter of hours there's nothing left.' She clasped the thing in her arms closer.

'Come on, let's get back to mine and put the kettle on. We'll settle the children and have a quiet talk.'

Luke smiled at her as she climbed into the passenger seat of Matthew's car.

Leaning in, he whispered, 'This is good of you.'

She felt the burn of embarrassment. It made a change to be on the receiving end of a compliment from him.

Driving past the police cordon, she noticed a crowd had gathered along with the press.

'Cover the children with the blanket,' she said, glancing back at Carmen.

'Why, I've got nothing to hide? We're the victims here. I won't give whoever did this the satisfaction of seeing us hide like criminals; not in my own village.'

It was the same indignation she'd heard from Rowan, and look where it had got her; banged up, charged with manslaughter. She thought of the bail application she would be up half the night preparing.

'You're right to be angry but someone lit the fire on purpose, someone who doesn't give a damn about you and your family. Why antagonise them further? It's what that type wants; an excuse.'

Eden peered through the window at the so-called moral high ground, waving their wretched placards, spreading the gospel of Hell and Damnation. The viciousness of the attack pointed towards one of those fanatics. They'd been outside the farm all day, maybe one of them decided to up the ante.

She half expected to see one of her old clients among them; the type only too happy to join any bandwagon if it meant a bit of gratuitous violence and a chance to get your face on YouTube but she recognised no one, until at the very back talking to one of the police officers, she spotted James Ferris. He was standing next to Sindy Raybald, the reporter who interviewed him earlier that evening and Eden wondered whether they'd arrived together. She could understand why James would be worried. If these people were capable of this, how on earth was he going to keep Elspeth's precious site safe?

FIFTEEN

Matthew carried a sleeping Maisy in before leaving for his girlfriend's house. Jago was awake but dead on his feet. Eden didn't feel much better. She made up a bed for herself on the settee, popped in a couple of slices of toast, brewed a pot of tea and waited for Carmen to finish settling the children.

Now they were inside, she could smell smoke on her clothes and in her hair. She was filthy and in need of a shower. She'd offer Carmen one too.

'They're both out for the count,' Carmen sighed, plonking herself down at the table.

'Tea?'

'Thanks, I'm parched.' She sniffed her jumper. 'I'm sorry about the smoke, you'll have to change those sheets tomorrow. I can take them home and wash them for you if you like?' she offered apologetically.

'There's no need. Take your things off and I'll put them in the wash. You can borrow a pair of my pyjamas. I'll do the same with the sheets tomorrow. They'll dry in the tumble dryer. Why don't you have your tea, then take a shower?'

'If you're sure?' Carmen replied gratefully.

'It's no trouble at all.'

Eden walked to the airing cupboard to fetch some clean towels. 'There you go.'

The woman hesitated as she took the towels. 'I've got something I'd like you to see.'

'Okay, but it can wait until tomorrow, surely?'

Carmen hesitated for an instant. 'No ... no it can't. I rescued it from the barn. I put it there after Rowan's arrest for safekeeping, in case the police searched the house.'

Eden was immediately concerned. She'd wondered earlier what the woman had clutched to her chest? It looked like a book and Carmen had braved the fire to retrieve it. She hoped for everyone's sake it wasn't something incriminating. The last thing she needed, was to be accused of concealing evidence pertinent to the criminal investigation.

'It's not Rowan's diary is it?'

'No, not Rowan's, she was never one for writing. This is old, very old. It's been handed down to me. I suppose it's older than I can even imagine. It's more a manual than a diary.'

Eden watched as Carmen retrieved a green leather parcel from the bundle of coats in the hallway. She placed it carefully on the table in front of Eden waiting for her to do the honours. Eden obliged, carefully unwrapping the soft kid envelope to reveal a scuffed darker leather binding, crudely etched with what looked to her like birds and Celtic symbols. She carefully opened it. Carved on the inside cover was a grotesque creature; a bird's body with a woman's head, talons poised, wings outstretched; the unmistakable shape of an egg nestled between the hideous beast's squatting legs. Eden recoiled, then remembered her conversation with James Ferris; *a shape with no beginning no end.*

'It was my grandmother's and her grandmother's before that. It goes back generations. I don't know how far.'

It looked ancient to Eden as she tentatively turned the well-thumbed pages; each covered with hieroglyphs of one kind or another; circles, triangles, pentacles, randomly drawn so barely a centimetre of paper remained blank. Superimposed in a lighter copperplate were instructions of a sort, like recipes each under a short heading.

My God, it's Grandma Lutey's spell book, she thought, as she began to read.

For an ulcer or foul bones
Walnut-tree leaves boiled in water
Bath morning and evening with a decoction of leaves and bind on.
For Windy Dropsy

Mix the juice of wild leek and elder.
Two spoons taken morning and evening.

Eden wasn't sure what windy dropsy was or whether there was a non-windy version. She struggled not to laugh, knowing Carmen would be deeply offended. Like any recipe book, it was stained and blotched with ingredients, albeit not cake mix. The recipes seemed sort of everyday to Eden who wondered what she'd expected; *tongue of toad, wing of bat?*

'I expected something different; I don't know what exactly, maybe spells, incantations?'

Carmen raised a disapproving eyebrow. 'Nothing like that would be written down; leastways not so ordinary folk could read it. It could be used as evidence against us if the book fell into the wrong hands. We learnt the charms by word of mouth. The symbols are hints if you like; to trigger the memory; used as bindings to the charms. Gran and Mother didn't need the book to work the craft, they used it mostly to teach us. The written down cures came later after the family learnt to read and write.'

Eden turned to the centrefold. A hand-drawn map spanned the pages; the surface peppered with a series of crosses and circles.

'What's this?'

'You need to turn it around the other way.'

Eden flipped the book vertically and could immediately see it was a plan of the site, similar to Elspeth's but less detailed. She could make out the road and the entrance, the wavy line of the stream ending at a grouping of stones amongst a clutch of trees.

'What's that?' Eden asked.

'The well,' replied Carmen.

'And the other marks?'

'The pits. The ones marked with a circle are empty, the gifts removed. They were successful, resulting in a child. Once the child was born the gifts were replaced.'

'Replaced with what?'

'The afterbirth.'

'The placenta?' Eden winced.

'Why so shocked? In many cultures, the mother eats the placenta,' Carmen said, eyes glistening with impish amusement at the lawyer's reaction.

Eden's lips puckered in disgust.

'Some say it's because it's nutritious; full of iron but it's more than that to us.' Carmen continued. ' Have you ever seen one, up close I mean?'

Eden shook her head.

'It's the original tree of life, you know. It's trunk is the umbilical rooted to the mother. The branches the blood vessels carrying life to the child. It sustains us in the womb and when buried it protects us through life too, like a guardian angel to a Christian. The old belief is when your life's done, your spirit returns to the place where it's buried.'

'Elspeth Fuller didn't mention any of this?'

'That's cos she doesn't know everything. Some things aren't learnt from books. All she saw was empty pits, the afterbirth would have rotted over time.'

'So, the ones with the crosses didn't work?'

'That's right.'

'And the offerings Elspeth showed me; the swan's pelt; the eggs came from pits that failed?'

'Yes.'

Eden suddenly saw them in a new light, imagining the heartache they represented. 'Carmen this is fascinating but why did you want me to see this?'

'It's this I needed you to see.'

Carmen, turning to the back of the book, pushed her fingers into a little pocket inside the cover and pulled out a folded envelope. 'It's a letter Gran wrote before she died.'

Carmen took the letter carefully from the envelope and smoothing out the thin sheet of paper, placed it on the table in front of Eden.

'It was wartime and everyone was jumpy. Back when this all happened, people would have been only too glad to accuse us. Gran was only thinking of the woman you see, and her husband, of course, she knew what it would mean for them.'

'What woman, what's this letter about?'

'It's about the other baby buried at the site.'

The hairs on the back of Eden's neck stood on end. 'The other baby?'

'Read it; then I'll tell you the whole story.'

Eden read with trepidation.

20th of November 1981

At about eleven on the night of 14th of November 1945, Mary Bluet the wife of John Bluet gave birth to a baby. The child died, born with the cord around his neck so all his breath was taken from him. No one could have saved him. I know that because I tried. Not wanting to cause trouble for Mary or distress to her poor husband, I took the baby boy and buried him in the pit I'd dug for Mary the previous spring. It's my dearest wish the child remains where he has laid all these years. I never spoke to Mary about the baby again. I never told her where he was and she never asked but I planted a Rowan tree above him to ward off evil and over the years I've tended the boy's grave. I hope my family will do the same when I'm gone.

I'm nearing the end of my life and have dug my last pit. I have delivered many babies into this world and some sadly didn't survive but I remembered this one and his loss almost every day. He was and is special to me. In case he is ever found and I'm not around to explain I have written the truth for whoever needs to know it.

Madge Lutey

Carmen patiently waited for Eden to finish.

'Why didn't she call a doctor to take care of everything; wouldn't that have been the thing to do in the circumstances?'

'The letter only tells half the story.'

'What do you mean?'

'There was something else about the baby. Gran knew Mary. She'd dug a pit for her the previous spring. She and her husband had been married for over three years and been trying for a baby for most of that time. Whenever he came home on leave, she hoped she'd fall pregnant but never did, not until Gran dug the pit and Bride listened.'

Eden remembered Elspeth talking about the goddess Bride but it was still strange to hear Carmen, a practical down-to-earth woman talk of her as if she were a real person.

'The baby wasn't expected so early. Mary had gone to bed feeling bad and then the pain got worse. There was no time to fetch the doctor from Truro and no way of getting Mary to hospital; no transport or phone.'

Carmen spun a gossamer thread to the past.

'Her husband was only home cause he'd caught some shrapnel in his leg in France; it was a terrible struggle for him to get to our farm. He needed a stick to walk and with the blackout, you couldn't see your hand in front of your face. Even with Gran's help, it took ages to get back to Mary. As they got close, Gran could hear her screaming and ran on ahead. The door was open and she went straight upstairs to the bedroom. The place was in darkness with the blackout curtains pulled and she could barely see by the oil lamp beside the bed but then as she got closer …' There was a tremor in Carmen's voice as she reached for her cup of tea.

'Go on,' encouraged Eden, 'go on.'

'It was terrible; so still and quiet. Gran thought the worse; that Mary was dead but then she heard her groan like a wounded beast she said. She lifted the sheet and there, between her legs was a baby. The bedclothes were soaked with blood and the baby was blue. Mary's husband was downstairs. Gran shouted to him to stay put. Back then men didn't sit in on the birth and he didn't argue. Mary was away with the fairies. Gran carried on talking to her, cause she needed to fill the silence; keep herself together. The baby had been born with the cord wrapped around his neck, but he was still warm, so she slipped it over his head to free him; rubbing his back hoping he'd come back but the poor little mite had gone.'

An image of Rowan's baby on the mortuary slab flashed through Eden's mind and she swallowed hard.

'He looked full term to Gran. Once she'd cut the cord, she moved towards the light to clean him up in case Mary wanted to hold him; just the once. She took the pillowcase from the other side of the bed and wiped away the blood. It was then she saw it wasn't the lack of air, or the blood, or the dim light making him appear dark; he was black, he was a coloured child.'

Carmen's face flushed with embarrassment as she said the words.

'I'm sorry, I know you mustn't say *coloured* now but that's what she said; Gran. She described the baby as coloured; "had a touch of the tar brush," she said.'

Eden reminded herself this was 1945 and *coloured* was probably as good as it got back then.

'It's okay.'

Carmen seemed grateful for the reassurance and she relaxed back into her story. 'All Gran could think about was the poor broken man pacing downstairs; wounded for his country and now this? Mary wouldn't even look at the child; turned her face to the wall when Gran tried to make her hold him. Gran didn't know what to do for the best. She told Mary she could take the child away, without showing her husband if she wanted her to; said she'd say the baby was early and wasn't right and it was best he didn't see it. She told her she'd bury him somewhere safe, and no one need know and that's exactly what she did. She took the baby and buried it in the pit she'd dug for Mary; gave the baby back to the earth that had delivered it; back to Bride.'

'And she never spoke to the woman about the child?'

'Never. Gran guessed Mary had become friendly with one of the Americans billeted not far from the village in the months leading up to D-Day. There were hundreds of them camped around the county waiting to leave for France. The village held welcome dances and there were all sorts of goings-on between them and the local girls and it caused problems. The black and white GIs had separate camps; because that's the way it was back where they came from.

Several local girls planned to start a new life in America after the war but never got the chance because so many of them boys never came back from France. Lots more brought up kiddies from those GIs and their husbands never knew or never wanted to. They made the best of it but Mary could never have pretended the child was her husband's and Gran didn't see the point of either of them suffering the shame, now the baby was dead. She kept the secret and only wrote the letter when she started to worry someone might buy the site from the council to build houses after she died. I need you to know in case they find the other baby and think Rowan was carrying on some awful tradition. I hope you understand why Gran did what she did in the circumstances?'

Eden was at a loss to know whether Carmen meant because she was a lawyer, or a woman, uncertain if either qualified her to judge Madge Lutey, given the risks the woman had taken for someone who never gave her back so much as a thank you.

***

Eden stayed up for a while after Carmen took herself to bed. She scanned the pages of the book into her PC and photographed the carved leather cover. When she finally turned in, she tossed and turned for hours; her body reluctant to drift into sleep, partly down to the lumpy settee but mostly because of the other baby.

She didn't know why the story bothered her so much. After all, the little boy had died a natural death; avoidable, with proper medical care, but natural, nonetheless.

Mary Bluet must have convinced herself the baby was her husband's; then when he wasn't, the shame stamped upon him for all to see, rendered him unworthy of her love, unworthy even of acknowledgement. She never spoke of him again. Madge Lutey may have planted a Rowan tree to ward off evil but the evil had already been done by then.

Whether the grief twisting in the pit of her stomach, catching the back of her throat was for the little boy, for Rowan's baby, or for herself, Eden wasn't sure. She too had faced abandonment by a mother who didn't want her. Her story was the same as theirs, only by pure luck she'd survived and been loved by those who took her in.

She wondered whether her birth mother had been able to erase her from her mind the minute she abandoned her? If someone hadn't found her or had it been winter, she would have died without a name. It would have been as if she had never existed, like Rowan's baby and the little boy born all those years ago to Mary Bluet.

Fists clenched tight by her sides, she clamped her mouth shut, knowing if she opened it the sobbing might never stop.

SIXTEEN

The air, yesterday sweet with the peaty scent of autumn, had been corrupted by acrid smog, slashing the back of Carmen's throat like a razor blade as she bundled the children out of the taxi. The charred bones of the old barn still smouldered and she steered them away from the pink ash glowing on the cobbles. At least the fire had seen off the last of the God squad.

The draft from the open door, sent tiny soot motes spinning. The sight of the thick layer coating the blue and white china on the dresser made Carmen want to weep. Matthew, busy emptying a bucket of filthy water into the Belfast sink, looked up as they entered;

'I rang the insurance company to see if I could start moving the debris but they said not to until their bloke had been to take photos and assess the damage. I told them the police think it's arson and they said it could hold up the claim; bloody typical.'

Matthew's face glowed crimson. Carmen worried about the effect all this was having on him. Her eldest son was not much for showing emotion. He'd had to be wise beyond his years; a sensible foil to Rowan's madcap wildness. She'd always had some plan or other on the go; first wanting to open a farm shop, then letting out yurts in the top field. Matthew was only a couple of years older but often had to be the wet blanket, reminding his sister of the practicalities of funding her projects and how they needed the fields for the dairy herd.

He'd held down his job at the garage and done all the manual work at the farm without complaint. Carmen didn't know how she'd manage when he finally got married and moved out. He'd offered to settle at the farm but Laura his girlfriend wasn't the farming type. She worked as a cashier in the bank and she'd never seen her out of high heels. Carmen had vowed she wouldn't be the one to ruin things for her son by making him choose between family and his future. She'd just have to pay for help when the time came.

'Sit down Matthew, you look done in. Have you had anything to eat?'

'I need to see to the bottom fence. It was damaged when the fire engine came through last night.'

'It can wait,' she insisted, 'sit down, I'll do you a cooked breakfast; it'll set you up for the day.'

Matthew slumped back down into his seat. She put the sausages and bacon into the oven and made her way upstairs to run a bath for the children.

'You two take your stuff off and get in the bath.'

'I'm not going in with *her*,' Jago protested, screwing up his face in disgust.

'Jago I haven't got the energy for this. You can go in together, or one will have to use the other's water, there's not enough hot for you both to bath separately till I've got the range going.'

Carmen ran her fingers along the landing wall, leaving a greasy trail through the smut-stained paintwork. She hadn't expected it would be as bad as this. The smoke had snuck in and had a good look around like a nosy neighbour.

Letting the bath run, she strolled to the end of the landing and opened the attic door. She needed to put the book back in the trunk. It was clear now it was as safe there as anywhere else.

It was a miracle she'd had the presence of mind to save it from the fire. After all those years of careful custodianship, it would have weighed heavily on her had she been the one to lose it. She was also glad she'd confided in Eden. She'd asked her to keep the letter for the time being. She'd know what to do for the best. It was a burden she didn't feel able to carry alone anymore; not with everything else going on.

Before all this, Mary Bluet's baby drifted into her thoughts once a year in early February during Imbolc, or Candlemas as Christians called it, when the silvery snowdrops flowered around the Rowan tree her grandmother planted all those years ago. Ever since the archaeologists turned up she'd worried daily one of them would find the baby's grave. She'd been so relieved when they'd finished their survey of the field and moved on to the coppice to excavate the ancient well. She'd prepared herself to keep the secret for the rest of her life, like her mother and grandmother before her. Then Rowan's baby was found and all hell broke loose. Making her way up the stairs, she paused to shout down to the children,

'Turn that tap off; you don't need to fill it to the brim. Jago, I want Maisy in that bath by the time I get back down, do you hear me?'

At the top, she reached for the light, gasping at the chaos confronting her as the room lit up. The place had been ransacked; the boxes piled up against the eaves all overturned. Children's toys, defunct electrical goods; newspapers and magazines were scattered across the floor. The contents of the trunk were strewn around its base: the horse brasses slung over the rusty wheel of an antiquated Singer sewing machine. Stepping carefully over Matthew's old skateboard, Carmen picked her way slowly towards the trunk, all the time clinging tightly to the book. Nothing seemed to be missing but it was a mess. Had the police been in the house and searched last night while they were away? Surely, they couldn't do that, didn't they have to have a warrant or something?

Then a more alarming thought crossed her mind; what if it wasn't the police; what if it was one of the lunatics hanging around the farm with those terrible banners?

'Matthew ... Matthew.'

Jago came to the bottom of the stairs. 'What is it, Mum? Maisy's in the bath I'll go in after.'

'Go get Matthew from the kitchen, there's a good boy.'

Carmen clung to the book like a life raft until Matthew appeared at the top of the stairs.

'Fucking hell?'

'Matthew language.'

'Sorry, Ma.'

'Do you think it's the police?' she asked.

'No, not them. When would they have done this? They wouldn't only search the attic, they'd have searched the rest too; more likely to be one of those bastards who torched the barn. Is anything missing?'

'No nothing I can see,' replied Carmen, scanning the room.

'There you go then; some nutcase.'

'But when did they get in?'

'Last night ... it had to be last night during the fire. I locked up before we left but the house was open during the fire.'

Carmen hated the idea of one of those people being in the house.

'What's that?' asked Matthew, pointing to the book.

'Oh, just an old book.'

The Lutey men weren't privy to the secrets of the book; it was the domain of the women. She'd never spoken to Matthew about it. He knew the basics of their Pagan beliefs and the family history; it was common knowledge thereabouts but she'd never shared the stories or the charms with him, the way her mother had with her and Morvah or the way she would have with Rowan if she hadn't chosen not to.

'Did you find it up here then?'

'No, no ... I didn't. It *was* up here but I took it from the trunk the other day.'

'What for?'

'To look up something or other, nothing worth worrying about.'

'Mum, Maisy's splashing,' Jago shouted.

'Alright, we're coming now,' yelled Carmen. 'Maisy stop splashing, that floor's lethal when wet, you'll slip and hurt yourself.'

Carmen followed Matthew back downstairs. She had to think what to do. Whoever it was had been looking for something and the only thing of any worth was the book. Only two other people knew it was there, one of them was Rowan; the other was Morvah.

She would have to bite the bullet and ring her sister but it would have to wait. A working farm couldn't stop. Animals had to be fed, fences secured and the filth swept away.

92

SEVENTEEN

Monday morning, Eden was about to leave home for the office for Rowan's bail application when the phone rang. It was Carmen.

'I'm so sorry to bother you again, I know you've got Rowan's bail hearing later today but I needed to ask you whether you know anything about the farm being searched by the police?'

'No nothing, I'm sure they would have told me if they had a warrant to search the property. They know Rowan wasn't living there when the offence was committed and they searched her flat on the day she was arrested. When was this?'

'Last night, but if it wasn't the police, then someone else broke in and whoever did it headed straight for the attic. I think they were looking for the book. The thing is no one knew it was there other than Rowan and my sister.'

'Morvah?'

'Yes, how do you know about her?' Carmen sounded surprised.

Eden didn't have time to tell her about Morvah's involvement in Rowan's pregnancy. 'Rowan told me you had a sister called Morvah and you'd had a falling out.'

'Yes ... that's right. Over nothing really. She thought I should have carried on with the family traditions and because I wouldn't, she felt I shouldn't have had the farm.'

'Do you think that too?'

'No, no, I don't. There's no need for the cures anymore. People have access to medicine and midwives. And I'm glad they do. Morvah's a nurse she should know better than anyone doctors should be treating medical problems not people like me.'

'Do you think Morvah would have broken in to look for the book?'

'No, of course not but I wonder if she's told someone else about it and they've let it slip, you know how these things happen; loose lips and all that. The book would be valuable now with all the press interest in Rowan's case and the dig.'

'Look, I'll ask the police in case it was them but I don't think from what you're saying it was. I'm afraid you'll have to talk to Morvah if you want to rule her out too.'

'I will and thanks Eden and good luck with our Rowan. It would be such a relief to have her home, where I can take care of her'

'Hopefully, you'll have her back tonight. I'm going to suggest a police presence because of the fire. If the fanatics who lit it know Rowan's back home, they might try again and this time your family might not be so lucky.'

'Thank you, I'll feel better having someone around.'

Ending the call, Eden speculated what Morvah might tell her sister if confronted. It wasn't going to help the rift between them, admitting she'd overseen Rowan's antenatal care knowing Carmen was in the dark about her daughter's pregnancy. Nevertheless, it might prove a useful exchange to help Rowan's case. Maybe she'd know something Rowan didn't or wasn't prepared to talk about. With that hope, she left for the office.

***

Agnes greeted her with a pile of telephone messages and e-mails she'd printed off and arranged in order of priority; most from disgruntled clients demanding a call-back. She scowled in the direction of another pile spilling from Eden's in-tray.

'These are the ones who don't want to talk to me, they want to talk to you *personally*.'

The words were delivered as a well-deserved reprimand.

It was looking more and more as if she was going to have to concede defeat and get a trainee to help out with her workload, especially if Rowan's case was going to monopolize so much of her time.

'I'm sorry I left you to juggle all this, Agnes. I've been so tied up with the Lutey case, everything else has had to take a back seat I'm afraid.'

'I'm sure you've got an uphill battle defending that one. The whole town is talking about that poor baby. Imagine someone burying a defenceless child alive. Pure wickedness is what it is.'

'Then it's just as well I'm not concerned with tittle-tattle,' she retorted, sweeping up the paperwork and moving through to her office.

An hour or so later, she'd finished apologising to clients, promising letters of advice and rearranging appointments. She was relieved to get off so lightly without a formal complaint to the Law Society. The final call was to a client summoned for 'a chat' with the Inland Revenue. She promised to attend with him the following morning, before scooping the pile of e-mails into the bin. She had two hours before Rowan's bail application in the magistrates' court to finalise her arguments as to why the girl should be released pending trial.

Despite ringing twice, she'd not heard back from the CPS and had no idea if they were opposing the application, although she saw little legal reason for them to do so. Rowan wasn't likely to skip the country; she didn't even have a passport. She had strong family ties locally and wasn't a risk to the public at large. Even if they believed she'd killed her child they must recognise it was out of ignorance or panic or because she was unbalanced? The circumstances dictated the crime and it was unlikely those circumstances would ever be repeated. No, she was pretty certain Rowan would get bail. Then the work for the trial would begin.

Her first task would be to lobby the CPS to get them to reduce the charge from manslaughter to infanticide but there was no guarantee she'd succeed. She'd spoken to a law lecturer friend who told her their decision might well be political. There was a backlash brewing from those who thought, in these days of gender equality, there was no place for a defence available only to women. Fathers affected by witnessing the birth, no matter how traumatic couldn't rely on it. Other critics, coming from a completely different stance, felt it had always been a device to cover up some pretty shocking statistics. History confirmed women from all cultures had, since records began, killed their unwanted children, especially in times of deprivation. No one knew exactly how many infant deaths were down to murders by desperate mothers, covered up by family members and sympathetic doctors, but times had changed. Children were no longer the property of their parents; they had rights too. The CPS was leaning toward manslaughter and even murder charges in such cases, especially where the child suffered a violent death. Social pressure had brought infanticide to the statute books to cover up an unpalatable truth and ironically another kind of social pressure may well get rid of it. Rowan could well be a victim of this policy decision.

The important thing was to get her out and arrange appropriate professional help. Deep down the girl must know what happened. Whether she was holding back on purpose or had buried it within her subconscious, it must be there somewhere, waiting to be exposed by therapy, hypnosis, or good old plain talking?

If she'd buried her child, unaware it was still alive it didn't make her a monster, it made her a victim of something terrible she'd carry for the rest of her life. If she didn't bury the baby, someone else did and Rowan had to have an idea who. Shuffling her papers back into the file, Eden slipped on her jacket and wandered back out to where Agnes was manning reception.

'I'm off to the magistrates. I've phoned everyone back and made some appointments in the diary. I'll be back after the application.'

'Good luck. I know other people think you shouldn't help that girl, you should let her rot if she's done what they say she has, but I said you wouldn't be defending her if you thought she'd done it, so good luck.'

Agnes was like everyone else. Even after all these years working for defence lawyers she still didn't get it. Eden didn't know if Rowan was guilty or not but she had a right to be defended and it was her job to do it.

EIGHTEEN

Carmen tapped in Morvah's number. She'd deleted her from her contacts but knew it off by heart having called a dozen times or more over the last couple of years only to cancel at the last minute.

Knowing Morvah would recognise the call was from her, she spent ten minutes looking at the screen in case she phoned back. She didn't.

When two hours later, her sister still hadn't returned her call, she telephoned the hospital and told the woman on the desk there was a family emergency and she needed to talk to Sister Lutey.

Morvah rang back within minutes.

'Carmen, what is it; is it one of the kids?'

'It's okay, everyone's fine.'

'But they told me there was a family crisis. I thought someone was hurt and what with Rowan and the fire and everything. I thought of smoke inhalation; sometimes that takes time for the symptoms to show … I didn't know what to think.'

'I needed to talk to you and you weren't answering my calls.'

'You frightened me half to death to get my attention? You're lucky I don't put the phone down; in fact, I think I bloody well will.'

'No don't, please … please listen to me for a minute.'

Morvah remained silent.

'I didn't lie, this *is* a family crisis. No one got hurt last night but someone easily could have. Whoever lit the fire didn't care about me or the kids and then, when I got home this morning, I found the attic had been ransacked. I think someone was looking for Gran's book.'

'They didn't get it; tell me they didn't get it?'

'No, they didn't. I thought the police might search the house and take it, so I hid it in the barn.'

'The barn, but what about the fire. They said on the news the fire started in the barn?'

'Don't worry, I managed to rescue it. It's safe with me but I needed to know if you've told anyone about it and where it was kept?'

'You don't know me at all do you? If you did, you'd know I'd never tell anyone. My beliefs are the most important thing in the world to me. If anyone should have the book it should be me but even though I know you've turned your back on Wiccan, I've respected Mum's wishes and never asked for it. I could have taken it hundreds of times; you wouldn't have known. When was the last time you even opened it, let alone practised the craft? It's the thing I value most, do you honestly think I'd let someone else have it?'

Carmen knew she'd made a big mistake. If she'd thought it through, she'd have realised Morvah wouldn't tell anyone about the book. She, unlike her, still believed in the power it held within its ancient pages.

'I'm sorry, I had to ask because only you and I know about it and I'm sure whoever broke in must have known it was in the attic.'

'And Rowan?'

'What do you mean?'

'Rowan knew about it; knew where it was kept. Three people knew; us two and Rowan.'

'Rowan's been in custody.'

'She might have told someone about it and with all the interest on the telly and the internet they might have seen it as a way of making a bit of cash by selling it to the media.'

'Who would she tell?'

'We won't know until we ask her.'

'Her bail application is today. Her lawyer, Miss Gray, has been very good.'

'Eden Gray?'

'Do you know her?'

'Only by reputation but I'm glad you've got someone to support you.'

Carmen bit her lower lip. 'I'd rather have my sister's support.'

Another long pause at the other end of the phone.

'Morvah?'

'Yes.'

Carmen could tell Morvah was crying;

'Are you okay?' she asked choking back her own tears.

'I'm so sorry; about everything and the farm. It was wrong of me.'

'Look it was a long time ago. Things have moved on. You've got your career. A senior midwife who could have imagined it? I'm so proud of you.'

'Can we meet, we need to talk and I can't do it over the phone, not here at work?'

'Yes, of course. Why don't you come to the farm? Rowan will be home later if everything goes to plan and she'd love to see you.'

Carmen understood Matthew might not be quite so happy. He'd taken Morvah's self-imposed estrangement personally. He'd always been close to her and when she broke all ties with them, it hit him badly. The two younger children probably wouldn't even remember her.

'No, not at the farm. I don't knock off until ten this evening. I'm off tomorrow though so could we meet at my place, say about eleven?'

'Of course, whatever's best for you.'

'I'll text you my address.'

'You're my little sister. Just because we haven't spoken for the last four years doesn't mean I've not been looking out for you.'

'Alright, I'll see you then,' Morvah sobbed.

'Good. And Morvah, I can't wait to see you.'

'Me too.'

Carmen held her mobile to her ear for a long time after the call finished, not wanting it to end.

NINETEEN

Luke was deep in conversation with Angie Evans from the CPS when Eden walked into the foyer of the magistrates' court. She knew Angie well. Though always on opposing sides, they got on. She'd even been to a New Year's Eve party at her house.

Angie was in her late forties but didn't look it. From Cardiff originally, she had a passion for rugby extending to her playing seven-a-side for a local ladies' team which kept her fit. Her other passions were Michael Bublé, tequila slammers and a Volkswagen camper van called Dilys she drove to festivals at weekends. Eden had never seen her flustered or grumpy.

Her mouth stretched in a welcoming grin as Eden approached. Luke, after a quick hello, left the women to talk in private.

'Hi, Angie. I tried ringing your office twice this morning. No one would tell me whether you were opposing the application or not?'

'Over here,' Angie whispered conspiratorially, moving them to a battered mahogany bench polished to a high shine by the backsides of successive fidgety defendants.

'It's been a bit of a shit storm if I'm honest.'

'What do you mean?'

'I got the nod they wanted to oppose the application.'

'Who's they?'

'Up the line.' She rolled her eyes at the ceiling as if the order had come straight from God himself.

'And ...?'

'I bloody told 'em it's ridiculous. The law's clear. I get there's no presumption of bail because of the manslaughter charge, but your client's got no previous; there's no threat to witnesses and she's not likely to abscond; all the usual shit; but they said they needed to be seen to be protecting the public. From what, a teenage girl who's been through a terrible experience, ending with the loss of her baby? They said they were under pressure from certain factions worried about the witchcraft thing and concerned things would get out of hand; public order issues.'

'What *witchcraft thing?* There is no *witchcraft thing.* It's something the press has concocted to sell papers. If the baby had been found in a dustbin or a public toilet like they usually are, they probably wouldn't even have reported it. They don't give a damn about the baby. The place it was found; that's what's got them all fired up and the gossip about my client's family. All the stuff not relevant at all.'

Angie's firm hand covered hers in a show of solidarity.

'I know, I know, you're preaching to the choir. Your girl's no bloody witch and she's no bloody risk either. Between you and me, I argued against manslaughter. This is infanticide.'

'If she did it at all?'

'What, you honestly think she didn't?' Angie looked surprised.

'Honestly, I don't know but something's not right.'

'That's where we differ. I think she did it but I don't think she's a criminal not in the true sense of the word.'

'So, the upshot is you've been told to oppose the application?'

'Afraid so.'

'Damn it.'

'But look, you go in there and do your bit. I'll oppose but I'm not going to break my neck doing it. Let's just say I've got a funny feeling I'm going to have a bad day at the office. I'll need conditions; she'll have to report to the station, not talk to the surrogate couple who hired her, but you'll get your bail.'

'Thanks, Angie.'

'You're welcome, my lovely. Now, what's going on with boyo over there? I've never seen him so down in the dumps,' Angie said nodding in Luke's direction.

'Oh, nothing much; the usual problems with my sister.'

'Ah, the lovely Thea. No offence mind, but it's about time he kicked that one into touch.'

'I think he would if not for my niece.'

'Well trust me, he's certainly got plenty of admirers in my office and then there's that new DS of his.'

'Denise Charlton?'

'Don't act so surprised.'

'Oh, I'm not, I'm just a bit jealous. Not about him. It's just I haven't got a lot of that kind of attention myself lately. I'm beginning to think I'm past it.'

'What? You're not telling me you've got trouble getting a date? Take a look in the mirror girl; gorgeous. God if I had legs like yours, I'd rule the bloody world.'

'You do all right as you are,' Eden winked. 'See you inside.'

To Eden's relief, the application went as planned. Rowan entered a not guilty plea and the case was bumped to the Crown Court for the first available hearing. Angie opposed bail on behalf of the CPS on the grounds the girl needed to be remanded in custody for more psychiatric reports; had been uncooperative and might interfere with witnesses and evidence. She also stressed Rowan might be in danger from certain elements and there was a risk of public order offences being committed on the back of her release.

As planned, Eden argued the behaviour of the public was not relevant and if the criteria were strictly applied, her client should be granted bail. She agreed conditions with Angie and Rowan was released into her custody to report to the local police station once a week. She was to stay away from the Marshalls, live with her family at the farm and be subject to a seven o'clock curfew, although she wouldn't be tagged. All in all, not a bad result.

Leaving the courtroom, she walked headlong into Luke.

'The press is outside. I think it's best if you talk to them. If you don't, they'll only hound the Luteys and they have enough to deal with,' he urged. 'My car is around the back. I can take Rowan home, if you like?'

'Thanks.'

She turned to Rowan. 'Are you alright with that? I'll be around later to talk over the conditions with you and discuss where we go from here.'

The girl shrugged and followed Luke.

Eden took a deep breath and headed out to face the wolves. The surge of reporters; their massive, furry caterpillar microphones thrusting in her face, nearly knocked her off her feet.

She spotted Sindy Raybald.

'Your client was released on bail today, Miss Gray. What do you say to all those young mothers frightened for the safety of their children now Rowan Lutey is out there, free to do what she wants?'

She wanted to run but Luke was right; they wouldn't let her leave until she gave them something.

'Firstly, my client has been released under strict bail conditions and secondly, she has not been found guilty of anything yet. People should reserve their judgement until after the trial but rest assured Rowan Lutey is not guilty of manslaughter.'

'What about your lack of judgement in taking this case? You must be aware of the backlash growing on social media aimed at you personally because of this client and others you've defended in the past?'

'I try not to engage with social media if I can help it. The only opinion I'm interested in is the jury's and until then I will keep my own counsel. I've nothing more to say at this time.'

She jostled her way past the rest of the reporters, avoiding eye contact.

'Do you still keep in touch with Mr Pearson, Eden?' someone shouted from the side.

Stifled by the weight of pressing bodies and the taunts of the crowd beyond, she thought she might throw up if she didn't get away and made a dash for it through the crowd down the steps; heart pounding. A shove from behind caused her to lose her footing and someone grabbed her elbow to save her from a tumble. Glancing up she saw Denise Charlton.

'This way,' she said, keeping a firm grip on her as she led her out of harm's way.

'Luke said you might need some help.'

'I didn't expect this. I don't understand where all these people have come from?'

'Rent-a-crowd ... and those bloody morons are only too happy to feed the sharks,' said Denise gesturing in the direction of the reporters overtaking them as they walked.

One scuttled sideways like a crab, snapping as he went. A couple more hovered at the end of the car park; shutters clicking. Eden realised with dismay they were photographing her car. As she got closer, she saw broken eggs shattered across her bonnet; the word BITCH scrawled in something unmentionable across the windscreen.

Denise flashed her warrant card, and the photographers scattered.

'I'm so sorry, Eden. We had no idea things were going to kick off like this. We would have got extra security had we known,' she apologised. 'I can get one of the court ushers to fetch a bucket of water to wash that lot off if you want?'

'No, it's okay,' Eden replied, desperately trying to keep it together as she slid into the driver's seat. 'I've got plenty of washer fluid; the wipers will get rid of the worst of it. I'll deal with the rest when I get home.'

'If you're sure?'

'Honestly; thank you but I'm fine,' she said gripping the wheel to hide the shake in her fingers. From her expression Eden could tell Denise wasn't convinced.

'Okay, but watch your back. Take extra precautions with your social media feeds; up your security at home if it's not up to scratch. This stuff has an edge to it I don't like.'

Denise circled the car once more to check there was no further damage, before finally retreating towards the court building.

Eden sat watching the windscreen wipers swish back and forth until they had cleared a small square big enough for her to see to drive. She'd barely driven out of the carpark when her phone rang. Once she was sure she wasn't being followed she pulled in. Her father had left a voicemail.

'Hi love, it's Dad. I need to talk to you about Thea. I know you're probably busy but you must call me as soon as you can ...

not on the landline ... on my mobile. I don't want Mum to know about this.'

She phoned him back and he picked up right away.

'Is everything alright, Dad?'

'It's about your sister. After we spoke, I tried to get hold of her. I called her mobile and left a message but she didn't come back to me. I called again several times with no luck. In the end, I phoned the gallery where she works and spoke to the owner, this Leon chappie she's been living with and he said he hadn't seen her for over a fortnight; said she'd gone off to Scotland with some Moroccan sculptor he's been exhibiting.'

'And what about Flora?'

'She left her with him but he couldn't cope, what with work and having to travel abroad to see clients and so one of his staff has taken her in; a young woman he's paying to make sure Flora gets to school and what-not. He was relieved I called.'

'I bet he was. Why didn't he call us?'

'Thea told him not to say anything in case it got back to Luke and he was fine with that for a couple of days but two weeks on, she's not answering his calls and he's had enough. He doesn't want to get her into trouble with the authorities but he's miffed about this other chap and let's face it Flora's not his problem.'

Of all the selfish reckless things her sister had done this was right up there with the worst of them.

'What do you suggest we do?' asked her father sounding desperate.

'Tell Luke of course. He has a right to know his only child has been dumped on strangers while Thea's gone off with yet another man that's blown into her life and will no doubt blow out again once he gets fed up with her antics.'

'But won't it affect the custody situation; won't she lose the right to keep Flora with her?'

'Yes ... she will and deserves to. She can sabotage her own life as much as she likes but not Flora's; she has no right to do that.'

'But maybe she's not taking her meds; maybe that's what's brought all this on?'

'And whose fault is that? All she has to do is take the pills but no … she misses the extremes; the rollercoaster ride; thinks the pills shackle her talent. Well, sod her talent.'

Her father fell silent on the other end of the phone and she was instantly guilty. It wasn't his fault after all.

'I'm sorry, Dad, but she's not a teenager anymore. She has to understand actions have consequences and not only for her.'

'I know … I know,' her father agreed wearily. 'Can I leave it to you to tell Luke? I'll text you the number and address of the girl who Flora's staying with and I'll keep trying to get hold of your sister.'

'Okay, but I think you should tell Mum, she's stronger than you think.'

'Alright, I'll have a go.'

Ending the call, she set out for the farm, wondering how best to break the news to Luke his daughter had been dumped on a virtual stranger. As she approached, she was pleased to see he'd had the presence of mind to post a car at the end of the lane. The officer waved her through and her stomach lurched at the sight of Luke's car in the courtyard. He was leaving as she arrived and she almost lost her nerve; afraid he'd shoot the messenger.

'Can I have a quiet word?'

'I can't discuss the case anymore,' he said too quickly. 'I helped Rowan out today because of that lot outside the court but she's been charged and it's an ongoing investigation.'

'I know and I'm grateful,' Eden replied, ' but it's not about the case; it's personal.'

Luke blushed and Eden wondered if he thought she was going to mention the message he'd left on her answerphone?

'I see.'

'I was going to call later but as you're here,' *she might as well spit it out*, 'it's about Thea.'

'I need to go fetch Flora,' he said when she'd finished telling him the saga.

'If you're on duty, I could go?' Eden offered, ashamed her sister had put him in this position.

'No, give me the address. Flora needs to know at least one of her parents is there for her.'

She didn't argue. Then, suddenly remembering the break-in;

'Luke, did anyone from your team search the house on the night of the fire?'

'No, we assumed it was an accident. We got everyone out of the house as soon as possible. I suppose the firemen might have gone in to check the fire hadn't spread, but no, we would have needed a warrant to search.'

'I thought so.'

'Why?'

'Oh nothing,' she replied, certain he was telling the truth. 'And Luke, good luck.'

***

Carmen, rushed towards her; arms outstretched, to give her a big hug.

'Thank you ... thank you so much for getting Rowan home.'

'This is where the work starts you understand. She's home under strict restrictions.'

'Yes, DI Parish explained everything to us. I'll make sure she sticks to the rules. You can be sure of it.'

Eden glanced across at Rowan, relieved to see she had more colour than she'd had earlier in court when at one point she thought she might keel over.

'The good news is I now know not everyone in the CPS feels happy about the charge of manslaughter. If we can keep the pressure on, I've got every hope we can get them to change their minds.'

Rowan yawned; eyes drifting up to the timbered ceiling. Eden felt the familiar pinch of frustration she was coming to expect from her conversations with the girl.

'You're tired, I don't expect you slept well last night? I'll see you tomorrow. I wanted to make sure you understood the bail restrictions. If you're happy you do, I'll leave you in peace.'

Carmen followed her into the hall.

'I've arranged to see Morvah tomorrow morning to talk but I'm sure she didn't tell anyone about the book.'

Eden knew exactly what Morvah wanted to talk about.

'She thought Rowan might have told someone.'

'Did she, who?' Eden leapt on any information that might give her insight into the life of her uncommunicative client.

'She didn't know, she thought I ought to ask her?'

'Well, we know it wasn't the police; Luke confirmed it just now. I think your sister's right; you should ask her. Someone's got the inside track on this and if you believe Morvah and know you haven't told anyone, there's only one person who could have.'

'I'm not going to say anything tonight. I'm so glad to have her home, I can't bear to spoil it.'

'I'll leave it to you to decide when the right time is but bear in mind at the moment we haven't a clue who Rowan is close to; who she confides in. If she told someone about the book she did so for a reason and we can be sure she was pretty damn close to whoever it was. If that's so she may have confided something else, something she's not telling either of us.'

TWENTY

Eden was roused at four the next morning by the sound of her mobile vibrating on the bedside table. She contemplated not answering before thinking better of it, in case it was work. She wasn't on call but it wouldn't be the first time she'd been asked to speak to someone kicking off in the cells when the other duty solicitors were busy. It was Luke.

'I'm outside in the car. Can I come up; I've got Flora with me?'

Under normal circumstances, she would say no but the mention of her niece's name meant these weren't normal circumstances.

'Sure,' she replied groggily, dragging herself from the warm bed and slipping on her dressing gown. 'I'll buzz you in.'

Five minutes later she was helping him unbundle a sleepy Flora into her bed.

'You look exhausted,' she whispered, closing the door quietly behind them.

'I drove there and back.'

'To London?'

'It helps when you can plonk a siren on the roof and put your foot down.'

'And the girl from the gallery; was she happy for you to take her?'

'I rang the number you gave me and explained who I was. She knew about me of course from Thea. I think the badge swung it. I guess she thought she'd rather get into trouble with Thea than the law.'

'And Flora? Is she alright; was she shocked to see you?'

'I'm not sure much shocks Flora these days. She's used to being passed around from pillar to post. She was asleep when I arrived. The girl – Lucy - woke her; told her I was there to take her back to Cornwall. She asked me about school; who would let her teachers know and when I reassured her I'd deal with all that, she gathered up her belongings quietly as if it was the most natural thing in the world and was asleep in the back of the car by the time we hit the A303.'

'Do you think Lucy will contact Thea?'

'I expect she'll try but whether she has better luck getting hold of her than us is anyone's guess.'

'Did you talk to her about this sculptor she's gone off to Scotland with?'

'Rafie; that's his name; no surname just *Rafie*. She wasn't sure if that's his actual name or the one he uses professionally. He makes massive installations from recycled waste; you know plastics from the ocean and stuff.'

'So, what happens now?'

'I go home and get some sleep. I've got an appointment with my solicitor tomorrow to get an emergency order, giving me care and control and if that goes to plan, I'll set about getting permanent custody and finding Flora a place in a local school.'

'And until then. What about work?'

Eden imagined he had more than enough on his plate without all this. She didn't particularly want to be dealing with another officer who might be less willing to share information with her about the case. Luke was no fan of Rowan's but at least he was fair.

'Well, actually that's why I brought Flora here rather than take her back to my place. I share with a couple of other guys in the force and it's not suitable. I was aiming to get a place of my own soon anyway so I could have Flora stay in the school holidays. That'll have to be brought forward now but until then ...'

'Now hang on ... I'm not set up to look after a child any more than you are. I've got the practice to run and the case ...' she protested.

'No ... oh no, sorry I didn't mean you. I was wondering if perhaps your mum and dad would be willing to help ... let her stay there until I get settled?'

'I don't know; that's not exactly going to go down well with Thea. She'll see it as treachery on their part.'

'Maybe, then again she might be glad they're in the mix. It's worth a try surely?'

'Okay,' she relented, 'I'll have a word but I can't promise anything. Last time I spoke to Dad he hadn't even told Mum about Thea doing a flit.'

'I know it's unorthodox but whatever you can do would be much appreciated.'

'Okay … okay,' she held her hands up in submission, 'I'll do my best.'

After he'd left, she crawled back into bed beside her niece and felt the warmth rising from her little body as she tossed and turned. Poor kid, what a mess.

***

Flora was sitting on the edge of the bed waiting for her to wake up.

'I looked for Daddy but he's gone.'

'Good morning, poppit,' Eden smiled as she tried to remove the crick in her neck. 'Daddy thought it best you stay here last night after your long journey. Don't worry we'll catch up with him later.'

'Will I be staying here again with you tonight?'

'No, I think you'll probably be staying with Nanna and Grandad for a while until Daddy gets a new place. Is that okay?'

Flora's face dropped. 'And Mummy? Will Mummy be coming down to Cornwall too?'

'Soon … but not right away.'

'Is that because she doesn't love me as much as she loves Rafie?' she said, head down picking at the corner of the duvet.

Eden swallowed the growing lump in her throat. 'Don't be a silly sausage,' she said, pulling her niece into her, 'your mummy loves you more than anyone in the world. We all love you to bits,' she murmured into the little girl's hair gritting her teeth so as not to cry. 'Come on … let's see what we can find for breakfast.'

She was pouring Flora's juice when the bell rang. She expected it was Luke calling in on his way to work but resisted the urge to open the door in case after Denise's warning yesterday it was someone else.

'Who is it?'

'Me.'

Agnes. Grabbing a sheet of kitchen roll from the worktop, she dabbed her loaded lashes before opening the door.

'God you look awful,' Agnes said, scanning her face with disapproval.

'I've got a bit of a cold coming,' Eden sniffled.

'You'd better take something. You've got a long day ahead of you. Have you got any lemons? Mother always swore by honey and lemon.'

'Agnes, what are you doing here?'

'I came to warn you.'

'Warn me about what?'

'I've had to shut the office. Reporters are blocking the door. I didn't know how to keep them out so I decided to come here. I picked these up on the way.'

Reaching into a huge red shopping bag, she pulled out a couple of client files and a clutch of newspapers.

'I thought you could work from home today,' she said coyly, plonking the files down in front of her.

Eden was more interested in the newspapers; one local and one national tabloid. They'd made the front page of the *Western Packet*. The story set out the bare facts. She'd have preferred no report at all but as it was; it was fairly innocuous.

Agnes was holding the tabloid rolled up like a weapon as if ready to bash someone over the head with it.

'What about that one?' queried Eden.

'It goes on about the Lutey girl coming from a family of weirdos and there's an interview with a woman from a local toddler group about how young mothers are afraid for their children's safety.'

'What local toddler group?'

'Beggared if I know; none I recognise. I think they make it up as they go along.'

'Go on then … show it to me.' Eden reached to grab the paper.

Agnes stepped back.

'What is it Agnes?'

'Nothing; I told you what it says.'

'Well then, give it here.'

'But …'

'What page?' demanded Eden, grabbing it from her.

'Centre spread,' sighed Agnes conceding defeat. 'I don't think you should read it but if you must, take no notice.'

'They've got to be joking?'

TEENAGE WITCH GETS BAIL

Lawyer, Eden Gray, was not willing to comment yesterday on whether she felt witchcraft had been a factor in influencing the magistrates to release on bail her client Rowan Lutey.

Lutey, the latest in a long line of notorious 'witches' was smuggled by the police from the back of the courtroom to avoid the crowd of protesters gathered at the front of the court building. Vanessa Pengelly, a young mother who runs Tiny Tackers toddler group in Truro expressed her concerns for the children in her care to our reporter.

"I think it's a disgrace letting her out. I know she's not been found guilty yet, and I'm a fair person, but who knows what she's capable of? As a mother I need to know my children are safe and I don't feel they are, with that girl wandering free."

Lutey's lawyer, Eden Gray, known for her radical feminist views and for defending notorious sex offender Carl Pearson, serving a twenty-year sentence at HM Prison Belmarsh, is more than happy to represent the young woman widely thought to practice witchcraft, accused of burying her baby alive. Gray's obvious love of defending perverts and child abusers more than qualifies her for her new role. Maybe Eden Gray would feel differently if she had children of her own?

Perhaps then she'd concentrate on protecting the weak and vulnerable rather than fighting for the release of her evil teenage client.'

Below the headline, a shot of her leaving court the day before. They'd caught her grimacing, her hand up to her face as if trying to hide. Eden threw the paper across the room, knocking one of the client files from the breakfast bar.

'What the hell are they trying to do; how can Rowan get a fair trial with all this crap circulating? Then again why bother with a trial, why not take her to the outskirts of town light a bloody great bonfire and burn her at the stake?'

Her head throbbed. Rowan was just a girl; witches didn't exist, surely everyone knew that, even the stupid sods who read the crap peddled by that rag. Not to mention all the stuff about her and her background. How dare they?! Surely people would see it for what it was and be just as outraged as she was?

Remembering Flora in the next room, she made an effort to calm herself. Agnes was busy retrieving the contents of the client file strewn across the floor. As Eden stooped to help, she remembered her appointment that morning with her client and HMRC. She was already running late. She needed someone to look after Flora.

'I've got to go. I've got that interview with Terry Medlin and the Inland Revenue at ten and I've got my niece here. She's in the bathroom at the moment but do you think you could look after her for a while?'

'You mean your sister's girl; what's she doing here?'

'Look it's a long story but Luke is collecting her later this morning to take her to my parents so it'll only be for a couple of hours, max.'

'No need.'

'What do you mean?'

'Mr Medlin cancelled; in fact, when I rang in to pick up the messages, the answerphone was full of calls from clients phoning to cancel. It's all over the internet; pictures of you at the Lutey farm and the links to witchcraft and about you defending that awful

Pearson man; all sorts of nutters are out there having their two-penneth.'

'This is wrong.'

'I said no good would come of defending that girl,' said Agnes, in a *told you so* tone.

'When did you say that?'

'Well, I thought it and I was right.'

Much as she hated to admit it, Eden had to agree.

After Agnes left, she sat on the floor in a daze next to her niece watching Tom and Jerry knock seven bells out of each other.

What to do next ... *Elspeth*?

She could explain the witch pits to the press the way she had to her; tell them they weren't about death but birth; new life. The professor would be able to confirm the Lutey women were midwives and healers, not witches and devil worshippers or whatever Netflix fantasy the papers were peddling. She had to speak to Elspeth.

She wasn't sure yet how much she should divulge about Grandma Lutey's book. She knew one thing for sure. If the press somehow got hold of the letter it would be a disaster. She decided to keep quiet about Grandma Lutey's confession for now but try and persuade Carmen to allow Elspeth access to the book. Elspeth wasn't swayed by gossip or melodrama. She was first and foremost a scientist. She dealt in hard evidence and the book was evidence the Lutey family were good people.

TWENTY-ONE

Carmen crossed the open space ironically re-named The Piazza by the council. Generally, the soulless wind tunnel hemmed in between Primark and the Job Centre bore little resemblance to the colourful Bougainvillea- strewn squares of Italy, but this morning there was a tented farmers' market and the place was a hub of activity.

She took a shortcut through the billowing white marquee, full of stalls, pausing to admire the flavoured oils glowing in their long-necked bottles; the spicy jars of pickles and preserves, balanced on saucers with stubby breadsticks for tasting. Normally by this time of year, she would have made and stacked away her jams and pickles for Yule. The kitchen would have filled with the heady perfume of cumin and cinnamon as the copper pans bubbled but all that had gone by the bye with everything else going on.

She cast an approving eye over a stack of freshly-baked crusty loaves; before moving on to the cheese counter where she reached for her purse, unable to resist a wedge of creamy Cornish Yarg, wrapped in its nettle leaf rind. The reversal of their surname by the local farming family who made the cheese was a clever bit of marketing and she wondered if Eden Gray was a relation.

Reminded why she was there, she waited for her change then made for the exit. Looking up at the clock perched high on the old Town Hall she thought she'd better get a move on; she was due at Morvah's at eleven and didn't want to be late.

Her sister's flat was part of a new complex built above the shopping precinct off the Piazza. It was undoubtedly convenient for the shops but Carmen couldn't help thinking it must be noisy especially at night when the pubs turned out. The view was pretty grim too.

Her gran had talked of a time back along, when the river came right up through there; lapped at the doorsteps of the houses of the gentry who lived on Lemon Quay; of a time when tall ships arrived with coal and sailed away with tin. Now that would have been a sight to see, she thought, walking into the underground carpark behind Marks and Sparks to take the lift up to the flats. She adjusted her hair before knocking.

Her sister came to the door immediately. She'd lost weight and it suited her. She'd always been the one with the looks; popular with the boys but never that interested. She'd had a few boyfriends before leaving home but nothing serious. She was too demanding, wanting everything on her terms.

'Coffee?'

'Lovely.'

'I can do you a cappuccino or a latte?'

'Oh, instant's fine.'

'I don't have instant.'

'Then anything; you choose.'

It felt strange, passing pleasantries as if they were strangers; feeling the need to fill the gaps with inconsequential conversation where once they would have stayed silent and thought nothing of it. They'd been inseparable since the day Morvah was born and her mother let her hold her little sister. She knew her better than she knew herself. She wanted to hug her; confide in her; share secrets and dreams as they once had but the years of not speaking had shattered the bond and they'd never be that close again.

She admired the open-plan room, envying the super-sleek vanilla coloured kitchen with its moulded sink and soft press units. She couldn't help but compare it to the chaos she'd left at home. Even before the fire, the farm kitchen was never this clean, what with the mud dragged in on wellington boots; not to mention the fine dust that blew down from the fields coating everything like icing sugar when the windows were open.

Carmen noticed there was nothing in the room betraying Morvah's roots. Guilt swamped her. Her sister had walked out leaving everything. It wasn't as if there wasn't enough clutter at the farm to go around; the attic and the barns were falling down with it. Maybe it was her choice; maybe she didn't want anything to take the sheen off her new squeaky-clean life.

'So, what did you want to talk about?' Carmen shouted above the high-pitched squeal of the milk frother as it ran short of steam.

Morvah put two mugs down on the table with a thud, so the contents slopped over the sides.

'Damn it. I'll get a cloth.'

'Leave it,' Carmen said, gently grabbing her sister's hand. 'What did you want to talk about?'

'Rowan; I want to talk about Rowan.'

'She's fine, or as fine as can be expected. Eden is hopeful of getting the charge reduced to infanticide and a non-custodial sentence.'

'What has she told you about the pregnancy?'

'Not much. I didn't know of course. I had no idea and I can't help feel responsible. If I'd taken more notice maybe all this wouldn't have happened and she could have had the baby and it would be alive.'

Carmen had swallowed her tears up until now for Rowan's sake, but here with Morvah her courage started to fray at the edges.

'It's not your fault. I should have told you.'

Carmen distracted, rummaged in her bag for a tissue to blow her nose.

'What do you mean?'

'I knew.'

'Knew about what?' she asked looking up.

'Everything; the pregnancy, the surrogacy, everything.' Morvah's eyes were fixed on the coffee cups.

'You knew everything, then why the hell didn't you tell me?' Carmen spluttered.

'Rowan made me promise not to.'

'An eighteen-year-old ... no, no, when she fell pregnant, a seventeen-year-old kid asks you to promise and you, knowing it's a stupid, reckless thing to do, go ahead and agree? You're a nurse, you should have known better than anyone how dangerous it was for her to be pregnant without medical help; without the proper support.'

Carmen was beside herself. She wanted to wrestle her sister to the ground like when they were children; pummel her until she admitted she was wrong.

'She got proper support. I helped her, I checked on her through the pregnancy, well at the beginning at least.'

'I can't believe I'm hearing this. Was this your way of getting back at me for Mum leaving me the farm, is that it?' Carmen's voice cracked like a brittle bone.

'No, of course not. Rowan contacted me. She begged me to help her. What was I supposed to do, turn her down?'

'Get her to tell me, of course.'

'Don't you think I tried? I tried again and again.'

'Not hard enough.' The heavy thrum of the air conditioning made it difficult for Carmen to think.

'I tried to stop her selling the baby. Then the Marshall woman and her husband got involved and wouldn't let me have any further contact.'

'Did you meet them; the Marshalls?'

'Not her. I met him once.'

'Where?'

'At the flat. I called one afternoon unannounced with some leaflets for Rowan I'd picked up from the hospital. I knocked and when she didn't answer, let myself in using the key she'd given me in case of emergencies. He was there with her.'

'What do you mean *with her?*'

'Sitting on the sofa with her and he was holding her … you know, close. They shuffled apart when they saw me and he left shortly afterwards.'

'Are you saying something was going on between Philip Marshall and Rowan?'

'There was something about the way they acted like they'd been caught, so when he left, I asked her outright but she wouldn't admit or deny it either way, but I knew.'

'You thought from the way they acted they were having an affair?'

'There was something; the way they pulled away when I walked in, plus I always got the feeling Rowan was seeing someone. Sometimes I'd go around and she'd be in her tracksuit bottoms, hair pulled back in a ponytail; not a scrap of makeup. Other times I'd turn up and she'd be done up to the nines and the flat would be tidier than usual. She'd try to get me out of there as soon as possible as if she was expecting someone.'

'You never saw anyone else; only Philip Marshall?'

'No, no one and I didn't see him there again. Rowan told me all about him and his wife though; how they'd been trying for a baby for years. They'd been through IVF, then therapy when it hadn't worked. It ruined their relationship. He couldn't bear the thought of Rowan getting rid of her child. So, he made a proposition to her. She would keep the baby and find a way to confide in his wife. He knew she wouldn't take much convincing to take the baby on, for a price of course, enough to allow Rowan to move on with her life and leave the county. Rowan had to promise never to seek contact with the child.'

Carmen listened to the sordid details of her daughter's life being rolled out and didn't recognise her. Did Rowan really hate them all so much she'd sell her child to get away from them? No wonder she wasn't talking. She was ashamed and rightly so. She felt ashamed too, for not seeing any of this coming.

'Morvah, tell me, do you know anything about the baby's death?'

'No, I swear. As far as I was concerned Rowan's antenatal care was being taken care of by her GP. I have no idea why the baby was born at home without medical help or why no one rang for an ambulance. I can't bear to think of Rowan going through that on her own.'

'But who took the baby and buried it alive; please tell me you don't think Rowan did that?'

'No, I don't, but I'm worried. Now the baby's gone and she's repaid the money. Why hasn't she told anyone about her relationship with Philip Marshall?'

'I don't know why she hasn't but it's about time she did. It's about time she started to tell the truth about a lot of things.'

TWENTY-TWO

Eden's father collected Flora at eleven. He didn't say much but as he left, laden with his granddaughter's things, he kissed Eden on the cheek.

'I told Mum and you were right, she's stronger than she seems.'

'Told you,' she smiled, 'we'll catch up later, I'll let Luke know you've got her.'

After he'd gone, she tried Elspeth's number several times but her calls went straight to answerphone. In desperation, she rang the museum.

'Can I speak to Professor Fuller? Tell her it's Eden Gray.'

'I can't tell her anything,' came the curt reply, 'Professor Fuller's not in today. She's not been in for a few days now. I can put you through to her assistant if you like?'

She could tell by the cool response the woman knew exactly who she was.

Eden had no intention of confiding in James Ferris but would have to talk to him. She had to get a message to Elspeth somehow and was running out of options.

'Yes, could you put me through to him please?'

'Who did you say it was again?'

'Eden Gray.'

The response was frosty. 'I'll check if he's available.'

The next voice Eden heard belonged to James.

'Hi Eden, how are you holding up?'

'Fine.'

His overly sympathetic tone annoyed her. Elspeth wouldn't have dreamt of asking.

'James, I need to speak to Elspeth and I'm having trouble getting hold of her.'

'I'm afraid she's gone away for a few days. She's at a conference on Brythonic Celtic traditions in Brittany.'

'Brittany?'

'She took the ferry to Roscoff a couple of days ago.'

'When will she be back?'

'The conference ends today but she said she might stay on for a bit to catch up with a few colleagues while she's there.'

'I thought she'd want to be on site with everything going on. She seemed concerned when I spoke to her before that the dig would be compromised by all the media attention.'

'She was at first, but decided maybe it was better to engage with the press.'

'Really?'

'Yes, to make the best of things and get some positive publicity on the back of the tragedy so at least some good comes of it. The coverage can bring what we're doing here to a wider audience and dispel some of the ridiculous misconceptions about what went on at the site.'

'And she decided to go to France rather than stay around?'

'She's on the end of a phone and I'm in contact with her daily. She thought I might be better placed to deal with the media attention, you know as part of the *infotech generation*.'

'Is there a landline I could ring?'

'Mmm, not really. I tend to ring her on her mobile in the evenings, you could try that. If I can't get hold of her I e-mail the college where she's lecturing but I haven't got any numbers for her friends over there and even if I did I wouldn't like to give out their details without permission but don't worry I'll pass the message on.'

She would have to take what she could.

'I saw your interview on the local news. You did well, all things considered,' she lied, hoping a bit of flattery might encourage him to remember her when he next spoke to his boss.

'Thanks, I think that's only the start. The BBC wants to film a documentary about the witch pits. It's all very exciting.'

'Yes, I'm sure it is for you: maybe not so much so for Rowan and the Lutey family.'

'No,' he paused, 'no … sorry I suppose not, but then again they're bound to be interested in interviewing the family and that'll give them a chance to tell their side of the story and counter the rubbish being bandied about.'

'And Elspeth's okay with all this?'

'She's all for it.'

Eden was confused. Elspeth gave her the impression she wanted to keep the dig under wraps. All she was interested in was maintaining the integrity of the site. How could she have got her so wrong?

'Could you ask her to call me please? Tell her I've something I have to discuss with her urgently.'

'About Rowan?'

'Yes, and the family.'

'Is it anything I can help with?'

Eden thought about it for a moment. 'No, I don't think so but thanks for offering. I've got something I need Elspeth to see.'

'Something belonging to the Luteys; to do with the site?'

He was persistent, she'd give him that.

'I think so, but I'm no expert. I'm sure Elspeth will tell you all about it in due course.'

She hoped Elspeth would get back to her soon. If she could speak to her in person she was sure she'd be able to tell if she really was as keen as James to have the press onboard? Once they'd had that conversation, she could gauge what she'd be getting the Luteys into if she showed her the book.

TWENTY-THREE

By mid-afternoon, having read the newspaper over and over again, she knew the piece by heart and had beaten herself up enough.

She decided to escape the confines of her flat and drive to the farm. Before she left she rang her parents to check Flora had settled in. She hadn't mentioned the news stories to her father earlier, not wanting to add to his worries. She was pretty sure they wouldn't have read any of the tabloids but just in case, she'd better warn them.

'Hi, Dad how's it going?'

'Fine, Flora's helping Mum bath the dog. He's rolled in fox poo.'

'Oh … great; a baptism of fire if ever there was one.'

'How about at your end?'

'Not so good.'

'But I saw on the news you got bail for your girl.'

'I did but there's a lot of people not happy about it.'

'What people?'

'Oh, you know, the press; trolls on the internet.'

'Since when did this family care what that lot think?'

'I know, Dad, but some of the stuff they're saying attacks me personally; focuses on me rather than the case.'

'Look, love, like I said before, you'll do the right thing. Take no notice of the press; don't engage, it's what they want. Stay true to yourself. You're strong, you've always been a survivor and you'll survive this.'

She put down the phone, galvanised, by his unwavering faith in her.

Hopefully, Rowan would be keen to start preparing for her defence now she'd tasted incarceration. There was nothing like a night in the cells to make you value your freedom.

TWENTY-FOUR

Carmen answered the door, red-faced as if she'd been running.

'Eden?'

'Hi Carmen, I'm here to see Rowan.'

'Yes, I know,' she replied, rooted to the doorstep.

'Is everything alright?'

For an awful moment it crossed Eden's mind she'd seen the newspapers and no longer believed she was the best person to defend her daughter. Perhaps she thought it would be better to have someone less likely to draw attention; someone male maybe? She hated herself for even thinking it. This case was forcing her to acknowledge prejudices she never thought applied to her. She was becoming increasingly deflated by the unwanted attention; the sexist innuendo dressed up as critique.

'Carmen, is there something you want to say to me?'

'Eden, I'm sorry; what am I thinking, keeping you on the doorstep? Come in please … come in.'

Eden followed her into the kitchen. There was no sign of Rowan and she braced herself for the sacking she'd convinced herself was coming. Carmen agitated, turned to face her.

'It's Rowan; she's gone.'

'What do you mean, gone?'

'I went in to wake her this morning and her bed hadn't been slept in. I've been racing around the farm like an idiot calling for her, then I telephoned the few friends she has left. No one's seen her. Where is she; where on earth is she?'

Carmen began to cry.

Rowan had seemed fine to Eden when she left her. She was due to report for the first time tomorrow and if she didn't, a warrant would be issued for her arrest and she'd lose her liberty, and do untold damage to her case.

'When did you last see her?'

'About nine last night when she went to bed. I didn't go in till late this morning. I let her sleep. I thought she could do with the rest.'

'Have you told anyone else?'

'Matthew but no one else.'

'Let's keep it that way for now. You realise how serious this is, Carmen?'

'Yes of course. I can't believe she's run away. She wouldn't up and leave … she wouldn't.'

Eden put her arm around the woman. 'Now come on, let's not think the worst. She may have cold feet or needed to see a friend you don't know about or to be on her own for a bit. We've got no reason to believe she's skipped bail; not yet anyway.'

'But what if she's not in her right mind, what if she does something stupid?'

Eden knew she meant suicide. 'She's not going to do that, Carmen. None of the preliminary psychiatric reports indicated any risk of self-harm or harm to others for that matter. I would have told you and made sure she was never on her own. I'm certain she'll be back home any time now safe and sound.'

She wasn't certain; the only thing certain about Rowan, was her unpredictability but she saw no point in adding to Carmen's distress.

'Let me make you a cup of tea,' she offered, reaching for the kettle.

'There's something else you need to know,' Carmen sniffed, pulling a handkerchief from her sleeve. 'I spoke to Morvah yesterday and she told me stuff about Rowan I can't believe or rather, don't want to believe.'

Eden poured two cups of tea. She was aware of Morvah's involvement in Rowan's pregnancy and the conversation made her uncomfortable. She would have to come clean if she could but confidentiality prohibited it. She was relieved when Carmen spilled the beans first.

'Morvah knew about Rowan and the surrogacy. She even helped her at first until things went sour. Can you believe that?'

'I have to tell you Carmen; I already know Rowan asked your sister to help her through the pregnancy and to keep it secret from you.'

'You do?' Carmen's face dropped.

'Yes, but Rowan is my client, and I have a duty to keep the conversations I have with her confidential. I'm glad you know though.'

'Do you know about Philip Marshall too?'

'I know Morvah didn't agree with the surrogacy and tried to persuade Rowan to keep the baby or have it adopted through the local authority.'

'No not that. Morvah told me Philip Marshall and Rowan were close; like there was something going on between them.'

It was as if Eden had been thumped in the chest.

'Did his wife know?'

'I don't think so. Morvah said it was probably nothing. Perhaps it was concern, you know for Rowan, her being so young.'

'Carmen don't you get it; what if there was something going on and his wife found out? The police believed everything Jessica Marshall told them because she appeared to have no reason to lie; but if she knew, if she found out her husband was having an affair with Rowan it changes everything. It impacts upon the credibility of her testimony and gives her a motive; a reason to kill the baby; to punish her husband and Rowan.'

If circumstances were different Eden would immediately be on the phone to Luke about Philip Marshall; telling him to scrutinise his wife's testimony but he had lots to sort out and at the minute all she had was Carmen's conversation with her sister; which was hardly evidence. She'd go and see Philip Marshall herself; see if there was any way his wife could have discovered he'd had an affair with Rowan and the baby was his. She knew it was probably a stupid idea. She was used to interviewing witnesses, including witnesses for the prosecution, and wouldn't be breaking any rules but this wasn't a formal interview. This was her playing detective and despite all the American TV programmes depicting it that way, it wasn't her job. She was planning to interview someone close to a suspect. What if Jessica Marshall was there; she might inadvertently tip her off?

She had to get Philip on his own; bluff her way through this; tell him she knew all about the affair and see what surfaced. It wasn't ideal but she had no choice. She would have to tell Luke Rowan was missing if they spoke. It was her duty as an officer of the court. No, the more she thought about it the more convinced she became she had to avoid any communication with him for the moment at least.

Anyway, it was possible the police knew all about Philip and had already checked him out. It wouldn't be the first time in her career they'd withheld information they considered not helpful to their case. They dealt in black and white; guilt or innocence. She looked for shades of grey; reasonable doubt. She didn't need to *prove* Jessica killed the baby. She didn't have to *prove* Jessica did anything. All she had to do was convince a jury the wronged wife had motive and opportunity and lay out a sufficiently persuasive scenario to raise reasonable doubt in their minds about the version of events being put forward by the prosecution.

'Carmen, what's the name of the Marshalls' cafe?'

'Samphire, you know, like the sea herb. Why?'

Eden tapped Café Samphire into Google to find the address. 'Oh, nothing; just for the file. 'I'm sorry I do need to go but only if you're going to be okay? Do you have someone who can collect the children from school for you?'

'Matthew's doing it. You go, I'll be fine until they come.'

'Okay, I'll be off now. Mind you call me the minute Rowan gets in touch.'

'Yes of course.'

'And if the police contact you for whatever reason, or anyone else asks for Rowan, don't let on you don't know where she is. Try and fob them off. We don't want to create a problem before we need to.'

'I understand.'

'One more thing; the book. Would it be alright if I showed it to Elspeth Fuller, the chief archaeologist at the site?'

'Not the letter though, not now with Rowan missing and all the fuss in the papers.'

'No, I promise; only the book. The press is spinning this witchcraft thing against Rowan. It sells papers. They're not going to listen to us, but Elspeth is an independent professional. She's widely respected within the academic community and her public support could be invaluable. Once she's had the chance to look at the book, I'm sure she'll be only too happy to tell the journalists the facts.'

'Okay if you think it will help Rowan, I'll go fetch it.'

Ten minutes later Carmen reappeared without the book, holding a small piece of paper. Her hands shaking. Eden slipped a chair underneath her and prised the note from her tightly clenched fingers.

'It's gone,' Carmen blinked.

Eden read the one word on the note: *SORRY*.

'Look, maybe Rowan's had the same idea as us. Maybe that's where she's gone, to show it to someone who might be able to help?' Eden offered, thinking all the time what a selfish little cow this girl was.

'What if it's something else she's sorry about, what if it's about killing the baby?'

'Carmen you can't let yourself think that way. The note doesn't say that; it's not a confession. In my experience when people confess to family they lay out their excuses. It's human nature to try and justify your bad behaviour to those who matter to you. Sorry just doesn't hack it.'

'I suppose so.'

Eden glanced at her watch.

'It's alright, you go. Matthew will be here with the kids soon.'

TWENTY-FIVE

Eden felt bad about leaving Carmen alone but now Rowan had gone AWOL, finding evidence that cast doubt on her guilt was even more pressing. She couldn't keep her abscondment a secret for long.

The showery morning had given way to a balmy afternoon and the trendy wireframed tables outside Café Samphire were all taken by escapee sixth-formers eating waffles and drinking cups of coffee so big you needed a wrist brace to lift them.

Eden dissected the hipster-chic interior. The uncomfortable mismatched furniture, reclaimed brickwork and industrial copper-pipe lighting met the retro gloom brief fashionable these days. A blackboard leaning at a jaunty angle against a rusty bicycle announced the daily specials;

Homemade Soup of the day
Crab Tacos
Salt and Pepper Squid and Aioli

At the counter, a man in his early thirties dolloped crème fraîche onto a pile of freshly made pancakes.

'I'll be with you in a minute,' he said chirpily, head down, sprinkling cinnamon over the cream.

When finished, he looked up and she could tell by the way his smile slid from his face like melted butter he recognised her.

'Mr Marshall?'

'Yeah?'

'I'm Eden Gray, Rowan Lutey's solicitor. Do you think I could have a word?'

He handed the pancakes to the girl waiting for her order, who immediately snapped a photo of her dessert before handing over her money. Marshall waited for her to join her friends outside before turning his attention to Eden.

'I know who you are, I've said all I've got to say. My wife and I have given statements to the police.'

'I know, but I think maybe there's something you haven't told them?'

'I've got customers to serve.'

There was no queue. The place was empty but for an elderly man in the window seat, finishing off a bowl of mussels.

'Okay, how about we arrange to meet later when the rush is over?' she said, trying to stifle the sarcasm.

'And why would I do that?'

'Because you may prefer I talk to you rather than to your wife?' Eden leaned in towards him. 'I know about your affair with Rowan.'

He glanced over his shoulder as if any minute, someone might creep up behind him and shout 'BOO!'.

'Keep your voice down,' he hissed.

'Like I said, why don't I come back later, when you can talk?'

'My wife goes to the Cash & Carry at four, come back then.'

Eden looked up at the clock, five to three.

'Fine, I'll have a cappuccino and some of those pancakes while I wait. They look delicious.'

'No, you bloody won't. I'll talk to you because you've forced my hand but I don't have to serve you. Sit in your car; go for a walk; do whatever the hell you solicitors do to kill time, I don't care but I don't want you here. If Jess sees you she'll flip.'

'Fine,' said Eden, genuinely disappointed to be missing a treat. 'Four then.'

She sat in her car reading her text messages. There was one from Agnes and one from Luke neither of which she read in case they interfered with her plans. She deleted both and put the phone back in her bag.

To be certain she didn't run into Jessica Marshall she waited until ten past the hour to go back in. The students enjoying the sun had all moved on now the pavement was in shade. There were no customers inside and Philip Marshall was sorting change from the till into banker's bags.

'Wait there, I'll take you through to the back. Jess won't be long; let's get this over with.'

She wondered if his hostility was fed by frustration that Rowan had told their secret.

He slipped the closed sign across the door before taking her to the back of the cafe through a pokey area subdivided into a store and kitchen. Shelves stacked with cans of olive oil, tinned tomatoes and massive jars of mayonnaise, looked as if they might topple any minute as Eden squeezed past a chest freezer buzzing like a swarm of angry bees. An even tinier area behind the store was set up with a slouchy old sofa and a couple of chairs. Eden guessed it was where the staff took their breaks.

'Have a seat.'

She immediately regretted taking the sofa as she sank back into its under-stuffed seat. She had to hoist herself forward to reach in her bag for her notepad.

'Hang on, I'm not happy about you taking notes,' Marshall objected.

'But you've agreed to talk, that's right, isn't it?' she said perching herself on the very edge of the cushion and crossing her legs to avoid sliding back.

'Yeah, but I'm a witness for the police.'

'There's no property in a witness. I'm allowed to talk to you. Call them and check if you like?'

'I'd prefer if this was off the record.'

She returned the notepad to her bag.

Marshall relaxed a little but still had the look of a man ready for a fight as he sat in the battered leather chair opposite; arms folded defensively.

Eden thought he wasn't bad looking if your taste ran to the brooding swarthy type, though his baggy jeans and faded t-shirt seemed at odds with the coiffured no-sock brigade the cafe seemed to attract.

'Alright, what do you want to know?'

'When did you begin your affair with Rowan?'

'It wasn't an affair; we weren't in a relationship, although it might have become more if she'd wanted to keep the baby.'

'You would have stood by her?'

'Of course. More than that, I would have left Jess for her; for the baby's sake.'

'Why couldn't you stay with your wife and support Rowan and the baby financially, plenty of men would have taken the easy route?'

'I didn't want to be an absent father. I wanted a proper relationship with the baby and that wouldn't have been fair on Jess; to have to watch my child growing up on her doorstep after what she'd been through.'

'You mean the IVF?'

'Yeah. Have you got children?'

'No … no I haven't.'

'Want them?'

She hesitated, not knowing what to say. If she was truthful, she and Andrew had never really talked about having kids, or if they had, only in a hypothetical way; the way they talked about owning a Banksy or visiting Japan to see the cherry blossom. They'd been too busy forging their careers, but now she wondered whether the unspoken decision had been joint or like every other choice made in the marriage, largely down to Andrew? It had certainly made it easier for him to leave.

'Maybe … one day,' she said.

'Well, if you make up your mind to have them, I hope you can. Jess and I didn't see the need to rush. We concentrated on growing the business; on financial stability. Once we were comfortable and could afford for Jess to take some time out, we started trying for a family but as the months passed and nothing happened, we began to realise there was something wrong. We tried for years, spent a fortune on IVF. Nothing worked. It was a big strain on the relationship and our finances. It cost a fortune and by the end, the financial safety net had unravelled too.'

The grim set of his face was mapped with the effort of bracing himself for bad news.

'So, you started a relationship with Rowan as a distraction?'

'I didn't start anything. I didn't make a conscious decision to have an affair. It wasn't some fling to cheer myself up if that's what you think.'

'I'm sorry, I didn't mean to sound trite.'

She could imagine how exhausting, how all-consuming, the treatment must have been for them both.

'After the final lot of IVF failed, we were both gutted. Jess needed a break and went to stay for a couple of months with her sister in Bristol. It happened while she was away.'

'You slept with Rowan?'

'She came in one evening to collect her wages, stayed for a drink and one thing led to another. I'm not proud of what happened, I know it makes me look a complete shit. It was such a relief to talk about something other than babies; to be with someone young, full of fun and willing to listen. I know it's a cliché but she made me feel like a real man, not a failed husband. Ironic, considering she got pregnant in those couple of months.'

'How far gone was she when she told you?'

'About six weeks, as soon as she knew for sure. I'd waited to hear *I'm pregnant* for so long, I was over the moon.'

'But you must have realised it would ruin your marriage?'

'Of course, I'm not a fool and hated myself for how I was behaving but the love I felt for that child, nothing else mattered.'

Eden watched his eyes cloud as he leant forward, lax and exhausted, fingers steepled. elbows resting on his knees. In that second she believed him. He'd never have harmed the baby.

'So, you planned to leave your wife?' she said sympathetically.

'Yes,' he coughed, rearming the defences he'd let slip for a second. 'I told Rowan we'd bring up the baby together. She laughed at me; said she had plans of her own and the last thing she wanted was to be tied to me and my kid. She wanted money for an abortion.'

'What did you say?'

'No, of course. We parted badly but after she'd gone, I got to thinking. She was pregnant and didn't want a baby but Jess and I did. Rowan wanted a new life and I could give it to her. It would mean another loan from the bank, like the one we'd taken for the IVF but it would be worth it. I knew without a baby my marriage was over anyway and the business would have to be sold if Jess and I split up. With all the debt, we'd be bankrupt. This way, by paying for the baby, I could keep it all and make Jess happy so I put the proposition to Rowan and she agreed. Ten thousand for the baby on condition she never told Jess it was mine. As far as everyone else was concerned, she was our surrogate and the money covered her expenses. It seemed the perfect solution.'

'Until everything went wrong?'

'Until that little bitch killed my son.' The anger had resurfaced.

'We don't know she did.'

Marshall pushed his chair away. 'He's dead. Probably the only child I'm ever likely to have is dead; suffocated, buried alive, in a bloody field. Who the hell else do you think did it? She took the money and then thought … I don't know what she thought. Maybe she wanted more; maybe she changed her mind? Maybe like the papers say, she killed the baby in some evil bloody ritual, who knows? But she did it. I know the way my gut twists every time I think of it; she did it.'

He began to pace. Within the confines of the tiny room, he looked like a caged animal. 'Are we finished? Jess will be back any minute and I don't want you here when she arrives.'

'I understand, I'll go. But one more thing.'

He was so tightly wound he could unravel when she asked her final question but she had to finish what she'd started and take her chances.

'Could Jess have found out the baby was yours; could she have discovered the truth about you and Rowan without you knowing?'

The rage she'd watch writhe across his face when he spoke about Rowan seconds before, morphed to open mouthed horror.

'How would Jess have reacted if she'd found out; discovered you were prepared to leave her for Rowan and the baby?' she pressed.

'The baby, not Rowan,' he said, colour leaching from his cheeks.

'With all due respect, she might not be able to see the difference. Why were you so worried about her finding out, what did you think she'd do to you and Rowan or the baby?'

The cafe door rattled; someone was trying to get in.

'You've got to leave, it's Jess. Through there,' he said, pointing to the back door before scrambling through to the cafe to let his wife in.

Eden stayed put, listening behind the storeroom door.

'Why's the dead-lock on. What's going on?'

Jessica Marshall's voice was shrill and accusing, like a woman who didn't trust her husband.

'Trade was slow, so I cashed up early,' he said nervously. 'thought we could have a talk before we open this evening.'

Eden, wishing she could be a fly on that wall, quietly slipped out the back door. Why was Philip Marshall so scared of his wife; was it because he understood what she was capable of?

She'd baited the hook, now she had to wait for Jessica Marshall to bite.

TWENTY-SIX

It was past five by the time Eden drove away from the cafe. She knew the minute she stepped inside the flat her thoughts would turn to the hateful stories in the paper. She still hadn't got any food in and didn't feel like running the gauntlet at the supermarket again. She'd do a shop online later. Tomorrow she'd have to fess up to Luke about Rowan breaching bail. For the moment, she needed space to process the information she'd gleaned from Philip Marshall and what it meant for her client when she finally turned up.

She headed out of Truro on the coastal road towards Perranporth.

The evenings were drawing in. The seafront gift shops were closing their shutters; weary eyelids rolling down; preparing for hibernation. The tourists had all but disappeared and the languid decline that always arrived at the end of the summer season lay ahead. She parked in the beach carpark and watched the last of the surfers leave the water whilst dictating the details of her interview with Marshall. She needed to get it down while it was still fresh in her mind. By the time she finished, it was nearly dark and she was starving. Shoving the machine in her bag, she walked through the carpark to the main street.

The neon lights of the fish and chip shop *Cornish Sole* called like a siren. The smell of battered fish and the steamy warmth of the fryers peaking her appetite. Two youths jostled in the queue in front of her. One grabbed a sachet of ketchup, flicking it against his mate's ear.

'Fuck off you moron.'

They looked edgy; bristling with nervous energy, Eden could tell they were on something.

'How long is it gonna be; we've been ere fifteen fucking minutes?'

'It'll be as long as it takes. I told you when you came in, I'd only then turned the fryers on. If you want soggy batter go somewhere else.'

'Yeah right, just get a fucking move on.'

The elderly man ignored the youth; looking past him to Eden.

'Want to put your order in, love? Like I told these boys, it'll be five minutes.'

'Cod and chips please.'

One of the boys looked around at the sound of her voice. Piggy eyes beneath a Peaky Blinder haircut giving her the once over before nudging his lippy friend who turned sharply, cracking a snide grin from a pot-marked face the colour of corned beef. Huge pupils stared from pale watery eyes; beads of sweat crawling along his forehead. Eden guessed amphetamines.

'There you go battered sausage and chips twice.'

The boy, turning his attention away from Eden, slammed a fiver down on the counter.

'He's got the rest,' he slurred, pointing at his mate who trawled a fistful of shrapnel from his pocket, holding out his palm for the man behind the counter to take what he wanted before returning the rest.

Eden rifled through the database of clients in her head to see if she recognised either of them as they lurched away.

'Scratters,' murmured the man. 'Sorry about that; barely seven o'clock and they're already off their bloody heads. How old were they do you think; twenty; twenty-two? Bloody idiots. Kids in men's boots. National service that's what they need, that would sort the buggers out. Cod and chips coming up.'

Her stomach rumbled as she watched the double-handed shake of salt and vinegar splatter the chips.

'Thanks,' she smiled, holding the warm bundle close as she walked from the shop across to a bench by the harbour wall to sit and eat her food. She wondered if the evening before, the cod she was munching had been swimming about oblivious to his fate. She should feel bad but the sacrifice was much appreciated. She ate the rest with greedy reverence.

Licking the salt from her fingers, she walked across to the nearest bin. Once the wrapping would have been newspaper, perhaps one of the rags she'd been reading this morning; *her* face coming out of court, soaked in grease. Today's news, tomorrow's chip paper, she thought.

'Oi?' The shout came from behind.

A little way back across the street; the two louts from the chippy.

'My mate says you're the one in the news; the lawyer trying to get that bitch who killed the baby off?'

Eden said nothing. She wasn't far from her car, she just had to walk slowly and calmly away from them. She heard footsteps crossing the street; catching up. She reached in her bag for her keys; quickening her step.

'Oi, I'm talking to you?'

Not far; keep walking, don't let them see you're scared.

She looked around for someone; anyone who might help her but the street was deserted, the approach to the carpark dark. Why hadn't she walked back to the chip shop when she clocked them?

They'd caught up and were right behind her. She could practically feel the spotty little shits' breaths on her neck. She tightened her grip on her bag. Her phone was in it and her notes on the case. She couldn't let them grab it; not without a fight anyway.

She could see her car now. Why hadn't she parked closer?

One of the youths overtook her, blocking her way so she had to walk around him.

'Like a bit of my sausage with your chips would you darling?' he leered, clutching his groin suggestively through his skinny jeans; thrusting himself towards her. 'Papers say you're a feminist; are you one of them lesbos. I can set you straight if you like?'

'Get out of my way.'

'Or what?' he snarled. 'You gonna cast a fucking spell on me?' He wiggled his fingers in her face. 'Has the witch been giving you lessons?'

'I'll call the police.'

'Good luck with that; by the time they get here we'll be long gone.'

He was right, the nearest station was a good fifteen minutes away.

'What do you want?'

'Well, if you're not gonna be friendly, your purse will do for starters.'

'Yeah hand it over, bitch,' the younger one chipped in.

Eden reached into her bag; fingers shaking, as she handed it to him. She knew it was the sensible option. She only had a few pounds in it but it held her credit cards, her court ID, her driving licence with her home address, her entire life.

He rifled through it pulling out the cash. Unzipping the purse compartment, he emptied the coins into his hand; passing them back to his friend.

'Arcade,' he said gleefully and Eden remembered the man in the chip shop; grown men acting like kids.

He threw the purse to the pavement. She left it where it was, knowing if she reached down for it, he'd kick it away and probably show her the toe of his boot too.

He leant in close and she could smell his breath.

'You'd better watch your step. See, I got a kiddie myself; two-year-old; lives with my ex. We don't like kiddie killers down 'ere or them that's their friends. We don't need your kind here.'

He shoved her hard against the rough pebble-dashed wall of the public toilets, before running off with his sidekick, back the way they'd come.

Eden's heart was hammering; blood rushing to her head as she bent to pick up her purse. She took a moment to steady herself before walking on shaky legs back to her car.

Safely inside she gripped the steering wheel, wringing it with trembling fingers, angry tears stinging her cheeks. It was a good five minutes before she felt safe to drive.

'Bastards; ignorant bastards,' she screamed at the windscreen. Who the hell did they think they were; telling her where she did or didn't belong?

She thought of her dad's advice; 'you're a survivor'.

She wasn't so sure.

TWENTY-SEVEN

Eden woke the next morning feeling bruised and violated. The press reports were bad enough but now they seemed trivial. It was one thing to read hateful things about yourself; it was quite another to witness its gut-wrenching ugliness up close. As she strained to look over her shoulder in the mirror at her aching back the difference showed in technicolour. She was black and blue.

She swallowed a couple of paracetamols and rang Carmen.

'Hi, Carmen it's Eden. I'm sorry I didn't ring last night, I …'

'Is she there with you?' the woman interrupted. She sounded desperate.

'No, I'm afraid not.'

Eden heard her deflate on the other end of the phone.

'I thought because you rang, you'd found her. What do we do now?'

'If she's not here by eleven she'll have broken her bail conditions and I'll have to tell the police.'

'To be honest, I don't care. At least then, they'll be looking for her. It's been nearly twenty-four hours and I'm worried sick. There are so many people out there who, if you believe what you read, hate her; wish her harm. Matthew told me about some of the stuff being said on the internet and it scares me to death.'

'Lots of people say things on the internet, it doesn't mean they follow through. Don't be too concerned unless there's anything you consider a threat or feel is inciting violence against Rowan or your family. If there is, you must let me know and the police can deal with it. No one has the right to terrify you and remain anonymous.'

Eden thought of her experience with the two louts the evening before and felt a hypocrite. She hadn't reported it to the police.

'It's so vile; so, outside my comfort zone. I know I shouldn't take any notice and Matthew only told me about it because Rowan's missing and we can't afford to ignore anything that might help us find her.'

'It's understandable you're worried and you're right. The most important thing is to find Rowan. As soon as eleven arrives, I'll call the police, I promise.'

With that reassurance, she ended the call.

The doorbell rang and she let the courier delivering her groceries in. At least she could have a decent breakfast before she had to report Rowan missing.

The smell of freshly brewed coffee made her feel better. As she tucked into a second croissant, she rehearsed what she'd say to Luke about Rowan and her interview with Philip Marshall.

She could see from her mobile he'd tried to ring her several times and had left an answerphone message on her home phone saying he had been round to her parents and Flora was settling in fine but had still not been able to contact Thea.

She hadn't rung him back.

When eleven o'clock came she forced herself to pick up the phone, call the station and ask for him.

'Eden, I've been trying to ring you.'

'Have you?' she replied nonchalantly.

'Thanks for the other night; for helping me out.'

'What else could I do. Flora's my niece.'

'And your parents have been brilliant.'

'Good … that's good.'

'Are you alright, you sound a bit … down?'

'Luke I wasn't ringing about Flora. It's Rowan, she's missing.'

'You mean she's skipped bail?'

'To be honest I just don't know. The trial is likely to be months away and if you're going to make a run for it you don't do it amid all this publicity. I'm worried. I haven't let on to her family but I'm scared someone else might be involved.'

'Stay put, I'm coming over.'

TWENTY-EIGHT

'When was the last time anyone saw her?' Luke asked when he arrived half an hour later.

'The night she was released on bail at about nine-thirty according to her mother.'

'Why didn't you let me know sooner?'

'I couldn't, I didn't know she'd gone. I thought she needed to catch up with her mates or something. She's a teenager and at that age friends are everything; you confide in them rather than your parents.'

'You thought a third party might talk some sense into her?'

'Possibly.'

'Well let's hope you're right and she's not done a runner. The media will be baying for blood.'

'I know, and there's something else.'

'Go on then, let's get it all out in the open.'

'Rowan and Philip Marshall had an affair. The baby was his; conceived the old-fashioned way.'

'You're joking?'

'No, I'm not. He admitted it to me.'

'When?'

'Yesterday. I went to see him and he admitted it.'

'What the hell were you thinking going to see him, how did you know he wouldn't react badly?'

'He's a bistro owner, not a serial killer. What was he going to do to me, spike my tagliatelle?' She didn't let on how angry Marshall had been.

'Did his wife know?'

'No, she didn't; well at least he doesn't think she did.'

'But if she did know?'

Eden was pleased they were thinking the same way. If it was Luke's first thought, it felt more and more likely a jury would latch onto the possibility; see room for doubt when weighing Rowan's guilt.

'She might have decided to punish them both?'

'But come on; after going through all those rounds of IVF she was hardly going to hurt a baby, especially one she expected to keep.'

'Think of the WPC in your team; the one with the attitude who had so much to say about Rowan. If she found out her husband had got another woman pregnant and paid her to keep quiet about it how would she react?'

'I get your point.'

'What if Jess Marshall found out and went around to the flat and confronted Rowan and she went into labour? What if she took the baby with good intentions but something went wrong? I don't know but it's possible.'

'There's a lot of *what ifs* in there, Eden. Why wouldn't she just take the baby to the hospital? I can understand her abandoning Rowan, letting her deal with her own mess, but the baby, surely she'd help the baby?'

'Perhaps Rowan wanted more money or told her Philip was going to leave her if she didn't get more? We only have Jess's word she arrived after the event. Perhaps she arrived before Rowan went into labour or during it? Rowan doesn't remember.'

'There's the problem, Rowan doesn't remember. It always comes back to that. Why not; if she's not hiding something why the hell can't she remember?'

'I don't know. Maybe she *is* hiding something. Maybe she's protecting Jess; agreeing to keep quiet about what really happened so long as Jess forks out more cash? I don't know and to be honest it won't be my problem. Reasonable doubt is all I need but from your point of view surely it's worth interviewing Jess?'

'Yes of course it is, but don't get your hopes up. It might be enough to cast doubt on Rowan's guilt but unless when confronted with the facts Rowan is willing to 'remember' and corroborates what happened, your girl is still in the frame as far as we're concerned. I'm going back to the station to circulate she's missing to uniform; giving them strict instructions not to alert the press. We don't need a bloody riot on our hands. Later, I'm going to pick up Jessica Marshall and try and get to the bottom of all this. I'll let you know how I get on. Where will you be?'

'I'll be at the site. I need to speak to Elspeth Fuller about something.'

'Okay, but Eden, do me and yourself a favour, in the future leave the detecting to us.'

TWENTY-NINE

Eden wasn't sure whether Elspeth was back from France but decided to try her luck at the site. There was another reason for going.

She wanted to see where Mary Bluet's baby was buried; the baby who, if he had lived, would have brought shame to his mother. She needed to gauge for herself the risk of him being discovered.

On arrival at the site, she was struck by the absence of flapping yellow police tape and the lack of reporters but guessed they'd bled the place dry for the time being. They were after a different quarry now. They were probably still blockading her office.

A heavy base beat echoed from the far end of the field where a group of students were working. They didn't hear her arrive.

The last time she'd been there the door of the prefab had been open; this time it was shut. She tried the handle – locked. Then banged on the door – no answer. She peered through the window. The place had a mothballed look about it. She walked back down the steps to the caravan - locked too.

Clearly, Elspeth was still away and there was no sign of James either. She wondered whether he was at the museum or busy building his media profile in some chat room somewhere.

The place was still a quagmire. She remembered what Elspeth had said about the natural springs criss-crossing the site. Her wellies had seen more outings in the last few weeks than they usually saw in a year. Pulling up the zip of her jacket, she slowly nudged her way along the planking towards the students.

'Hello?' she yelled above the thud of music blasting from the radio.

'Oh, hi,' returned a pretty blonde, looking like she'd stepped out of a promotional video for the Sunshine State; all wholesome

American tan and smile so dazzling it was enough to make any orthodontist pee his pants with pride.

The others were a motley crew in comparison; pasty-faced and geeky, in their waterproofs and woolly hats. Eden guessed, unlike Miss California, they were homegrown.

'Can I help you?' asked an earnest-looking beanpole, pulling himself up out of the trench onto a precariously balanced aluminium plank. 'I'm Sam.'

'I'm looking for Professor Fuller?'

'Are you a journalist?' asked the American girl quite unashamedly adjusting her neckline and holding out her hand. 'I'm Carrie.'

'No, I'm not a journalist.'

'She's Rowan Lutey's solicitor,' said Sam. 'That's right, isn't it? Eden Gray?'

'Yes, that's right.'

The girl looked disappointed and turned her back on them, returning her attention to an infinitely more interesting patch of dirt.

Sam, she guessed, was in his mid-twenties with a gangly awkwardness of someone younger. His large hands and feet looked too big for his body as if the rest of him needed a chance to catch up.

'Elspeth isn't here.'

'That's a shame I was hoping she might be back.'

'James is in charge while she's away, but he's not here either right now.'

'Oh well, that'll teach me not to ring before turning up. Would it be okay if I take a look at the pit where the baby was found, I noticed the police tape has been taken down?'

'Sure, I'll take you then, walk you back to your car if you like?'

'Thanks.'

The Rowan tree stood alone in the far left-hand corner of the field; a verdant patch of grass around its base. Clusters of brilliant berries like rubies glowed in the milky autumn sun; paradise amidst a muddy monochrome wasteland.

'What a beautiful tree.'

'Yes, the Rowan. Your client's namesake. The Celts planted them to ward off dark magic and evil spirits, although of course, that one's not very old, less than a hundred years.'

Eden knew exactly how old it was. 'The berries are quite striking,' she said.

He paused as they walked to stare off at the tree, almost as if seeing it for the first time. 'I suppose they are. The Druids used to dye their vestments with them and you can brew them into a pretty potent spirit if you've got enough of them, so I'm told.'

'I'm surprised it's not been damaged with all that's been going on.'

'There's nothing much at that end of the field and Elspeth's keen to show the site respect. It's bad luck to cut down a Rowan. She's very strict about things like that even though it's not subject to a tree preservation order or anything.'

Eden was relieved. 'It's quiet; no press?'

'Not for a couple of days now. I suppose James isn't here and it's him they usually talk to. The rest of us are under strict instructions not to give interviews.'

'From whom, the police?'

'Elspeth; she hates the idea of them crawling all over the site. What we've found here is unique. It could provide years of academic research in many specialist fields. It's a part of our social history. It could be one of the most important finds in Western Europe.'

There it was again that enviable passion for the job.

'So, Elspeth's not keen on press involvement; she doesn't think the publicity will help finance the dig or bring it to the attention of a wider public?'

'God no, she's very old school; believes in sound research. She's not interested in playing to the crowd. The danger with a site like this is everyone gets distracted by the witchcraft thing and then the serious academics lose interest. It's always happened with important finds; think of Tutankhamun. Everybody knows about Howard Carter's discovery; about the curse written on a cartouche in the tomb. The thing is it didn't exist, no curse was found. No one really knows how much sound archaeological research was lost because the press got hold of the bogus story and the whole world descended on the Valley of the Kings. The place has been a car wreck ever since.'

Eden didn't think it was the time and place to tell Sam about rubbing Iset Tayef Nakh's forehead for luck.

'And that was before social media,' the boy continued, 'today one person could tweet about this place and it could go viral; work would have to stop.'

'But James Ferris told me Elspeth was on board with all the publicity; that she'd had a change of heart?'

'Well, if that's right, it's a massive turnaround. She was furious when I found the baby. She knew it would mean the police and unwanted press interest.'

Eden's ears pricked up. 'I'm sorry, *you* found the baby?'

'Yes.'

'So, you're the one who nipped off for a cigarette and spotted the witch pit had been disturbed.'

'Not quite; I don't smoke for one thing. I was digging in trench number three over there and James came across and asked me to go and look at a pit where the marker was down and the ground looked disturbed. I did as he asked and that's when I found the baby about fifteen metres ahead of us. Pit Ten.

As they approached the baby boy's last resting place, Eden wondered why James' version was different. Maybe in the mayhem that came after, the chronology got muddled? It wasn't surprising. Nevertheless, something about it made her uneasy. Then there was Elspeth. Sam seemed convinced she still wasn't happy about the publicity and that accorded with her conversations with her but James was adamant she'd changed her mind. She needed to talk to her in person to find out who was telling the truth but she was proving elusive.

She took out her phone to take a photograph of the pit now covered once again, the earth slightly darker already turning to mud.

'There was nothing in this pit when you first excavated it?' she asked.

'No, not all of them contained offerings. Some were empty. We don't know why.'

Eden did. She remembered her conversation with Carmen on the night of the fire. The woman who commissioned the Lutey family to dig the pit must have conceived. It had been blessed until the baby had been buried there. How easily a place could be corrupted. Pit Ten would be forever remembered as a place of horror rather than joy. She turned to Sam.

'I don't suppose you know when Elspeth is back from Brittany?'

'Brittany?'

'I understand she's been at a conference in Brittany about Celtic rituals.'

'Really, that's the first I've heard of it? She usually gets me to help with the presentation if she's lecturing. She's not great at PowerPoint.' He looked puzzled.

'Sam is something wrong?'

'No, I'm surprised that's all. I thought she'd gone to visit her family in Ireland; some crisis or other. I wonder why she didn't let on about the conference?'

Eden didn't know what to think or say. What on earth was Elspeth playing at?

'I probably got the wrong end of the stick. I've got so much going on, my mind's like a sieve at the moment. I may well have.'

He didn't look convinced.

'Sam, when are you expecting her back?'

'This weekend. We begin excavations on the Crystal Well at the weekend. She wouldn't miss that.'

'Carmen Lutey mentioned she'd heard you'd finished with the witch pits and were moving on to a well.'

'Yeah, it's really exciting. We're pretty sure it will contain all sorts of talisman and votive offerings; pottery, personal items; scraps of cloth with messages written on them if we're lucky. The peat has preserved everything in the pits to such a fantastic degree, we hope it's done the same for the stuff in the well and you never know we might find something really valuable. In the past, gold coins and intricate stone replicas of human heads have been found down wells like this.'

'It was used in rituals; like the pits?'

'We think so, especially at the time of the Spring Equinox when the moon seems low enough to touch it. It would have looked amazing back then in the firelight; the moon reflecting off the crystals in the granite; magical.'

'Well good luck with it, and should Elspeth make contact before the weekend can you tell her to call me?'

'Of course, but it's more likely to be James she speaks to. He talks to her every day but I'll be sure to tell her when I see her.'

Her mobile rang. It was Luke.

'I'm sorry Sam, I've got to take this.'

'No worries,' the boy smiled, lifting his hand before returning to the others.

'We've got a problem,' said Luke.

Eden's heart sank.

'What now?'

'I was seen.'

'What do you mean, *seen*?'

'By the press, coming out of your place in the early hours of the morning.'

'And?'

'This is so embarrassing; they've got completely the wrong idea; I've seen the photograph and I look like … like I've spent the night with you. They phoned the superintendent's office for a comment.'

Eden felt her cheeks redden at the thought of her and Luke together in that way.

'So, you're in trouble?' she coughed.

'You could say that. I've been suspended … and Eden they told me we could expect something in the papers tomorrow.'

'What?'

'And…'

'Go on then, it can't get any worse.'

'It can,' he sighed, 'the press know Rowan's missing.'

Embarrassment gave way to dismay.

'This is a bloody nightmare.'

'One we're not going to wake up from any time soon that's for certain. I've told my superiors the reason I was there but they still aren't happy I didn't tell them about the family connection before. I suppose I assumed everyone already knew. It's not like I've ever tried to hide the fact you're Thea's sister, but there it is. I think we should keep a low profile for a couple of days until things have a chance to blow over and we've found Rowan. I'll text you when I think it's safe.'

'Luke, I'm so sorry.'

'It's hardly your fault but it does mean I'll have to tell my superiors about Flora; all the private stuff about Thea I didn't want them knowing. Even so, I think it'll be too late to stop what's gone to print already. I just hope Thea doesn't get wind of it.'

Eden could imagine her sister's reaction; the accusations and threats. She would love the drama; anything that placed her centre stage.

THIRTY

Luke adjusted his tie in the bathroom mirror.

He'd managed to secure a reprieve; one last attempt to put things right before his disciplinary on Monday morning. He was about to interview Jessica Marshall.

It was still his case and even though they didn't like it, the powers that be had to admit he was the best one to do it. She'd come in voluntarily after he'd called her. He'd asked for her to be taken to interview room three because it had a two-way mirror. He knew his bosses would want to keep an eye on him. They'd want to jump in if they thought he was compromising the case. Entering the room, he glanced directly at them, raising a disdainful eyebrow for the benefit of his live audience.

'Good afternoon, Jess. Thanks for coming in. I called you in to ask you a few questions about your statement if that's okay with you?'

'Yes.'

'You understand you are here voluntarily; that means you can leave at any time.'

'Yes, I know, like before.'

'Yes, like before.'

'There are some elements of your statement that need clarification in the light of what has unfolded since. In particular the discovery of the baby.'

The woman sighed heavily. 'I understand.'

'I'm going to hand you a copy of your statement so we can go through it together.'

'Okay.'

'Now, before we start could you read it through to check there is nothing you have omitted; nothing you feel you forgot at the time and ought to rectify now.'

'I'm not sure what you mean?'

'Well, when you gave your original statement you had no idea that there was a possibility Rowan had killed her baby. With the benefit of that knowledge there may be something she said or did, you didn't notice at the time but which in the circumstances might now come to mind.'

Jessica read through her statement slowly, studying every word, while Luke waited patiently for her to finish.

'No, I think it's all there.'

'You're sure there's nothing else?'

'What are you getting at?'

'Jessica, I'm going to tell you something I get absolutely no pleasure in telling you.'

Luke braced himself as the woman's eyes pooled with tears.

'Is it something about the baby, I don't want to know the details … I don't think I could stand to hear about how he died?'

'It is about the baby but not about his death.'

Luke watched her shoulders relax a little.

'Jessica did you know your husband was the biological father of Rowan's baby?'

No answer.

'Jessica?'

'I don't want to talk about this.'

'I'm afraid I'm going to have to press you. If you have concerns, we can stop the interview at any time, or if you like you can have someone else present.'

'Do you mean a solicitor? Is that what you mean when you say I can have someone else present? Are you accusing me of something?'

'No, I'm not accusing you of anything but you should understand, should something arise that does implicate you in any way, it's important you appreciate your rights. If that occurs for whatever reason, I will stop the interview and formally caution you.'

'Me, how can I be implicated? I'm the victim here; me and the baby.'

She was agitated but still hadn't challenged the allegation concerning the child's parentage. Luke sensed something odd here, maybe she was in denial?

'I'm also going to bring in a female police officer if that's okay and I think it best if we record this interview so we don't misinterpret anything.'

Luke looked up at the two-way mirror and nodded. Denise Charlton came into the room and pressed the button on the tape recorder.

'Present DI Luke Parish and DS Denise Charlton. Interviewing Jessica Marshall. 20th of September 2019, time fifteen-thirty.'

Caution dealt with, he continued.

'Now Jessica a short time ago I told you that your husband Philip Marshall was the biological father of Rowan Lutey's baby. The question is, did you know?'

Jessica said nothing; her eyes glued to her statement.

'Jessica are you alright to continue?' said Denise Charlton gently.

'You said I didn't have to say anything.'

'That's your prerogative of course but I'm rather surprised at your reaction. I just told you your husband had an affair with Rowan Lutey and you don't even seem upset.'

'How do you know how I feel?' she mumbled.

'I don't but I'd imagine hearing about your husband's infidelity and the deceit that followed would make you angry?'

'I don't think she ever intended to hand the baby over to me.'

'Why do you say that?'

Jessica bit her lip. She'd been folding and unfolding her statement and it was now dog-eared and creased, 'because Rowan likes being in control.'

'Control?'

'She doesn't play by the rules.'

'What rules, Jessica? Do you mean the money; the fact she chose to change her mind. Did that make you angry?'

'Of course it made me angry. By then it felt like my baby. She didn't want it. She encouraged me to think of it as mine; that's what we agreed.'

'But it wasn't your baby was it, Jess? You were not its biological mother even if Philip was the father. Rowan was free to change her mind; the law allows her to. You must have thought of that possibility; it's common in surrogacy and adoption cases so I'm told and you got your money back.'

Luke knew he was being callous and insensitive but he wasn't a social worker, He was here to wheedle out the truth.

'She broke her word. She promised me. She broke the rules from the very beginning.'

'Are you saying she broke the rules by having an affair with Philip; is that it, Jess, is that what made you angry?'

'I'll tell you what made me angry. Her telling me the baby was gone and giving me back the money as if that was all this was about; after everything we'd gone through and all the sacrifices I'd made.'

'What sacrifices, Jess? I understand you were upset and disappointed. I can appreciate you'd want to know where the baby was, but if you didn't know about Philip's affair, I can't see why you felt so entitled. So entitled and outraged you reported it to us here at the station.'

'I was worried about the baby. Rowan wasn't making any sense. She wouldn't tell me what had happened or where it was. It was about more than the money. She destroyed my life.'

'And your marriage Jess; and your marriage?'

Her statement was now in tatters. She'd shredded it as she talked reducing it to confetti. There were tears in her eyes as her face twisted with emotion.

'Yes, and my marriage.'

'So you did know. You found out and wanted to punish them by taking the baby?'

Her body stiffened as she looked up; her voice, shaky and disbelieving.

'What?'

'Were you angry enough to take the baby, Jess, to punish Philip and Rowan? It's natural enough; it must have been awful for you?'

'No … no, you've got it all wrong.'

'Did Phil say he was going to leave you for Rowan and take the baby with them? Is that why you went to the flat, Jess?'

'I didn't … I didn't take the baby. The baby was gone when I got there. I told you.'

'You've said, but you can see why people might think you had a motive; to take the baby before they took it from you.'

'No, I didn't. She'd already got rid of him. That bitch had already killed my son. You may think you know her but you don't. I thought I did too but she's a liar and just like she played me she's playing you lot too.'

Denise was glaring at him as if to say; *what the hell are you doing?*

'Jess would you like us to stop the interview so that you can call a solicitor?' she said when her silent warning failed to raise a response. Luke took Jessica's silence as his cue to carry on.

'The problem is Rowan had no motive to kill the baby. It was her ticket to a better life. She didn't have to keep it. She was free to take the money and leave.'

'But I wouldn't kill him. I loved him.'

'I'm sure you did, but that would make the loss worse once you learnt your husband would rather be with the mother of his child than you. Was it then you decided to take the child you'd paid for; the product of an affair he'd had while you were recovering from IVF?'

Luke knew he almost had her. He could see the words spinning in her mind.

'NO … NO … NO. I knew; so there. Now you know; I knew all along. Why would I be jealous when I'm the one who asked Rowan to sleep with Phil? It was my idea in the first place.'

THIRTY-ONE

Eden settled in her car. Once the news broke Rowan was missing, the shit would hit the fan. She couldn't stay at the flat. If the story the paper intended to print gave any hint of the location, she could expect protesters and more reporters to set up camp there.

She rang Agnes. 'Hi it's me could you do me a favour?'

'I'm here to serve.'

'Agnes, Rowan is missing. The police know and soon, so will everyone else. I thought she'd come home but she hasn't and everyone will assume she's on the run and if she's done a runner, she must be guilty.'

'Well, you know my views on that girl.'

'Yes, I do Agnes but there's something else,' she took a deep breath, 'tomorrow the papers are running a story about me and DI Parish.'

'What sort of story; about the case?'

'Not exactly.'

How was she going to put this without Agnes losing focus?

'It's about our relationship. He was seen coming out of my flat in the early hours and they think we spent the night together.'

'DI Parish, but he's your brother-in-law or would be if he and your sister had ever bothered to get married. He's a catch mind, I'll say that for him. He's tall. Mother always said it was nice to have height in a man or at least someone taller than you and that's quite difficult for you, and he's always been friendly to me when he's called about a case. You could do a lot worse … compared to that husband of yours, Luke Parish is a prince.'

'Agnes, listen. There is nothing and I mean absolutely nothing going on between me and DI Parish. He was dropping Flora off, that's all.'

Her tone was firm and the woman quit jabbering.

'The press will spin this so it looks as if the case has been compromised by our relationship. They could even say Rowan has been able to escape justice because of it. It's rubbish of course, but that won't make any difference to them. As far as they're concerned a baby killer is on the loose because we were too busy having sex to do our jobs properly.'

'You can see their point mind when you put it like that. It does look a bit iffy.'

Eden let that one go.

'Listen, I need your help. There's an extra key to my flat in my desk drawer at the office. My place is going to be crawling with reporters by tomorrow. I need you to go there and throw some clothes and toiletries into a bag and meet me.'

'Where?'

'The multi-storey in town. I'll be on the top level, so we won't miss each other. You can do that for me, can't you?'

'It's all very cloak and dagger.'

'I know it sounds that way but it's so I can carry on trying to find Rowan without all this crap getting in the way.'

'Where will you go?'

'To my parents, but please, don't tell anyone else and make sure no one follows you.'

'I'll be careful, it's quite exciting really; like something out of James Bond.'

THIRTY-TWO

Carmen hadn't slept despite brewing Valerian root tea the evening before. She was dozing in the chair when Denise Charlton turned up to tell her the authorities were aware Rowan had skipped bail.

'Mrs Lutey, have you any idea where Rowan might be?'

'No, of course not; if I did, do you think I'd be in this state? I'm worried sick.'

'It's a shame you didn't let us know earlier she was missing.'

'I thought she'd be back; that she needed some space. I'm so worried something's happened to her. I've tried all her friends and no one's seen her.'

'Well, we're on the case now. I'm sure we'll find her soon but if there's anything you think of that might help, here's my card; give me a ring.'

'What about DI Parish; he was with you before?'

'He's no longer on the case. Call me if you think of anything.'

Once she'd gone, Carmen phoned Morvah.

'Can you come over? I'm at my wit's end. I can't talk to Matthew; his girlfriend has told him to keep out of it and I can't say I blame her.'

To Carmen's relief, Morvah replied without hesitation.

'I'll be over after my shift. I finish at five.'

'Come for your tea then.'

'Alright, it'll be nice to have someone cook for me for a change.'

'You looked thin when I saw you … good thin though; not *bad* thin.'

She didn't want to say the wrong thing now everything was back on track with her sister.

'Make sure you do plenty of spuds, then.' Morvah joked.

'I will. Roasties!' Carmen laughed, her mood lifting at the prospect of her sister's company.

She busied herself preparing dinner the rest of the afternoon; glad of the distraction. She roasted a chicken and retrieved some of the blackberries she'd picked from the freezer to make a blackberry and apple pie for after. By the time the kids arrived back from school the kitchen was full of the smells of home cooking and for a moment she was able to fool herself everything was normal.

'Something smells good,' shouted Matthew over the thunderous *thump, thump* of Maisy and Jago running upstairs to ditch their school bags.

'Morvah's coming over for tea.'

'Morvah?' He looked surprised.

'Yes, we've had a talk and decided life's too short for fighting; family needs to stick together at times like this.'

She hadn't told Matthew about Morvah's involvement with Rowan during her pregnancy; not sure how he'd react.

'Suppose so,' he said, pinching a biscuit from the barrel. 'Is there any news? It's been on the radio Rowan's missing. They're talking like she's done a runner.'

'The police have been around; a young woman officer, Denise something … who came here before, told me DI Parish is off the case.'

'Did she say why?'

'No but I suppose now they've charged Rowan; he's moved on to something else. She seemed certain they'd find her. I'm just glad they're looking.'

'It'll be alright, Mum.'

He moved across the room to where she stood peeling potatoes and put his arm around her. 'You know what our Rowan's like; she does stuff like this. She's probably just had enough and bolted. Remember how when things went wrong at school or she got in trouble over something or other, she'd run off and we'd all worry where she was? She'd be hiding in one of the barns or up the top field with the horses, cooling off. She always came back in the end.'

'I know Matthew but it's those people out there, the ones with the placards. They hate her and they hate us too. It's this witch stuff and all the nastiness on the internet; that's what frightens me. It's escalating and I'm worried for your sister's safety.' Carmen's voice quivered, her hand was shaking and she dropped the potato peeler into the muddy water. 'Damn it.'

'Come 'ere,' comforted Matthew hugging her close. 'It'll be alright.'

She buried her head in her son's shoulder; happy to stay there for a while until making a conscious effort to pull herself together, she drew away. She rubbed her eyes with the heels of her hands and looking up at him tried a smile.

'Are you staying for your tea?'

'No, I don't think so Ma. I told Laura I'd go around hers tonight and you've got Morvah. It's better if I'm not here; you can have a proper talk then.'

'Whatever you think best. Thanks for picking up the kids again.'

'That's alright; only I'm not sure I can do it for much longer. The boss is getting a bit funny about it … about me taking the time off. I work my lunch hour but it doesn't seem to make any difference.'

'It's alright, I understand.'

She didn't want the children taking the school bus; not with everything that was going on. Another thing to worry about, she thought, as she watched her son drive away. At least she had the weekend to sort it.

***

Morvah arrived still in her uniform.

'I couldn't be bothered to go home and change. I came straight from work.'

'Who are you then?' asked Maisy.

'That's Auntie Morvah,' Jago said, pleased to know something his sister didn't.

'What, like Auntie Madge down the shop in the village?'

'No, you numpty *she's* not our real auntie. Everyone calls her Auntie Madge. Morvah's our real auntie; she's Mum's sister.'

'Like Rowan and me?'

'Yes like Rowan and you.'

Morvah traipsed upstairs to change, returning in jeans and a sweater.

'I'll just pop these back in the car.'

' Okay, I'll start serving up.'

Carmen had felt strangely nervous preparing the food as if she were cooking for visitors rather than her sister but as Morvah took her seat between the two children she relaxed and couldn't help regret all the family time they'd wasted over nothing.

'Where 'ave you been before then?'

'Maisy stop asking questions; let Morvah sit down,' scolded Carmen.

'It's fine,' said Morvah, turning to face the little girl.

'Me and your Mum had a bit of a falling out but we've made friends now, so I hope to be seeing a lot more of you and Jago.'

'And Rowan and Matthew,' insisted Maisy.

Morvah looked up at Carmen, 'and Rowan and Matthew.'

'You're a nurse. I saw your uniform.'

'Yes, I am.'

'Do you live in the hospital then, is that why we ain't seen you?'

'No, I don't live there, although it feels a bit like that sometimes,' Morvah smiled. 'I work there.'

'Stupid!' teased Jago. 'Nurses don't *live* in hospitals.'

Maisy paused to poke out her tongue, before returning to her interrogation. 'What kind of nurse are you; are you a bad leg nurse or a bad head nurse? Matthew, come off his motorbike once and broke his leg didn't he, Mum? He had to see a bad leg nurse.'

'Yes, he did,' said Carmen.

'I look after ladies who are having babies; then I help the babies when they're ready to come out of their mummy's tummy.'

'Our Rowan killed *her* baby.'

There was a loud clatter as Carmen dropped a saucepan sending carrots, scattering across the quarry tiles. 'What did you say?'

The little girl looked up at her mother; 'Our Rowan killed her baby; that's what the boys are saying at school.'

'Who said that?' Carmen banged the kitchen table so hard, the knives and forks jumped and clattered.

Maisy stared at her wide-eyed. 'Michael Edyvean.'

Carmen struggled to hold it together. 'Well ... I'll be having a word with your teacher about him on Monday morning.' She was furious but didn't want to frighten her daughter, whose bottom lip was beginning to tremble.

Morvah jumped up to help recapture the escaped veg and finish putting the rest of the dinner on the plates so they could sit down to eat while it was still hot.

Jago and Maisy moved on to new conversations; tucking into their food, squabbling occasionally, while Carmen did battle with a growing lump in her throat, she knew would prevent her swallowing a single mouthful. She held her knife and fork in her fists like weapons, rolling them from side to side not knowing what to do with them.

Morvah reached across and touched her hand. 'It's alright to be upset. You're entitled to get angry,' she soothed.

The touch opened up a flood of emotions Carmen had been holding back with sheer willpower. Now the gates were breached she couldn't stop the deluge.

'What's the matter with Mum?' asked Maisy through a mouthful of roast potato.

'Nothing,' Morvah said, 'Mummy is a bit upset about the carrots.'

'I don't like carrots anyway, Mum. I like peas better and we got lots of peas ... look!' she said, flicking one at Jago.

'Hey!'

Carmen looked at her daughter's grinning face and despite everything; began to laugh. 'Oh, Maisy ...'

They all laughed; loud childish guffaws that made them snort. All the time Morvah held Carmen's hand, steadying her like the master of the ship through the tidal wave of feelings spilling across the kitchen table.

***

Once the children were in bed, the two women moved into the sitting room where Carmen lit a fire. Curled up on the sofa, they sipped whiskey in silence watching the logs crackle and spit. After several minutes Carmen spoke.

'Thank you.'

'For what?'

'For being here this evening; for bringing some peace back to this house.'

'I'm not going anywhere till we find Rowan ... until this nonsense is over with.'

'Thank you.'

'Stop saying *thank you*, that's my only condition.'

'Alright.'

They listened to the children jumping around upstairs, not quite ready to fall asleep; the occasional giggle seeping through the ceiling until finally, everything was quiet.

'Where is she Morvah, where could our girl be?'

'I don't know, but we could try and bring her home.'

'How do you mean?'

'You and me, we could try and cast a charm to call her home.'

'I haven't done anything like that since mother died.'

'I know you haven't,' said Morvah. 'I know you don't believe but what harm could it do? The police are doing their job and we've got to let them get on with it but you said yourself you feel useless sitting here doing nothing. This is at least *something*.'

'I wouldn't know where to start?'

'Maybe not, but I would.'

'We'd need the book and we haven't got it.'

'We don't need the book. I know every charm, every remedy in there. I learnt it from cover to cover and more besides.'

Carmen sat up, 'Really, you did that?'

'I had to.'

'I'm so sorry Morvah, I should have let you have it when Mother died.'

'It doesn't matter now; what matters is we try to bring Rowan back. Here and now, you and me. If we were Christians we'd get down on our knees and ask Jesus for help and no one would think anything of it. We need to pray in our way; the way we were taught. Here and now, together.'

'We'll need an altar,' said Carmen.

'Have you kept everything?'

'It's put away but I'm not sure if it's all here. I never really took much notice when mother was alive.'

'Show me.'

Carmen wandered to the far end of the room where she lifted a small blue pottery jar from an alcove dug into the cobb wall. Tapping its contents into her palm, she retrieved a brass key she used to open the door of the antique mahogany sideboard beneath.

She pulled out a wooden box, pitted and ebonised with age; the size of a canteen of cutlery, which she carried back to Morvah.

'What there is, is in here,' she said, handing it to her sister.

Morvah shuffled towards the light, then placing the box on her lap, slowly opened the lid to reveal the contents; a round mirror, a stub of chalk, two long white feathers, three smooth white pebbles, two jam jars, one filled with earth another with salt, a pack of matches and four brown beeswax candles.

'Is it all there?'

'Not everything, but enough. Have you got a white candle … a large one?'

'I think so, somewhere.'

'Fetch it and something to stand the other candles on; a plate or table mat will do … oh, and a small bowl of water.'

By the time Carmen returned Morvah had already laid everything out on top of the sideboard. She placed the table mat, bowl of water and large white candle down with the rest, then with the chalk, began to draw a circle on the dark polished surface. Within the circle, in one deft motion, she drew a pentacle.

Carmen looked on, mesmerised at her sister's dexterity. She could never have drawn the protective symbol, not without practice and even then, doubted she'd be able to do it correctly so that each of the five points touched the outer circle.

'How were you able to do that so quickly?' she asked.

'Don't you remember, Mother showed us?'

'Vaguely but I'd never be able to get it right.'

'Do you at least remember the meaning? The circle symbolises eternity, the Circle of Life. The four points the elements; Water, Air, Fire, Earth and finally pointing upwards the fifth, the spirit; the Quintessential.

As she spoke Carmen had a vivid memory of her mother drawing a giant version on the flagstones in the kitchen and explaining it to both of them. She had sketched it out as swiftly as Morvah, in one movement without the chalk leaving the ground once. She'd then added the symbols of the elements at each of the five points finishing with a circle at the top to represent the Spirit.

'We've got all the symbols for the Goddess here,' Morvah said, pointing to the items she'd laid on the left-hand side of the Pentacle; 'the Swan feathers, pebbles and water. The salt and earth will have to do for the Masculine.'

Carmen watched her unscrew the jam jars and position them on her right side, then place the mirror in front of the Pentacle and set the white candle in the centre of it. Finally, she took three brown candles from the box and set them on the table mat, before lighting them.

'There, now all we need is a photograph of Rowan and some hair from her hairbrush; one or two will be enough.'

Carmen was operating on automatic pilot, following instructions as if she was ten years old again and it was her mother talking when all this was part of daily life. Now, it seemed alien to her. She imagined this must be how a lapsed Catholic forced to go to confession would feel; out of sync and insincere but she didn't want to offend Morvah. Her sister still believed and she needed to respect that. She didn't want to lose her again and like she said, what harm could it do? Maybe it would bring Rowan back; maybe not but it was better than doing nothing.

She returned with a photograph of Rowan taken the year before on her birthday and a couple of long dark hairs she'd picked from the collar of one of her jackets hanging on the hook in the hallway.

'Will these do?'

'Yes, fine,' Morvah answered, laying the hairs carefully across the photograph.

'Let's light the white candle.'

Carmen recognised Morvah planned to cast a candle spell. It was pretty basic stuff they'd learnt when they were kids. She had a vague memory of them working the same charm when they'd lost one of the farm dogs. She guessed her mother had hoped it might comfort them in the same way Morvah hoped to bring her comfort now. She could remember holding the candles and chanting but couldn't for the life of her recall the dog's name, or if it ever came home.

'Now,' said Morvah, 'kneel next to me and think of Rowan. Focus on her, not what she has or hasn't done. There must be no negative energy as the candle burns. Channel your love for her. It's your love she'll feel; your love that will bring her home.'

Carmen did as she was told. She knelt beside her sister, holding the white candle balanced on the mirror in both hands, reflections dancing upon her face; lips moving in silent prayer. Her eyes glinted hazel and green as they drifted across the random items placed carefully to form the Wicca alter; the feathers, the pebbles, then the earth.

Please, she prayed, please bring her home.

She thought of her daughter; her difficult, querulous daughter and longed for her to be safe. She thought of the farm; of Matthew, Maisy and Jago, and her and Morvah walking hand in hand down the lane; of her mother and her grandmother, of the Rowan tree and the baby boy buried beneath it. Then of Rowan's baby; the grandson she'd never know, suffocated in the pit.

Time after time her eyes drifted to the jar filled with earth.

Images filled her head of Rowan and the baby but her thoughts always drifted back to the suffocating earth.

THIRTY-THREE

Eden pulled into the multi-storey and waited for the arrival of Agnes's Fiat Punto.

Only a few cars ventured to the top level. There was always masses of space out of season, nevertheless, she watched Agnes drive up the ramp and park as far away as possible.

Her secretary emerged two minutes later wearing dark glasses, a headscarf and an oversized trench coat turned up at the collar. She gave Eden a perfunctory nod, then scuttled to the boot to retrieve a large holdall Eden recognised as hers.

With an enormous effort, she heaved it onto one shoulder and shuffled across the tarmac towards Eden's car, arriving dishevelled and out of breath; glasses slipping off her nose. Eden was thankful there was no one around because without a doubt she would have drawn attention. With her awkward gait and blanketed disguise, she was about as incognito as the Elephant Man.

Eden put the bag in the boot. 'Thanks, Agnes, this is good of you.'

'No problem, I drove around the block a couple of times before coming in, in case anyone was following me.'

'Well done,' Eden said, thinking, she's loving every minute of this. 'Were there a lot of reporters at the flat?'

'No, it was quiet but I expect it's the lull before the storm. They'll be there tomorrow mark my words, once the story's out. It's already been on the local news about Rowan. They're telling everyone not to approach her; to call the police.'

'What the hell do they think she's going to do, bring down a plague of frogs?'

Agnes pursed her lips. 'Do you need anything else? I can always bring stuff to your parents' place if you want. It's no trouble now I've got the hang of this.'

'This is fine for now,' Eden said, adding when she noticed she looked a little crestfallen, 'I'll keep in touch though and thanks again.'

Eden watched her secretary scuttle back to the car and drive off. She wished she found this as exciting as she seemed to.

Driving to a parent's house, she knew she'd have to tell them about Luke but decided it could wait until morning. Tonight, she needed to sleep.

THIRTY-FOUR

The next morning, Eden woke in her old bedroom and for one glorious second, as the light played familiar patterns on the ceiling, she was sixteen again without a worry in the world except whether to wear flip-flops or Converse because Garry Pellow, her latest crush, was a bit of a short-ass and she didn't want to spend their date looking at the top of his head.

She'd lived in the house her entire life up until she went to uni; well for the extent of the life, she remembered at least. She had no recollection of the old farmstead on the outskirts of St Ives where she'd been found. Her legs felt heavy and useless like she'd been tasered. She realised the dog was lying across them. He'd obviously sneaked in when she'd gone to the loo in the middle of the night.

'Go on boy, down.'

Castro opened one lazy eye, gave an unimpressed shuffle of his back end and promptly went back to sleep. Sensing she'd lost the battle, Eden dragged herself out from under him.

Unlike the rest of the house, littered with pottery and artworks her room was stark; practically monochrome, despite her parent's mission to free up her inner rainbow. When she was little, they'd decorated it with murals and hung dreamcatchers above her bed. They sent her to a Montessori school where she could enjoy a child-led education meant to nurture creativity. Thea took to it like a duck to water but she had spent most of her time trying to shut out the relentless racket; her nose in a book. Aged ten, she'd finally found the courage to ask if she could go to a proper school and paint her bedroom walls magnolia. The result was a haven of minimalist calm in the technicolour dream-coat house.

Once dressed she made her way downstairs for breakfast. She wanted to get an early start. She needed to buy a copy of the paper. Her parents hadn't pressed her the evening before. They had heard

Rowan was missing on the radio and she'd admitted being concerned about reporters turning up at her flat but that was all.

Desperate for a coffee, she knew she'd have to do with mint tea but her mood lifted when she spotted her father in the kitchen scrambling eggs.

'Do you want some? I'm allowed them on Saturdays; it's your mother's one concession to cholesterol. I can do you an omelette if you prefer?'

'That would be great; where is Mum?'

'Gone for a walk with Flora. She usually takes the dog but couldn't find him this morning. They won't be gone far; down to the beach and back; Mum likes to keep up her step rate.'

'Castro's on my bed.'

Her father smiled. 'He probably can't believe his luck.'

Eden took a deep breath. 'Dad, you know last night we talked about Rowan? Well I didn't tell you everything.'

'Hmm ...' he murmured, manoeuvring her carefully rolled omelette from the frying pan onto her plate, 'there you go.'

'Thanks,' she said, wondering how long it had taken him to perfect his technique.

'The press think I've been seeing Luke ... romantically, I mean'.

'But that's ridiculous, don't they know about Flora ... about him and Thea?'

'They've been put straight now but they photographed him coming out of my flat in the early hours; put two and two together and made five.'

'But if they know the truth. why are they going ahead with the story?'

'They said it was too late to pull it. But being cynical, I think they don't care as long as they sell papers. Luke has tried to limit the damage, but the inference is he was too wrapped up in personal matters to keep his eye on the job and so in a roundabout way he's enabled Rowan to skip bail.'

'And what about you? Were you distracted by all this stuff with Thea, because if you were, it's my fault?'

'No, of course not. Rowan had already gone by the time you rang me and as soon as I told Luke she was missing, he reported it.'

'So, you've done nothing wrong?'

'No.'

'But what will your client think when she eventually surfaces?'

'I don't know, she's so difficult. Luke has been kind to her; he even tried to give her a route to a lesser charge but she wouldn't take it. To be honest she reminds me of Thea; the way she won't be told anything, even if it's for her own good.'

Her father's expression was sympathetic. 'And her family, will they understand?'

'I don't know.'

'Well, they're the only ones you should worry about, they're the ones you owe a duty. Now eat, before it gets cold, or the chef will throw a wobbly.'

Eden obeyed. 'This is delicious,' she mumbled, her mouth full; wondering why her father didn't do more of the cooking given her mother's culinary incompetence, which at times, bordered on assault.

'So, what's your plan?'

'I'm going to walk to the village to get the paper. I know you think I should ignore it but I need to know exactly what it says. I've already lost clients because of the way I've handled this case. If I'm going to defend myself, I need to know what I'm up against.'

'Then I'm coming with you and that lazy mutt can come too.'

***

The village newsagent was about a mile from her parents' smallholding. It was easy-going; a flat walk all the way.

'He doesn't usually get to lie on the beds,' said her father, giving Castro a tug on the lead to get him going. 'I sense when you leave it might be difficult to break the habit.'

'I'll make sure he doesn't do it again.'

'Probably best; it's the way of things. Once you get the idea you're entitled to the run of a place, it's difficult to adjust to new rules.'

Eden had the feeling they weren't talking about the dog anymore.

'You mean me?'

Her father sighed, confirming she was right. 'You've always naively believed people are fair and when faced with a well-presented argument they'll reach the logical conclusion. Truth is, you couldn't be more wrong. The world is full of mean, ignorant people who get to have a say because they shout the loudest. They might be up in arms about that poor baby but it won't stop them from reading the gory details. Add a witch or two into the communal cauldron and a salacious sex scandal and you might as well be back on Pendle Hill. The fact the girl's solicitor is a woman, and a lefty feminist at that, is a gift to them. It's the same old crap that's always out there under the surface. All the press is doing is raking up the shit hidden under the rose bush.'

'Dad!'

'What? I'm telling you in their world a woman like you is either a bitch or a slut, take your pick.'

Eden was shocked at his directness. She'd gone to university; worked hard and become a lawyer without obvious sexist obstacle. It didn't mean she didn't appreciate the struggle of others; it just didn't seem to apply to her. Now her father was telling her she was delusional? She wondered if he was being oversensitive; that this was his politically correct, left-wing chip on his shoulder talking?

He leaned in to give her a reassuring squeeze. 'I'm sorry, love, but it's true. The other day; when I said you were a survivor, I didn't only mean your difficult start in life, I meant you've had to fight ever since. It doesn't matter you've never realised you were in the battle. The difference with this case is it's so obvious you can't fail to recognise it.'

Was this how it truly was, Eden thought? Did others see her sex before they saw anything else and for some was that where it began and ended; was that all they needed to know to make their judgements about her? She'd always believed it was what she had to say that mattered. She was a lawyer; she proved her worth in intellect and words. How often had those words been ignored; how often her intelligence questioned, her opinion dismissed because she was a woman, without her knowing? Had her gender cost some of her clients their liberty?

'You can call yourself a feminist, love; you can call yourself what you like but don't expect it to mean anything unless you're prepared to take the fight to the enemy.'

'I don't know I am strong enough, Dad. It's this case; it's a bit too close to home. Thank God the reporters haven't got hold of the fact I was abandoned as a baby. That would be the icing on the cake for them.'

Her father was quiet and it made her anxious.

'There's nothing I should know is there; nothing about my birth mother that could come out?'

'Mmm.'

'Dad?'

'Your mother didn't want to be found. The police tried; you know the story.'

He was right of course she did know the story, backwards and sideways, she had listened to it so many times.

Her parents moved to Cornwall in the late seventies straight from St Martins to join an artists' commune. Her mum had misgivings from the start but her dad was Cornish and persuasive, bombarding her with stories of St Ives and its thriving artist community but by the time they arrived the cracks had begun to show. Two of the group had received offers to exhibit in a smart West End gallery and utopian ideals had gone tits up, as those with cash got to make all the decisions. Not radical enough to suspend farm animals in Perspex or brave enough to join some of the others and invest in a fully operational polytunnel and grow weed, her parents decided to leave and would have, if not for the abandonment of a baby girl in one of the derelict barns.

'I know the story but just tell me again,' she said.

'Why for goodness sake?'

I don't know … to make me feel better?'

He took a deep breath before beginning the monologue.

'That night … the night of the summer solstice, it hit me and your mother it was the last time we would celebrate it with our friends in that place. Most of us weren't particularly spiritual, not like the hippies who descended on Stonehenge back then but loads of people always turned up; old friends from far and wide and a few from the town, although the locals generally held their celebrations by the standing stones on the road to Sennen. The longest day was a great excuse for a party. Trees hung with paper lanterns; soft half-light until eleven-thirty at night. Food and dancing and no neighbours to complain. We usually gathered around the last of the fire. waiting for the sun to come up; it was wonderful … truly magical, but this time tinged with sadness for us. Tensions were running high. I drank too much and at some point in the early hours your mum and I argued. Nothing terrible, you understand, I was emotional, that's all. She ran off to one of the barns to be alone and there you were; fast asleep in an old wooden crate someone had rescued from the beach to use in a sculpture. You were about a year old. No one had a clue who your mother was. Some of the group wanted to call the police but the feeling was we should wait a couple of days to see if she came back. In the meantime, we took a vote and named you Eden. Three days later the police were called but despite all the appeals your birth mother never claimed you. We left the commune, got proper jobs teaching and visited you every day at the children's home in Truro until we convinced the authorities we were suitable candidates for fostering. After a trial period, we were eventually able to adopt you.'

'And you took no photographs of me until that day.'

'And we took no photographs of you until that day because we would never have borne the agony of looking at them had we not been allowed to keep you.'

She grabbed his arm; hugging him close until they reached the village.

'Tie up the dog or he'll be off chasing squirrels,' warned her father.

In his dreams, thought Eden tying up Castro who immediately flopped to the pavement with a yawn.

The bell tinkled cheerfully as they entered the newsagents but the good news ended there.

'Morning Ken, you know my daughter?'

The stout man behind the counter nodded; a look of unsavoury triumph on his face as he announced with all the flourish of a town crier; 'I see she's in the papers today.'

'I believe she is,' her father said glibly, slapping his paper down on the counter. 'Thought I'd get a copy; wouldn't normally wipe my ass with this rag but what can you do when your daughter's a celebrity?'

Two women huddled by the magazine racks stopped chatting; their eyes lifting from the opened pages of the tabloid they were reading, to tut their disapproval.

Her father shot them a sideways glare. 'Anything interesting, ladies?'

Eden looked on in disbelief as he sauntered casually towards them, the grin on his face at odds with the contempt in his eyes. 'She'll autograph that for you if you ask nicely; won't you, Eden?'

Tilting his head in her direction he gave an exaggerated Carry-On wink before rolling his newspaper under his arm and walking out of the shop; slamming the door behind him with such force, it shook in its frame.

'He didn't pay for that!' stuttered Ken.

The woman holding the tabloid, closed it with a flourish; mouth tightening to a bow of indignation.

Eden stepped sheepishly up to the counter to pay for the newspaper and the jar of coffee she'd been clinging to before scooping up her change and leaving.

Her father strode ahead at such a pace she had to run to catch up, only to realise in her agitation she'd forgotten Castro. By the time she'd run back, untied the dog and waited while he sniffed every tree trunk along the verge, her father was out of sight.

Eden had never seen her easy-going hippy dad so angry and had never loved him more.

THIRTY-FIVE

Luke's car was parked outside her parent's house when she got back.

Her mother was on her hands and knees weeding the herb bed beneath the kitchen window. 'You've got a visitor,' she said, creaking to her feet.

'It's Daddy,' piped up Flora, who was helping, 'he's in the sitting room; he didn't want a drink.'

I bet he didn't, thought Eden, pulling the jar of coffee from her coat pocket.

'And your sister rang,' her mother said, brandishing her trowel. 'She sounded upset, poor thing and not very happy with you ... something about you and Luke, I said you'd ring her back.'

Eden had known it wouldn't be long before one of Thea's old school friends blabbed about the story on WhatsApp but she hadn't reckoned on it being this soon.

She took out her phone; three missed calls. She'd been trying to contact Thea for days. Her sister had chosen to ignore her and she'd be justified in doling out the same treatment but Thea wouldn't give up. She might as well get this over with and, wandering down the garden out of earshot, pressed return call.

She was met with an immediate onslaught.

'First, you steal my daughter but not satisfied with that, you had to go and steal her father as well,' Thea ranted.

'Now hang on a minute ...'

'You've always begrudged every bit of joy that's come my way. Just because I'm not clever or have the added cachet of having been abandoned or in foster care doesn't mean I don't deserve to be listened to. Flora's my little girl ... mine, not yours and if you think you and Luke can cast me aside like old rubbish you can think again ... and don't think being a lawyer will help ... I'll get my own lawyer or better still maybe I'll talk to the press; tell them how on top of all that witch stuff you're trying to steal my child now.'

A vein pumped in Eden's temple. She was angry; angry with the press, with those people at the shop and at her fool of a sister.

'Let me get this straight; you're actually suggesting I was lucky to be abandoned; is that it, because if it is, you've finally lost the plot? You left Flora with strangers. No one knew where you were; you didn't answer your calls; what did you expect Luke to do? All I did was help him out the same as Mum and Dad are doing now. You should be glad he put Flora first; grateful he's a good father.'

'Grateful … grateful,' Thea shrilled. 'Do you know how difficult it is to get a minute to myself; to be able to paint or keep a relationship going with a small child? No of course you don't you only have to think about yourself.'

There was a little girl whine in the voice now and Eden thought she could hear a man in the background trying to calm her sister.

'If it's such a strain why don't you let Luke have Flora more often; why make it so difficult for him?'

'Why should I?'

'But I'm sure he would help out more if you asked. He misses her so much.'

'Is that why you slept with him; are you his consolation prize, or is this payback for me winning him in the first place?'

'You know I would never do that. The press saw him coming out of my flat in the early hours after dropping Flora off; that's all. I can't believe you'd think either of us capable of doing that to you.'

'Then why isn't he answering my calls … guilty conscience?'

'He's got nothing to be guilty about. Maybe he's finally had enough and who could blame him?'

'Well, you can tell him I'll get my daughter back. He can bank on it, so you can forget any dreams you have about being a happy little family right now.'

The phone went dead.

Luke was scrolling through the messages on his mobile when she walked in. He looked up as she entered. 'Thea; she's been texting me non-stop all morning.'

'I've just spoken to her, or rather tried to reason without success.'

'She's heard then?'

'Afraid so.'

'I'm ignoring her. My solicitor's told me not to engage in case it prejudices my application for custody.'

She noticed the newspaper on the table in front of him.

'Snap,' she said, holding up her copy.

'Page four,' he sighed.

She shuffled next to him and opened the paper to read the headline;

SLEEPING WITH THE ENEMY

DI Luke Parish of Devon and Cornwall Police was caught leaving the flat of lawyer Eden Gray in the early hours of Tuesday morning. Ms Gray is defending child killer Rowan Lutey the teenager accused of murdering her baby by burying it alive.

The paper went on to describe the grizzly contents of the witch pits.

The notorious Lutey family has practised witchcraft in the small rural community for generations striking fear into the hearts of their neighbours. The recent release of Rowan Lutey on bail pending her trial has raised concern for those rightly outraged by this atrocity. Their worst fears were confirmed yesterday when the police announced Lutey has absconded and is on the run. Questions need to be answered. Not least if DI Parish had been concentrating on Lutey instead of Ms Gray perhaps a dangerous and unpredictable criminal would not be at large and young parents could sleep at night knowing their children were safe. Parish was too busy playing Adam and Eve in his Garden of Eden to do his job properly.

Yet again Rowan Lutey and Eden Gray have been allowed to cast their spell over the powers that be and the good old British public are the losers.

There was no mention of Luke's suspension.

'They don't actually come out and say we're having an affair.' she offered unconvincingly.

'Come on Eden; the headline says it all. It's a character assassination if ever there was one.'

'It wasn't as if we didn't know the press was sniffing about,' said Eden, dropping the paper down on the table, 'we should have seen this coming.'

'I never imagined they'd run with this nonsense but it's done now; we'll just have to roll with the punches and concentrate on finding Rowan. Denise is in charge of the investigation. I'm off the case.'

'Will she keep you in the loop?'

'Not sure; she's ambitious and could see this as a way of getting a feather in her cap. That said, she's a good copper. If anyone can find Rowan, she can.'

'Did you get to interview Jessica Marshall?'

'I did.'

'And?'

'I don't think she was involved either with the abduction of the baby or its death.'

'How can you be sure?'

'You're not going to like this but Jessica Marshall set Philip and Rowan up to have sex. She purposely took herself off for a couple of months and gave Rowan five grand to get Philip into bed.'

'What, on top of the ten thousand?'

'Yep, only Rowan didn't give the five back. She said she'd earned every penny of it.'

'Bloody hell.'

'So, Jessica didn't have a motive; she was willing to risk her marriage for the baby. The last thing she wanted to do was kill it. The two women concocted the plan for Rowan to tell Philip she didn't want to be with him and wanted an abortion. Jess knew everything. It's put a strain on the relationship, largely because she's had to hide the fact, she knew about the affair all along. Nevertheless, she was certain she and Philip could get through it once the baby was born. Her original story holds up and we're back to square one.'

'Rowan's certainly not the girl I met that first time at the station or the daughter her mother thinks she is, come to that.'

'No, and you may have to face the possibility she's run because she's guilty.'

'That's not lost on me either but there's still something missing here. Rowan's not stupid, she knows her selective amnesia is not doing her any favours. It makes her look guilty and she knows it but I still get the feeling there's more to this; she's protecting someone. I don't know who but I'm certain if we find her, we'll find them too.'

His phone pinged with another message.

'Thea?'

'No, Denise. She's told Carmen Lutey I'm off the case. I think the least we can do is explain ourselves in person before she reads this crap.'

THIRTY-SIX

They travelled in separate cars in case there were reporters at the farm. As it happened there were none.

Carmen was hanging curtains on the line when Eden arrived.

'These are the last of them,' she said. 'I've had to wash all the ones in the house to get rid of the smoke.'

'Have you had any reporters here today?'

'One or two, early on, asking if I knew where Rowan was and if I had any comment about DI Parish. I didn't know what they were talking about. I know he's off the case but I have no idea why?'

'Well, actually, that's why I'm here.'

As they were speaking, Luke drove into the yard.

'Talk of the devil,' Carmen said, 'not that I do often,' she smiled, 'just in case you get the wrong idea.'

Eden was glad to see despite everything the woman hadn't lost her sense of humour.

Luke arrived as Carmen pegged the last wet curtain on the line.

'You'd better come in,' she said, swinging the empty laundry basket into her arms.

They followed her into the house.

'Cup of tea?'

Eden knew it was futile to refuse.

Maisy was sitting at the table, painting a picture of a house with a red roof, spiky green grass and an inch-wide strip of blue sky along the top.

'That's a lovely painting,' commented Luke, sitting next to her.

'I know,' said Maisy confidently, adding a yellow-eyed daisy.

Luke thought of the colourful crayon scribbles drawn by Flora pinned to his fridge.

'Have you got any news?' Carmen asked hopefully, 'or are you out of the loop now you're off the case, you are off the case, aren't you?'

'Yes ... I am.'

'Carmen could we talk privately?' asked Eden, looking down at Maisy and back to the girl's mother, who took the hint.

'Maisy, why don't you go outside and find Jago? He was looking for slow-worms last time I saw him. He might catch you one if you ask him nicely?'

'I can catch my own,' protested Maisy, drawing a long black squiggle through the green paint before plopping her brush into the water and stirring until it turned a muddy brown.

'What's that?' asked Luke, 'is it a snake in the grass?'

'No, silly it's a slow-worm,' she laughed liking the phrase, 'Ss ... snake in the grass ... ss ... snake in the grasss ... s,' she chanted, holding up the picture.

'That's lovely,' Carmen said, 'let it dry and we'll put it on the wall later. Now off you go I want to talk to Eden and Luke.'

'I want to stay.'

'Off you go, I said.'

'Alright, but if I find a slow-worm can I keep it in my bedroom tonight? He can go in the doll's house Matthew made me.'

'I don't think that's a good idea. How about you keep it in one of these until bedtime, then let it go?' Carmen reached into the cupboard under the sink and handed her daughter an empty ice cream container.

'Alright,' Maisy said grudgingly, running through the kitchen into the yard to find her brother.

'What is it you need to tell me?' asked Carmen once she'd gone. The woman looked as if she was bracing herself for more bad news. Her face was a granite mask; her lips tight. Only her eyes betrayed her tattered nerves, as they darted between Luke and Eden as she struggled to lock herself together.

Eden suddenly realised Carmen thought they had bad news about Rowan.

186

'Oh no … it's not about Rowan. We've heard nothing about Rowan's whereabouts, and we're no wiser about what happened to the baby.'

'Oh, thank goodness. I thought when you asked to speak to me without Maisy being here …'

'How stupid of me; I should have thought,' apologised Eden, reaching for the woman's hand.

'So, what's it you want to tell me?'

Eden sought out Luke for reassurance.

He nodded.

'It's about this.' Eden pulled the newspaper from her bag, placed it on the table and turned to page four.

'What is it?' asked Carmen. 'I'll have to get my glasses if you want me to read it.' She retrieved a pair of battered-looking spectacles from the window sill before sitting back down. 'That's better.'

Looking up from the page only for an instant to scrutinise Luke's face, she read the article in silence. Eden felt an uncomfortable heat creep up her neck.

Luke wandered to the window, sipping his tea.

Finally, Carmen spoke. 'Is it true, are you two seeing each other?'

Eden wiped her sweaty palms across her jeans.

'No not at all and even if we were; in no way would we have let it hurt Rowan's case. I promise you, I'd never do that. Luke and I are connected through my sister. He has a child with her; that's why he was at my flat. He was dropping her off.'

'I trust you're telling me the truth but I don't see it makes a lot of difference from Rowan's point of view. You're still connected and that's bound to make things worse because it draws even more unwanted attention to the case. It's another stick to beat us with.'

Eden knew she was right.

'I'm so sorry.' She knew her apology wasn't enough.

'Is this why they took you off the case?' Carmen asked, turning her attention to Luke.

'Yes,' Luke said, returning her stare; 'yes, it is.'

'I suppose to me *you're* the enemy. To the public Eden is and the police are the good guys but not to me. You're the ones who believe Rowan is guilty; you're the ones who charged her with manslaughter.'

'But I'm the one who's let you down,' said Eden. 'Luke has done his best to help Rowan but he has his job to do.'

'I know you've been kind to Rowan,' Carmen said softly to Luke, 'but things seem to get worse every minute. I'm so sick of bad news.'

Eden knew she had to tell Carmen about Philip Marshall and the deal Rowan struck with Jess but didn't know how.

Luke put his cup on the table with a thud, making her jump.

'There's something else you should know Carmen, something that's come out in the investigation. We know who the father of Rowan's baby is.'

'Don't tell me it's one of the village boys and I'll have some mother on my doorstep any day now.'

'It's not a boy from the village. It's Philip Marshall.'

'Are you sure? I know Morvah said she thought there was something going on but that was after Rowan was pregnant.'

'I'm afraid the affair started before the baby. It ended with Rowan getting pregnant and wanting an abortion. He offered her a way out, suggesting he and his wife took the baby. Rowan agreed, for the money. What Philip didn't know was his wife knew all along. She'd given Rowan five thousand pounds to sleep with her husband in the hope she'd get pregnant. When Rowan did, she was delighted. The only problem was her husband might not like the fact he'd been set up.'

'They both lied. They were both keeping secrets,' muttered Carmen.

'Yes, he wanted to keep the affair secret and she wanted to keep the fact she knew all about it from him.'

'And there was our Rowan in the middle taking the money, bargaining with a child's life like it was livestock.'

The woman's face leached colour as she clung to the back of the chair; her back rounded, stomach caved as if she'd been punched.

Eden noticed for the first time she no longer looked sturdy, the way she had the first day they met. The stuffing had been knocked out of her. She'd aged in a matter of days and didn't look like she'd ever retrieve those runaway years.

'Are you alright?'

'Not really,' she said, her voice freighted with despair. 'You think you know your children. You assume they're made in your image, only better because you've taught them not to make your mistakes. You hope you've armed them with the tools to know right from wrong. Then you find out they've been slowly turning their backs on you; breaking free, making a new them you barely recognise or want to. You still love them but at the same time despise what they've become. That's how I feel about Rowan.'

'She's young, we all make mistakes when we're young. She may have taken the money and slept with Philip Marshall but she wouldn't be the first to have a lapse of judgement. It doesn't make her a killer; you mustn't lose sight of that.'

'It explains why she wouldn't tell me though, doesn't it? She knew how I'd react, and she was right. The only thing worse than this is if she's killed that baby. I don't recognise her at all and if you asked me right this minute whether I think she did it or not, I wouldn't be able to tell you. Terrible as it is for me to admit, that's the truth.'

Eden helped the woman sit down.

'Thanks, but don't worry, I'm not going to cry. I'm all cried out; I'm too tired. I need her home so I can look her in the eye and ask her to tell me the truth. I need to ask her if she killed my grandson.'

Eden didn't know what to say and was relieved when Luke finally took the pressure off by taking the lead.

'Carmen have you got an up-to-date photo of Rowan? The police have got the one they took when they arrested her but she looks tired and dishevelled in it; not a bit how she looks normally. A picture of your average teenager firstly might mean she's more easily recognised and secondly might help dispel the image the papers are busy creating.'

Carmen got up. 'I've got one in the other room,' she said, walking wearily into the hall, through to the sitting room where she and Morvah had cast the charm the night before.

As soon as she left, Luke moved towards Eden.

'Well done, that was hard for you,' he said, touching her shoulder.

'Harder for her,' nodded Eden in Carmen's direction.

'Is he your boyfriend?' Maisy asked, grinning from ear to ear as Eden caught sight of her standing in the doorway.

Carmen joined them and handed the photograph to Luke.

'Is he?' Maisy repeated.

Carmen hadn't heard her daughter's initial question. 'Is he what?'

'Is he Eden's boyfriend?'

'Never you mind, Miss.' Carmen said, then changing the subject to save her guests' further embarrassment added, 'What have you got in your container?'

'I got a slow-worm, only Jago said they aren't worms at all, they're lizards. They're not, are they Mum, lizards got legs?'

'I think they are,' answered Luke.

'Maisy's face dropped, then the smile slowly crept back; 'Are you her boyfriend then?'

'No, but we are friends,' said Luke.

'Ha! That's not the same; our Rowan's got a proper boyfriend,' she squealed, pleased she'd trumped them.

'Maisy, I've told you before, you mustn't tell fibs,' scolded Carmen.

'I'm not fibbing, I've seen him.'

'Maisy, why don't you come over here a minute and tell me all about it?' Luke said sitting down at the table.

The two women joined them.

'When did you see him?'

'When I was poorly; you know Ma, when my throat was croaky and sore and you and Matthew were lambing, so Rowan looked after me?'

'Where, here at the farm?' asked Eden.

'No. Rowan had to go to work so Maisy went with her to the cafe,' explained Carmen.

Eden looked at Luke. 'Philip Marshall?'

'Not Mr Marshall, silly,' Maisy said, 'he's old and he's got a wife, he can't be Rowan's boyfriend. He gave me ice cream for my sorely throat.'

'That was nice of him,' said Carmen, brushing a stray curl out of her daughter's eyes.

'Maisy,' said Luke, 'how do you know this man was Rowan's boyfriend?'

'Because he kissed her,' she giggled batting her eyelashes.

'Do you remember his name?'

The girl rolled her eyes back into her head as if she was physically trying to fish the name from inside. 'Nope, don't know.'

'Try my lover,' said Carmen, 'try and remember, it's important. Rowan might be with him and we need to find her.'

'Why?'

'Because we need to talk to her about something very important.'

She paused to think again. 'Nope, still don't know,' she said turning her concentration back to the ice cream container and the slow-worm inside.

'He feels so shiny,' she said stroking the creature's silky copper scales. 'Cold too.'

'He's brilliant,' said Eden not keen to have a feel herself. She didn't particularly care whether he was a slowworm or a lizard, he looked like a snake to her and she couldn't bear snakes of any description. 'How about we have a proper look at him in a minute?'

Eden could tell the girl was losing interest in her revelation. They needed to find out who this man was, right now.

Jago walked through the door. He was filthy but Carmen barely noticed and her disinterest seemed to alert him something important was going on and his younger sister was at the centre of it.

'What you gone and done now?' he asked her in an exasperated tone.

'Nothing I ain't done nothing; I told 'em about Rowan's boyfriend and her kissing him.' She puckered her lips and made a loud kissing noise.

'Ughh,' winced Jago, 'that's disgusting.'

'Did you know about Rowan's boyfriend, Jago?' Eden asked.

'Only cos Maisy told me. I didn't take no notice; it's just 'er being soppy.'

'Did she tell you his name; your sister can't remember?'

'No, she didn't say, but why don't you ask her what he looked like?'

'Good idea,' said Eden. 'Maisy, can you tell me what the man looked like?'

'Like a man but not as old; like Matthew, a big boy.'

'Did he look like Matthew?'

'No.'

'What did he look like then, was he tall?'

'Bigger than our Rowan.'

'I know,' said Jago, running to the table. 'Ask her questions, like in Who's Who; she's good at that, she always beats me.'

'I do. I always beat him, don't I, Ma?'

'Yes, you do my lover. Now you listen to Eden and she'll ask you questions.'

'Right here we go, Maisy. Did the man have black hair?'

'No.'

'Did the man have Mummy's colour hair?'

'Yes.'

'Did he wear glasses?'

'No.'

Every time, Maisy vigorously shook her head emphasising the importance of her reply.

'Did he have black skin or white skin like Luke's?'

'Not black but not white like him,' she said, pointing at Luke.

'You mean like Sanjeev in my class at school?' Jago said, getting back to quizzing his sister.

'No, I mean with the sun like Matthew when he's been on the tractor all day.'

'That's true I don't get to see much sun these days.' said Luke, examining his arm for signs of an elusive tan.

'Good, okay Maisy, let's try again. Did he have a beard?' asked Eden.

'Yes, he did,' said Maisy excitedly, 'he did, he did have a beard. A proper beard not bristly like when Matthew doesn't shave, a proper, proper beard and a jumper; a nice green jumper. I liked it cos it had a horse on it.'

'You mean a picture of a horse on the front?'

'No, a little horse with a man on it here.' She pointed with her index finger to a spot on the left-hand side of her chest.

'Ralph Lauren,' shouted Eden.

'Who?' asked Maisy trying to remember the name from the board game.

'I think I know who this is,' continued Eden excitedly. 'James Ferris, Elspeth Fuller's assistant. I've seen him in that jumper and he has a beard. He's the right age too and tanned from working on the dig, I think it's James Ferris.'

'Well done. love,' whispered Carmen in her daughter's ear.

Maisy peered into the ice cream container. 'Can I go and play with him now?' she asked looking at her mother.

'Of course you can but keep him in the box. I mean it.'

'I will,' she said, lifting the container from the table. 'Come on you old snake in the grass,' she giggled as she skipped away.

THIRTY-SEVEN

'James lives in a caravan on-site,' said Eden, once both children had disappeared upstairs.

'We need to interview him,' said Luke.

'The excavations on the well begin today; it's a big deal. One of the students, Sam, told me about it when I went to see Elspeth. She's been away on some conference in France, although Sam knew nothing about it. He thought she was visiting family in Ireland. Either way, he was certain she'd want to be back to supervise the setting up of the well excavation given its importance. It's over six thousand years old; can you imagine? If Elspeth is going to be there you can bet James won't want to miss out.'

'What's your impression of him?'

Eden thought about it for a moment. 'When I first met him, I liked him. He's passionate about what he does and was helpful. He seemed a genuinely nice lad but lately, his head seems to have been turned by all the attention the site is getting, and he comes across as full of himself and a bit callous.'

'How do you mean?'

'He seems hell-bent on getting as much publicity as he can on the back of the discovery of the baby's body no matter how distressing it is to others. The story's gone global and he's managed to raise the profile of the site and of course his own importance. I'm not sure that's what his boss thinks because I haven't been able to get hold of her since she's been abroad. It may be James hasn't had much choice and has had to ride the wave of publicity. If Elspeth has chosen to take herself off, he's inevitably been forced into the limelight. What concerns me is he's been caught out with a lie a couple of times.'

'Lies?' asked Luke.

'Firstly, about Rowan. I gave him ample opportunity to say they were an item but he never mentioned it. He knew all about the family. We talked about them and their history in some depth.'

Eden glanced at Carmen, for signs of offence but there were none and she was pleased they were past all that.

'It was the obvious thing to say he was dating Rowan or at least acknowledge he was a personal friend.'

'But he didn't?'

'No. Then there's the conversation I had with Sam; he's the one who discovered the baby, though according to him it didn't happen quite the way James told me.'

'How's that?'

'James told me the boy went for a smoke and came back to him to report the ground had been disturbed at one of the pits. They both went to investigate and discovered the baby.'

'So how does that differ from Sam's story?' asked Luke, curiosity working across every contour of his face.

'Well, Sam is adamant he doesn't smoke. He says James noticed it was disturbed and told him to go and look at the pit. I know it's not much and it doesn't make any difference who discovered it.'

'It does,' Luke contradicted, 'if the person who alerts everyone to the disturbed ground knows what's there. If he's pointing them in the right direction?'

'Are you suggesting he buried the baby? But why would anyone point people in its direction if they did that?'

'Because he wanted it to be discovered?'

'Why would anyone want a crime to be uncovered if they were involved?'

'Publicity. What if the whole reason for burying the baby in a witch pit was to draw attention to the dig?'

'Are you serious?'

'Absolutely; you have no idea how many times murderers join the search party and how often they gravitate towards the body. For them, it's the thrill of playing the concerned neighbour or grieving father; fooling the police. Here it's something more cynical. We're not dealing with some sick pervert. This was done for purely mercenary reasons; to get publicity for the site. The celebrity status he's achieved for himself is a fortunate spin-off.'

'Are you saying he killed the baby to do this?'

'No, I'm not going that far. It sounds to me as if James Ferris is an opportunist. That doesn't make him a killer. It might be Rowan confided in him and he saw the potential.'

'He was keen to lead me off track by telling me Rowan would never bury a dead baby at the site; that it was against her beliefs.'

Eden glanced at Carmen. They both knew that wasn't true. Rowan had no beliefs and there was the other baby Madge Lutey had buried. James at best had been making up what he didn't know; at worst he'd deliberately sought to deceive.

'And do you think Elspeth Fuller knew about all this?'

'I doubt it, but there's only one way to find out. Ask her.'

THIRTY-EIGHT

Alone in the car, they were able to talk freely.

'You know Rowan better than me; you've talked to her outside a police interview room; is she the type of girl to be led on by her boyfriend?' asked Luke.

'Not from what I've seen of her and heard from others but she does hanker for more than life on the farm and James Ferris is ambitious.'

'Does she want it enough to pull a stunt like this, that's the question?'

'That, I don't know. It certainly casts doubt, on the whole, *I don't remember a thing*. If she's been protecting someone from the off and the person is James, what's the betting she's been with him since she went missing? I still can't believe either of them buried the baby alive on purpose. I don't think they have it in them. I know you probably think that's a stupid thing to say?'

'Not at all. There are two types of criminals; those who fall into crime and those who choose it but I thought you lawyers didn't care which kind you represent?'

Eden didn't say anything and Luke didn't press her and the conversation dwindled as he concentrated his attention on driving the impossibly narrow road.

Eden took a sly sideways scan of his face. He seemed eager; leaning over the steering wheel like a bird of prey. She on the other hand felt like something awful had her in its sights; pinned by a cat's paw.

'Will you get into trouble for this? Shouldn't you let Denise in on it?'

'In on what? We've not verified anything yet. I've heard there's an important excavation going on today and I've come along with you to have a look. If something else comes out of it pertinent to the investigation, I will of course, like a good boy let her know.'

As they neared the site entrance, she could see there were more vehicles parked than before; cars and a pick-up with winching machinery on the back, around which men in high-vis vests and safety helmets were milling about; kicking at the earth impatiently.

Eden spotted Sam talking to one of them, a mountainous man who dwarfed the boy and who looked like he should be in charge.

'That's Sam,' she said, nodding in his direction, 'he's the one I told you about.' She looked around. The group of students she'd met before congregated around the prefab; their muddy multi-layered clothes giving them the look of Victorian vagabonds.

'He looks so young; talk about David and Goliath.'

'I don't see Elspeth or James for that matter.' said Eden. 'Perhaps they're already at the well, controlling operations?'

As they got out of the car Eden noticed Luke reach into his back pocket and bring out his warrant card.

'Shouldn't you have handed that in?' she murmured to him as they walked towards Sam.

'No one asked,' he smiled.

He'd held onto the card for the interview with Jessica Marshall and had forgotten to hand it over before he left the station.

'DI Parish,' he said, flashing the card. 'It's Sam, isn't it?'

'Yes, that's right; can I help you?' He held out his hand to Luke, then, turning to Eden said, 'Hello again.'

The thick-necked foreman hesitated, before reluctantly lumbering away to join the rest of his crew.

'It's certainly a hive of activity here today.' said Eden

'You can say that again. Is this about the excavation?' he asked obviously worried. 'We cleared everything with the police. They said they'd finished with the site and we could press on with the dig.'

'No, it's fine,' reassured Luke, 'you can carry on. We're here to speak to Elspeth and James; can you tell me where I can find them?'

'You tell me. The men need someone in authority to sign off the paperwork for health and safety and neither Elspeth nor James are here. I've tried ringing them but both phones go straight to voicemail. I've got all these people waiting to start excavating the well and it's costing loads of money.'

The boy looked flustered. 'Carrie's not turned up either. She's the one who normally deals with this sort of thing when James and Elspeth aren't here but I got a message she's been called home because of an unexpected opportunity with another project for UCLA.'

Eden wasn't surprised. Carrie hadn't seemed the type to miss an opportunity, even if it meant letting others down.

'When was the last time you spoke to James?' Luke asked.

'Days ago, and to Elspeth even longer.'

'Has anyone other than James, spoken to Elspeth?' queried Eden. increasingly worried about the woman.

'No, not as far as I know. Although when I went back to the trench after speaking to you the other day and told everyone Elspeth was in France, Carrie said she knew, so maybe she'd spoken to her? Then again, she's very close to James, so maybe it came from him?'

'What do you mean close?' asked Luke.

'It's not official or anything but there have been a couple of mornings she hasn't had to travel far for work.'

Sam glanced across at James's caravan.

'They're sleeping together?'

'That's what we all think but we don't know for certain. It's the way Carrie sticks up for him. I've been moaning about how it's not right he's not here while Elspeth's away and she always jumps to his defence saying he's busy promoting the site and how all of us will have him to thank when our careers rocket on the back of working here.'

Eden, spotting the titanic foreman was on the warpath again, gave Sam a nudge.

'Oh god, him again. He wants a decision.'

'Sorry to interrupt mate but we need to get going. We'll lose the light early this afternoon and this has to be done today; we've got other jobs to go to tomorrow.'

Sam looking as if he was about to cry threw up his hands in a final gesture of surrender.

'Go on then … just go ahead,' he spluttered.

Eden saw doubt shadow his face the second he signed for the job. He was not a man to leave in charge and it seemed incomprehensible to her Elspeth would abandon her team at such a crucial time.

Sensing the boy was wavering, the foreman signalled his driver to start up the truck and, gathering the rest of his men, marched them off across the aluminium planking towards the coppice before Sam could change his mind.

'What exactly are they doing?' shouted Eden above the deafening racket of moving machinery.

'We have to go down into the well to excavate it. It's about thirty feet deep and quite narrow. They've got to pump out the water to get to the sediment; attach wooden panels to the sides so that the construction isn't compromised, then fix a ladder so we can get up and down safely.'

'Quite an operation?'

'Yeah, look I'll have to go. The water has to be filtered in case there's cloth or coins, bits of pottery and they'll be waiting for me so they can begin.'

He glanced across to his friends, who, busy chatting and smoking something smelling suspiciously like old socks, were hardly chomping at the bit.

Poor Sam, Eden thought.

'Okay, you go,' said Luke, 'but is it alright if I have a look in Elspeth's cabin?'

'I'm not sure … I?'

Yet another decision beyond his pay grade, thought Eden. 'I promise I won't let him steal anything,' she joked, trying to lighten the mood; hoping he'd see the irony.

The boy was too harassed; his sweaty face blanked with stress.

'It's only I told him about all the finds and he'd like to see the site plan,' mollified Eden.

'Okay, but you mustn't touch any of the samples or the finds in the numbered plastic containers in the back room. They can only be examined under controlled conditions. Elspeth will go mad if I've let anybody anywhere near them. You'll need the code to get into the prefab it's 1066.'

'Obviously,' joked Eden, 'what else would it be?'

'Sorry, I have to go,' said the boy hurrying towards the rest of the team.

'Something's not right,' said Luke.

'No shit,' joked Eden. 'Where the hell is everyone? Elspeth should be here and James for that matter and what about that Carrie girl?'

'You met her?'

'Yes, the other day. It's not likely that Rowan's with James if Carrie is going out with him surely?'

'Who knows, maybe he likes to play the field?' Luke shrugged, 'Come on, let's have a look in there,' he said walking towards the portacabin.

Eden tapped in the code; 1066.

The room was stiflingly hot; the stench of formaldehyde or whatever it was Elspeth used was even stronger than before. They left the door open to let the air circulate. The place looked much as it had the last time she visited; the plan of the site spread out on the table; the jars lined up along the shelves.

Luke wandered around peering at the contents; grimacing at the labels.

'*Nail Clippings*' he read aloud, 'disgusting.'

'Through here is where Elspeth keeps the most important finds,' Eden said walking towards the tiny room at the back where she'd been shown the swan's pelt and mummified chicks. It was unlocked. She turned on the light, bathing the room in the same artificial glow as before. There was a pile of papers on the desk which Luke reached for.

'Looks like invoices for equipment; final demands.'

'That's strange, Elspeth told me they didn't have any funding issues.'

Luke dropped the invoices on the desk. 'Well someone's not doing the housekeeping. Let's look at this swan thing then.'

'No, you heard what Sam said. I haven't got gloves or anything, Elspeth wouldn't want anyone opening the containers without her here.'

'I've got gloves,' he said pulling out a pair of blue police issue from his pocket.

'No!'

'Oh, go on,' he cajoled, 'as we're here and Elspeth hasn't bothered to show up.'

Eden took the gloves trying to pull them apart.

'Blow into them. You know how to blow, don't you?' Luke grinned.

'Oh, ha bloody ha,' she said, trying not to laugh but secretly relieved for a break in the tension building since they arrived. Suitably gloved up, she made her way to the back of the room from where Elspeth had retrieved the plastic containers previously. They weren't there.

'They're gone; all the containers are gone.'

'Are you sure?'

'Of course, I'm sure. They were all stacked numerically at the back here.'

'How many were there?'

'I don't know exactly. She showed me the swan pelt and that was number thirty-something, so I guess at least that many.'

'Perhaps they've been taken somewhere safe because of all the press and nut cases hanging around since the baby was found?'

'Maybe but why did Sam specifically tell us to leave them alone; not to open them. Surely he'd know if they'd been moved somewhere else?'

'Watch yourself, you're sounding like a detective,' Luke joked. 'What's in the filing cabinet?'

Eden tried the top drawer of the cabinet next to the desk.

'It's locked.'

'Look in the desk drawer, nine times out of ten filing cabinet keys are kept in an unlocked desk drawer.'

Eden opened the drawer and began sifting through the pens, and paper clips until she found a small bunch of silver keys. She was about to shut the drawer when she spotted something else, right at the back; Elspeth's phone.

'Luke?' She held the phone up. 'It's her phone; it's Elspeth's. I remember it from the other day. I remember trying to guess how old it was; how it was typical of her to have never upgraded.'

She could see from the knit of his eyebrows he immediately understood the significance of the find.

'The battery's dead,' said Eden looking around for a phone charger.

'I think I saw a charger in the other room,' said Luke, taking the phone from her.

'Shall I still look in the cabinet?'

'Yes, but keep the gloves on. I'll try and get some juice into this.'

Adrenaline ripped through her. She fumbled with the small bunch of silver keys, finding the thin rubber gloves impossible to master. Eventually, she found the key, unlocked the cabinet and pulled out the drawer. She had no idea what she was looking for but expected a stack of files. Instead, there was a Sainsbury's bag containing something bulky. She had to pull the drawer fully out to extricate it. Inside was a handbag.

'Luke?' She could hear the panic in her voice.

'What is it?' Luke shouted from the other room.

She carried the bag next door to him.

'Look.' She held up the battered bag by its long strap.

He immediately stopped what he was doing.

'Open it,' he said, 'you've got the gloves on.'

She laid the slouchy tan leather bag on the table and carefully, her fingers shaking, undid the zip. Slowly holding the bag upside down, she shuffled the contents onto the desktop. Tissues, an old lipstick; two brightly coloured scrunchies, loose coins, hairbrush full of Elspeth's distinctive purple-grey hair, cigarettes and lighter, four biros a purse and a bunch of keys on a woolly pom-pom key ring.

'Open the purse,' said Luke looming over her shoulder, in police mode now.

Eden slowly opened the heavily stuffed red leather purse. Unfolding it, she was met with Elspeth's photograph staring up at her from her pink driving licence tucked inside the clear plastic window. She lay the purse flat on the desk. Within its folds, she could see there was some cash along with a debit card and Elspeth's museum staff ID.

'She's not gone anywhere without that lot,' said Luke, his breath hot on the back of her neck.

'What are you saying?'

'I'm saying she's missing and I bet if we contact her family or whoever she's meant to have been with in France, neither has seen her.'

'Luke you're frightening me. Do you think something awful has happened to her?'

'I don't know but I have to say it's not looking good. Let's see if we can get into her phone. It might cast some light on things. Put everything back in the bag and bring it with you.'

Luke stared down at the phone which had now charged enough to turn on.

'It's password-protected.'

'Try 1066 again,' Eden said hopefully.

He tried; nothing.

'What about another date; you know something else historical?'

'Go on then mastermind.'

'I don't know, Waterloo 1815?'

Luke tapped in the number.

'No, definitely not an Abba fan. Look, I've only got one more chance, perhaps we should go and ask Sam if he knows?'

'17… something…12; 1712 James told me that's the date of the last witch trial in Cornwall.' said Eden. Try 1712.

Luke typed in the numbers. 'Bingo, we're in.'

Row after row of missed calls and texts lit up the screen. Twenty voicemails but nothing sent from her for days.

'Perhaps there's an explanation. Perhaps she forgot her handbag and her phone but needed to catch a plane and ...' Even as she was saying it, Eden realised it sounded ridiculous.

'Maybe,' said Luke, 'but it's strange there's not a single text or call from James Fuller.'

'So?'

'Well, it means either he knew she'd forgotten her phone and was calling her on another number or he was lying when he said he was in regular contact with her.'

Luke's train of thought was interrupted by a commotion outside; shouting and the sound of men's feet thundering along the aluminium planking towards the cabin.

The foreman peered around the door of the prefab, face red, gulping for breath;

'Earlier ... when you were talking to the boy... did I hear you say you were police?'

'Yes,' answered Luke, handing the phone to Eden, 'I am.'

'Then you'd better come quickly; we've found a body in the well.'

THIRTY-NINE

Eden watched through the window as the grim-faced man, so keen to start work earlier, talked to Luke. When finished, he bent his hulking frame over double; hands-on knees, gulping for breath.

Luke looked towards the portacabin. He was obviously expecting her to be right behind him but she was rooted to the spot, Elspeth's phone clasped in one hand; her bag in the other.

There was a nauseating sway to the room. Dropping the phone into the bag she grabbed the edge of the table as Luke walked back in.

'Are you coming?'

'Give me a minute. I'll follow you.'

'Okay, but make sure you lock the door.'

'I know what to do, you go on.'

She watched Luke follow the foreman across the field.

Peeling off the blue gloves she reeled a little at the smell of sweaty rubber. She'd feel better when she got out of there.

After depositing Elspeth's bag onto the back seat of Luke's car, she set off following the sound of machinery; heading along the bouncing aluminium planks.

Hearing voices, she glanced up at a couple of girls she recognised as two of the urchin lookalikes from earlier, heading her way. Arms wrapped around each other; they were crying and didn't acknowledge her as she stepped aside to let them pass.

Quickening her pace, she stomped towards the woodland.

Up ahead she caught sight of a wall of hi-vis vests. Luke, his back to her, his finger in his right ear, was on his phone, shouting above the loud whirring of the pump on the back of the pickup.

'The whole team yeah; access is difficult though … hang on a minute, I can't hear a bloody thing.' He broke away from the crowd to yell across to the pickup driver.

'Turn that damn thing off.'

The pump engine clattered loudly to a halt; its mechanical din replaced with the deafening squawk of rooks fleeing the canopy. Once it passed, Luke continued his conversation.

'I'll clear the site at this end and we need forensics too; ASAP. No, it's not an accident.'

Eden burrowed between the workmen's broad backs then stopped in her tracks.

On top of a spread tarpaulin lay what appeared to be a dead animal, slick with black mud. Although she could make out four limbs, she could not make sense of its form. What should have been a leg was bent upward, dislocated so it touched the head which faced away from her. The foreman said they'd found a body not a carcass, so surely it was a person?

Curled up in that odd position she wondered if whoever it was had been down the well for centuries, like some ancient corpse from an episode of *Time Team*. So, what was Luke talking about, why did they need forensics? Why had those girls been crying, surely this was what every budding archaeologist hoped for?

She glanced up at the workmen standing grim-faced around the body like a Roman guard.

Luke sidled up to her. 'I've got to clear the site. I've called it in. Denise is on the way with the SOC team and the pathologist.'

'Isn't that a bit over the top. Surely this is one for the archaeologists. There's enough of them here for goodness sake?'

'What do you mean?'

'It's ancient. The well is what … six thousand years old or something. It's probably been down there for centuries surely it can wait a bit longer, it's not an emergency is it, not like Elspeth?'

Luke took her by the forearms, turning her towards the body.

'Look again.'

She was confused. What was he on about, she'd already had a good look at the disgusting slimy thing?

'Look again.'

'Okay but I'm not sure what I'm supposed to be seeing?'

Taking a long, exasperated breath, concentrating hard, she scanned the contours of the thing. The curved back; legs pulled up; knees bent in a twisted foetal position. She could see now the arms were pulled behind the back; the wrists tied together with something long and thin. She saw a glint of metal; a buckle; the hands were tied around the wrists with a belt; and on one of the wrists, the circular face of a watch. The back of the head was covered by a mass of vegetation; moss or seaweed… or hair? a massive tangle of muddied hair. She gasped.

'It's Elspeth,' said Luke.

'It's not,' she protested in disbelief, 'it can't be … you're wrong … it's not.'

She looked at the hair again; the mass of unruly hair, then at the belt tying the hands; the man's belt she'd seen holding up Elspeth's baggy jeans. She couldn't believe it; didn't want to.

Eden looked up; averting her eyes from the archaeologist's poor broken body. Autumn's colour wheel spun orange and red through the trees above her. She heard sirens in the distance; their Wah Wah Wah coming nearer and nearer and then nothing else.

FORTY

She had no recollection of how she got back to the car but it was where she found herself a few minutes later, Luke leaning over her; eyes concerned.

'You fainted,' he said, gently brushing her hair away from her face. 'Look I'm needed here. I don't think you're fit to drive so Sam is going to borrow my car and take you to your parents but first, he has to debrief his team and send them home so we can do our job. Is that okay?'

Her mind was defogging slowly.

'Yes, fine but what about James, do you think he did that to Elspeth?'

'We won't be able to tell whether she's been murdered until the pathologist has examined her but it's looking that way at the moment, and James has to be in the frame.'

'Unless something's happened to him too?'

'It's unlikely. The body's been down there several days during which according to James he was talking to a dead woman. We've alerted the airports and the ports so unless he's skipped the country already, he won't get far.'

'What about Rowan; do you think she's with him?'

'Who knows but if she is and he's done this she's not safe; he's dangerous.'

'Oh god,' Eden moaned.

'Look I need you to sit in the car while we break into James's caravan.'

'Can't I come with you?'

'I'm afraid not; this is a crime scene now. You stay put.'

She leaned back in the passenger seat; door ajar. Denise Charlton was giving instructions to the yellow-vested workmen, who sat cross-legged on the ground by the prefab like a pack of overgrown cub scouts. Now and again, a police car pulled onto the gravel and two or three officers jumped out. Men in rubber boots and white protective clothing weaved their way up and down the glinting planks.

Eden heard Luke's voice barking orders from within the caravan. Moments later he emerged carrying Elspeth's stripy jumper in a sealed plastic bag.

He handed it to one of his colleagues and walked over to Eden.

'Where did you find that?' she asked.

'Stuffed under the bed.'

'Was there anything that looked like it belonged to Rowan in there?'

'No, but I found this.' He held up a small bag of cannabis. 'This too.' It was a selfie of James and Carrie, heads close together, him smiling, her kissing his cheek.

'They *are* an item then?'

'Looks like it.' Luke paused, staring at the photo. 'Right, got to get back to the others. Are you okay here, Sam won't be long?'

'I'm fine ... honestly.'

'I'll pick you up later and we'll go and collect your car from the farm.'

'Don't worry, Dad can drop me. Go on, you've got stuff to do. I can wait.'

She watched him walk away, joined by yet another white-suited alien. She thought of Elspeth and her work. She'd seen the site as something unique, teeming with history and tradition. Now look at it ... and Carmen; what would she think if she could see it now? Her family had preserved it for generations; carried out their rituals and kept the secrets of the women who longed to be mothers. Yet in a matter of months of outsiders arriving it had been denigrated to a muddy battlefield of death and decay. She knew she'd have to tell her about Elspeth and she'd inevitably worry even more about Rowan, if that were possible. She'd hear about it whether she told her or not. It wouldn't be long until the papers sniffed out the body. The sound of sirens and police vehicles racing through the narrow Cornish lanes in the middle of the afternoon would be enough to get everyone talking. It was not an everyday occurrence; not like in a big city.

She closed the door, wanting to shut out the noise and the image of Elspeth's body. She turned to look out of the back window at Sam talking to his friends. They were in bits. She wondered if some might be put off by this; might have a change of heart about their chosen career path? Sam looked as if he might be one of them.

She noticed Elspeth's bag was still on the backseat. Luke had forgotten to take it with him. She lifted it by the handle, heaving it into the front and onto her lap. She wondered if she should walk it over to Denise so she could put it with the other evidence but Luke hadn't told her to and maybe he had some reason to hold onto it.

Her lawyer's brain began to click into gear. She wondered why James had dumped Elspeth here, knowing she'd be found. He knew the workmen were booked to pump out the well; why hadn't he taken her somewhere else? There were plenty of places to get rid of bodies in Cornwall. He could have thrown her down one of the many disused mine shafts littering the county; she'd never be found. Or he could have pushed her off a cliff and made up some story she'd gone walking and disappeared. It had been done before and the accused had walked free. Why had he chosen probably the only *modus operandi* to see him convicted?

She knew she shouldn't but before she could stop herself, she'd unzipped the bag, felt inside for the large pom-pom keyring, re-zipped the bag and returned it to the backseat.

The rap on the window from Denise made her jump, dropping the keys to the floor between her feet, she wound it down to speak to her.

'I'm glad you're still here. Luke asked me to come and collect a bag he said was in his car.'

'It's there, in the backseat,' she gestured, knowing she couldn't put the keys back now. She shouldn't have taken them in the first place. She'd tampered with evidence.

Denise opened the back door and lifted out Elspeth's bag.

'Denise, is Luke back on the case then?'

'He's back on *this* case, put it that way. We're not crawling with detectives with homicide experience. We can't afford not to have him with us on something like this.'

She felt relieved but hoped she hadn't cocked it up for him again by her actions.

Sam returned to the car. 'Ready to go?' he asked.

'Whenever you are.' said Eden. 'See you, Denise.'

'You sure you're okay?' Denise asked, leaning in the window to take a good look at Sam. 'You look as shaken as she does. I can get one of our officers to drive Eden if you prefer?'

'No, it's okay,' interjected Eden touching Sam's hand, 'we'll be fine. He can sit down for a while at my parents' house. I'm sure he just needs a bit of time to process all this, like me. That's right, isn't it, Sam?'

'Yeah,' said the boy, cleaving to the steering wheel.

'Fair enough, if you're sure?'

As soon as she'd gone. Eden reached down and picked up the bunch of keys from between her feet.

'Sam, did Elspeth live in the village?'

'No, she lives… lived in Truro in a flat on Lemon Street to be near the museum. Since we finished digging the pits she's been there as much as at the site; until we found the baby that is.'

'Did anyone live with her?'

'No, she's single, although James stayed with her for a while last winter when the roof leaked in his caravan and it took weeks to fix because they couldn't work out where the water was coming from.'

James had a key, Eden thought. 'Right let's go if you're ready?' she said. 'I'll give you detailed directions when we get nearer. For the moment you can take a left at the end of the lane, then the first right heading towards Devoran.'

FORTY-ONE

Eden waved Sam off. Despite his youth, he looked shrivelled; desiccated, as if all the moisture had been sucked from him. He'd been silent the entire drive and didn't want to come in.

Eden's father emerged from his studio in the garden as they arrived.

'Back again already? Gosh we're seeing a lot of you lately. Not that I'm complaining; far from it.'

'Oh, Dad.' She ran towards him, sinking into his familiar shape as the tears flowed.

'Shush now ... now this isn't like you; what on earth has happened? Who was that young man driving Luke's car?'

'Sam,' she gulped, 'one of the archaeologists from the site. He brought me home because Luke is tied up there. Dad, it was horrible; we found Elspeth Fuller's body down a well. They think she's been murdered.'

'Come inside and sit down ... come on now,' comforted her father.

'No, no I need air.'

'Over here then.' He ushered her towards a bench overlooking her mother's herb garden. 'Sit there, I'll go and get you a drink, something hot and sweet. You've had a terrible shock.'

Eden caught her breath. She was still holding Elspeth's keys; squeezing the pom-pom between her fingers like a stress ball.

'Your mother's bringing out some coffee. You left the jar earlier.'

'Did you tell her anything?'

'No, I wasn't sure it was for general release?'

'Good, she'll only worry. Dad, will you take me into Truro?'

'Yes of course but don't you think you're better off here rather than alone back at your flat?'

'No, not my flat.'

'Where then?'

'Can you drop me in Lemon Street?'

'What on earth for?'

'I need to check something; then I'll go straight home and wait for Luke, I promise. He's picking me up later so I can collect my car from the Luteys' farm.'

'I can drop you there if you prefer?'

'No, Lemon Street will be fine.'

Her mother came out with a tray and placed it on the battered sun-cracked garden table. 'Coffee?' she said disapprovingly as if delivering a mug of nuclear waste.

Eden stood. 'Thanks, Mum, but I have to go.'

'But you only just got here. Tell her she can't leave yet.'

'Love, I don't think it's the right time,' her father said reaching out to her mother.

'If not now when; when is it ever going to be the right time?' she snapped, pulling away.

'It's just, Eden's had a shock.'

Her mother didn't answer, instead, rising from her seat, she walked towards the door.

'Wait here; it's high time I showed you something.'

'What's going on, Dad?'

'I told your mum about our conversation earlier about how we found you.'

'And?'

'She said you were right to be worried.'

'What are you talking about? It was just me fretting about the press; needing a bit of reassurance.'

'The thing is we haven't told you quite everything and when you and Luke left and I told your mum about our conversation and those bloody women in the newsagents she said I should have spoken up then, rather than the press somehow getting hold of it and you finding out that way.'

'Finding out what?'

Her mother arrived back five minutes later, carrying a small brown envelope.

'Hold out your hand,' she said, hesitating for a second, before tipping something soft and light as a feather onto her outstretched palm.

Eden carefully lifted it to take a closer look; marvelling at the delicate auburn and golden copper strands, finer than cotton, entwined to form a ring, finished with a tiny love knot.

'It looks like hair?'

'Yes.'

'Whose?'

'Yours, and your mother's. I don't know why I haven't given it to you before. I probably should have but I thought it might frighten you when you were small and assumed one day when you were ready, you'd ask me more questions but you never did. I didn't want to be the one to rake it all up, upset you for no reason other than to salve my conscience but with the press snooping around all the time someone might talk.'

Eden couldn't speak. She stared down at the ring as if it were a beating heart.

Her mother reached inside the envelope again, this time pulling out a matchbox-sized sliver of wood, painted with the image of a tiny robin; its delicate brown and red feathers flecked with gold; emerald moss clamped in its beak. It hung from a short leather necklace.

'Tell me … you have to tell me.'

'I might as well start on the night I found you.' Her mother seemed wistful, her eyes dark and serious as she continued.

Her dad sat silently on the bench.

'I looked around expecting to see someone. I called out but no one answered. You were all alone. I was about to run for help when you opened your eyes and stared at me, your bottom lip curling, ready to cry. I lifted you and you nestled into me and dropped off again. That's when I saw the envelope tucked beneath your blanket. I knew whose child you were the minute I saw the painting and the colour of your hair.'

Eden began to pace; heart pounding, her mind filled with questions she wasn't sure she was brave enough to ask.

Her mother gave a sideways glance to her father, who nodded back indicating it was no time to stop now.

'About six months before, a girl had turned up at the farm asking for art lessons. She was about sixteen and brought the pencil drawings she'd done; beautiful intricate sketches of wildlife; insects, birds, a couple of the family dog all drawn on scraps of paper, bits of cardboard anything she could lay her hands on. It was clear she didn't need lessons but had no money for materials, so, we let her use ours and the studio. She was no trouble; came and went as she pleased then stopped. We thought nothing of it. Like I've told you before, people passed through that place all the time. Some stayed for days, some like us, for years. When I saw the painting, I immediately recognised it as one of hers. Then when I saw the ring; her copper-coloured hair I knew for certain.'

Eden imagined the girl's delicate fingers twisting the hair ring, painting the intricate feathers.

'What was her name?'

'I don't know.'

Eden's throat tightened, 'She must have had a name?'

'I only knew her by the nickname we gave her; "Star", because that's what she was, so talented.'

'But the police they must have been able to find her if she was local?'

Her mother's eyes drifted back to her lap. 'We never told the police.'

'What ... what about my time in the foster home; my adoption?'

'We made it up. We all agreed to keep you until she came back; not inform the authorities in case they took you into care.'

'But I have my adoption certificate?'

'We lived with talented artists. It was pretty easy to forge the paperwork once we knew what it was meant to look like.'

'And she never came back or contacted you about me?' Eden's voice broke.

Her mother shook her head, her eyes brimming with tears. 'We asked in the town about her but no one knew who she was, and we realised we'd only assumed she was local because she came and left every day. We stayed on at the commune for another year waiting but by then the place was breaking apart; everyone going their separate ways and it was decided we take you with us. I was glad to leave. To my shame, I didn't want her to come back and take you away from me. I thought of you as mine, a sort of parting gift.'

It was like listening to a story about someone else. Eden couldn't believe her parents with their uncompromising ethics could have done such a thing.

Her mother brushed away a tear skirting her jawline before reaching inside the envelope again and pulling out a small bundle of polaroid photographs which she handed over.

Her father moved again to comfort her and this time she accepted.

Eden held her breath as wave upon wave of feelings threatened to topple her. Her hand was shaking as she took them and unwound the elastic band holding them together.

Most were of her and her parents with other commune members and their children; on the beach or at the farm, feeding the animals. She looked at them one by one. It was easy to spot her; fat baby cheeks rosy with the sun, curls escaping the straw hat plonked precariously on her head. The missing years she thought lost forever.

The last was of a teenage girl; taken in profile, long braids of copper hair hanging down her back over the straps of her denim dungarees. Hunched over a table, paintbrush poised between delicate fingers; her pale lashes curtaining downturned eyes, she was a study in poise and concentration. Eden turned it over. One word was scrawled in blue biro on the back.

STAR.

'She knew we'd take good care of you.'

'And you all agreed to keep the secret?'

'We were family; we kept each other's secrets but we should have put our feelings aside and told you the truth once you were grown up and knew no one could take you away. We were worried we'd lose you; you'd hate us because of what we'd done. We wanted you to stay our little girl. Later we had Thea and you know how much I love her but it wasn't the same. No one could have felt more for a child than I felt that first time I held you. How could I risk losing you?'

Her mother looked so tiny; head bent, tears dripping onto the empty envelope.

How could she be angry with her? She had put her before everything else and it was humbling. Her birth mother had cared in her own way. She had left her tokens as proof of it but that was all they were, tokens. They were nothing compared to the years of parenting; years of hard slog put in by her mother and father.

Eden pulled them close, as they cradled each other; as she tried to choke back breathless sobs, sticking in her throat like broken glass.

FORTY-TWO

Two emotional hours later, her father dropped her off at the bottom of Lemon Street as planned. She was all cried out.

'Are you okay?'

'Yes, a bit confused but I'm glad you told me.'

Her dad reached across, hugging her tightly. She could feel the heave of his dry sobs as he pressed his face into her hair.

'I'm so sorry, love.'

'It's okay, Dad … it's okay.'

Although shocked, she could honestly say she felt nothing but love for him. How could she be angry about what they'd done? Before this, she'd thought they'd sold out for her; joined the ranks of the nine til fives but this was so much more. They'd risked everything. Nothing had changed; her birth mother had still left her no matter which way you looked at it but at least now she had some understanding of why. She'd been so young; her whole life ahead of her, she must have felt overwhelmed. At least she cared enough to leave something for her to remember her by; showed she cared.

She was glad her parents hadn't told the authorities. If they had she may well have ended up in some children's home passed from foster home to foster home without any real hope of finding a proper family; worst still, they might have found her mother; forced the teenager to take her on. Who could say she wouldn't have blamed her for ruining her life; who's to say she wouldn't have reacted just like Rowan?

As she waved her father off she knew if this came out there would be repercussions for all of them but at least they'd face them together.

***

The elegant sweep of the buildings set on either side of the wide avenue ascended the steep hill from the centre of the city. A miracle of early eighteenth-century town planning, the honey-coloured stone houses could easily be mistaken for a Bath terrace.

Once the homes of mine captains and wealthy merchants eager to spend the fortunes they'd earnt trading tin and copper, the properties were now largely relegated to commercial use. On one side of the street, the multi-paned facades had been replaced with plate glass and housed a hub of trendy restaurants and high-end estate agents selling properties the locals couldn't afford. The side Eden chose housed mostly offices. Only very few of the grand three-storey buildings retained their residential status. Those that did were sub-divided into flats. These, Eden knew were mostly positioned towards the bottom of the hill from where she began her search. Lifting the keys from her bag, she pressed the fob, scanning the parked cars for any reaction; nothing.

She'd hoped to find Elspeth's vehicle parked up. Back to square one, she had no idea what number she was looking for and wished she taken a closer look at the driving licence when she'd tipped out the contents of the woman's bag. She could try ringing the museum to see if they knew her address but given how unhelpful the receptionist had been the last time she phoned, she doubted she'd be forthcoming. Luke would probably know of course or at least be able to find out but she had no intention of calling him. He'd only tell her to turn around and go home.

She concentrated on the houses with nets at the window rather than vertical blinds or advertisements. Making her way along the road, house by house, past insurance brokers, hairdressers and basement wine bars, she narrowed her search down to three properties.

She decided to try the first of these; a three-storey house accessed directly from the wide granite pavement via four steps. She noticed the narrow stairway leading down to the basement flat with its dingy courtyard. No doubt it had once been the servant's entrance. She stepped tentatively up to the glossy dark green door and pressed the brass doorbell.

If this was Elspeth's flat, she wouldn't expect anyone to answer but needed to make sure the coast was clear so she could use the key without arousing suspicion. She was about to reach into her pocket for the keys when the door opened and she was faced with a dapper grey-haired man, sporting a leather patched cardigan and red corduroys.

'Can I help you?'

'I hope so. I'm looking for a friend of mine. I'm meant to be calling around for coffee but have completely forgotten the address. I only know she has a flat in Lemon Street.'

'Well, I can probably help, there aren't many of us; we're a dying breed. I know most people who live hereabouts. I'm the chairman of the window box committee.'

Eden glanced across at the immaculate window box filled with vivid pink petunias and trailing purple lobelia.

'How lovely,' she gushed.

She watched as pride curled the corners of the man's mouth into a wide smile.

'What's your friend's name?'

'Elspeth … Elspeth Fuller.'

'Elspeth … of course, the museum lady, she's in the basement flat below. There's a bit of luck,' he smiled. 'I often take in deliveries for her from all over the place. China, South America, all over the world when she's out. I took one down this morning. It came yesterday but she wasn't in. Perhaps you could take it with you and save my legs?'

Eden could barely contain the relief she felt at finding the right place at the first attempt and now with the parcel she had an excuse to be there if anyone asked.

'I'd be delighted.'

The man walked back into his hallway and picked up a small parcel from the side table.

'You will tell her I tried earlier, won't you?'

'Of course.'

She could tell the old boy would have gladly talked all day given half a chance.

'Lovely to meet you but I really must go,' she said waving the parcel, 'Elspeth will be expecting me. I'll make sure she gets this.'

Eden walked back down to the pavement and turned left. Why the hell wasn't he closing the door?

Holding tightly to the wrought iron handrail in case she tripped, she made her way gingerly down the narrow granite steps to the basement flat. She could feel the man's eyes on her back and it crossed her mind he might be checking up on her in case she chose to do a runner with the package. Looking up, she waved; giving him her best smile. She remembered now why she'd never joined the neighbourhood watch committee at her complex. She heard the door above slam shut.

Finally, she thought.

Below ground level, she felt less conspicuous.

She peered through the window. The place was in darkness. As expected, it didn't look like anyone was in. Retrieving Elspeth's keys from her pocket she took a good look at the lock, trying to recall whether it could be classified as breaking and entering if you had keys to a property. Of course it could, if you stole the keys in the first place. Then again, how can you steal from a dead woman? In any case, she had no intention of permanently depriving anyone of them. When she'd finished, she'd deliver them back to Luke and that would be that. Someone had killed Elspeth and they had to have a reason. The most likely candidate was James and he and Rowan were in a relationship. Rowan was missing and she owed it to her and her family to try and find her, or more importantly to protect her from the same fate as Elspeth.

She had no idea why she'd taken the keys or how the nebulous notion had developed into this but something told her she'd find answers here.

She picked out the only Yale in the bunch looking as if it might fit. Slipping it into the lock she turned it and opened the door.

FORTY-THREE

The passage ran from the front to the back of the flat and was dark; even darker once she closed the door behind her. The black and white tiled floor gave it an echoey, chilly feel and she shivered. The three doors to her right were closed but through the open archway at the end, she could see into a room with patio doors out to a garden beyond. She could hear nothing but the steady beat of her heart thumping. Inhaling deeply, she steadied herself before continuing. The last thing she wanted was to faint again.

Hugging the wall; dado rail digging into the small of her back, she moved slowly and quietly, half expecting one of the doors opposite to fly open. At the end, she peered into an empty room stretching the width of the building and listened for signs of life before entering cautiously.

At one end was a small kitchen area. The rest of the room was taken up with a sofa and two enormous armchairs, placed on either side of an unlit wood burner. The furnishings looked comfortable but a musty dankness Eden remembered from her basement-living student days lingered in the air; a memory reinforced by a pair of jeans drying on a radiator.

Although the flat was obviously Elspeth's; two alcove bookshelves stacked with historic memoirs and an etching above the hearth of the ancient world, testimony to it; there was an incongruity troubling her. Scanning the mantlepiece with its carefully positioned shards of broken pottery she realised it was the general lack of clutter. The room was extraordinarily tidy. It had none of the haphazard eccentricity she'd expected.

Eden knew only too well how living on your own afforded you the luxury of not having to consider others. There was no one to complain if you shaved your legs in the bath or left the washing up until the next morning. If last Sunday's supplements were still on the table unopened a week later so what, you'd get around to reading them when you were good and ready. It was one of the perks of a single life and one she didn't relish ever giving up again.

She'd met Elspeth and there was no way this anally retentive tidiness was down to her. She had a clear picture of how the professor's flat would look. Stacks of books on the windowsill; colourful coats and scarves hanging on the back of the door; an old radio, lots of half-dead pot plants and long grey hairs clinging to the back of the soft furnishings. This place looked like a show house with a viewing booked that afternoon.

She opened the fridge. Unlike her own, it was full. Milk, eggs, chicken fillets; the bottom drawer brimming over with salad and veg. She picked up a bottle of semi-skimmed and sniffed it; still fresh.

Piled neatly on the small breakfast bar was the post. Putting down the parcel, she checked the details. It was all addressed to Elspeth. Nothing interesting; a couple of bills, what looked like a bank statement and a glossy invitation for a private viewing at a local art gallery a few doors down.

Eden was about to steal herself to search the other rooms when out of the corner of her eye, she noticed the dishwasher light was on. She walked over to it. Unlike her one at home which she rarely used (a couple of cups and a takeaway container not warranting the electricity) this one was almost silent and she hadn't noticed it was on before then. She felt the warmth and whir of the machine under her hand.

Someone else is here; she thought, someone's running the bloody dishwasher and one thing's for sure it's not Elspeth. That's why the fridge is full; why the place looks like this.

For a second, she was completely thrown. She tried the patio door leading to the rear garden; locked. The only way out was the way she'd come. She'd had some crazy notion of finding clues to her client's whereabouts but what if she'd stumbled upon a killer instead? James had a key to this place. The murder weapon could be in the dishwasher and he could come back at any minute to put it back in the drawer so no one would be any the wiser. She'd be trapped.

She needed to get out of there, fast.

She headed for the front door; heart bashing against her chest cavity as she reached for the catch. As her clumsy, fumbling fingers grabbed it, a voice echoed from behind.

'Eden?'

She froze. Unpeeling her fingers from the latch.

FORTY-FOUR

She turned to face Rowan.

The girl stood in the hallway as insubstantial as a ghost.

Wearing only a thin baggy t-shirt and her knickers; her feet and stick-thin legs bare; she looked like a sleepy child who'd stumbled into her parents' bedroom in the middle of the night.

'What are you doing here?' she asked, her voice groggy.

'I might ask you the same thing,' Eden replied. 'Have you any idea of the trouble you've caused; how worried your mother has been?'

Rowan turned her back on her and began to walk along the corridor to the living room. Eden followed, incredulous at the girl's *laissez-faire* attitude as she watched her stretch up to take a glass from one of the kitchen cupboards and run some water from the tap as if she had all the time in the world. She drained it in four large gulps before filling it again and carrying it to the mantlepiece. Slumping down into one of the armchairs next to the unlit wood burner she pulled a crochet blanket across her legs.

'Well, sit down then, if you're staying?'

Eden was furious.

'What the hell are you playing at? You're facing a manslaughter charge and have breached your bail conditions. There's a warrant out for your arrest, yet you're acting as if you haven't got a care in the world. I've asked you before and I'll ask you again; are you taking drugs because frankly, I'm beginning to think you must be? You seem to be unable to comprehend how much trouble you're in. If you don't tell me what the hell's going on right now, you can find yourself another lawyer because I've had enough.'

Eden felt her phone vibrate in her back pocket. It was Luke. She knew she had to speak to him. He'd only call again if she didn't.

'Hi, how's it going?' she asked, trying not to sound like she was about to burst a blood vessel. She glanced over at Rowan who was staring vacantly out towards the garden. Should she tell Luke she'd found her?

'I rang to check you're okay and to let you know Rowan's DNA results are finally back and she is as we thought, the baby's biological mother. I know you said you'll be applying to exclude the DNA evidence at trial but I thought you should know. At least you'll be able to run the infanticide defence, that is if we manage to find your client, of course.'

He paused and she didn't know what to say, her cheeks burning with the deception.

'Sam brought my car back. He told me he dropped you back at your parents' place.'

'Yes, he did.'

That much was true at least.

'They've arrested James and Carrie at Gatwick. boarding a plane to LA. They're on their way back to Cornwall to be interviewed.'

'What about Elspeth?'

Rowan's head shot around at the mention of the name.

'Her body's been taken to the pathology lab. SOCO are still at the site but I'm going to make my way back to the station to prepare for the interview. I'll catch up with you later. Make sure you take it easy.'

'I will,' she said, 'see you later.'

She felt bad not telling him the truth but she would see to it Rowan reported to the station. She would drag her there by her tatty hair if she had to.

'Who was that?' asked Rowan.

'DI Parish.'

'Does he know you're here?'

'No.'

'Why didn't you tell him you've found me then?' Rowan asked, a satisfied smirk creeping across her face.

'Oh, don't worry I will, but I want to talk to you first. I want to allow you to tell me what you know without the benefit of your convenient memory loss.'

Rowan shrugged. Curling her legs under her in the chair she pulled the blanket up to her chin.

Creating a physical barrier, Eden thought. Okay if she wants to play it like that.

'Right,' she said, 'let's approach this another way. How about I tell you what I know first?'

Rowan said nothing, her expressionless face a study in muscular atrophy.

'Luke has just told me your DNA results are back and they confirm the baby's yours. So, with one half of the equation complete why don't you tell me who the father is?'

A twitch of the lip.

'I'll take that as no comment,' Eden continued undeterred. 'It doesn't matter, I already know the answer. I know Jessica Marshall paid you five thousand pounds to sleep with her husband hoping he'd get you pregnant and that the two of you kept the plan a secret from Philip who remained petrified his wife would find out he was the biological father of your child. I know the poor man is grieving for his dead son and his grief is real. I know you on the other hand have shown not the slightest sign of remorse for the baby you have lost or what you've done to that couple.'

'It's not my fault things went wrong. Jessica came up with the idea. They started this,' Rowan muttered.

'Yes, I'll give you that, but you finished it, didn't you? You finished it in spectacular style when you killed the baby, or should I say when you and James Ferris killed the baby?'

Eden watching the girl's expression change was determined to keep chipping away at her stony-faced resolve. 'Yes, I know all about you and James.'

'You don't know anything about us.'

'Oh, but I do. In fact, I'm pretty sure I know more about James Ferris than you do. For instance, I'm sure you don't have a clue where he is right now whereas I do; I know exactly where he is and what he's been up to.'

'Where ... where is he?'

'He's with his other girlfriend on the way back to Cornwall to be interviewed by the police.'

'What other girlfriend; what are you talking about?'

Rowan threw the blanket onto the floor and lunged towards Eden, wielding an accusing finger like a knife.

'Sit down,' Eden shouted, grabbing the jeans from the radiator and throwing them at her; 'put some bloody clothes on and sit down, or I call DI Parish back.'

The girl seemed taken aback at the ferocity of her reprimand, and to Eden's relief backed down. She watched her wriggle into the jeans and sit, gripping the arms of the chair as if she wanted to kill it.

'James was arrested with Carrie, the American girl from the dig. They were stopped boarding a plane to Los Angeles.'

'You're lying.'

Rowan was up from her seat again, this time pacing the room.

'He wouldn't leave me. He's meant to be picking me up later when it's dark. He wouldn't leave me ... he wouldn't. We love each other. He's coming for me tonight and we're leaving this dump for good; we've got a plan.'

'He's got a plan alright; I think he's had a plan all along only you've overplayed your part in it; outlived your usefulness and his plans don't include you.'

Face like thunder, Rowan looked as if she might hit her.

'You don't know anything. What could you possibly know about love? You, with your fancy job; living on your own; you haven't got a clue; you frigid bitch.'

'I know what love isn't. It isn't wheedling your way into the affections of a young girl desperate to escape her boring life because you think she might have inside information that could benefit you.'

'That's a lie.'

'It's not lying to your employer, then killing her when she finds out.'

Rowan stopped pacing. 'What do you mean, killing his employer?'

'Elspeth Fuller is dead. Her body was discovered earlier today. She's been murdered; her body thrown naked down the well at the site.'

The girl buckled. Eden grabbed her and sat her down, handing her the glass of water from the mantlepiece. She took a sip and handed it back, her face grey.

'James wouldn't. He never ... he wouldn't kill Elspeth. Why would he? She knew all along what was going on. It was her idea.'

'What?'

'You need to see something.'

Rowan slid from her seat and shuffled to the doorway. Pausing for a second to steady herself against the frame, she walked out of the room into the hall and opened the first door to her left. Eden followed.

Curtains pulled, the room was dark until Rowan switched on the light, to reveal it was piled high with boxes of all shapes and sizes; all numbered and stamped;

FRAGILE HANDLE WITH CARE

'What is all this?'

'The finds from the site; that box over there's the swan pelt.' Rowan pointed to a large square box in one corner of the room. 'The numbers are catalogued on Elspeth's computer, that's how I know.'

'Why aren't they at the site?'

'They're here to be picked up and taken by boat to France; then shipped to collectors all around the world.'

'Collectors?'

'Do I have to spell it out for you?'

'I think you better had.'

'Elspeth deals in artefacts; some from the site, some from excavations she's been involved with in the past and some via connections she's got with other archaeologists abroad doing the same thing. The finds get sent to her and moved on.'

'And she gets paid for this?'

'God yes; loads. According to James, there are tons of collectors out there, wanting to get hold of stuff like this. That it's illegal makes it all the more attractive for people like them, with money to burn. It doesn't matter they can't show them off; that they've got to be locked away. They know they've got them and to a collector that's all that counts.'

'Elspeth didn't seem to be the kind of person to care about money. She seemed committed to what she did.'

'Oh, she is …was committed alright. She used the money to fund more digs. If she didn't sell the artefacts to pay for the excavations, they wouldn't happen. She was all about unravelling the history and all this was the price she had to pay for the privilege. She didn't care about the stuff going to collectors as long as they took care of it. She didn't think us plebs could be trusted with it anyways.'

'But she told me the council was funding the excavation?'

'Yeah right, like they're awash with money with all the cuts. The funding came from Elspeth; from the money she got from selling this stuff.' Rowan waved her arm across the boxes.

Eden thought of the package the neighbour had given her and rushed back to the kitchen to retrieve it from the counter where she'd left it. She tore open the padded brown envelope, ripping free a tight binding of grey plastic bag to reveal a wad of cash; twenty-pound notes, about five thousand pounds altogether.

'Told you,' Rowan said, over her shoulder.

Eden had never heard the girl talk so much.

'When you say she wanted publicity do you mean the publicity that came with the discovery of the baby?'

'Not at first. She thought it would draw unwanted attention but James pointed out to her it was a way of escalating interest in the site. She needed some publicity, not for the site as such but to ramp up the interest in the artefacts. She hadn't had much luck getting interest before because the finds weren't the usual pots or jewellery and didn't have a context, that's why she wanted Mum and Morvah on board. She'd rung both of them asking them for stuff on the family history; the witch pits and the old rituals but Mum wasn't interested and Morvah wouldn't even answer her calls. James knew the notoriety would prompt collectors to come forward. After that she encouraged him to start a blog and post on Facebook about fertility rituals and stuff. She didn't know about him and me of course or it was my baby.'

'Did the plan work?'

'Yeah, too well. James underestimated the public reaction. Then when I was arrested, with the police presence, although they had loads of interest from all over the world, not only from the usual collectors but from those into the occult and all that shit, they were afraid to transport the finds from the site. In the end, she brought the whole lot here with the aim of moving it on without attracting attention.'

'Rowan, when did you first meet James?'

'He came to the cafe to ask me what I knew about the witch pits and Wicca. I told him not much, which was the truth. I'd seen a few things about the house to do with the rituals and I knew Mum had an old book in the attic that had been handed down to her full of symbols and charms but not much else.'

'And the romantic relationship started almost immediately?'

'Yes, but how did you know; we didn't tell anyone?'

'Maisy.'

'Maisy?'

'Maisy saw James kiss you.'

'Maisy ...' sighed Rowan. 'We started seeing each other and it got more serious but I was already pregnant and knew I had to tell him.'

'How pregnant?'

'A few weeks.'

'With Philip Marshall's baby?'

'Yes.'

'Is that why you wanted a termination because you didn't want to tell James?'

'Of course, but then it all got out of hand. Philip wanted the baby and Jess had paid me already. It was all so fucked up. I was going to end it with James but then he confided in me about Elspeth.'

'You mean about the smuggling?'

'Yeah. He told me that when he started on the dig, he didn't know what she was doing; had no idea what was going on but then stuff started disappearing and he got suspicious. He held back because he needed the job and by the time he was sure, he was already involved and scared because he knew too much. He needed money to get away. So, when I finally told him about the baby, he was pleased. We planned to take the ten thousand and the five Jessica had given me before and leave as soon as the baby was born.'

'Did James ask you to get the book for him?'

'Not then, that came later when I'd lost the baby and had to give the money back. He said it was our way out. He said whatever it contained was valuable and we needed it, so I told him I'd get it but then I was arrested. I didn't know if I'd get bail, so he had to get it himself. That's why he started the fire.'

'James started the fire in the barn as a distraction?'

Rowan hesitated; 'Yes, but he didn't mean for it to go up like it did. He looked for the book during the fire but it wasn't there?'

'So, you took the book when you ran away?'

'Yes, James has it now …' Eden noticed she hesitated slightly as if running something through her head before continuing. 'Elspeth never knew anything about the book. It was our insurance, something to bargain with but things didn't go as planned.'

They were finally getting somewhere. Now for the part Eden had been dreading.

'Rowan, I need to know what happened the night the baby was born?'

'I went into labour early.'

'I need you to take me through it step by step.'

Rowan took a deep breath. 'Like I said I went into labour. James came around to the flat that night. He brought a pizza and a bottle of wine, though, I didn't drink, because of the baby. I was fine all evening. We watched a film and James had some weed on him and we had a smoke.'

'Hang on you told me you passed on the wine because of the baby; now you're telling me you smoked weed?'

'Weed doesn't harm them; it's brilliant for morning sickness.'

Eden couldn't believe what she was hearing.

'It's not illegal everywhere, loads of countries have legalised it,' Rowan said, eyes wide as if aghast at Eden's ignorance.

'Yes, I do know that but I'm questioning whether it's appropriate for pregnant women to take it?'

'Well, all I know is when I first got pregnant, I was sick all the time. Working in the cafe was hell. The constant smell of food made me throw up; I couldn't keep anything down. Then I read up about what might help and weed came tops. I didn't take much; a couple of puffs during the day and suddenly I could keep food down. When the sickness stopped, I stopped.'

'If that's the case, why were you taking it the night the baby was born?'

'I hadn't had a good night's sleep for days. The baby was getting bigger and kicking all the time and no matter which way I turned in the bed, I couldn't get comfortable. James suggested it might relax me and help me get off to sleep, and it worked.'

'You went to bed?'

'I don't remember falling asleep. The next thing I remember is James waking me and telling me the baby had come.'

'Are you asking me to believe you slept right through the birth?'

'You can believe it or not, that's what happened. I woke and James was standing over me. The covers were off and my legs were apart; you know with my ankles together but my knees splayed and he was holding the baby.'

Eden's stomach roiled.

'It was fine at first. I laughed; had a fit of the giggles. I'd been dreading going into labour and I'd had the baby in my sleep, it was brilliant but then I noticed James's expression.' She hesitated slightly and took a sip of water. 'He looked, like, disappointed as if something had happened and when I asked him what was wrong, he didn't answer.' She pulled the words from deep inside her, regurgitating them slowly as if each one caught in her throat like a cherry stone.

'So, I looked properly.'

Eden reached out instinctively to touch her hand.

'I saw the baby wasn't moving. It lay there all bloody, between my legs and I looked at James and he looked at me and we both knew the baby was dead.'

'How did you know; why were you both so sure; who said it first, you or James? It's important who knew first.'

'Neither of us said anything. I looked at James's face, then down at the baby. I was there when Morvah delivered Maisy. I know what a baby looks like when it's born and this one wasn't wriggling or making any noise; it just lay there grey and lifeless.'

Eden wanted to shout; it wasn't lifeless because it was still breathing when it was buried.

Rowan had slept through childbirth. Hadn't it occurred to her the baby might have slept through it too; the poor little thing's system was full of cannabis, like hers, and if they'd called for help it might have survived? Eden bit her tongue.

'What happened next?' she asked.

'I told James to cut the cord. I'd seen Morvah do that too. I told him to get some scissors and he did it.'

'Then what?'

'I kept falling back to sleep; I was so tired. I think James took the sheet from the bed and wrapped the baby in it.'

'What was he going to do with it?'

'I didn't ask. I knew it was too late to do anything; it was dead. I knew we'd have to give the money back.'

Eden felt a wave of revulsion, knowing Rowan thought about money at that moment. She'd just given birth; witnessed the death of her baby and all she thought about was the loss of her reward. Her mind turned to Mary Bluet, more concerned about her reputation than the loss of her child. At least she felt shame. Rowan felt none. Eden couldn't imagine anything worse than witnessing the death of a child; any child, yet Rowan was relaying the most horrific of stories imaginable and talking about it as if it was something she'd seen the night before on Netflix. She'd only shown emotion once when she talked about James's face; that he looked disappointed. Eden suddenly realised what she meant. He was disappointed because they wouldn't get the money for the baby, now it was dead. She swallowed her disgust.

'So, the story you told me and the police about searching for the baby was a lie?'

'Yes.' It was the first time she'd looked ashamed.

'Do you remember anything after that?'

'No.'

'When did you find out the baby had been buried?'

'James told me when he got back early the next morning, he'd buried the baby in one of the empty pits. He said they'd stopped the digging there so it was safe but then that boy on the site found it.'

Eden knew the truth. James had engineered the baby's discovery and poor Sam had been targeted as a useful decoy in a bigger plan just like Rowan, but there was no point telling her. Rowan's loyalty to James wouldn't be shaken by anything she had to say.

'Did he say why he hadn't rung for help?'

'He panicked because we'd been smoking weed. He thought they'd call the police and there would be an investigation.'

'So, let's be clear Rowan.; you're telling me James took the baby and buried it thinking it was dead and you both continued to believe that until you heard from the police the child had been alive when buried?'

'Yes.'

Eden believed her. Rowan had been reckless, selfish beyond belief, but she hadn't been physically capable so soon after giving birth of burying the baby and for what it was worth although James had engineered its discovery she believed he, like Rowan, thought the child was dead.

Her client wasn't innocent by any standard but she wasn't guilty of killing her baby. She needed to get her to the station so she could finally give a full statement but first, she needed to take her home to see her mother. She owed Carmen that much.

FORTY-FIVE

Luke received the call from Denise on route to the station.

'Are you on the way?' she asked.

'Yeah.'

'Could you pull over for a second to look at some photos e-mailed through from the pathologist? I think you might want to take a detour to the lab before you come here once you've seen them.'

'Where are Ferris and the American girl?'

'They've been picked up from Newquay airport. By the time they've been in front of the custody officer and separated for interview, it'll be a good couple of hours. You've got time to get there and back.'

'What's in the photographs?' Luke asked, curious what could be so urgent.

'I can't describe them; you'll have to see for yourself but I think you'll want to take a proper look before you conduct the interview. The pathologist is waiting for consent to take fluids. He's got nothing yet other than what's in the photographs but it's relevant.'

'Okay send them through. I'll pull over and ring you back once I've had a gander.'

Luke pulled over into the next layby and turned off the engine. He reached for his phone, clicked the message then waited patiently for the attachments to download. Peering at the tiny screen it was difficult to make them out. A series of fine lines drawn across a pale background. He wondered what this had to do with the mud-covered body of Elspeth Fuller until he realised, he was staring at her lily-white skin, washed free of its slimy coating. The pictures were close-ups, making it hard to identify what part of her body he was looking at.

He clicked each of the attachments in succession. He discerned from the only photo taken sufficiently far back to give any perspective, it and the others were of Elspeth's torso; in particular her back. What the marks represented and what they'd been made with was not so clear. Eventually, he managed to achieve the best resolution possible and saw the lines joined to make a series of symbols. They meant nothing to him and were partially obscured because of the flat angle of the shot, taken from the bottom of the gurney by Elspeth's feet. However, one thing was clear; the lines weren't drawn they were carved; etched into Elspeth's bloated flesh. Whether the disfigurement was post-mortem he couldn't tell. If not, the woman must have suffered. The skin was puckered and engorged around the point of impact and was now inlaid with black mud; shallow ditches across her swollen back.

He called Denise, who answered right away.

'You've looked at them?'

'Yeah but my phone's not great and the definition's not that good. What did the marks look like on the larger screen; did you think the lines had been carved into her rather than drawn?'

'Definitely; that's what the pathologist thinks too.'

'It looks like some kind of symbol to me rather than random gashes.'

'At first, because of the shape he thought it was one of those Russian tattoos, you know the kind you see on gang members, recording their prison history; but then we all thought about it and wondered if it was something Celtic or Pagan, but we're all guessing, no one knows.'

'That's hardly surprising, they don't come across many Russian gangsters or ritually carved victims in the Truro path lab.'

'No, I don't suppose they do. Is there anyone else who might know?'

'Well James Ferris might but we can't rely on him. We need an independent opinion.'

'It certainly narrows down the list of suspects.'

Luke suddenly had an idea. 'There is someone else who might be able to help,' he said. 'Look rather than go to the path lab I'm going to see Carmen Lutey; she should at least be able to tell us whether or not the symbols are Pagan or Celtic.? It's only a short detour. You process Ferris and the American girl and I'll get there as soon as I can. If you have to start without me, take the girl first. She might tell us something useful we can use against James in his interview.'

FORTY-SIX

Eden decided not to ring ahead in case anything went wrong. Carmen had suffered enough disappointments. It wasn't until she'd paid the taxi driver and they were through the front door she was certain Rowan wasn't going to make a run for it. She'd managed to persuade her she needed to confess to her mother before telling anyone else.

Rowan had initially been intent on going straight to the station; desperate to see James. In fact, James seemed to be the only one she cared about. It was only after Eden told her she wouldn't be allowed to see him she backed down and agreed to go home.

The front door was open but Carmen was nowhere in sight. Rowan entered carrying the small rucksack she had left with; walking confidently through to the kitchen as if she hadn't been missing the best part of a week. She wandered nonchalantly to the fridge; looked inside then shut the door without taking anything.

Carmen emerged from the hallway carrying a stack of tea towels which she dropped on seeing her daughter.

'Rowan, I've been so worried,' she cried, suffocating the girl in a bone-crushing maternal squeeze.

'Mum you're smothering me.'

Eden watched the ice-princess thaw in her mother's embrace.

'I've been beside myself thinking all sorts. To have you home; I can't tell you how thankful I am.'

Holding Rowan at arm's length; she scrutinised her face for signs of trauma, injury and hunger, Eden guessed, as frowning, she walked to the bread bin, cut a thick slice of bread and pushed it in front of a daughter.'

'Eat!'

'I'm afraid this is a flying visit,' said Eden. 'I need to get Rowan to the station. They'll want a statement. I haven't let them know

I've found her yet but she's breached her bail conditions and I think they'll keep her in custody tonight given everything that's going on.'

Carmen looked hard at Rowan now. 'Where have you been all this time?'

The girl took a strategic bite of the bread.

'Rowan has a lot to tell you and the sooner she starts the sooner we can sort things out. I'm going to leave you two alone to discuss things for half an hour and then I'll take Rowan with me. Okay Rowan?' She gave the girl a fixed stare, to make it clear she had no room for manoeuvre.

'Okay,' Rowan replied so meekly it made Eden immediately suspicious.

'I'll wait for you in the car. I trust your mum to make sure you don't run again. It'll only be worse for you if you do.'

'Don't worry, I won't let her out of my sight.'

***

Eden left the pair to talk, knowing much of what Rowan had to say would be unpalatable. The drugs; the sordid way the baby died; the scheming and lying but she also knew her client had enough bare-faced cheek to spin it so she appeared an innocent bystander; it was her speciality. In her version she and James would be victims of circumstance; star-crossed lovers with Elspeth Fuller the villain of the piece. Once, Carmen would have fallen for it hook line and sinker but now, Eden wasn't so sure. She, like everyone involved in this case, had come to expect the unexpected; to understand people were not necessarily all they seemed. She hadn't mentioned Elspeth's murder, realising it might be too much for Carmen to handle in one sitting. She wondered if Rowan would divulge it or at least tell her about Elspeth's plans to sell the artefacts. If she did, Eden was sure it would be on the back of defending James.

The car felt like a safe and familiar place to rewind the day's events. That morning seemed a lifetime away; sitting in the kitchen talking to the Lutey children and working out James Ferris was Rowan's boyfriend.

She pulled out her notebook. She needed to remember her role here. The boundaries had been blurred. She'd turned into one of those lawyers straight out of a novel, working out the back of her car. It was satisfying, she couldn't deny it; perhaps a little too satisfying? She needed to leave the investigating to the police from here on in. Her duty was to build a defence and it was already worming its way through her mind.

Rowan had told her things she needed to record contemporaneously before they had time to change in the minds of the teller and the listener. Looking at the facts it was hard to see how the police would be able to continue with the manslaughter charge. Yes, she'd taken drugs but she hadn't taken them with the view to hurt the child. On the contrary, she thought the cannabis was harmless.

She truly believed she'd given birth to a stillborn baby. It could be argued she should have reported it to the authorities but she was so far out of it when this happened, she was not fit for anything and events took over. James was the reckless one. He was the one who had supplied the drugs and it was he who decided not to report the birth to the authorities and bury the child.

It wouldn't be necessary for the prosecution to argue he did it on purpose for the manslaughter charge to stick in his case. He'd been negligent and that was enough to secure a conviction. Rowan on the other hand was not capable of making decisions and was not complicit until after the event. She had of course perverted the course of justice by lying but that was a very different proposition than a manslaughter charge. She had the benefit of mitigating factors leading directly from the traumatic birth of the child and its subsequent discovery. She had no doubt Rowan would avoid a custodial sentence.

Eden had all but finished her statement of events when she heard a car surge into the courtyard, prompting her to look up. It was Luke. There was no point trying to hide, he'd already seen her. Dropping her notes on the passenger seat she got out of her car and walked towards him. Luke's eyes locked on hers. She had no idea why he was here. He was meant to be at the station interviewing James Ferris; it was him who asked the question first.

'What are you doing here, you're meant to be with your parents?'

'I was, but I got dropped off in town and took a taxi here. I need to talk to you before you go in.'

'I'm in a rush. I need to ask Carmen her opinion on some photos of Elspeth's body.'

'Photos?'

'She could tell from his face he wasn't going to divulge anything else.'

'It'll only take a minute; I need to fill you in.'

'Okay, but five minutes is all I can spare.'

A drop of rain fell on Eden's cheek.

'Shall we sit in my car?'

As soon as they settled in their seats the skies opened and the few drops turned into a squally downpour, battering the roof.

'Rowan's inside,' Eden said.

'What, she's come home?'

'Not exactly. I found her at Elspeth's flat.'

Luke turned to face her. He didn't speak and she almost blurted out the whole story in her desperate need to fill the accusatory silence.

'What the hell were you doing at Elspeth Fuller's flat?'

'I don't know and that's the truth; I don't know why. I thought I'd find Rowan, and I did. Sam told me James had stayed there before and I had a feeling she might be there.'

Disbelief scuttled across his face.

'Are you telling me you broke into a murder victim's home?'

'I didn't break in; I used her keys.'

'Her keys?'

'From the bag; I took the keys before I gave it back to Denise.'

'For Christ's sake, Eden.'

'Well, I found her didn't I, which is more than you lot did? She's inside now with her mother. I found something else as well.'

'Go on then,' he said, 'surprise me.'

'She pulled the parcel of notes from her bag and handed it to him.

'What's this?'

'One of the rooms was packed with boxes and when I asked Rowan what they were she told me they were artefacts. She said Elspeth was planning to sell them to private collectors and she'd done it before. It's all here.' She handed him her notebook. 'I've written everything down. The money must be from one of Elspeth's customers.'

'Was James in on this?'

'A reluctant participant according to Rowan but she might not know the true position, after all, she certainly didn't know about Carrie.'

Luke's eyes travelled up and down the page several times until finally he closed the notebook and handed it back to her.

'Thanks,' he said with reticence, 'you did well, although it was probably the most reckless, stupid thing I've ever come across. You didn't have a clue what you'd find. We don't know who killed Elspeth; what if you'd come across the killer? James is a suspect, nothing more as yet. It was a stupid thing to do, Eden.'

She knew he was right.

He reached for the door. The car was steamy with conversation and it was good to feel the fresh air. The rain had eased but it still felt muggy, and walking to the house they had to dodge the rivulets of muddy water trickling through the cobbles.

Opening the door, the din of laughter hit them. The children had been forced in from their play by the rain. Carmen was rubbing Maisy's hair dry with a towel. Jago warmed himself by the range. Rosy faces turned on them as they entered.

Rowan was at the table, a large bowl of soup in front of her.

'You called him,' she said, her face rigid with contempt, 'you said you wouldn't.'

'I didn't call him,' Eden replied. She was tired of having to constantly re-forge the links she made with the girl.

'I came here of my own accord to see your mother,' said Luke.

Rowan didn't reply.

'Eden can follow me to the station with you when you've finished eating.'

Eden sensed his patience with the girl was wearing thin. He knew she'd lied through her teeth and any sympathy he may have felt for her now evaporated like the condensation in the car. She felt much the same way. She was finding it increasingly difficult to disentangle the girl from the acts or omissions leading to her baby's death. She'd continue to defend her; she'd taken on the job and she'd see it through to the end but her instincts had been right about her. She was a self-centred little bitch.

'Carmen, do you think I could speak to you for a minute alone, I've got something I need to show you?'

'Me?'

'Yes, if you don't mind?' He looked at his watch. 'Now, if that's okay with you, I'm in a bit of a hurry.'

'Of course,' she said, giving Maisy's hair one last rub before slipping the wet towel over the range to dry. Do you need Rowan too?' she asked, looking at her daughter.

'No just you, thanks,' Luke smiled gently at the woman who, perturbed, was putting on a brave face for the children's sake.

Rowan remained silent, spooning tomato soup into her mouth.

'Come on you two,' Eden chirped; taking up the task of drying the children in the absence of any move by their big sister to help.

'What's he doing with Mum? asked Jago. 'He's not taking her away like he did our Rowan is he?'

The little boy's face was awash with worry.

'No, of course not. Your mum's very clever; he needs her help.' Eden felt his tense little shoulders relax under the towel with the reprieve.

'Look at my hair. It goes all curly with the rain,' said Maisy, pulling a ringlet out from her head and letting it spring back with a giggle.

'Don't you ever shut up?' sniped Rowan.

'I do when I'm sleeping.'

'Pity you're not asleep more often, perhaps then you'd mind your own business and keep your mouth shut.'

The little girl's bottom lip curled.

Eden knew Rowan was referring to her sister spilling the beans about her and James.

'That's enough, Rowan.'

Rowan looked up; dark eyes defiant as ever.

'Why don't you two go and play in your bedroom now you're dry?' said Eden herding the children towards the door. Glad to take up the suggestion, they ran off.

'That was spiteful and uncalled for; she's a little girl.'

'A pain in the ass is what she is but that's what comes of having babies when you're too old for it. Matthew and me never got away with half as much as her and Jago do.'

Eden didn't bother to answer. The chip on Rowan's shoulder was cavernous and would never be filled; she enjoyed having it far too much. It was something she'd come to rely on as an excuse for every wrong she committed, every mistake she made and it was tedious. Just as it was with her sister. Like Thea, it would eventually blight Rowan's life and that of everyone who loved her.

FORTY- SEVEN

Carmen led Luke into the sitting room. He could tell she was nervous; not knowing what to expect. He wasn't at all sure how to prepare her for what he intended to show her; he wasn't sure you could prepare anyone for that.

'Carmen, I don't know if Eden told you but we found Elspeth Fuller's body down the old well at the site earlier today; we believe she was murdered.'

'The archaeologist lady you mean? That's terrible; who would do such a thing?' Her face was a study of concern.

'We don't know but think it could be James Ferris. Apparently, Elspeth was involved with selling artefacts from the site to private collectors. It may be something to do with that; we don't know but Elspeth's body was marked.'

'Marked?'

'With symbols. We're not sure what they are but they must have some relevance. I wonder whether you might be able to identify them; tell us whether they're Pagan? Don't worry if you haven't a clue. That in itself will be helpful; it will rule out certain lines of inquiry. I don't want you to guess, only tell me if you definitely recognise the symbols and if you do, what they mean?'

'I see,' she said, nervously. 'I'll do my best.'

Luke handed over his phone. 'Take your time,' he said, watching the woman carefully scroll through the photographs. She paused at each one saying nothing but nodding occasionally in what he hoped was recognition. When she reached the distance shot; the one definable as an image of a dead woman's body, she shuddered and moved quickly on.

'Yes,' she said solemnly, handing back the phone.

'Are you saying you recognise the symbols?'

'Yes, I'm afraid I do. The first; the one drawn on her stomach is the Triple Moon, the moon in all its phases. The full moon in the centre; to the left the waxing moon; to the right, waning. The moon is feminine. It is a symbol of feminine power.'

Luke scribbled as she spoke.

'And the other; the one on her back is the Witch's Knot. If drawn in a single stroke it has protective powers, others use it to bind or control. Some say it can even control the weather. Then there are the other two.'

'I'm sorry; what other two?'

'Look at the third photograph.'

Luke punched in his code, opening the attachments again.

'Look at her shoulder blades.'

Luke could see nothing. 'Show me,' he said handing the phone back to Carmen.

She took it and zoomed in on the marks she'd seen.

'There, do you see them; three lines like the imprint a bird makes in the sand, on each of her shoulders?'

Luke looked again; she was right. On each shoulder the sign of the letter V with a single line drawn vertically from the centre.

'What does it mean?'

'The symbol of the goddess Bride. Whoever made these marks understood their relevance. The first two are mainstream; they could be found in any book on Wicca or Celtic symbolism but the two on the shoulder blades relate directly to the site. They are the bird's foot; the sign of the Swan.'

With those words, Carmen began to roll up her sleeve. There, tattooed on the pale inside of her wrist was the same sign. She rolled the sleeve back down again.

Her eyes swept the floor. 'That poor woman, to think someone could do that to her. Do you think it was done while she was alive?'

'Probably not,' he was glad to reply.

'Well, that's something, I suppose.'

'Thank you, thank you so much; that's helpful and it couldn't have been easy.'

They joined the others in the kitchen.

'All done?' asked Eden eager to know what had been said.

'Yes; are you both ready to go?' asked Luke.

'As ready as we'll ever be,' replied Eden.

Carmen hugged Rowan. 'Bye, my love. Now you listen to Eden, she's been a good friend to you and this family; you do as she says.'

Rowan silently hugged her mother back.

***

Carmen's throat ached as she waved her daughter goodbye. Terrible as it was to think of what lay ahead for her, it was not as terrible as the other thought that began to smoulder in her mind; a thought she couldn't stifle no matter how much she tried. The smooth regular lines perfectly drawn; the Triple Moon, Witch's Knot and of course the sign of Bride. Only the most practised could draw them so perfectly even with a pen and paper. To carve them into a person's back and stomach so precisely took skill of a different kind. There was only one person who could have made those marks with such accuracy; only one person who truly knew their meaning and understood their power.

FORTY-EIGHT

They arrived at the station in tandem. It had been a long and exhausting day and it wasn't over yet. Luke walked them to the main doors. Sidling up close to Eden he whispered,

'Give me the keys.'

'What?'

'Elspeth's keys, give them to me.'

Eden reached into her pocket and surreptitiously slipped the pom-pom keyring into Luke's hand, their fingers briefly touching.

'Let me do the talking,' he mumbled under his breath.

There was a different atmosphere in the station; the high-octane vibe that accompanied a breakthrough in a murder enquiry and an unmistakable buzz of anticipation.

Luke ignored the hubbub, directing his attention to the custody officer behind the desk.

'Evening Mike, I've got Rowan Lutey here with her solicitor. She's surrendered to custody.'

'Seen sense at last then, has she?' replied the man flicking a wry look at Rowan from under the rim of his glasses as he flipped to a clean page in the record.

'Do you want to interview her? I'm only asking because two and three are occupied already.'

Eden guessed he meant they were occupied by James Ferris and his American friend.

'I don't need an interview room yet but I need someone to take a statement. Denise can take it in my office if there's nowhere else available.'

'Fair enough, she said to let you know when you got here. She wanted to speak to you before you got started, she said to say she's heard more from the pathologist.'

Eden listened in. She was pretty sure he'd want to talk to Denise too before she took Rowan's statement. He'd want to brief her on the information she'd given him in her notes.

Once he'd finished booking Rowan in, he nodded to Eden to take a seat with her client.

'Where's James?' whispered Rowan as they sat down.

'I don't know. Probably waiting to be interviewed downstairs, where you were interviewed before.'

'Why can't I see him?' she whined.

'I told you why; you are both suspects in the same crime.'

'But I had nothing to do with Elspeth.'

'I mean your baby, Rowan.'

'But …'

Eden wished the girl would shut up. She was trying to hear what Mike was telling Luke, but Rowan persisted.

'Why can't you help him; at least sit in on the interview?'

'Because I can't. There's a conflict of interest, shush now … let's wait quietly.'

Luke and Mike were talking about Carrie.

Rowan persisted. 'But it's not fair; he hasn't got anyone to help him. Why can't you help both of us?'

'Because one or other of you is going to carry the can for this and he might choose to incriminate you to save his own neck. From what you've told me you were not the main protagonist, whilst James on the other hand is the prime suspect in Elspeth's murder, not to mention his involvement in smuggling artefacts.'

Eden rose from her seat. She needed to get closer to hear what the two men were saying.

'Do you want some water, Rowan? Eden asked, walking towards the water tank in the corner of the room and pulling a plastic cup from the holder.

Rowan shook her head.

Eden listened as she pressed the lever and filled her cup.

'The American girl has demanded her own lawyer from London. Her parents are loaded apparently and there's some swanky brief on his way.'

'So no interview with her until he comes?' sighed Luke.

'Doesn't look like it.'

'What about Ferris?'

'Interview room two. His solicitor's already with him.'

'Good, I'll give them a few minutes.'

'As I said, Denise has got some information from the pathologist for you.'

'Is she upstairs?'

'Yes.'

'Give me fifteen minutes and I'll start with Ferris.'

Turning to Eden he said, 'DS Charlton will come and collect Rowan in about twenty minutes to give a statement.'

'Fine,' said Eden, before taking a sip of her water and making her way back to Rowan.

Thirty minutes later, Denise Charlton arrived to take them upstairs.

'It'll be fine,' reassured Eden as they took the lift to the first floor; 'just tell them what you told me about the smuggling.'

FORTY-NINE

It was eight o'clock before Carmen could get away. Matthew had to change his plans and babysit but she told him it was important and true to form he'd come through for her.

'Take your time, Ma, I'm going to spend the night here anyway.'

'Is that alright with Laura?'

He didn't answer and Carmen guessed he'd probably had words with his girlfriend and she'd be in her bad books again. She wondered whether she should tell him where she was going but he hadn't asked and she thought he probably assumed she was going to see Eden to discuss what was next now Rowan had turned herself in.

She wondered what she was going to say to Morvah; how do you ask your sister if she's a murderer?

She hadn't called ahead. Morvah had said this was her weekend off and had invited her round for a takeaway and a film. Rowan was still missing when she'd asked and Carmen had declined wanting to be at home in case there was any news.

Morvah opened the door in her exercise gear, surprised to see her.

'I didn't think you were coming? she said, letting her in. 'I just got back from my run, excuse the sweat I haven't had a shower yet.'

With her hair pulled back into a neat, high ponytail she looked like she had when they were at school and Carmen's heart twisted a little.

'I should have phoned. I've had some news and I wanted to tell you in person.'

'What news?'

'Rowan turned up today.'

Morvah smiled broadly; tossing her damp towel into the washing machine.

'There, I told you the candle spell would work. We called her home; you and me; together. I told you it would work.'

'Yes, you did. I'm so relieved. I know she's in custody and we've still got a long way to go to prove her innocence but at least I know she's safe.'

Morvah reached for two glasses and poured them some wine.

'Not for me, I'm driving.'

'It's a celebration, one won't hurt. Will she be allowed to come home?'

'I don't know. She's gone with Eden to the station to make a statement. So much has happened since you came to the farm. Rowan's finally told me everything.'

Morvah's hand trembled a little as she placed her glass on the table.

'What do you mean everything?'

'How she was paid to sleep with Philip Marshall by his wife and how she knew the baby was his.'

Morvah looked incredulous. 'Did she tell you about the birth?'

'Yes, she did.'

'So she was lying when she said she didn't remember anything?'

'To a certain extent. She and her boyfriend were smoking pot that night, so the whole thing is a blur.'

'Her boyfriend?'

'James Ferris from the archaeological dig; the one who was on the telly after the baby was found.'

Morvah shuffled in her seat.

'Did you know she was seeing him?' asked Carmen.

Morvah looked away, unwilling it seemed to meet her eye.

'Not when I was helping with the pregnancy. Like I told you I had suspicions there was someone but I thought it was Philip Marshall. It was only later I found out about James from Rowan.'

Carmen didn't push the point she'd withheld that crucial information, knowing she had to tread carefully. She needed to unfold the facts and see what Morvah was prepared to reveal in return. It was a game of cat-and-mouse she had to play with feline stealth.

Carmen continued. 'As I said, the night Rowan gave birth, the pair of them had been smoking cannabis. She didn't think it would harm the baby. Did you tell her that?' Despite Carmen's best efforts, it sounded like an accusation.

'Of course not; what do you take me for, I'm a nurse remember?' Morvah answered indignantly.

'Okay, I believe you but whether she heard it from someone or on the internet that's what she thought. She had the baby in her sleep. James delivered it and both of them, in the state they were in, thought the baby was dead. It wasn't of course, we know that now; it was the effect of the damn drugs.'

Carmen's throat swelled with emotion as she spoke of her grandchild.

'Why didn't they call me; I would have helped them? I would have known the child was alive.'

Morvah's face puckered with remorse. had lost all its after-run flush. 'I shouldn't have gone along with what that bloody Marshall woman wanted. I should have made sure Rowan knew to call me in a crisis.'

'You should have told me what was going on from the outset,' snapped Carmen, 'then none of this would have happened; none of it.'

'Don't you think I know that?'

Carmen forced herself to reel in her temper. She still had questions she needed to be answered and didn't want this to disintegrate into another slanging match. She tempered her tone;

'What's done is done. At least we know Rowan had nothing to do with burying the baby. Ferris did that alone. Rowan's adamant he didn't know it was alive and I'm pretty sure no one could be evil enough to bury a baby thinking it was. I can only assume he was as high as Rowan, who by then was fast asleep in her bed. When she finally came to and realised it wasn't all a dream it was a shock and that was how Mrs Marshall found her when she turned up.'

'She's innocent then; if she didn't know anything about it. I've seen women fall asleep during labour when they've had an epidural. I could tell the police that if you want?'

'It's not quite that simple; after all, she took the drugs knowing it was illegal. You can't endanger a child's life like that, but we know from the autopsy the drugs didn't kill him and so according to Eden, she cannot be guilty of manslaughter. James on the other hand could have called the authorities; he could have taken the baby to the hospital to be sure, but he didn't because he knew the fact they'd been taking drugs would come out. Eden says that was reckless and that's enough for him to be guilty. Rowan, thinking the baby dead already, went along with him; to protect him.'

'They must have known the Marshalls wouldn't leave it after all they'd invested.'

'Who knows? I suppose Rowan thought she'd given back the money and it was none of their business anymore. She knew they had no legal rights once she'd done that. Stupid, and I know, but I don't think she was thinking straight. I think she wanted it to be over and then it suddenly dawned on her she didn't have the money. She and James had planned to go away together but without the money, they wouldn't get far. That's when they came up with the plan for James to engineer it so that the baby's body was found. He hoped the site would get some publicity and he'd raise his profile. He hoped to be able to make some money out of it and they'd be able to go away together as they'd planned to do after the baby was born. That's what the police think anyway. James is in custody right now. He was arrested at Gatwick Airport.'

'Carmen, what if it was someone else who wanted the publicity?' What if it was that Fuller woman the one in charge of the site?'

Carmen wanted to buy some time; not introduce Elspeth into the conversation quite yet. She certainly had no intention of revealing she knew she was dead, let alone the grisly details. Not yet.

'You sound as if you might know something I don't?' she said.

'I know that woman knows everything about what went on there and I know she's a fraud and a thief.'

'What exactly are you saying?' Carmen downed the contents of her glass. She knew she couldn't meet her sister's eye, without revealing Rowan had told her about Elspeth smuggling finds from the site.

'She's been stealing; digging up the offerings buried by our family without any respect for their meaning or our heritage and selling them to the highest bidder. She's nothing but a thief and a liar.'

'And how do you know this?'

'Rowan told me.'

'When you were caring for her, you mean?'

Her sister didn't reply.

'When, Morvah?'

'She came to see me before she ran away.'

'What?'

'I know I should have told you but she asked me not to. She told me about her and James and about the site and his involvement; that he knew and hadn't reported it. She told me if I could give her a couple of days' grace, she'd be able to stop the next shipment of finds and then she and James would give themselves up. She said James intended to get all of the information and give it to the police; dates, times, destinations of all of the artefacts Elspeth had stolen from this site and all the others around the world. She hoped by stopping Elspeth and telling the police about the racket she was involved in they would be lenient with them. She hoped they could make some kind of plea bargain on the back of it.'

Carmen was incensed. 'So you knew all along Rowan was okay; you saw me worrying about her and knew she was safe and sound and the candle charm … was a bloody charade? You knew she'd be back and you have the nerve to call Elspeth Fuller a fraud?'

'No … no it wasn't a charade. It was for us. I suggested it to bring us closer. I wanted us to work the craft together. She came home, didn't she?'

'The craft, what craft, listen to yourself, it's all nonsense. Rowan came home because Eden Gray found her and dragged her home, not because she wanted to and certainly not because of some stupid charm.'

Her sister's face darkened.

'You don't believe in the gifts you've been given; everything our family did?'

'No, I don't, any more than I believe in a God with a bushy beard sitting on a cloud or confessing your sins to a man wearing a black frock.'

Morvah was practically frothing at the mouth. 'You're a traitor,' she spat, 'look no further than yourself as to why this is all happened. You have offended our mother and grandmother's memory. You have offended Bride by denying her; by denying your past.'

'The only one I've offended is you and if you're honest, really honest, you're not offended, you're angry and not about anything spiritual … nothing as high-minded. You're jealous of bricks and mortar because I got the farm. You're as materialistic as the next person and if you were angry about Elspeth stealing those things it's because deep down you believe they belong to you.'

Morvah had her back to her. Her body hunched over the table. 'Shut up … you don't know what you're talking about.'

'Well, they don't belong to you or me, or any of us. They belong to the poor sad women who asked us to work our so-called charms for them. Our family took their donations whether the charms worked or not. The pits with the offerings still intact are a testament to our family's failure. They didn't work, that's why they're still there. So, what if Elspeth Fuller took them? Those poor women hoped for a child, they never got. Some women can't conceive; women like Jessica Marshall for instance. It was a lie, Morvah.'

'It worked for some,' Morvah said quietly.

'Granted some of the women got pregnant but you're the nurse; you know those women would have got pregnant with or without the offerings. Maybe like Mary Bluet, it was their husband at fault and as soon as they looked elsewhere, hey presto!'

'You've never believed.'

'No, I haven't; what's more, I hate it. It's brought nothing but trouble. It's made us outcasts and look at us now. All this because the baby was found in a *witch pit.*'

Carmen was ramping things up to deliberately rile her sister; prodding her until she told the truth but as the words left her lips, she realised much of what she said reflected her true feelings for most of her life. 'Elspeth Fuller was no different than us; benefitting out of other people's misery.'

Carmen felt light-headed with the exhilaration of venting her emotions in one violent outburst.

'I want you to leave,' said Morvah quietly.

Carmen needed a minute to gather her thoughts. She couldn't leave yet; not until she'd got what she'd come for. She was feeling hot and light-headed.

'I will, don't worry I've got nothing more to say to you but I need to use your bathroom before I drive home if that's okay … two minutes and I'll be gone.'

'It's through there,' Morvah said pointing to the door at the end of the corridor. Deflated, her head was bent and she rubbed her temples.

Carmen followed the corridor. She was about to open the door to the bathroom when she noticed the door to her left was ajar. She assumed this was Morvah's bedroom. Once she would have breezed into the room to take a peek at the colour scheme and to rifle through her sister's wardrobe for something to wear but not anymore. Nevertheless, out of sheer curiosity she gave the door a small shove, expecting the crisp co-ordination prevalent in the rest of the place.

What she saw rooted her to the spot.

Pastel grey walls. Wall to wall wardrobes and Egyptian cotton sheets as expected, but above the headboard, covering the space was drawn a huge pentagram and in its centre a circle; two curved lines representing horns protruding from the top from each of which hung the symbol for a Celtic torc. It was the symbol for the horned god, Cernunnos, to the Cornish Kernunnos.

This was not a symbol used by her family. They were concerned with what happened after conception; the child and its safety in the wound. The horned god was masculine, violent and visceral; nature and sexuality in its wildest form. She shivered.

Bolting the bathroom door, she tried to hold herself together. Ever since seeing the photographs, the nagging fear Morvah was involved had played on her mind. Now she'd seen the symbol and knew her sister had motive, it seemed impossible it could be anyone else.

She should have learnt something from her dealings with Eden and DI Parish and kept to the point. She wouldn't mention the symbol; she needed to go back out there and try and get Morvah talking again.

She pulled the flush and ran the tap for a second before opening the door. Morvah was exactly as she'd left her. She took a deep breath, stealing herself to finish this.

Carmen dropped her bag on the settee and walked over to her.

'I'm sorry. I do have a connection with the past. You … you're my connection. I respect what Gran and Mum did; helping women when they went into labour and finding remedies for their ailments; it's the religious side I find difficult. But I do respect your beliefs, I do, and I shouldn't have said what I did. I was angry you'd lied again. Learning you knew Rowan's whereabouts all the time; I just so angry.'

She touched her sister's shoulder and felt the heave of a sigh under her hand.

'Is there anything else you need to tell me because now is the time? There must be no more lies or secrets; everything must be out in the open if we are to remain sisters do you understand?'

'There's nothing else, I swear.'

'Nothing about Elspeth?'

'What do you mean?'

'Did you ever meet her for instance?'

'No, she phoned a couple of times and left messages but I wanted nothing to do with her and I didn't phone her back.'

'You never spoke to her?'

'No, I was against the dig and wanted nothing to do with it; even less when I heard about what the Fuller woman was up to.'

Carmen heaved a sigh of relief.

'Thank goodness,' she said.

'Why, what is it?'

Elspeth's body was found at the bottom of the crystal well this afternoon. She'd been murdered.'

Morvah's eyes widened. 'Murdered?'

'Symbols were carved into her body; The Triple Moon, The Witch's Knot and the Swan's Foot on her shoulder blades.'

Morvah recoiled.

'You thought it was me didn't you, that's why you came here this evening?'

'No of course not. Who knows who could have done it? It could be one of the lunatics hanging around since the baby was found and the dig went viral. Usually, we'd spot strangers in the village but not now the place is awash with them; the press, those damn protesters and all the new age crowd camping out where they can.'

'But the Swan's Foot; no one would know about that?'

Carmen blushed. 'Okay, I said no lies. So, to tell you the truth, because of that symbol I did think it might have been you; there I've said it.'

'Me?'

'I saw how perfectly the symbols were carved on the body and could only think of one person who could do that and guessed you'd found out about the smuggling.'

'I'm not the only …' Morvah said, then hesitated, 'wait a minute, I'll be right back.'

She moved quickly towards the bathroom. Carmen followed her and watched as her sister opened the cabinet above the sink and began moving the contents around, looking for something.

'It's not here,' she said, panic in her voice.

'What are you looking for?'

Morvah swept the contents of the cupboard into the basin. Bottles of cough medicine and vitamin tablets clattered against the porcelain. Carmen looked on bemused.

'A scalpel; there was a scalpel in here. I took it from work. They recycled the old ones and I took it because they're useful for jobs around the house when you need something really sharp.'

'And it's missing?'

'It was here until a few days ago. I know because I used it to cut a piece of coir matting I bought for the door well.'

Carmen thought of the marks on Elspeth's body; the fine unbroken lines etched into her pale skin and how they'd been made with something viciously sharp; a scalpel. The narrow blade built for accuracy used to cutting into flesh; able to cut to the bone with the lightest of touches. Morvah had said Rowan visited her after she skipped bail. She braced herself for her daughter's name. Rowan knew about Elspeth and she'd had the book to copy the symbols from.

'Rowan ... you think Rowan took the scalpel and killed Elspeth, don't you?' she blurted out.

'Rowan? No, she's never been interested in the craft; she's like you. She always thought it was nonsense,' replied Morvah dismissively.

'But she had the book she could have copied the signs?'

'But you said the lines were unbroken; that they were drawn precisely and there's only one person who could do that or certainly used to be able to; one person I taught to draw the Swan's Foot, the Triple Moon and the Witch's Knot.'

'Who?'

'Matthew, I taught Matthew when he was a boy.'

FIFTY

Denise Charlton showed them into Luke's office. Eden immediately noticed how tidy it was. No files stacked on top of filing cabinets; pens neatly arranged in their holders; an elastic band ball next to an angle-poise lamp. It was the antithesis of her own. Most of the time hers looked as if burglars had ransacked the place.

There was a photograph of Flora on the desk sitting proudly on a tricycle; face beaming under a shiny silver helmet.

She was glad the station was old and the office wasn't the glass goldfish bowl variety common these days. Rowan liked an audience and Eden didn't want spectators. She needed her client to make a statement without the melodramatics she was apt to revert to when under stress. Before this it had been about the police proving her guilt, now it was about her making sure they knew the evidence pointing to her innocence.

Given an inch, Rowan would try to manipulate the truth to make sure she didn't implicate James. She'd toss in excuses and alibis for him. Long term it would only serve to prove her a liar.

'Take a seat.' said Denise. 'Rowan this is not an interview. There is no tape facility in this room. You are here as a witness to give a statement detailing what you know about the trafficking in artefacts and Elspeth Fuller's involvement, nothing more. Do you understand?'

'Yes, but I thought I could tell you about the baby as well, clear myself and James too?'

'No, not at this stage. You are still under caution in respect of that crime and if you wish to provide us with further information, we will need to interview you on tape when a room comes free.'

'Who's in the interview room now; is it James?' Rowan asked.

Eden glared at her; 'Not now Rowan, let's concentrate on your statement.'

Rowan unabashed, carried on. 'Has he got a lawyer? Eden says she can't represent him because there is a conflict but I can't see any conflict, can you? We both want the same thing; we're both innocent after all.'

Denise raised her eyebrows at Eden. 'Is your client willing to give a statement dealing solely with what she knows about Elspeth Fuller's alleged involvement with smuggling artefacts or not?'

Before Eden could reply Rowan interjected.

'I don't know why you're so concerned about getting evidence about Elspeth, she's dead anyway.'

Eden watched a flicker of interest cross Denise's face. Realising why, Eden preferred to explain before she ran away with the wrong idea. 'I told Rowan Elspeth was found dead in the well. She didn't know before that, did you Rowan?'

'No,' replied Rowan.

Eden winced at the annoying upward lilt of her voice making her answer sound like a question.

'But I'm not surprised,' Rowan continued, 'a witch pit for an old witch. She made James's life a misery involving him in goodness knows what against his will.'

Denise looked frustrated. Eden knew the ambitious DS would far rather be at the main event, interviewing James and Carrie.

'Denise,' Eden interjected, 'can you give me a minute with my client? Just a minute alone so I can explain why she's here? I know you're extremely busy and I don't want to waste any more of your time.'

Once Denise left the room Eden lay into Rowan; softly, softly, obviously had no effect on her.

'All they want from you is a statement covering what you know about the smuggling that's all. A woman has been murdered. They'll assume if she was immersed in the kind of criminal enterprise you've described, she had links with all sorts of unsavoury types who might be involved in some way. If you can help with that, all well and good. They don't need a character assassination of the victim. Stick to what you know that's all; understood?'

She hoped Rowan had taken heed of her mother's advice as they'd left the farm.

To Eden's relief, forty minutes later, Denise Charlton had a signed statement.

As it turned out, Rowan knew very little about the scam, only what she'd been told by James and had already passed on to Eden earlier that day. She'd never met Elspeth herself. James had become embroiled unwittingly, thinking he was taking items from the site to be sent off for expert analysis. It was when his caravan roof leaked and Elspeth let him stay at her flat, he discovered some boxes in a cupboard in the spare room, destined for addresses abroad and got curious. Opening one, he found an artefact he recognised from the site.

He confronted Elspeth who admitted what she was up to, warning him if he told anyone she'd say the plan was his and it was he who'd been caught red-handed by her. James wanted nothing to do with it but had no means of escape. That's why he was delighted when Rowan told him about the surrogacy and they hatched a plan to take the money from the Marshalls and leave once the baby was born. He took none of the finds for himself other than the book which Rowan admitted stealing for him after his failed attempt to find it after setting the fire.

Denise to her credit didn't press Rowan about the child and Eden was grateful for her integrity. Afterwards, she led them back downstairs, leaving them with the custody officer to book Rowan into a cell for the night. She was to appear before the magistrates in the morning. They'd decide whether to re-grant her bail.

Rowan remained nonchalant about all of it, and when Eden asked if she was okay, she turned misty-eyed and asked,

'Will James be in the cell next to mine?'

Eden exasperated, couldn't wait to get out of there.

FIFTY-ONE

Carmen felt as if she'd been beaten around the head with a heavy object. A stupefying paralysis overwhelmed her and she could barely open her lips to whisper her son's name.

'Matthew?'

'I taught Matthew all of the signs and many of the incantations when he was small. If you remember we were very close at one time,' Morvah said wistfully. 'Rowan was always so demanding but he was quiet; always in her shadow, despite being older.'

Carmen listened remembering how Matthew had gravitated towards Morvah. Rowan was a handful from the beginning. As a baby, she didn't sleep and when she did manage to put her down and should have made time for Matthew, she was too tired. He was often left to amuse himself. His father's work as a trawlerman took him away for months on end and when he was home, he was busy helping out on the farm and had little time to play with his son who barely knew him. When their relationship ended, he saw him once a year if he happened to be in the area. Nowadays neither he nor Rowan heard from him at all.

Morvah had made it her business to take Matthew under her wing. She taught him how to swim; showed him how to deal with the animals and how to mend the dry-stone hedges if they toppled in winter. Carmen was more than aware of the bond they had.

'I talked to him about Mother and Gran,' Morvah continued, 'about the family history and the pit ceremonies and he was gripped by the stories. I'd take him on walks and point out the plants used for healing and when he got older, how to prepare them and he'd write it down in his little book. I loved being with him; he was my joy.'

Carmen felt wretched as the tears streamed down her sister's cheeks and passed her a tissue from her bag; gulping down the last of her wine to steady her nerves.

Morvah paused, obviously waiting for some reaction from her.

Carmen swallowed hard. 'Go on,' she said, 'you need to tell me.'

She listened as if in a dream, imagining her little boy holding Morvah's hand, wandering through the woodland near the farm; gathering doc-root and wormwood as the dappled light played upon his golden hair.

'He was eager to learn how to use the cures. So, when any of the animals got sick or needed a tonic, I showed him how and he made them better. He had a real gift for healing. I taught him the blessings and incantations and the candle and water charms. I showed him how to draw the symbols like Mother showed us and he practiced and practiced until I didn't have to help him anymore. He could remember every one and what they meant. He was like a sponge sucking up every snippet of information I gave him ... until the day it all ended.'

'Why, because I got left the farm and we fell out?'

'No. He was about ten. We were in the barn mixing a poultice for one of the sows whose ear had been bitten by the hog who'd covered her, and he asked when he could start using the charms on people. I told him he couldn't because he was a boy and tradition dictated only the girls in the family could practice the craft. He shouted at me; threw the bowl and all the herbs across the barn floor and ran out. It took me ages to find him. He was curled up in the hen coop; sitting with the chickens. "Why didn't you tell me before?" he said, "why did you let me think I was special?"'

Carmen groaned, 'Poor Matthew.'

'We never spoke of it again. He said "no" whenever I asked him if he wanted to come with me to forage. He was only interested in learning about the farm stuff; about the crops and the machinery. Then you got the farm and that was that.'

Carmen forced herself to ask the question, 'The scalpel; when would he have taken the scalpel. I don't understand?'

'He visited me when Rowan was on the run. She'd phoned him wanting him to meet her with a change of clothes. He refused; told her she had to come home. Rowan being Rowan gave him a mouthful about how he was like you, always right and how I at least understood her and had promised to keep my mouth shut about where she was until she'd sorted things out. He came around here furious with me, like you were when you found out just now. I explained what I knew about the baby and about James and Elspeth stealing and selling the offerings. He was angry; incensed, said Elspeth needed to be stopped, the family had suffered enough. I thought he meant he was going to the police. I managed to calm him down before he left and then when I heard nothing more, I guessed he'd thought better of it and decided not to get involved; what with his girlfriend and all, until today, when you told me the woman was dead.'

'And the scalpel?'

'I used it that day. I'd been cutting the mat to size when he turned up. He took the off-cuts away with him to save me having to put them out with the rubbish. He said he'd put them on the compost heap. I couldn't remember if I put the scalpel back in the bathroom cabinet where I keep it; that's why I looked just now but it's not there and I'm certain it's nowhere else. It can mean only one thing; Matthew took it.'

'But Morvah, you can't think he did this; not our Matthew?'

As Carmen stood up the room reeled. Her body felt heavy and unresponsive. She could feel a tightness in her neck and the stiffening seemed to be travelling into her jaw like the start of a toothache. Her stomach felt as if something terrible was fermenting there; something which any minute would burst out of her mouth. Her peripheral vision was blurry, fading like an old photograph at the edges. She felt Morvah pushing her back onto the sofa; lifting her legs and heard her voice, distant and echoing calling her name,

'Carmen ... Carmen.'

She saw her sister's face, pressed close to her own; drawn and worried; searching. Then pain, terrible pain as if rocks were being loaded onto her chest; burying her alive.

She could hear noise all around; men's voices. They were calling her name. Then another face, a young face; a man she didn't know. She tried to speak but although the words formed in her head, she knew instinctively nothing left her lips.

'Carmen, you're okay,' the man was saying, 'I'm a paramedic. You've had a heart attack. I'm going to give you something to ease the pain and then we'll get you to hospital as quickly as possible.'

She thought she nodded but couldn't be sure. She felt a small prick in her hand, followed by a feeling of release; the smell of rubber as a mask covered her mouth and nose.

'I'll go with her in the ambulance.' she heard Morvah say before she closed her eyes and darkness engulfed her.

FIFTY-TWO

Denise filled Luke in on the latest from the lab;

'I'm not sure you're ready for this,' she said. 'but the pathologist has reported in to say Elspeth Fuller met a particularly violent death. She was, get this: bludgeoned, garrotted and finally had her throat cut. The toxicology results aren't back yet but he believes she was drugged beforehand. He thinks the blow to the head killed her and the rest came later. The symbols were inflicted post-mortem. They still haven't got an exact time of death but his best estimate is she'd been down the well for at least forty-eight hours before she was found.'

'Bloody hell; if that's not overkill, I don't know what is? Elspeth was slightly built. It would have been relatively easy to topple her into the well when she was dead but it sounds messy. Did forensics find any rope at the site or the murder weapon; whatever was used to hit her? It would be a miracle if they found a knife as well. Christ talking about it out loud it sounds like a game of Cluedo.'

'No, nothing. The pathologist did say the same knife was used to cut her throat as was used to carve the symbols. He said it was a small blade; extremely sharp. The scene of crime boys found traces of blood on the stones around the well but it's rained over the last two days and most of it has been washed away.'

'Okay, the custody clock is ticking. I better get on with this.'

***

James Ferris waited in the interview room with his lawyer, Robert Weller. Luke knew Weller. He was a local solicitor off the rota. Ferris, unlike his American girlfriend, had had to make do with what he could get, which wasn't much. Weller would be peeing his pants with excitement at getting a murder suspect. He'd be clocking up the fees in his head. He wasn't up to it and the boy would dump him if he had any sense after this interview.

James fired a nervous glance at Luke as he walked into the room. Luke had seen Ferris holding forth on the television several times and met him briefly when he'd gone to the site after the discovery of the baby's body. The cheery, self-confident young man cut a different dash than the dishevelled, jumpy individual sitting in front of him now. Looking at Ferris, Luke was confident this would play out one of two ways. Either he wouldn't trust himself to talk at all and give a no comment interview, or he'd crumble and spill his guts. There was seldom a middle road for his type.

'Hello James. I'm DI Parish; we've met before. I'm going to turn on the recorder now before we begin the interview. Luke flicked the switch waiting for the end of the steady purr to cease then said jauntily, 'Present DI Luke Parish; James Ferris and his solicitor Robert Weller. James, I have to remind you, you are still under caution following your arrest at Gatwick Airport earlier today. Do you understand?'

'Yes, but I don't understand why I've been arrested. I didn't kill Elspeth. I didn't even know she was dead until you lot stopped me from getting on the plane.'

'With your girlfriend, Carrie Devereaux?'

'She's not my girlfriend,' James barked.

'Then what is she?'

'She's a business colleague.'

'I see.' A practiced smirk of feigned disbelief lifted the corner of Luke's mouth.

Dramatically flipping open the buff-coloured folder in front of him, he slipped out the photograph of Carrie kissing James on the cheek. He slid it in front of James, watching for his reaction.

'Where did you find that?' asked James a flush of embarrassment sweeping his cheeks.

'In your caravan. We found lots of interesting things in your caravan. You look a little more than friends in that,' he said pointing to the photograph, 'and I understand from some of your workmates Carrie stayed in your caravan overnight on several occasions?'

'She did, but not with me. I wasn't there with her.'

'So where were you James?'

'I was with someone else.'

'Rowan Lutey?'

James fired a look at his lawyer, who was too busy writing to pick up on it. Luke continued.

'We know all about you and Rowan Lutey, James. Rowan is making a statement right now.' The boy's head dropped like a coconut from a shy, into his hands.

'James, look at me please,' cajoled Luke. 'We know it was you who delivered Rowan's baby and buried it in the empty witch pit; that's old news to us.'

Weller woke up at that point.

'My client has not been cautioned in respect of that crime. I'm advising him not to answer any questions relating to that incident.'

'Fair enough; if he doesn't want to answer any questions, I won't question him but I can tell him what I know about the weed he and Rowan smoked that night and about this.

Luke pulled out a small evidence bag from the case sitting beside him and held it up in front of James. 'For the purposes of the record, I'm holding up an evidence bag containing a quantity of cannabis resin. We found this in your caravan too.'

Luke could feel James's leg shaking the table. He watched the boy take a large gulp of water from the glass beside him. His stare drifted towards the bag as he ruminated over the implications. Luke knew from experience adrenaline was now pumping through him like poison making him feel clammy; his mouth impossibly dry. He took another gulp draining the glass and Luke poured him some more from the jug.

'I never sold the drugs; they were recreational, just for me.'

'I know you're not a drug dealer James, but you shared them with Carrie. You both look pretty high to me in this photograph and you gave them to Rowan too, didn't you, the night she gave birth?'

'Yes, but I didn't know it could harm the baby; neither of us knew.'

'James I'm advising you not to say anything about this,' Weller interjected.

James ignored him.

'When the baby was born, I freaked. I thought it was dead and if I reported it, the authorities would get to know about the drugs. Everything turned to shit so quickly. I couldn't think what to do with it, so I wrapped it up and buried it. I couldn't bear to look at it. I took it to the site, opened up the pit unwrapped the sheet and put it in.'

'James,' said Weller more sharply this time. 'I'm advising you to say nothing more; say nothing.'

Weller was doing better than expected, Luke thought.

'You should listen to your lawyer, James,' Luke agreed, with an expression saying; *don't listen to him; the man's a fool.*

'No, I have to tell someone. I couldn't look at it; I didn't even use a torch; I didn't want to see. I pulled the sheet away, dropped the baby in then shovelled the earth on top. I can't let people think I knew it was alive when I didn't; I didn't. I didn't want to look at it,' James sobbed.

'My client needs a break.'

'Good idea,' said Luke.

'For the purposes of the record, interview suspended at twenty-one-thirty DI Luke Parish leaving the room.'

Next, the smuggling and finally Elspeth's murder, Luke thought. He was setting up the charges like a row of dominoes but wasn't so confident about toppling the final one. Looking at James he had serious doubts he was capable of the brutal murder the pathologists described. It was one thing to kill someone in a fit of temper or panic but to mutilate them was something else. It was the act of a madman or someone with balls of steel. He didn't think James was either.

Denise Charlton walked around the corner carrying an evidence bag.

'What have you got there?' asked Luke

'A book. It looks ancient. It was found in Ferris's suitcase and his prints are all over it. I've looked through it and as well as some pretty disgusting recipes I won't be trying any day soon, there are drawings of symbols, some of which look like the ones on Elspeth Fuller's body.'

'Did he steal it from the site?'

'No, I've just finished taking Rowan Lutey's statement. She told me she took it from the farm when she absconded. She said James wanted it because it was valuable. He'd tried to take it before. He lit the fire and broke into the farm to get it but Rowan's mother had hidden it.'

'Ahh,' mused Luke remembering his cryptic conversation with Eden following the fire. 'What else did Rowan say?'

'She confirmed what Eden told us. Elspeth masterminded the operation. James was drawn into it and wanted out.'

'Did she mention Carrie Devereux?'

'No, she didn't seem to know anything about her.'

'James says she's not his girlfriend, she's a colleague.'

'That would fit with Rowan's take on things. According to her, she and James are pretty loved up. Eden's gone home by the way. They've put Rowan in the cells until her bail application tomorrow.'

Her train of thought between Rowan and James and him and Eden didn't go unnoticed.

Denise continued. 'I was going to take Carrie next but her lawyer hasn't arrived yet. He's a bit of a name in the City apparently and the powers that be don't want to step on his toes, especially as Carrie's a US citizen and we haven't got any evidence to link her to a crime.'

'If that's the case why don't you sit in on my interview. It might work tactically to throw him a curve ball? He's got used to me. As you're fully up to speed, why don't you take the lead?'

'You don't mind?' Denise grinned. Luke noticed how her whole face lit up when she smiled.

'Go for it.'

Luke finished off his coffee with a grimace, then they returned to the room together.

Luke positioned himself to one side, next to Weller.

'Hello James,' said Denise, I'm DS Charlton. I'll be conducting the rest of the interview.'

FIFTY-THREE

'I've advised my client not to answer any more questions about the death of the baby.'

'Of course, I wouldn't dream of asking him anything about that. If you could resume recording please,' she said to Luke. 'Interview resumed at ten minutes past ten. Present DI Parish, DS Denise Charlton, Mr James Ferris and his legal representative Mr Weller.'

'Now James, why were you at Gatwick Airport today?'

'I was going away on business.'

'To Los Angeles with Miss Devereux?'

'Yes.'

'What was the nature of this business?'

'Promotional work about the site. There is some interest in making a film about it; a drama. Carrie's parents know a lot of people in the industry and they arranged a meeting with one of the networks.'

'We can check all this can we, with the relevant parties?'

'Yes ... yes you can. Carrie has all the details.'

'Good,' said Denise smiling warmly.

'So, interest was aroused because of the discovery of the baby and the publicity from it?'

Luke could see Weller about to jump in again, as could Denise who immediately changed tack.

'Who arranged the trip, you or Elspeth?'

'Me, or rather it was Carrie's suggestion. She'd arranged to go home to work on another dig and suggested it would be a good time for me to go too. She arranged everything and I went along with it.'

'When?'

'Oh, the talks began a while ago but I decided to go in the last day or so.'

'And you decided to go even though you knew excavations of the well, probably the most important find at the site, were due to start today?'

Good work, thought Luke.

'I thought Elspeth would be there.'

'You checked with her then?'

'Yes.'

'When?'

'Yesterday or the day before maybe?'

'Which is it, James, yesterday or the day before?'

'Yesterday, yes definitely yesterday.'

'But that's not possible, James.'

'What do you mean?'

'It's not possible because Elspeth has been dead for several days; days you claim you've been talking to her; now why would you do that, James?'

'It's not what you think.'

'And what do I think?'

'You think I killed her, but I didn't.'

'So why lie about speaking to her?'

'I was scared. I haven't been able to get hold of her. I've had calls from all over; from people she's promised stuff to. Then the bloke from the company doing the scaffolding for the well wanted paying and there was no money in the account. I thought she'd done a runner leaving me to carry the can.?'

'The can for what exactly?'

She's good, thought Luke.

'For smuggling the artefacts; it's what she threatened to do if I told.'

'I think my client needs another break.'

'Do you need a break, James?' asked Denise smiling.

'No, I need to tell you about her. You need to know this was her, not me. Now she's dead I'm the one all this is going to be pinned on and it's not right.'

'When *did* you last actually talk to her, James?'

He looked down at his hands, picking at his nails.

'Four days ago.'

'And when you couldn't reach her, you made up the story about her being in France at a conference?'

'France? Oh yeah, to Rowan's lawyer.'

'And the story of a family crisis to your team?'

'I didn't want anyone to know she was missing. I was scared word would get around and people would target me instead.'

'Who James, who would target you?'

'I don't know,' he spluttered. Gangsters, international smugglers, one of the lunatics off the dark web who is interested in the creepy stuff. Mean bastards who don't give a shit about peoples' lives. Look, I'm small fry. I'm nothing to do with it all really but I know enough to get me into deep shit. What if they kill me like they killed Elspeth?'

'But you said you didn't know they'd killed Elspeth, James, not until you were arrested at Gatwick?'

'I didn't ... I mean. I didn't know. I knew we'd not been able to move the stuff as easily as before because of all the people at the site all the time and thought she might be being watched. I knew some customers wouldn't be very happy. They'd be worried they weren't going to get what they'd been promised. These people don't fuck about.'

'You haven't properly answered my question, James. Why did you think Elspeth might be dead; not missing, dead?'

James slumped back in his chair. 'I found her bag and a bundle of her clothes in her prefab; the shitty stripy lucky jumper she always wore and her jeans and I knew she wouldn't go anywhere without them.'

'What did you do with them?'

'I locked the bag in the filing cabinet because I'd seen her do that sometimes and hid the clothes in the caravan. I was going to burn them.'

'Not the smartest of moves.'

'No, I know, I know ... I panicked. I didn't want anyone else to find them. They were lying on the floor, like some sort of warning. I freaked.'

278

'So, you chose to run?'

'Yes, when Carrie invited me it was a godsend.'

'What about Rowan?'

'Rowan?'

'Yes. Were you going to leave her behind? She was expecting you to collect her today so you could leave together. It came as a bit of a shock to her to find you were at Gatwick Airport leaving with another woman.'

'I was going to ring to explain she couldn't come with me because she didn't have a passport.'

'Come on, James, we've seen Carrie. She was a better prospect, wasn't she? That's why you abandoned Rowan.'

He didn't reply.

'Let's go back a little. When did you decide to set Rowan up in Elspeth's flat?'

'I had a key. I went there looking for Elspeth but there was no sign of her. Rowan and I were going to try and find some evidence about the smuggling and give it to you lot.'

'Very public-spirited of you, I'm sure.' said Denise sarcastically. 'So, what made you change your mind?'

'I started thinking what if you took the information from me and then wouldn't protect me? What if Elspeth had disappeared because she'd done the same thing, only she told you lot it was me who masterminded the whole thing and someone got hold of her to punish her for it?'

Paranoia was seeping from every pore.

'Who were you likely to believe, her or me? I'd already lied about Rowan. As soon as you found out about her and the drugs and it was me who buried the baby; why would you believe me over some hippie archaeologist with an Oxford degree and a perfect reputation?'

'Why indeed?' replied Denise.

Luke noticed Weller had stopped writing with the mention of the word *gangsters*. He guessed this case was a little too rich for his tastes. Luke had the impression if he could, he'd run like his client had.

'Didn't you worry about leaving Rowan alone in Elspeth's flat with all the finds, that she might be in danger from all these *gangsters* you were afraid of?'

'Yes of course I did but where else was she to go; she couldn't come back to my caravan?'

'She could have stayed at her mum's and reported for bail like she was supposed to. She would have been safe then, wouldn't she?'

James said nothing. He looked exhausted.

'As I said several minutes ago, I think my client needs to be allowed to rest now,' chipped in Weller. It's eleven o'clock.'

'One more thing. Did you use the symbols in the book Rowan stole from her house as a template for the marks you carved into Elspeth Fuller's body after you killed her?'

Weller teetered on the edge of his chair. 'What? I must object to this; what book?'

'Carmen Lutey's book containing her *spells*.' Denise raised her hands like a magician about to conjure a string of handkerchiefs from her sleeve. 'I'm sure those filmmakers in LA would love to get their hands on that? All those incantations and Celtic symbols. Those American audiences love a bit of witchcraft.'

'I don't see where you are going with this, DS Charlton?' interrupted Weller.

Denise turned on him. 'Your client has been hiding a bail absconder in the murder victim's flat. He is, on his own admission, implicated in the theft of artefacts along with his accomplice who also happens to be that murder victim. I am questioning him now about the theft of a book containing symbolism used in the crime. Is that clear enough for you?'

Weller looked like he'd been hit with a wet fish.

'I didn't steal it. Like you said, Rowan took it from her house. The book is as much Rowan's as anyone's. She has a right to it. Her mother never used it; why shouldn't Rowan make a bit of money from it?'

'Or you James, or you? After all, it's the reason you got friendly with Rowan in the first place, isn't it. I'm sure after all you'd gone through you thought you deserved a payday?'

This is almost too easy, thought Luke.

Denise didn't wait for an answer. 'So, you never set fire to the Lutey's barn to create a distraction so you could enter the house to take it? Think very carefully before you answer, James.'

'How do you know all this?' James moaned.

Weller shuffled his papers.

'Okay. Yes, but I didn't mean for it to get so out of hand. I thought it would be put out sooner. I didn't realise it would go up like it did.'

'And the marks on Elspeth's body?'

She's mixing it up now; clever, thought Luke.

'What marks? I don't know what you're talking about?'

'The marks on Elspeth's body; Pagan symbols like the ones in the book, carved into her dead flesh.'

Denise was on a roll and Luke could tell she was enjoying the feeling.

'Wasn't it enough to have bludgeoned her to death; then strangled her and cut her throat? Did you have to mutilate her? Why did you do it, James? Publicity? To be clever? Or were you being ironic? Or was it an act of defiance; your way of having the last word on the body of the woman you were too scared to stand up to when she was alive?'

'I didn't … my god no. You mean it was a ritual killing; she was killed three ways in the Celtic tradition?'

Luke had to say something. 'Three ways?'

'The Celts carried out human sacrifices. They sacrificed their enemies and their own, even their kings if they didn't perform. They killed them three times over to appease their gods. A blow to the head; garrotting, then they slit the victim's throat and let the blood spill over the land. Are you saying someone killed Elspeth like that and then carved into her? I can't believe it … my god.'

James looked grey; his body heaving. 'I'm going to be …'

He vomited all over the table.

'Interview suspended at twenty-three hundred hours,' said Denise, grabbing her papers from the desk before they were soiled.

She turned to Weller. 'Your client will be staying in custody overnight.'

The lawyer didn't argue.

FIFTY-FOUR

'Well, what do you think?' Denise asked once lawyer and client had left.

'I hate to say it after all your good work in there but I don't think he killed Elspeth.'

'Me neither. He confessed to all the rest so quickly, I barely needed to raise the subject and he fessed up. He's one of those who need to talk.'

'Well done by the way; impressive.'

Denise blushed. 'Thanks but it leaves us with no suspects for the murder.'

'No, but it confirmed one thing. Whatever Elspeth was tied up in was big. Ferris is terrified. He thinks there are people out there who wouldn't want anyone knowing about their involvement in this and would do just about anything to silence those who look like they might talk or don't live up to their side of the bargain.'

'Do you think the Devereaux girl is involved at all, perhaps she'll know something?'

'Don't bank on it. If you ask me, she sounds like a little rich girl spending Daddy's money on a sabbatical in Ye Olde England; getting down with the peasants.'

Denise laughed, 'I'm going to see if we've heard anything from her brief. It would be good if we could get an early start tomorrow with both James and her. Are you off home now?'

'Yep, bed's calling.'

'Yours or Eden Gray's?' Denise teased.

'Ha bloody ha, 'Luke retorted. He knew his friends at the station understood the story in the paper was nonsense, knew the truth about him and the Gray family, but most hadn't dared mention it; treading on eggshells knowing the reaction they'd get if they did. It felt a relief to have someone come out and say something even in a cheeky roundabout way and it felt even better it was Denise. The disciplinary hearing had been cancelled and he would probably get a one-line apology in the paper now Rowan was back in custody but it was still a source of huge embarrassment and there would always be those who thought there was no smoke without fire; Thea being one of them.

Arranging to meet Denise tomorrow morning at nine o'clock sharp, he walked upstairs to get his coat. Having gathered his things, he was about to switch off the lights when Denise came rushing through the door.

'She's gone,' she puffed.

'Who?'

'Carrie. Her brief arrived when we were in with James He kicked off and the word came down from the Super the CPS said we had to let her go.'

'Who the hell is this girl?' said Luke, 'and why would the Super become involved?'

'I don't know.'

'Well, we'd better find out,' sighed Luke, throwing his coat back down and turning on his computer. He waited impatiently for the screen to light up then typed in Carrie Devereaux.

There was nothing on the police database. She wasn't a UK citizen and as a student volunteer wasn't registered with the DWP either.

'Did they take a copy of her passport downstairs?'

Denise rang Mike to ask. Slamming the phone down she said, 'No.'

'Bloody hell.' said Luke, exasperated.

'Try Facebook,' suggested Denise.

'I haven't got an account.'

'Move over,' she said edging him out of his seat.

She typed in Carrie Devereaux; nothing. There were lots of Carrie's spelt every conceivable way but none were her.

'Let's see if there are any photos of the dig online.'

She pulled up the dig's website. There were plenty of photographs some listing the names of the volunteers. One of them was Clarissa Devereaux.

She searched again; this time using Carrie's full name along with the words Los Angeles and up it came; pages of it.

Clarissa Devereaux with her friends in New York shopping.

Clarissa Devereaux at the Viper Room for her eighteenth birthday.

Clarissa Devereaux at some artist's opening show; and on and on.

'Loaded,' exclaimed Denise.

'Looks that way but in itself, it wouldn't be enough to get the Super in a spin.'

'Go back a couple of frames,' said Luke. 'I thought I saw a photograph of her with some older people.'

Denise scrolled through the earlier pictures.

'There,' said Luke.

Clarissa Devereaux with her parents, Deputy Ambassador Mark Devereaux and Mrs Devereaux, with philanthropist Robin Kirkwood at a charity ball at Newport Beach in aid of the Los Angeles Historical Society.'

They tapped in Robin Kirkwood; chairman of numerous charitable foundations and a large contributor to many universities; a New Yorker, who studied history at Yale and then took a Master's in Medieval Studies at Oxford.

'James said Elspeth studied at Oxford,' said Denise, 'and they're about the same age?'

They read in silence all about the illustrious career of Carrie's father, now on the Ambassador's staff in Paris.

They didn't have to read any further.

'That's the end of that then. We won't be seeing her again.'

'No.'

'Have the finds been removed from Elspeth's flat?'

'I don't know but I can check.'

She phoned downstairs to get the answer.

'Yes, but we're not keeping them; they're off to some archaeology lab tomorrow. We haven't got the right conditions to store them apparently.'

'That's something, I suppose. At least we know they're not on some boat heading god knows where.'

Do you think Carrie and this Kirkwood bloke were mixed up in this; involved in the murder?'

'I don't suppose for one minute we'll ever know. If they were, neither would have done it themselves. People like them never do. They pay others to do their dirty work for them. I believe we've been looking too close to home wondering how anyone on our list had the bottle to do something like this. To a paid killer it would be a walk in the park.'

'And the method and symbols?'

'A bit of window dressing; red herrings to lead us off track, probably from information provided by Kirkwood who seems to know his stuff. With all the nutters hanging around the site since the baby was found they knew we'd be led in their direction and away from the scam Elspeth was running. They didn't reckon on James blabbing or rather they did and took the decision to fly him over to their side of the pond where they could keep an eye on him.'

'We can ask James about Kirkwood tomorrow when we interview him again,' said Denise.

'We can; but even if he admits to knowing him, it's meaningless. We haven't got a cat in hell's chance of finding out who did this if this was a contract killing. The best we can hope is we've got this wrong.'

FIFTY-FIVE

Eden was about to climb into bed when the phone rang.

She looked at the screen; Carmen.

She was probably ringing to see what happened at the station and to ask whether Rowan had been kept in custody. She answered, knowing the woman would be up all night worrying if she didn't.

'Hello?'

'Is that Eden Gray?'

'Yes, it is.' She didn't recognise the voice.

'This is Morvah Lutey, Carmen's sister. I'm calling on her phone. She's in hospital. She's had a heart attack.'

'My god, is she okay?'

'She's stable. They'll keep her in overnight then fit a stent tomorrow. It's a blessing really. She could have had an attack anytime. It might have been fatal if I hadn't been there to call an ambulance. This way she'll at least get the treatment she needs.'

'That is a blessing,' agreed Eden. 'Give her my best wishes and tell her Rowan is in custody but I have every hope she'll be released on bail once the manslaughter charge has been dropped.'

She wasn't sure, given Rowan had broken her bail conditions before, but Carmen didn't need to know that right now.

'I will … but Eden there is something I need to tell you. Someone else might need your help.'

'Who?'

'I'd rather not say over the phone; could we meet?'

'When?'

'Now? Can you come to the hospital?'

'Now?' Eden was so tired she felt like one of the walking dead. 'Can't it wait until the morning; surely you need to concentrate on Carmen tonight?'

'It won't wait, I'm afraid. It's about Elspeth Fuller's murder.'

'Don't you think you should speak to the police if you've got information, rather than me?'

'No … not the police.'

Morvah's voice wavered on the end of the phone. 'I need to talk to you first. I need your advice on what to do.'

'Okay, where shall we meet?' asked Eden reluctantly. She didn't feel she had any choice; the woman seemed determined and so she arranged to meet her outside the main entrance of the Royal Cornwall Hospital. She had no idea what was so important; it must be something major. From what little she knew of Carmen's sister; she wasn't the hysterical type.

When she arrived fifteen minutes later, Morvah was already waiting. Eden pulled up and she got in.

'I'll park up and we can talk.'

'No. I need you to drive to the farm.'

'The farm? Why?' Eden asked, even more confused.

'I'll tell you on the way.'

Eden took a good look at the woman next to her. There was little physical similarity between the sisters. She was dark like Rowan but unlike her niece, had a refined beauty, the upward curve of her chin; her profile, just short of haughty. Morvah's raven hair was pulled tightly back and she was dressed in running gear. She looked fit; her body a sinewy toned advertisement for the gym. She had none of the full-figured cosiness her sister possessed.

As she drove, Morvah relayed the conversation she'd had that evening with Carmen; about her meeting with Matthew and finally about the scalpel and how Elspeth's broken body had been carved with Pagan symbols.

Eden was too stunned to do anything but listen as the woman unwound the tale.

Finally, when she was certain Morvah had finished, she spoke.

'Where is Matthew now?'

'At the farm babysitting the children. I rang him before you arrived to tell him about Carmen and said I was on the way.'

'Did you tell him why?'

'No, I told him I was coming to look after the children so he could go to the hospital to be with his mother.'

'And me?'

'I told him you were giving me a lift because I'd ridden in the ambulance to the hospital and had left my car at my flat.'

'Did he believe you?'

'I think so. It was half true after all and he was so worried about Carmen I don't think he thought anything of it.'

'What are you proposing we do when we get there?'

'Confront him of course; convince him to confess. You need to tell him how it will be better for him in the long run and will save his mother going through what she's had to with Rowan.'

'I'm not sure that's wise. If what you believe is true and he has murdered a woman in cold blood, he's bound to be in a heightened emotional state already. Add to that the news about his mother. It might be enough to tip him over the edge. Don't forget there are two young children in the house.'

'Don't worry, he'll listen to me. He's always listened to me. I'm the one who taught him all of this stuff. If I hadn't taught him the craft and the family history, he would never have felt so strongly about what Elspeth did. Now I have to sort this out. I owe it to Carmen.'

'I have to tell you I'm uncomfortable with this,' said Eden. 'I don't feel either of us are equipped if something goes wrong.'

'Trust me, Matthew won't harm us. He won't lie if I ask him outright and point to the evidence. He was a pragmatic honest little boy, unlike that sister of his, and will do the right thing.'

'Is that how you're going to deal with this? Are you going to come straight out and ask him if he killed Elspeth; is that why I'm here, as a witness to his confession?'

'And to help him. I know if he confesses you can't pretend he's innocent but he must be a very sick boy to have killed the Fuller woman like that; to have clubbed her; strangled her, cut her throat and then carved her dead body. He needs professional help and you can make sure he gets it. You can protect him the way you protected Rowan. She didn't deserve your help; Matty does.'

Eden hadn't been privy to Luke's conversation with Carmen earlier so when Morvah had told her about the symbols it was the first she'd heard of it. Now she'd divulged the terrible way Elspeth had been murdered, she was finding it difficult to equate the mild-mannered young man she'd met with the fanatic Morvah painted.

'I can't understand how anyone could kill someone that way; it's barbaric.'

Morvah hesitated. 'Carmen told me when she came around. I'm sorry, I shouldn't have said. She told me not to say anything. The police told her in confidence about the markings and the method used to kill Fuller.'

Eden remembered the shocked look on Carmen's face when she came back into the kitchen after speaking to Luke.

Morvah continued. 'It's a Celtic ritual you know, the Threefold Killing, carried out to appease the gods when they have been angered.'

'And you taught Matthew about it?'

'Not how to perform it obviously but yes, I taught him about it. It's part of our culture; I taught him about the symbols and Wiccan. I assume he read about the rest. He was always an avid reader and it's widely documented.'

As she drove into the now familiar courtyard, Eden felt Carmen's absence. Her motherly presence gave the place its warmth. Knowing she wasn't inside hovering about in the kitchen changed its character for Eden. The granite walls suddenly seemed cold and uninviting; the wet shine on the cobbles treacherous. Matthew came to the door the minute the car pulled up.

'Is Ma alright; please say she's going to be okay?' He spotted Eden. 'Hello Miss Gray.'

'Where are the children, Matthew?'

He looked confused. 'In bed of course.'

'Of course, yes of course they are,' said Eden, trying her best to muffle the tense tone of her voice.

'Morvah's going to stay and mind them while I'm at the hospital. Thanks for dropping her off, Mum will be relieved. Who says solicitors aren't worth the money?' he smiled pulling on his coat.

'There's no rush Matty,' said Morvah, 'She's only now been put on the ward. There's plenty of time; they'll have given her something to sleep. Just as long as you're there when she wakes up. Sit down with us for a minute, I'll make a pot of tea and fill you in on what the doctors have told me.'

She moved behind Matthew, took off his coat and hung it back up in the hall.

'Where was she when she had the attack?' Matthew asked.

'With me, at my flat,' replied Morvah, re-entering the room. 'She'd come to tell me Rowan was home. I'll make that pot of tea now.'

'I'll make it if you like?' offered Matthew.

'No Matty, I'll do it; I can manage. I'll put two sugars in, you've had a shock but you can do something for me while you're waiting, Eden's interested in the symbols; you know, the ones I taught you when you were little; the Swan's foot; the mark of Bride. Can you show her what it looks like while I'm doing this? It's some background for Rowan's defence. That's right, isn't it Eden?'

'Yes, that's right; some background so I can build up a picture,' Eden lied.

Matthew walked to the dresser and came back with a pad of paper and a pencil. He drew a circle and a V with a straight line rising from the vertex so it resembled a bird's footprint. He drew carefully, concentrating, so each line touched the edge of the circle.

'There,' he said, pushing the pad towards Eden.

'Good,' said Morvah glancing over her shoulder at the drawing, 'have you remembered all the signs?'

Matthew dragged the notebook back; took the pencil and drew a pentacle.

'Yeah most of them I think, but I haven't drawn them for years, not since I had that fit about not being able to do the charms; that was sexism, that was,' he laughed.

Morvah smiled at him. 'Yes, I suppose it was.'

Morvah handed Matthew his tea. Then made one for Eden who thought it looked like the weak Fairtrade stuff her mother used to serve up, but it was hot and sweet and she took a sip needing the sugar hit.

'Your mother also told me Elspeth Fuller, the archaeologist, is dead. Someone murdered her,' Morvah said.

Matthew looked completely taken aback. 'Murdered?'

'Yes, and they found marks on her body.'

'What do you mean, marks?'

'Cuts. You know you can tell me anything, Matty, I'll always be on your side, no matter what,' said Morvah touching Matthew's hand as she slid down next to him.

'Tell you what?' queried Matthew looking bemused.

'I know you were angry when I told you about Elspeth selling the offerings to collectors abroad. I understand how strongly you feel about the sacred places. I know how you feel; I'm angry too.'

'What are you talking about, selling stuff from the site? Are you saying she's been doing that?'

'Matthew, I told you so when you came around to mine to tell me off for keeping Rowan's whereabouts a secret.'

'I've never been to your flat. I don't even know where it is.'

Morvah shot a glance at Eden, then turned her attention back to Matthew. Holding his face between her hands, she looked straight into his eyes.

'You don't have to lie, Matty. Eden and I are here to help. Whatever you've done I'll stand by you; all of us will, but you need to tell the truth. Eden can only help you if you tell the truth.'

Matthew's mouth dropped open. He pulled away. 'Stop calling me Matty, I'm not a bloody kid anymore. What the hell is going on here, are you trying to make out I did this, that I killed this woman?'

'Matthew you came around to my place, ranting about Rowan and I told you how she was involved with James Ferris, the archaeologist from the site, and he and Elspeth Fuller had been defiling the ground and selling the sacred offerings to the highest bidder.'

Matthew looked to Eden; pleading for help.

'I don't know what she's talking about.' His eyes were wild and frightened and Eden watched as he staggered slightly when he tried to get up, then toppled back into his chair. He grabbed at his hair and for a moment he reminded Eden of Rowan in the police interview room. She wondered whether, like his sister, he was a bloody good actor or whether as Morvah said, he was disturbed and needed help. She wasn't happy with this. If this had been a police interview and Matthew was her client, she would have stopped it.

'Morvah, I think that's enough,' she said.

'No,' Morvah retorted tersely, 'you need to tell the truth, Matthew. This family is being ripped apart by lies. You're a good boy; you need to tell the truth. Where's the scalpel you took from my flat?'

'What scalpel? What are you talking about?'

'Matthew I was using a scalpel to cut a piece of coir matting when you came around. You took the remnants away with you to put on the compost heap.'

'I didn't … I didn't.'

He was floundering now; his words sounding slightly slurred. Eden wondered if this was what a mental breakdown looked like. The plummet into denial; a total disconnection with reality. It must be terrifying for him.

Morvah sighed heavily as she got up. 'Well let's go and see, shall we?'

'Yes, let's go and see,' repeated Matthew, rising shakily to his feet.

Eden jumped up. She needed to bring this to a swift conclusion.

'No, tell me where the compost heap is and I'll go and look. You two stay here.'

'It's around the side by the dustbins. There's a light on the side of the building. Carmen puts the kitchen waste there. Just lift the lid.'

Following Morvah's directions, Eden made her way around the side of the farmhouse to where the bins were lined up. At the far end was a compost bin made out of old pallets; a plank of wood lying across the top. She lifted it, her hand trembling and there, amongst the carrots, cabbage leaves and eggshells, peeking out from a ripped brown paper bag were several strips of coir matting.

Eden had hoped they wouldn't be there; that they'd got this wrong, for Carmen's sake. She lifted one of the strips. Shaking a potato peeling from it, she walked it back into the kitchen and laid it on the table.

Matthew looked at it with disbelief and horror.

'You see Matthew; it's as I said,' whispered Morvah.

'But I don't remember putting it there. I don't remember any of it? Why don't I remember, Morvah?'

'You're not well, Matthew. I think you've been more upset by what's been going on than any of us knew. All this with Rowan's baby and the site and you trying to hold this place together single-handed. I think you snapped and now you need help. Do you remember where you hid the scalpel?'

Matthew looked desolate; his face was a ghostly grey, his eyes sunken. 'I don't know I don't know.'

Morvah put her arms around him. 'Oh Matty, you poor boy.'

Turning to Eden she said quietly, 'Can you look around to see if you can find it?'

Eden thought they should call the police but something in the woman's voice propelled her forward.

'Where should I look?'

'I don't know. It might not even be here. Maybe he's thrown it away already. It might be down the well, I suppose?'

'The well?' Matthew said clinging on to her.

'Yes, my love, that's where the woman's body was found. I don't suppose you remember that either, my poor lamb.'

Matthew said nothing.

Eden glanced around. She had no idea where to start.

'Surely the police will find it if it's anywhere here? They'll have to conduct a proper search.'

'Yes, I suppose they will. I'll tell you what, check his jacket. I don't suppose for one minute it's there but I wouldn't want him to get hold of it and do something silly.' She gave Eden a knowing glance. Eden understood. Morvah was worried Matthew might make a run for it when the police turned up and do harm to himself. She walked to the hallway and felt the pockets of his coat. She was relieved to find a fiver and a petrol receipt in the first but when she felt inside the second, she recoiled at the touch of cold steel. Tentatively, she reached back in and lifted the scalpel out with her fingertips. Oh god, he must have been keeping it for something. A shiver grazed the back of her neck. He'd probably known all along they were on to him and intended to get rid of it on his way to the hospital. Hands shaking, she carefully carried it back into the room.

Morvah rushed to take it from her. 'Where did you find it?'

Eden looked at Matthew, his head in his hands.

'In his pocket.'

'Oh Matthew, you still had it with you? You wouldn't want to do anything silly now, would you? You have to realise, you're not in control of your feelings at the moment. I brought Eden with me to help you. She will make sure no harm comes to you. If you are unwell no one will blame you for what has happened.'

Matthew groaned.

'I think we have enough,' Eden whispered. 'We need to call the police now; they should deal with this from here.'

'Okay, you call them. The phone's in the hallway.'

Eden's stomach cramped. 'I need to go to the bathroom too; are you okay here with him on your own?'

Morvah nodded. "There's a cloakroom at the end, first on the left.'

She left the two of them in the kitchen, closing the door behind her so Matthew couldn't hear her conversation with the police. She didn't want to distress him any further.

She felt sick. She knew Luke would be tied up interviewing James Ferris. If she called the emergency services they'd come lights flashing, sirens wailing. She had never actually seen a gun in the house but if Matthew didn't have a shotgun he'd be unique amid the farming community. If he panicked they could find themselves in a hostage situation. On the other hand, if she called the station they were likely to make a note of the call and pass it on to Luke as the investigating officer, but what if he was unavailable? She decided to cut out the middle man and try his mobile. If she had no joy it would have to be 999.

Eden bolted the door and punched in Luke's mobile number. The phone seemed to ring for ages. 'Come on, please come on,' she willed him to answer. When he finally did, he sounded groggy, as if he'd been asleep.

'Were you in bed?' Eden asked wishing desperately she was too. She was beyond tired. If she sat down again, she knew she'd fall asleep.

'No, I fell asleep in the chair. Are you okay, you sound a bit odd?'

'I'm at the Lutey farm with Carmen's sister, Morvah, and Matthew. Carmen is in hospital; she's had a heart attack. Luke, I think Matthew killed Elspeth Fuller. Morvah called to tell me about the symbols carved on Elspeth's body and she thought it was Matthew. He knows how to draw the symbols. She taught him and he took a scalpel from her house. Then she told me about the Threefold Killing; the way Elspeth was ritually killed and it's terrible and …' The words spilled from her mouth like spaghetti onto a plate.

'Hang on … slow down. When did she tell you about the Threefold Killing?'

'In the car on the way here. She said Carmen told her. She knew she wasn't meant to; that it was confidential but she told her anyway.'

'But Carmen didn't know. I didn't know about it when I spoke to Carmen about the symbols earlier; nobody knew except the pathologist.'

'But Morvah said …'

'Where are you right now?'

'In the cloakroom.'

'Is anyone with you? Can anyone hear what you're saying? Be very careful how you answer if they can.'

'No, I came in here so Matthew couldn't hear me call you. Morvah stayed with him in the kitchen. She said she left a message at the station for you to come.'

'If she did, I didn't get it. Stay exactly where you are and keep the door locked. Do you understand me?'

'Why, what's going on?' Her brain felt like cotton wool. She couldn't understand what he was on about.

'There's only one way Morvah can know how Elspeth was killed; she's the killer. Morvah's the murderer, not Matthew, and if she's vicious enough to carry out that kind of killing and calculating enough to frame her nephew for it, she's extremely dangerous. If she gets even an inkling, you're on to her, your life is in jeopardy. Do not move and do not open that door.'

FIFTY-SIX

Eden's head was spinning as she ended the call. She turned, lifted the toilet lid and retched into the bowl. When she'd finished vomiting, she held her head beneath the tap, slurping up the water to rinse her mouth; splashing her face to keep her wits about her.

Pulling the flush, she listened at the door. She couldn't hear a thing. Matthew was on his own with Morvah but she couldn't risk going back. At least he was strong. It was one thing to overpower Elspeth; quite another to get the better of Matthew. He was muscular and fit from the relentless routine of manual work on the farm. In any event, she didn't think Morvah intended to harm him. She didn't need to. She was relying on his trust in her and her ability to make him believe he'd done something heinous he couldn't remember. She was a clever manipulator. She'd only met her once but she'd been able to convince her Matthew was a murderer.

Luke had ordered her to stay put but the children were upstairs. She had to get them out of there and to safety. Tentatively sliding the bolt and opening the door an inch, she peered into the hallway. The kitchen door was still closed. She could hear the thrum of voices, but not what was being said. She slowly sidled out of the cloakroom to the bottom of the stairs to try the back door. It was locked and no key.

They couldn't get out that way and she couldn't take them through the kitchen. She had no choice; she'd have to hide them and hope for the best.

'What are you doing?'

Morvah's voice made her jump.

'Checking the door's locked … in case Matthew decides to make a run for it before the police arrive,' she lied, turning to face the woman she now knew to be a killer. Eden wanted to scream; tell her the police were coming for her but there was something unnerving about Morvah's expression. Eden could imagine this woman, jaw set, cold and chillingly calm, slitting Elspeth's throat and not breaking a sweat and knew she was no match for her.

'Is Matthew okay alone? I mean, don't you think you should be watching him until the police arrive?' she asked, her voice high-pitched and unconvincing.

Morvah moved closer. Eden backed away, but as the door handle dug into her back knew she had nowhere to go.

'Are you alright Eden? You look unwell. You're trembling.'

Eden willed herself not to run. 'I … I'm. It's the shock; first Carmen then Matthew …' she said, her lips sticking to her teeth as they parted in a nervous smile.

'Hmm,' sighed Morvah, 'Well now you've told the police what's happened here, we can all get back to normal. Come on, let's go back to the kitchen and wait for them together.'

Eden knew she had to move quickly. She didn't want to be with this woman when the police arrived. She didn't trust her not to lose it when she realised her plan to frame Matthew had failed and they were there to arrest her.

'Perhaps I'd better look in on the children, to check they're alright. I won't be long. I'll be back down in a minute.'

Morvah paused by the kitchen door. Eden held her breath, waiting for a response which to her relief was nonchalant.

'Okay, but don't be long.'

Eden remembered the attic where Carmen had originally hidden the book. She'd take the children there. It was risky. There was no escape if they were cornered. There were probably no windows. Even if there were, the children were too small to attempt any acrobatics onto the roof.

She made her way upstairs and along the landing trying to work out which room might belong to the children. Noticing one door was slightly ajar, she remembered her mother always left her door open when she was little and gently pushed it.

Blackout curtains designed to stop children lying awake on long summer evenings. tarred the room pitch-black. She didn't want to put the light on; didn't want to frighten them. As her eyes slowly adjusted, she made out two single beds and guessed she'd made the right choice. She could hear soft breathing in the dark.

Feeling her way around the bottom of the beds towards the window she pulled back the curtains as quietly as she could. The room was immediately bathed in silvery light from the full moon hanging like a Christmas bauble in the sky.

She shuffled towards the first of the beds with its Spiderman duvet cover. Guessing it was Jago's, she balanced lightly on the edge, hesitant suddenly at the thought of scaring him. She wasn't exactly a stranger but he was bound to be scared if jolted out of sleep. She tentatively reached out and shook him softly.

'Jago … Jago,' she whispered, 'wake up.'

The boy moaned and rolled over.

'Jago,' she repeated, a little louder this time.

He rolled onto his back and peeled open his eyes.

'What? Ma, is it the fire?'

He was half asleep, thoughts of being woken not so long ago to the smell of smoke to the forefront of his mind.

'No Jago, it's Eden. Don't worry, there's no fire. Mummy has asked me to come and wake you. It's nothing to worry about but she told me to tell you it's important to do exactly as I say. She needs you to be a big boy and take charge.'

Jago slowly pulled himself up, rubbing the sleep from his eyes.

'What's happening; where's Mum?'

'She'll be here soon but she asked me to come and take you to the attic to wait for her because she's got a surprise for you.'

'I'm too tired,' he yawned.

'Jago,' she said, more urgency in her voice now, 'it is very, very important.'

She was starting to panic. She didn't have long before Morvah began to wonder where she was.

'Jago, please. You have to help me with Maisy because she's little and can be silly sometimes.'

'She can,' he said smugly; 'she can be a real fruit loop.'

'Yes, you're the clever one and you can help me and your mum by waking her now very slowly so she's not scared because we need to keep as quiet as mice. You must tell her she has to come with us up to the attic and wait for Mummy. Can you do that for me, Jago?'

She watched as his chest pumped out a little with the prospect of being in charge of his sister.

'Alright,' he said swinging his legs over the side of his bed and walking to where Maisy lay fast asleep.

'Maisy … Maisy,' he hissed in her ear, shaking her roughly, 'wake up … wake up.'

The little girl sat bolt upright. 'What?' she shouted, pushing her mass of unruly curls from her face; puffing out her sleep flushed cheeks. Wide eyes rested on Eden.

'What you doing here?' she demanded.

'Be quiet,' shushed Jago, clamping his hand over her mouth. 'We need to whisper. It's a surprise. We need to go up to the attic and wait for Mum.'

'What sort of surprise?' Maisy lisped, between thumb sucks. 'Why do we have to go upstairs?'

'Because Eden said so and Mum said to do what Eden says.'

Eden admired his logic and was sorry she seemed incapable of the same unquestioning rationality when told what to do. It certainly made life easier.

'It's a game,' he added for good measure.

'Yes,' joined in Eden, 'it's a game; hide and seek. We've got to go now or else we won't win a prize.' With the word *prize*, Maisy bucked up.

'Okay then,' she huffed, 'can I bring my blankie?'

She pulled a manky-looking blue blanket from beneath the sheets.

'Yeah, now come on,' said Jago dragging her off the bed.

'Jago you lead the way; you're in charge,' whispered Eden, checking the landing was clear. 'Don't run, remember we have to be as quiet as possible.'

Jago crept along the landing towards the door at the end. Maisy toddled on behind, dragging her blanket. Eden reached down and took her hand; feeling her hot chubby fingers tighten around her own.

Closing the door to the attic room behind them, Eden felt for the light switch.

'The bulb's gone,' said Jago, 'give me your hand.'

Eden hoisted Maisy up onto her hip and as the child rested her head on her shoulder a wave of feeling filled her with a resolve to protect these two from harm. She took Jago's hand.

'There's a light that works up here. I can turn it on if you like but if we're hiding, it's best the light's off. I know the way,' Jago said with authority.

'Then let's leave it off. I'll follow you.'

The boy navigated them around the cluttered room filled with boxes and old furniture, leading them to the far end.

'We've got a camp down the back,' he said.

'It's a fairy castle,' whispered Maisy in her ear.

'No, it ain't, it's an army camp, stupid.'

'Okay, you show me,' said Eden.

Jago led her through to the back of the attic space where a tarpaulin had been draped over some upturned chairs to form a tent.

'Here,' he said, 'come inside; we can all fit.'

The children had piled old cushions and blankets to form a cosy hidey-hole. Maisy cuddled into her.

Eden listened. She could hear nothing from downstairs. She wasn't sure how long she could keep them quiet; how long she could keep up this pretence.

'Right, both of you lie down and keep as quiet as you can.'

'Sleeping Lions,' said Maisy.

'Yes, Sleeping Lions,' said Eden, remembering the game loved by parents the world over.

Maisy lay her head on a cushion. Within minutes she was drifting back to sleep. Eden ran her fingers through her springy damp curls.

Jago lay on his stomach; aiming an old table leg through the flap as if it was a rifle.

'Jago, you stay here and keep watch. I'm going to give you my phone. I'm going back downstairs for a moment but if I don't come back say by the time you've counted …' she paused trying to think of a suitable number, a thousand, I want you to phone DI Parish.'

She handed the boy her mobile. 'All you have to do is press the number five and the phone will dial his number.'

'What do I say?' asked the boy looking confused.

'Tell him you and Maisy are here in the attic and I'm with Matthew and Auntie Morvah downstairs; tell him to hurry up.'

'Is this part of the game; is he bringing Mum?'

'Yes, that's right. You're being such a big brave boy. Mummy will be so pleased when I tell her.'

The boy grinned from ear to ear.

She lifted the tent flap and crawled out.

Straightening up as best she could; remembering to avoid the low beams, she felt her way through the darkness, to the stairs. She needed to get back to Morvah before she came to find her and discovered the children weren't in their beds.

She tip-toed down the stairs like a thief, keeping to the far edges of each step; fearing every creak. At the bottom, she closed the door behind her as quietly as she could and listened. She could no longer hear voices and for a split second nearly lost her nerve and turned back, then remembered Matthew. He was Carmen's child too. Taking a deep breath, she quickened her step along the landing towards the main staircase.

She let out a gasp as Morvah walked out from the darkened room to the left of her; blocking her way.

'Where have you been? Matthew and I got tired of waiting.'

Eden stopped in her tracks, desperately trying to steady herself; She touched her throat, her voice shaky as she asked,

'Is Matthew okay?'

'Stop asking that … is Matthew okay; is Matthew okay?' Morvah flared.

'I'm sorry …' Eden stuttered.

'Never mind Matthew; where are Maisy and Jago?'

'In their room … sleeping. Maisy stirred when I checked on her so I waited until she was back asleep.'

'Are you certain they're both asleep now?'

'Yes … yes, they're fine.'

'Is that so?' Morvah hissed, leaning forward; eyes narrowing. 'Shall we go and check, to be sure?'

Eden caught the glint of the scalpel clutched in the woman's right hand.

'No… there's no need; we'll only wake them. Let's go downstairs and wait for the police like you said.'

'No,' she snapped. 'What would Carmen say if she thought I was leaving the babysitting to the family solicitor?'

'I don't mind.'

'Ah, but I do.

Morvah grabbed Eden's arm; pulling her towards the children's bedroom.

Moonlight licked the scattered toys, the dinosaur wallpaper; the obviously empty beds. Eden knew she was busted.

'So, are you going to tell me where the children are?'

'I don't know.'

'Liar,' Morvah shrieked, digging her nails in.

Eden winced.

Morvah lifted the scalpel; until now held tight against her leg. 'Do you know most people wrongly think you slit your wrists this way?' she said, twisting Eden's wrist, palm upwards, before purposefully running the cold blade horizontally across it; 'lots of suicides fail because of that. You have to cut this way.'

Eden's fingers tingled as she felt the icy sharpness trace her veins.

'That way you take no time at all to bleed out. It's almost painless.'

'Morvah, please,' Eden pleaded. 'What are you doing?'

'How did you guess it was me who killed the Fuller woman?' Morvah asked; jaw set, her face close enough for Eden to feel her breath, as she traced a perfect oval with the blade on the surface of Eden's palm; drawing blood. 'How?'

The yell made Eden jump and the blade dug deeper.

'The Triple Killing,' she blurted. 'You said Carmen told you but she didn't know about it; no one knew … except the killer.'

'Stupid…stupid.'

Eden felt the woman's grip relax slightly as she chastised herself, and for one fleeting moment thought of fighting her way out of this. She could scratch with her free hand, pull hair; bite, kick, scream; all the things she'd always told herself she'd do if some lunatic ever singled her out for a beating, only real life wasn't like that. When the two louts attacked her in the street, she was too petrified to do anything; this was the same. She was a lawyer not a fighter; reason her most reliable weapon. Also, she had to think of the children; If they heard screaming, they might come down. She couldn't risk it.

Keep talking, Eden; keep your head and keep talking, she told herself.

'The police will be here any minute. Why make matters worse for yourself? Things have got out of hand but the situation isn't irretrievable.'

Morvah gave an unnatural, hysterical laugh.

'I'm not one of your clients; I don't want to retrieve anything. I'm not willing to say I'm sorry; argue I'm mad or damaged by my upbringing, or what other crap you lot cook up to get people off. I don't need anyone's approval or forgiveness; I answer to a power far greater than the justice you serve,' she smiled. 'I'm glad I did it and it was so easy. She came willingly; you know, to the well. It was important she did; that she was a willing sacrifice. All I had to do was tell her the site's secrets, and do you know when I bound her hands behind her back and pushed her to her knees, I felt she finally understood in the scheme of things, her life, like yours is unimportant.'

Eden couldn't help herself. 'What about Matthew? If you're so bloody proud of what you've done, why frame Matthew?'

Morvah let go her wrist; her grin twisting to a grimace.

'I didn't want to hurt Matthew; I love him, he's the son I never had, but now I'll have to say he killed you too; that I couldn't stop him.'

Eden noticed her eyes soften as she spoke her nephew's name.

'But you're bound to lose him then, no matter how you spin it he'll never believe he's killed me.'

The reprieve was fleeting, Morvah's expression flint and ice with her next words.

'He's already lost to me, like Carmen and that little bitch Rowan; they've lost their way. It's too late for them but I can do so much good once they're gone. I can live here and lead Maisy and Jago towards the true path; instruct them in the old religion. I can begin to dig the pits again; follow my true calling.'

Inch by tentative inch, Eden widened the gap between them.

'But why would Carmen do that, why would she let you raise her children?'

'She wouldn't be here. She's had one heart attack, what's to say she'll survive another? Next time I'll get the dosage right.'

'What?'

'Aren't you supposed to be the clever one; can't you work it out for yourself?'

'You tried to kill Carmen; you gave her something to induce her heart attack?'

'Guilty as charged; give the lawyer a round of applause; pity you'll never get the credit for solving the case. You'll be dead; another tragic victim of a disturbed boy,' Morvah scoffed.

Words swarmed in Eden's throat. She could hold them in no longer.

'You don't have a calling, you mad, delusional bitch. You're jealous, pure and simple; jealous of this place; of Carmen's life; her children. You probably only helped Rowan in the first place to spite Carmen. Everything has been for you; to get what you've always thought should be yours. Well, it won't work because the police know what you've done and you're going to prison. No one, not even me, can get you off.'

Eden scrambled onto Maisy's bed. If she could keep her balance, the height advantage would make it easier to fend Morvah off. If the woman lost her cool, she might just make a mistake.

'Carmen's alive and this place is hers and her children love her. They could never love a sad twisted bitch; a murdering monster like you!'

'Shut your bloody mouth,' Morvah screamed, lashing out with the scalpel.

Eden stumbled, bouncing slightly.

'Why is the truth so hard to swallow?' she taunted, remembering the two kickboxing lessons her friend Kate dragged her to before she made an excuse to quit.

Leaning back against the wall for support, she flicked out her leg, landing a perfect blow to Morvah's nose, splitting it open like a ripe fig.

The woman reeled, sinking to her knees.

Eden felt around on the shelf above Maisy's headboard for anything she could use as a weapon. Her fingers ran over soft toys, picture books, cobbled together models made from cereal boxes and loo rolls, then something round; heavy. She lifted it towards the light. A snow globe; glitter falling around a prancing pink unicorn. Eden held it in both hands and brought it down on top of Morvah's head.

Morvah looked up, her bewildered expression changing to fear as blood trickled slowly down her forehead and either side of her smashed nose.

Eden didn't hang around to watch her keel over. She leapt past her onto Jago's bed, then to the floor and ran for the attic, pulling the door shut behind her.

Jago peered down at her from the top of the stairs as she leaned all her weight against the closed door.

'Turn the light on Jago, throw down anything you can lift.'

The boy didn't ask why. Eden's expression warned this was no longer a game.

As things tumbled down the stairs, Eden piled them up behind the door; books empty tea-chests, an old tricycle. She ran up to collect the heavy items until the debris blocking the entrance reached the door handle. It wouldn't hold forever but would buy them time until Luke arrived if Morvah gained consciousness and came looking for them.

As if reading her mind Jago said; 'I called him; when I reached one thousand, like you told me.'

'Good boy,' she smiled, collapsing exhausted on the dusty attic floor.

'I did ten lots of a hundred but I lost count once or twice and had to start again. I heard shouting and was too frightened to wait any longer.'

'That's okay; you did the right thing,' she reassured, hauling herself up onto wobbly legs, taking his hand and letting him lead her back to the tent.

All they could do now was wait.

The dim light through the tarpaulin cast a green glow across the cushions and blankets. Go on, Jago, you go back inside with Maisy. I'll be outside. She knew she'd have to fight for them if Morvah broke through. She grabbed the table leg Jago had used as a toy gun earlier. It was solid; she'd hit her again if necessary.

Jago looked up at her, his head tilted to one side.

'But Maisy's not here.'

'Mmm, what?' Eden smiled down at him, thinking she had misheard.

'She said she'd had enough and she didn't care if she won the stupid old game; said she was thirsty and was going downstairs to the kitchen for some juice. She went before you came back; before I called Luke, didn't you see her?'

'No ... No ... No.'

She scrambled down the attic stairs pulling things aside as she went; clawing at the pile of furniture and boxes blocking her way. Jago stared at her like she was mad.

'Help me Jago ...'

'But we only just piled it up there.'

'I know, I know but it was a mistake ... please Jago, help me ... help me.'

They threw aside the debris. Eden pulled at the handle making a gap big enough to slide through, pulling Jago through after her.

308

'Wait here,' she said, rushing into the children's bedroom.

The snow globe lay shattered on the floor. Morvah was gone.

'Jago, stay behind me as we go downstairs.'

They had barely crept halfway down when they heard the sirens.

FIFTY-SEVEN

'Why can't you ever do as you're bloody told?' Luke scolded, handing her a glass of water.

Denise Charlton was tending to Matthew. He seemed asleep; head tilted backwards. She peered into his face. 'He's out for the count. I think he might have been given something,' she said lifting the teacup to sniff the dregs. 'I think it's in the tea.'

'Morvah made it.' said Eden.

'We probably ought to make him vomit,' said Denise.

'Charcoal,' said Jago, 'that's what Mum used one time when our Rowan got drunk on cider. We got loads since the fire; she won't mind. It's in the cupboard. It makes you sick.'

Jago pulled one of the chairs from the table; got on it and reached into the kitchen cupboard to retrieve a jar of black powder from its spot next to the Marmite.

'You mix it with water and swallow it down quick. It makes your teeth black but Mum said in olden days they used it as toothpaste.'

Denise spooned some of the powder into a small jug, mixed it with water from the tap, then, holding Matthew's nose, poured it down his throat. Seconds later he was hunched over the sink spluttering black bile.

When he'd finished, Denise asked,

'Matthew, where's Morvah?'

'Dunno,' he said, wiping his mouth with his sleeve. 'One minute she was here saying I'd done all sorts, then the next she said she'd made a mistake and left. She didn't come back as far as I know. I think I fell asleep.'

'Did she say anything else; give you any idea where she might be going?'

'No, she said sorry; that she knew I hadn't done what she'd said; asked if I could forgive her. I didn't understand; I was so tired. I half thought I'd dreamt the whole thing.'

'Did she have Maisy with her?'

'I don't know,' he groaned.

Gut-loosening fear swelled in Eden. She'd assumed Maisy was there with one of the other officers.

'We've got to find Maisy,' she screamed, heading for the door.

Luke grabbed her. 'Stay calm, I've got men searching the farm buildings and the upper fields.'

'But if she's got her?' Her voice trailed off as she remembered Jago was there.

'Was there anything else, try to think, Matthew?' Luke pressed.

Matthew's brow furrowed as he struggled to remember; his voice hesitant, carefully weighing each word. 'She said not to worry; she knew what she had to do to put things right … no not put things right; to right the circle, those were her words; to right the circle.' He looked up; eyes pleading for a sign his memories were of use. 'The next thing I knew, you were pouring that muck down my throat.'

A constable barged through the kitchen door.

'Sir, Miss Gray's car is gone.'

Eden felt a surge of panic. 'I hit her pretty hard. I'm not sure she's fit to drive.'

She remembered Morvah's fingers tensing on the handle of the scalpel; her fear of the blade rending her flesh.

'Did you find the scalpel? I think it slipped under the bed when I hit her but didn't stop to check?'

'Denise, go and see,' Luke said. Then, addressing the police officer in the doorway, 'Get the car's description out there. We're looking for a woman and a little girl.'

'Luke, if she harms her … it's my fault. I shouldn't have left them … I shouldn't have.'

Luke reached out to steady her. His grip was firm; his face earnest.

'We'll find Maisy. I promise you; this is not your fault, Eden.'

'I need to see Mum,' slurred Matthew.

He looked young; hair dishevelled; lips black as if he'd been eating liquorice.

'You'll be able to see her soon,' reassured Luke.

Pulling Eden to one side he whispered, 'We think Morvah might have tried to kill Carmen.'

'She did, she told me as much and intends to do it again.'

'We've got a team at the hospital guarding her and someone at Morvah's flat in case, but she's unlikely to risk going back there. Is there anywhere else you think she might go?'

'The site?' offered Eden; Elspeth's broken body ghosting through her mind.

'I've searched the bedroom floor; no sign of the weapon.' shouted Denise from the bottom of the stairs.

Neither commented but Eden was sure the same sickening thought crossed Luke's mind; Morvah had the scalpel with her and would use it again if pushed.

'Denise and I will go to the site,' said Luke. 'You stay here with Jago. One of my team will take Matthew to the hospital to get checked out.'

'No, I'm coming too,' insisted Eden, 'Maisy knows me and won't be so afraid if she sees I'm there.'

Luke paused for a second but to Eden's surprise didn't argue.

'Denise get one of the boys in here to wait with these two. Tell them any sign of Lutey or the girl they call us.'

Eden felt a tug on her jumper; Jago.

'Where's our prize then? We won, didn't we?'

'Yes, we did and your prize is …' Eden couldn't think of anything meaningful to say. She wished she could present him with his little sister; promise him she'd soon be back causing mayhem as usual but how could she promise that?'

'A ride in a police car, and you can put the sirens on and flash the lights and wear a police hat, then tell your mum all about it after,' said Luke saving her from the lie.

FIFTY-EIGHT

Denise drove. Eden parked herself in the back seat behind Luke. No one spoke; worst scenarios crowding their imaginations with outcomes so terrible they couldn't be uttered.

They were on their way to the site when they got the call to say Eden's car had been found on the road to Swanpool. Denise did a U-turn, taking the back lanes towards Falmouth and the coast.

The place was already cordoned off by the time they arrived. Police cars blocked the road; torchlight licking the trees as officers searched the woodland at either end of the beach. They pulled in behind Eden's car. It had been abandoned on the verge, the driver's door open, internal lights on. There was no sign of Morvah or Maisy.

Luke turned to her before getting out of the car.

'If I let you come with us do you promise to stick to me and Denise like glue no matter what; no going off on your own?'

'I promise.'

He was overestimating her capacity for bravery. She had no intention of doing anything stupid. They got out and walked towards her car. Her stomach jolted as she spotted Maisy's blood-stained blue blanket draped across the passenger seat.

'That's Maisy's ... but the blood. Oh god, Luke ...'

She steadied herself against the bonnet.

The moon so helpful earlier, now shrouded in wispy clouds like widows' weeds, gave no light to speak of and whilst she could hear the tidal shuffle of pebbles, it was impossible to make out where the water met the shore. Across the road, the still inky pool that gave the place its name no longer looked like a fun place to be. A handful of rowboats at the near end, bobbed listlessly under the jaundiced glow of the only working light in a carpark strewn with rubbish from bin bags ripped apart by seagulls; not a swan in sight.

'Sir?'

Eden jolted at the sound of the constable's voice.

'The suspect seems to have sustained an injury, the blood leads from the car down to the beach but then we lose it. We've called for the dogs but they haven't arrived yet.'

There was an unmistakeable excitement in the officer's voice. Who could blame him, it wasn't every day you were part of a team on the trail of a murderer? He could spend the next twenty years in the Devon and Cornwall constabulary waiting for another case like this.

'Show me,' said Luke, gesturing to the man to hand over his torch.

They followed the trail of barely visible blood along the road. Once they reached the sandy pathway onto the beach it was more obvious. There was a lot of it.

'How far down the beach does the trail go?'

'It stops to your right, Sir.'

Luke shone his torch directly onto the spot where a clot of blood splattered the smooth white pebbles and the trail stopped abruptly.'

'Those are the same pebbles Elspeth showed me; the ones she said were placed in the pits. She said they came from here. Luke, where's Maisy? You don't think it's Maisy's blood?'

'There's only one set of footprints. If she has the child with her, she's carrying her. Whatever happened, happened here; this is the beginning of the trail, not the end. The blood leads *back* to the car.

Didn't you think to check in the other direction for other trails?' Luke asked.

'I … I'm not sure, Sir. We saw the blood and followed it down the beach.'

'Gov …' It was Denise stumbling over the pebbles towards them.

'Elspeth Fuller's Jeep has been found in the underground carpark below Lutey's flat; her prints and the victim's blood are all over it.'

There was shouting... 'There's someone up by the pond.'

They scrambled back up the beach.

'Quick, shine the lights over there; to the left ... there in the rushes by the edge of the water.'

A bright white beam from a massive light fastened to the roof of a RNLI jeep moved across the pool.

'Morvah ... Morvah Lutey,' Luke shouted.

No reply. Luke took a deep breath to shout again. All other calling stopped; everyone fell silent.

'Morvah Lutey. We know you're there. You need treatment; you've lost a lot of blood. We have a medical team here ready to help. You need to come slowly towards us with Maisy. She must be cold in her nightclothes without her blanket.'

Eden knew this was Luke's way of letting Morvah know they'd found the child's blood-stained comforter.

The searchlight panned the pool like something from an old WW2 film.

'If you don't want to come out, will you at least confirm Maisy's okay; that she's not injured.'

'Why are you here? You people don't belong here.'

The voice came from the far end of the pond. The light hit her. Morvah stood alone on the shore, arms raised, shielding her eyes. She was stripped to the waist; her face, forearms and chest covered in blood.

'God almighty ...' whispered Denise.

Eden's stomach clenched as she remembered the cold steel against her wrist and Morvah's chilling advice; '*You have to cut this way ... that way you take no time at all to bleed out.*'

'She's cut her wrists ... with the scalpel; she's cut her wrists,' Eden exclaimed, 'it's her blood ... not Maisy's ... not Maisy's.'

'Right, everyone, we need to move quickly,' said Luke. 'You men, that way; Denise you're with me. We'll approach from the other side with the medic. You lot keep radio contact. We still don't know where the child is. The suspect must be feeling weak but she's got nothing to lose; caution is the watchword. Keep the light fixed on her.'

'What should I do?' asked Eden.

'Nothing, the last person she wants to see is you. You stay right here with the rest of the team.'

Luke, Denise and a nervous-looking paramedic set off skirting the left side of the pond towards Morvah. Three other officers, set out to the right, both teams keeping out of the light.

'What are you doing, where are you?' Morvah shouted.

No reply.

'Answer me!' she screamed. 'Turn the light off. I swear I'll kill the child. I will … turn that damn light off and keep away from me … keep away. If you move, I'll know.'

'Turn those lights off,' Luke shouted, his voice echoing across the black water, 'lights all off.'

They were immediately plunged into darkness.

'Okay, Morvah, the lights are out; we've done as you asked. Now, why don't you let Maisy come to us? You're badly hurt, if you've slit your wrists, we don't have long to get to you.'

'Shit we can't see a bloody thing,' one of the men stumbled behind Eden, 'and where's the girl; there's no sign of the kid?'

The impulse came too quickly for Eden to check it.

'Morvah, it's Eden,' she yelled out across the water. 'Please let Maisy go. Think of Carmen; think of Matthew and Jago … please, Morvah.' She knew enough not to mention Rowan's name.

'Eden Gray; still playing Mary Poppins?' Morvah shouted back; her speech slurred. 'I tried to tell you … but you wouldn't listen. It's pointless … all this. You and your tiny life; meaningless. Bride calls me. I am her faithful servant. She will take me under her wings and I will be reborn. This is not my end; this is my beginning.'

There was a massive splash.

'Turn the light on; turn it on,' shouted Eden.

There was no response.

'Turn the fucking light on,' she screamed.

The light shone across the water in time to see Morvah's body disappear beneath the surface.

Luke and Denise took off at speed. Eden followed, running as fast as she could; heart pounding; eyes fixed on the spot where the woman had gone under. Luke discarded his jacket then falling to the floor, pulled off his shoes, before jumping in.

Eden caught up with Denise and together they watched him disappear beneath the oily surface. Each time he came up to take a breath he scanned for any sign of Morvah but there was none. He disappeared again and Eden felt Denise grip her arm as both women held their breath waiting ... waiting for the surface to break again. Denise pulled away.

'I'm going in after him.'

Eden grabbed her as the water rippled and Luke emerged gasping for air, arms flaying as he laboured back to shore.

'Get a medic over here and an ambulance,' shouted Denise running towards him.

'I need ... to g ... go back in.' Luke stuttered as he hurled himself exhausted onto the grass.

'Yeah right,' said Denise 'like that's gonna happen.'

Eden watched the DS slip off her jacket and wrap it around Luke, holding him close; letting the warmth of her body leach through to his until the ambulance came. He was in good hands. The look of relief on Denise's face betrayed a concern far greater than that of a colleague. He was okay; wet, cold shaken up but alive. But where was Maisy?

'Maisy ... Maisy,' Eden screamed at the top of her voice.

Grabbing Luke's torch, she scrambled through the undergrowth, shining the light amongst the reeds where Morvah had stood minutes earlier. Nothing; no sign of the child.

Her throat was hoarse with shouting. Maisy wasn't the type to keep quiet. If she could hear she'd shout out, unless of course she couldn't hear her because she wasn't there or worse.

Defeated, legs buckling. she stumbled back to where Luke was being helped into the ambulance.

'What's going to happen now?' she asked Denise.

'We'll keep looking but there's a limit to what we can do in the dark. First light the divers will go down to retrieve the body and search ... in case ... you know Morvah had already ...'

'Oh god no … please don't say it. Perhaps she dropped her somewhere on the way here; perhaps she's safe?'

'Until we find a body there's hope,' soothed Denise. 'Do you want to go with Luke in the ambulance to the hospital?'

Eden began to weep. 'I can't. I can't leave until I know about Maisy; how can I face Carmen?'

'Look, it's probably best. You look done in and he could do with your support. This will have been hard on him; with him having a kid around the same age.'

'I hadn't thought about that,' Eden sobbed, thinking about Flora.

'He keeps his personal shit to himself, but something like this is bound to touch a nerve.'

Eden was seeing a different side to Denise. The woman was professional - there was no doubt about that - but she was also loyal. She had stuck by Luke when her own cause may have been better served by placing her allegiance elsewhere. He could do a lot worse than Denise Charlton.

Luke, wrapped like a Christmas turkey in foil to keep him warm, looked up when Eden stepped into the ambulance.

'Are you okay?' she asked.

'Yee … es,' he shivered. 'Maisy … did you find Maisy?'

'No … no but they're still looking. Denise won't give up; she's not the type. You've got a lot in common.'

FIFTY-NINE

Denise watched the ambulance drive away; sirens echoing into the night. Her heart was still racing and she paused to compose herself before joining the rest of her team.

She'd been taken off guard when Luke dipped under the water the last time and her throat had tightened with the realisation she might never see him alive again. When he'd resurfaced and she'd held him close on the grass she had surprised herself with the strength of her feelings for him.

She could see the forensics team were still working on Eden's car; Maisy's blanket in a plastic bag on the bonnet, tagged and ready for the lab.

'Has anyone checked the boot?' she shouted to no one in particular as she approached.

'No keys, the suspect must have had them on her. We can gemmy it if you like?'

'Check under the mat beneath the driver's seat first.'

The man bent down and rifled beneath the mat, pulling up a set of keys. Walking to the back he paused for a second to adjust his blue latex gloves, then clicked the fob. The boot opened. Stepping back, he shouted,

'She's in here; the girl's in the boot …'

Everyone fell silent.

Denise held her breath. She couldn't bear to look.

'She's …'

'Please don't say it,' Denise whispered to herself.

'…Fast asleep … she's fast asleep.

The cheer was deafening.

SIXTY

Six months later

Carmen had telephoned with a request for her to meet her at the site. She'd asked why she wanted to meet there and not at the farm and she'd said something about a cleansing ceremony; something she would like to give her as a thank you for all she'd done.

She'd last seen her at court for the handing down of Rowan's suspended sentence for conspiracy to pervert the course of justice. She'd promised her a proper goodbye and true to her word had agreed to meet.

Morvah's ragged body had been dragged from the pond the morning after her suicide. She'd filled her jogging bottoms with small smooth pebbles from the beach; the same pebbles found in each of the witch pits. She'd slit her wrists with the scalpel and waded in knowing she wouldn't be able to change her mind.

Maisy had been given the same sedative as Matthew. She spent the night in hospital but in the morning was as good as new. She remembered nothing.

They'd waited several days to break the news to Carmen that Morvah was dead. When she was eventually told, she cried for the sister who had once been her only friend. When she learnt she'd confessed to killing Elspeth, she was relieved it was not Matthew and ashamed she had ever believed her steady, gentle boy capable of such a thing.

The trial of James Ferris for the manslaughter of Rowan's baby occupied the papers and the local TV for the next couple of months. When, as Eden expected, he was found guilty and sentenced to three years' imprisonment, Rowan, as was her way, moved on.

Despite everything, the case, in the end, enhanced Eden's reputation and business was brisk. Reluctantly admitting she needed help she'd hired an assistant to keep the wheels on the bus. Molly, her new trainee had turned out to be a grafter and a success with clients and, to Eden's surprise, Agnes too.

She'd handed back the keys to the flat in Truro and moved back in with her parents temporarily, glad for the time to re-connect with them whilst the beach house was finished.

With her dad taking on the role of project manager productivity soared, nevertheless it had been New Year before the work was finally completed under budget despite the hand-built kitchen she'd forked out for because the circular building meant standard units weren't an option.

She woke in her own bed that February morning, to the sound of seagulls stomping on her roof; watery light bouncing off the rafters. She pulled her jumper over her pyjamas and padded downstairs to throw a log into the wood burner that had kept the place cosy through the night. It was the only heating she needed. Warm air funnelled around the circular open-plan room up the spiral staircase to her bedroom above. The money she'd saved on a central heating system had helped pay for the one real luxury buy, a wet room big enough to store her board, complete with a full-size drying cabinet for her wetsuits. Built as an add-on to the ground floor, to avoid traipsing sand through the place, it was where she'd headed once she'd drunk her coffee, the only thing on her mind as she opened the dryer door and smelt the neoprene, catching the tide.

Board tucked under her arm she started down the sandy path to the beach, deserted but for the clutch of like-minded die-hards gathered at the far end around the wooden shack loosely referred to as a cafe, drinking hot chocolate.

The wind was bitter. The wet sand, sparkling with early morning crystals cold and hard under her bare feet. She passed an old boy walking his terrier.

'Looks like snow,' he said, looking up at a grey sky pillowed with clouds.

'Surely not?'

Cornwall rarely saw snow.

'Mark my words, forty years at sea you get to know the weather, but you'll be alright in there,' he nodded towards the ocean, 'the water's always warmer than the land.'

It was true, the water did feel warm and steam rose from her wetsuit when she walked back up the beach an hour later.

After she'd showered and changed, she headed for the site. The weather forecast on the car radio announced snow was expected. She turned the heater up. It would be the first time she drove her car since Morvah stole it. It had been impounded as evidence until now and although it had undergone a professional valeting to remove the gore, she felt uncomfortable and worried the sight of it might upset Carmen. She'd trade it in as soon as possible.

A dusting of frost had left the hedgerows brittle and unyielding; the fields sheened with the pink light of the low winter sun. The tiny painting of the robin dangled from the car's mirror. She didn't know why she'd hung it there but ever since her mother handed it over, she'd been unable to stop looking at it. It bounced up and down with the rhythm of the bumpy lane, its gold paint glinting. She hoped it would serve as a talisman against another car coming from the other direction forcing her to reverse.

Carmen was already there when she arrived. She was alone and Eden was relieved. She didn't feel up to seeing Rowan's sullen face or facing one of Maisy's interrogations.

Parking up, she felt for Madge Lutey's letter in her pocket, it was time to hand it back.

'Eden,' Carmen called, rushing forward and wrapping her arms around her.

Eden was happy to hug her back. She could feel she'd lost weight.

'You look well.'

'Thank you. I've shed a few pounds; no more cakes for me. I need to watch myself these days. I've been given a second chance and I'm not going to muck it up.'

'How's everyone else?'

'All well. Matthew's moved in with his girlfriend and Rowan has gone back into the sixth form to re-take her A-levels. Hopefully, she'll be off to university next year.'

Eden hoped this meant a fresh start for Rowan; she'd leave her old self behind as she embarked on new adventures but something told her she would carry her baggage with her. Like Morvah, she would always feel slighted. When her grades were poor or she didn't clinch the job she hoped for, it would always be somebody else's fault and they'd have to pay. She wouldn't be surprised if their paths crossed again.

'She's moved out of the farm and is sharing a flat with friends in Falmouth near the college so it's just me and the little ones now,' Carmen continued, 'that's why I'm selling up.'

'You're selling the farm?' Eden couldn't disguise her surprise at the news. She'd expected Carmen would stay there and pass it on to Matthew.

'Yes, a developer has bought it. He's going to convert all the outbuildings and rebuild the barn. It fetched way more than I could have hoped.'

'Where will you go?'

'Away; I owe it to Maisy and Jago to start afresh somewhere else; somewhere the family history won't follow them. I might not be eating cakes but I can still make them for others. I've bought a little tea shop in Devon but don't worry they'll be getting cream teas Cornish style; jam first.'

Eden laughed.

'The shop is at the front with the living quarters at the back. It's a pretty little place by the harbour with a good school nearby.'

Eden nodded. She could see the wrench it would be for Carmen. Her words were hesitant and loaded with regret though she was doing her very best to put on a brave face.

'And this place?' Eden asked; looking around the site, now empty. Elspeth's prefab and the caravan had been towed away. From the frosty crunch underfoot, she could tell grass had sprouted over the quagmire left by the archaeologists and the police investigation that followed.

'There's nothing for me to protect anymore; no secrets left; only him.' Carmen stared in the direction of the Rowan tree at the far corner of the field where the baby boy was buried.

Eden felt a familiar pang and found herself twiddling with the ring on her finger.

Carmen noticed; 'That's new.'

'Yes, it's from my mother; my birth mother I mean. She left it to me.'

'Can I see it?'

Eden slipped it from her finger; handing it to her.

'A knot ring, how lovely. Mostly they're made from one piece of hair woven continuously, representing unity and eternity; no ending and no beginning but yours is two strands of different hair woven together. That means two paths. Two people on different paths but forever connected wherever they are, no matter how far apart.'

Eden couldn't help herself; hot tears stinging her freezing cheeks.

Carmen handed her back the ring, closing Eden's icy fingers around it with her own.

'Now, now don't take on so. It's a lovely thing for her to have done so you could have her with you always.'

Eden wiped her eyes, trying to gain her composure.

'You said something about cleansing the site?' she coughed.

'Yes, the last thing I have to do; if you can help?'

'Of course.'

'We'll start with the well.'

Eden remembered the last time she'd been there; the day they'd found Elspeth's corpse, then remembering the artefacts, thought of something else.

'Can you wait here a second' she said, 'I need to get something from my car.'

She was back two minutes later, having unhooked the tiny painting from its hanging place and put it in her pocket with the letter.

They walked together across the field where the aluminium planks had once been. Eden pulled her coat around her, feeling the chill now the sun had dipped behind the trees. The landscape seemed muffled; nature retreating at the sight of the ever-thickening sky.

She could smell snow in the air now.

When they reached the well Carmen dipped into the bag she was carrying and lifted out a white candle; a feather, a lighter and a small copper bowl, into which she tipped a bag of what looked like potpourri which she lit.

Once the incense had caught she blew out the flame.

Eden breathed in the sweet-smelling smoke, recognising sage from her mother's herb garden and a deeper, woody smell like aftershave; cedar.

Using the feather Carmen fanned the smoke over them, letting her hands hover as she traced the outlines of their bodies.

'What do I do?' asked Eden, coughing as a waft of smoke hit the back of her throat.

'Walk with me.'

Lifting the bowl with both hands, Carmen began slowly walking anticlockwise around the well. Eden followed as her friend chanted quietly under her breath.

Completing the circle, Carmen changed direction, leading her clockwise around the well one more time before returning to the spot where they'd begun. They did this three times in total.

Then Carmen stood the candle upright on the granite rim of the well and lit the wick.

'Smoke, air, fire and earth, cleanse this place. Shine on this place; let light return and cast out all evil.'

Eden listened as Carmen recited the same words over and over again.

During the prayer her head was lifted upwards, eyes closed and there was a radiance about the woman; a peace that spread through Eden as she watched.

When she'd finished, Carmen opened her eyes, blew out the candle and emptied the glowing contents of the bowl onto the ground. Reaching into the bag again, she pulled out a jam jar filled with white liquid.

'What is it?' asked Eden, thinking for one horrible moment she might have to drink the contents.

'Milk and honey to purify the land.'

She poured a little of the milk into the warm bowl before handing it to Eden, keeping the jam jar for herself.

'Now follow me, sprinkling the ground as we go.'

Eden looked around to see if anyone was watching before following Carmen's lead; dipping her icy fingertips into the bowl and sprinkling liquid onto the ground as they made their way around the perimeter, finishing up at the Rowan tree.

'Do we need to do something here too?' she asked.

'No,' puffed Carmen.

The walk around the field had been brisk. Eden hoped she hadn't overdone it.

'Gran cast a charm when she buried him; sprinkled salt around the tree.'

Eden looked up at the branches, bare now of their delicate fronds and ruby berries. A few of the lower ones had strips of fabric tied to them, the messages written upon them hard to read now the weather had done its best to fade them.

'The people who come here now have turned it into a Cloughty Tree and I suppose that's a good thing all in all,' Carmen said, following her gaze.

'A what?'

'A wishing tree. Mind you, they're in the wrong place. The Cloughty used to be by the well before it toppled over in a storm when Mum was a girl. Back then, lovers used to drop pins into the water. If they stuck to each other it meant true love; course the craftier lads would rub them on their jumper first; magnetise them so they'd always attract. For centuries before that, folk used to dip their wishes in the sacred well before hanging them on the tree but what does it matter what people did back then or whether it's the right tree or not, as long as it gives comfort? The Rowan tree knows why it's here; for remembrance.'

Eden reached into her pocket; 'I have your gran's letter here.'

'Keep it; I know it's safe with you.'

Saying nothing, Eden put it back. It was bitterly cold and she kept her hand in her pocket; twisting the leather necklace between her fingers.

Carmen took the bowl from her, returning it to her bag with the rest of the items they'd used for the blessing and they stood together in silence for a while.

'Will you come back?' Eden finally asked.

'Once a year maybe, when the snowdrops come,' Carmen answered, her eyes fixed on the tree. 'The past tethers us whether we like it or not no matter how often we slip the leash, something pulls us back.' She looked up at the loaded sky adding, 'I ought to get back. I've got a feeling the children will be sent home early from school because of the weather and I've still got packing to do.'

'Can I give you a lift?'

'No, it's only a short walk across the fields; the exercise is good for me.'

'In that case, I'm going to stay for a bit.'

The women hugged.

'You'll make a good mother,' Carmen whispered, peeling away.

'I'm not planning on becoming one any time soon.'

'Sometimes, we don't remember our dreams. It doesn't mean they won't come true.'

Eden looked to her for an explanation, but she was already walking away.

Turning towards the tree, Eden lifted the necklace from her pocket, then, reaching up as high as she could, looped the leather chord over one of its skeletal branches; watching the tiny, brightly coloured bird spin as the first flurries of snow floated down like feathers.

She shivered, suddenly cold. Pulling her collar up, she set off across the field in the direction of the entrance, worried now the snow was falling heavily, if she stayed longer, she might have trouble getting out of the lane.

Her phone pinged with a text from Luke;

'I'm at the site entrance. Are you on your way, the snow is drifting here already?'

She could see him now; sitting in his car, wipers swishing to keep the windscreen clear.

As she got closer, he wound down his window and smiled.

'What are you doing here?' she asked, leaning in, enjoying the rush of fanned heat wafting from the dashboard vents.

'I need to talk to you. I called and your mum said you'd come here to perform some mad ceremony with Carmen Lutey.' His raised eyebrows told her what he thought about her foray into Celtic mysticism. 'I saw the forecast and thought you might get yourself stranded and by the looks of it I was right.'

He nodded in the direction of her car. There was no way she'd be able to reverse it without digging it out first.

'Get in. I'll drive you home. We can tow it out tomorrow if this sticks overnight.'

She slid into the passenger seat, glad not to be driving herself.

'Eden, there's something I need to ask you.'

'What?' she asked thinking he meant something to do with Flora.

'I've been offered a promotion.'

Eden examined his expression trying to gauge whether this was cause for celebration or not.

'That's a good thing, isn't it?'

'Well yes it would be under normal circumstances but it means a move up the line.'

'To where?'

'Leeds.'

'Leeds?' she exclaimed, unable to hide her alarm. 'But that's miles away. Flora's started school and what about Denise? I thought you two were an item?'

She hadn't raised the subject of Denise Charlton before, although Flora had let slip, she had come around for pizza one evening. Maybe things would work out for them, maybe not, but at least Luke had finally cut the cord as far as Thea was concerned.

'We've been seeing each other a bit, but nothing serious. Denise has ambitions of her own she won't be able to fulfil down here in the sticks. When the opportunity arises, she'll be off for sure. I can't put Flora through something like that, not after what she's been through already. It's a great opportunity for me and of course, Flora would be closer to Thea.

There it was the T-word. Certain ties were obviously more difficult to break than others.

Luke had received a grudging apology and a pat on the back for solving Elspeth's murder and exposing the trade in stolen artefacts. He had also won his custody battle for Flora.

Thea had stood her ground initially, only throwing in the towel once Eden had agreed to sink some of her divorce settlement into the gallery she and Rafie were setting up in Edinburgh. Eden had promised to keep the funding to herself so long as Thea religiously took her meds and stopped causing trouble for Luke. In consequence, things had been relatively peaceful on the Thea front. Flora saw her mother once a month and stayed with her grandparents when Luke worked nights. She had started at the local school and blossomed with the benefit of a settled routine.

Eden turned away. She couldn't look at him. She had got used to having her bright little niece around and her mum and dad would be devastated. She had to use every ounce of self-control to stop herself from opening the door as she tried to breathe through the suffocating realisation of the loss.

'But weighing it all up, 'Luke paused, 'I've decided to stay put. I wanted to check you think that's the right choice because I value your opinion?' he said slipping the car into gear.

'Yes I do,' she mumbled, 'I do,' her eyes brimming as she stared out of the window across the field towards the Rowan tree, its branches weighed down with snow and the wishes of so many people.

Relieved she leant back in her seat and closed her eyes.

Carmen was right; she never remembered her dreams but as they pulled away, she found her mind drifting to a place where paper lanterns glowed in a lavender sky and the frozen ground turned green. She heard the jangle of windchimes; caught the glimmer of copper hair; golden freckles as sun-blushed skin, warm and musky with the scent of Patchouli brushed her baby cheek. She imagined the roots of the Rowan tree reaching down; deeper and deeper, into the earth; winding around the baby boy's bones, cradling him; keeping him safe. She had left him the painting of the robin because he needed it more than her.

She had people who loved her; she could spare him some of that love.

THE END

A LETTER TO MY READERS

Thank you for taking the time to read *The Bitter Fruit Beneath*.

I decided to write this book after reading about an archaeological discovery a few miles from where I live in Cornwall which uncovered forty 'witch pits'; small deep holes filled with fertility offerings, the earliest of which dated back to the early seventeenth century. Stranger still, it was rumoured they were dug by successive generations of women from one family tasked with performing this secret ritual up until the nineteen-eighties, when perhaps because of the availability of IVF, the practice came to an abrupt halt. My fascination grew on learning each pit was unique; customised for the individual whose inability to conceive it sought to remedy. I began to create backstories for these desperate women, joined together over the centuries by the invisible thread of infertility but found the lawyer in me constantly drawn back to the family who dug the pits. How despite ostracism and the risk of capital punishment in less enlightened times, they remained constant in their commitment to help women conceive until science took over. As a lawyer practicing in a rural community, where rumours breed like flies and grudges fester for decades, I began to wonder what might happen to the descendants of such a family if their bizarre past were to catch up with them and how a rational feminist lawyer like Eden Gray would deal with the pressures of a modern-day witch trial?

I have always been fascinated by the schizophrenic character of the windswept Cornish peninsula my family has been lucky enough to call home for generations. Occupied by a cast of reluctant bedfellows, city-slick escapees and us locals who carry the remnants of our myth-ridden history etched on our backs like tattoos, it teeters between the bucket and spade domesticity of modern-day tourism and a superstitious past, riddled with Pagan traditions.

The resultant clash of cultures and sensibilities causes friction, resentment and drama. My aim, through my writing, is to explore what happens when these divergent worlds collide to expose a darker reality at odds with the picture-perfect landscape. Whilst I was lucky to enjoy a fantastically satisfying career as a lawyer I cannot now imagine anything more joyous than being able to sit at my desk and write knowing others might read and connect with my words. Cornwall has captured the hearts and imaginations of countless wonderful writers through the decades; their vivid images now woven into its rich tapestry. If I can add one colourful stitch I will be happy.

Would you like to read more of my work? **Then visit my website www.cornishcrimeauthor.com to join my list.** You will be given the opportunity to become a member of my readers' club and receive free downloads, sneak previews and fascinating insights into the characters and places featured in my novels. These goodies are exclusive to members and currently include a **FREE** novella in the **CORNISH CRIME SERIES**, *THE ROSARY PEA What's Your Poison?* I look forward to meeting you there and on Facebook (www.facebook.com/julieevansauthor).

A final request...

If you've enjoyed this book I would be so grateful if you could leave a review on Amazon.

As an author, it is a great thrill to know someone has enjoyed your work, and it will help other readers find my books.

Thank you.

Julie

Printed in Great Britain
by Amazon

22726889R00188